She is every man's desire, but she longs more than anything to be . . .
THE DUKE'S INDISCRETION

Lady Charlotte Hughes lives a double life. By day, she is the plain, demure sister of a domineering brother who wants her married and out of the way. By night, she is Lottie English, an intoxicating, glamorous woman of mystery—a famed opera singer who drives men wild with wanting her. But the only man Charlotte wants is Colin Ramsey, Duke of Newark, though the dashing nobleman would certainly *never* risk his reputation on a woman like her. Imagine her shock, then, when the duke reveals himself as a smitten fan...and, while attempting to seduce her, inadvertently discovers her true identity.

Charlotte will submit to the handsome duke's every wish, but only as his wife—a proposal Colin eagerly accepts. But his secret duty to the Crown—to expose Charlotte's nemesis—threatens the fiery, very real passion that consumes them. And when Charlotte herself is suddenly imperiled, Colin must choose where his loyalties lie—and risk everything for the remarkable lady who has so thoroughly captured his heart.

By Adele Ashworth

THE DUKE'S INDISCRETION
DUKE OF SCANDAL
DUKE OF SIN
WHEN IT'S PERFECT
SOMEONE IRRESISTIBLE

*If You've Enjoyed This Book,
Be Sure to Read These Other*
AVON ROMANTIC TREASURES

AND THEN HE KISSED HER *by Laura Lee Guhrke*
AUTUMN IN SCOTLAND *by Karen Ranney*
CLAIMING THE COURTESAN *by Anna Campbell*
SURRENDER TO A SCOUNDREL *by Julianne MacLean*
TWO WEEKS WITH A STRANGER *by Debra Mullins*

Coming Soon

THE VISCOUNT IN HER BEDROOM *by Gayle Callen*

The Duke's Indiscretion

ADELE ASHWORTH

An Avon Romantic Treasure

AVON BOOKS
An Imprint of HarperCollinsPublishers

This is a work of fiction. Names, characters, places, and incidents are products of the author's imagination or are used fictitiously and are not to be construed as real. Any resemblance to actual events, locales, organizations, or persons, living or dead, is entirely coincidental.

AVON BOOKS
An Imprint of HarperCollins*Publishers*
10 East 53rd Street
New York, New York 10022-5299

First Avon Books paperback printing: May 2007

Avon Trademark Reg. U.S. Pat. Off. and in Other Countries, Marca Registrada, Hecho en U.S.A.
HarperCollins® is a registered trademark of HarperCollins Publishers.

Printed in the U.S.A.

10 9 8 7 6 5 4 3 2 1

This book is dedicated to the memory of
Maxine Harrison Garlick, my favorite
vocal instructor and musically gifted grandmother,
who chose love over fame by giving up
stardom on the operatic stage to elope
with a trumpet-playing marine biologist
in 1930s Seattle.
I miss you, Grandma!
And yes, I will practice . . .

Chapter 1

London, England
February, 1861

Colin Ramsey, third distinguished Duke of Newark, had been in love with Lottie English for three and a half years. Oh, that probably wasn't her legal name, and of course he hadn't actually been introduced to her formally. But the part of her that so engaged him when she sang upon the stage never ceased to capture his imagination, and, he suspected, would remain at the center of his very erotic fantasies until his dying breath—or at least until he bedded her.

Just such a vision of her lingered in his mind as he entered the magnificent Royal Italian Opera House in Covent Garden, vowing that tonight he would meet her face to face at last. He'd attempted to make her acquaintance twice before by calling on her behind the stage after her performances, but she'd cleverly eluded him, offering her final curtsy to her adoring public, then hastily leaving the theater by hired hack to places unknown before he could reach her.

That was the mystery of Lottie English, and, Colin supposed, why she endured as his fantasy, haunting his dreams. Nobody knew who she was, aside from her persona as one of England's greatest coloratura sopranos.

Tonight, however, performing as Susanna in Mozart's *The Marriage of Figaro*, he would watch her as always, but his plan had changed from all previous attempts to introduce himself after her performance. Tonight, he would catch her unawares during the final interval. Because he was the Duke of Newark, she could hardly deny him a request for an audience.

Highly confident, Colin felt as giddy as a schoolboy as he spied his friends, Samson Carlisle, the Duke of Durham, and the man's new wife, Olivia, sipping champagne in the center lobby of the opera house. Of course everybody he personally knew had, over time, become quite aware of his lustful infatuation with the lovely Lottie, and they were all, one way or another, rather amused by it, enough to tease him on occasion, as they undoubtedly would tonight.

The magic of the impending performance charged the air, as Colin graciously nodded to a few ladies who curtsied to him as he passed through the crowded foyer, lit brightly by wall sconces and crystal chandeliers. He'd dressed formally this evening, choosing his finest evening suite in black silk with velveteen collar and cuffs, a white shirt with pleated frills, and a charcoal-gray waistcoat and matching cravat secured by an onyx tie pin. He'd brushed his hair back from his face, shaved closely, and wore only a trace of musk cologne. Nothing but the best for Lottie English.

Olivia noticed him first, her dark blue eyes sparkling knowingly as he walked up to stand beside her. "I see you're looking your best for Lottie English."

Sam snorted.

Colin grinned, grasping her gloved palm and leaning in to kiss her cheek. "I was just thinking the same thing."

"You never seem to think of anything else," Sam drawled. "At least not lately."

He shrugged. "It *is* the winter opera season."

"Indeed," Olivia agreed. Then with a nod of her head to beckon them, she moved to her side a little so that she closed in on the wall to her right, taking them away from the growing crowd. After a sip of champagne, she murmured sneakily, "I've heard a rumor about her . . ."

Colin's brows rose. "Oh? I adore rumors."

"Especially if they're about you," Sam said, trying not to smirk.

He ignored that, gazing at Olivia with ardent anticipation. "Well?"

She began to swivel back and forth, teasing him with a crooked smile. "I just left the ladies' withdrawing room, where several people who apparently 'know' said they've heard she's the daughter of a viscount."

Sam chuckled and raised his full champagne flute to his lips. "Ridiculous gossip."

It sounded beyond credible to Colin as well. "Daughters of nobility don't work on the stage," he said with an exaggerated sigh. "Just another dead end, I'm afraid."

"And yet rumors are sometimes true, are they not?" Olivia piped in, twisting a loose tendril of hair at her neck with a finger. "At least the rumors I've heard about you seem to be."

"Madam," Colin asked in feigned shock, "what has your husband been telling you?"

Sam answered for her. "Nothing that I'm certain she didn't hear whispered first in the ladies' with-drawing room."

Colin tipped his head toward her. "If that's where you've heard these rumors, then yes, they're all true."

"Oh, really?" Olivia mused. "Quite the ladies' man, aren't you?"

Colin lifted a flute of champagne from the tray-carrying server walking by. "I'll know for certain later tonight."

Sam shook his head, smiling dryly. "Here we go again. I suppose you'll let us know if you manage to woo her."

He'd said that as a statement, not a question, and Colin only shrugged. "I guarantee to both of you, right now, that the lush and lovely Lottie English will one day swoon at my feet." He took a sip from his flute, then pointed it toward them, "Mark my words."

Olivia laughed again. "Determination counts for something, right, darling?"

Sam shook his head but offered nothing in re-sponse.

"And what are we discussing this blustery evening?" came the gruffly cheerful baritone voice from behind him.

Colin turned to acknowledge his longtime friend and immediate supervisor in his work for the Crown, Sir Thomas Kilborne, a stately, rotund gentleman with pinkened cheeks and thinning black hair that he combed over his head from one ear to the other.

"Good evening, Sir Thomas," he remarked good-naturedly. "We were just discussing the ladies who swoon at our feet."

"Ah. Lottie English, again."

Olivia took two steps to kiss the older man's cheek. "Good evening, Sir Thomas."

"Madam, you look as lovely as ever," he replied, pulling back a little to view her person, dressed richly in dark red satin. Then he turned to Sam and bowed slightly. "Your grace."

Sam returned it with a nod of his own. "And where is your lovely wife?"

Sir Thomas sighed with feigned exaggeration. "I've no idea. She left me to mingle with a group of ladies as soon as we entered."

"They tend to do that, don't they?" Colin commented.

Sir Thomas's lips twitched up making his side whiskers flair. "It's a nice reprieve, actually. She'll be tapping me with her fan all evening to make certain I stay awake."

"You sound as excited to be here as I am," Sam offered in light sarcasm.

Olivia scoffed, smacking her husband in the arm

with her fan, as it apparently worked for all women. "Sometimes it's necessary to make sacrifices for the pleasure of those we love."

The older man chuckled, patting his hair down atop his head. "She dragged you here, didn't she?"

Sam took a sip of champagne. "I won't go into the nasty details, but yes. She did. My passion for opera extends only beyond my passion for cleaning my teeth."

A bell sounded above the clamor of laughter, rustling skirts, and a thousand and one voices, reminding them that only a few minutes remained before the performance would begin.

"Well," Olivia teased, wrapping a palm around her husband's elbow, "we don't want to miss the introduction, do we, darling?"

"I can hardly contain myself," Sam replied slowly.

"I can't either," Colin added, his own excitement no doubt far greater than any other man dragged in this night.

Stalling his departure, Sam looked at his friend askance. "And just why are you so confident in meeting the famous Miss English tonight?"

Colin grinned again and pretended to straighten his tie. "I'm going to jump up on the stage and declare my love during her first aria. She can hardly evade me when I'm standing in front of her."

"Good God," Sir Thomas interjected. "Just don't start singing."

Olivia giggled.

Sam stared at him. "You know that if you do such a disgraceful thing I'll have to disown you as a friend."

Colin shrugged. "The cost of love."

Olivia patted his cheek. "You need a wife."

"Like I need my teeth cleaned," he grumbled. "Unless, of course, Sam intends to rid himself of you."

"Fat chance, that," Sam said far too casually.

Olivia beamed. "Well, then, since I'm taken, maybe Lottie English will marry you."

He took a swallow or two of his champagne. "I consider that highly unlikely."

Sir Thomas scoffed. "That's because she wouldn't dare. Not if you make a fool of yourself by jumping up on stage during a performance. You'll become the laughingstock of England."

Olivia cocked her head, studying him with amusement. "So, how do you *really* expect to meet your intended . . . what? *Friend*, shall we call her?"

Colin lightly lifted a shoulder in a shrug. "I'm going backstage to introduce myself during the last interval."

All three of them laughed, including Sam, which meant not only did they consider him a lovesick puppy, they didn't actually believe him.

"In the *interval*," Olivia repeated, brows furrowed in awe.

Colin winked at her. "What else is a forlorn and desperate man to do?"

Sir Thomas cleared his throat. "Well, while you're contemplating your, uh, proposal—"

"You mean his attack," Sam cut in. "Poor woman."

"Yes, undoubtedly," Sir Thomas agreed. "But I would like to have a word with you, Colin, before you lose your head to the beauty on the stage and they cart you off to Bedlam."

"Ye who have no faith . . ." was his only response before finishing off the contents of his flute.

"We do need to sit, darling," Olivia urged again as she tugged at her husband's sleeve. "I know you wouldn't dream of missing the opening."

"The thought never crossed my mind," Sam lied, trying to suppress a smile as he gazed at his wife.

Turning her attention to the older man, she lifted her skirts to depart. "Well then, Sir Thomas, perhaps we'll see *you* during the interval."

He bopped up on his toes. "I'll be here, of course, with my wife. *I* have my dignity in check."

"Good. And Colin dear," she admonished, shaking her head as she looked him up and down, "you behave."

"I'll do my best to contain myself, madam," he replied with mock seriousness. "But I guarantee it'll be a night to remember. At least for me."

Olivia straightened her shoulders and sighed. "Then naturally I expect to hear the details. For now, however, we shall see you in your box." With that, she turned and practically dragged her husband toward the inner doors, now filling with theater patrons as they slowly made their way inside for seating.

Colin placed his empty champagne flute next to several others on a small sidebar to his left, then silently, he and Sir Thomas strolled to the far end of the large foyer, waiting for the crowd to disperse even more before beginning their discussion. His nervousness about meeting the famous Lottie intensified as the seconds ticked by, and it made him ever more determined to get their business done, to watch the curtain rise and lights shine down upon the woman of his fantasies.

"What do you have for me?" he asked as soon as they were alone, squelching his impatience.

Sir Thomas glanced around him intently, skillfully, without looking as if he were doing so. "Charles Hughes," he said quietly, lifting his champagne to his lips.

"Charles Hughes?" he repeated, rubbing his palm across the back of his perspiring neck.

Sir Thomas frowned, his jowls drooping over his starched collar as he nodded. "The Earl of Brixham. Seems he's into some rather interesting dealings with foreign governments."

Colin clasped his hands behind his back to keep his growing agitation restrained. "What kind of dealings?"

Sir Thomas inhaled a full breath, held it for a moment, then let his out slowly, staring at the carpet beneath his feet. "Not certain, but we suspect he's trying to sell some kind of information he's gleaned from his involvement in various committees inside the House."

The House of Lords. Colin thought about that for a moment. He didn't know Earl Brixham except by name and perhaps a shared handshake once or twice. But such a suggestion of illegality on the man's part seemed thoroughly unlikely without reason.

"Why?" he asked simply. "What do you have on him?"

Sir Thomas looked up at him again, countenance drawn into serious contemplation, his dark brown eyes sharply focused. "He's desperately in debt. Gambles badly and all that." He paused in thought, then added, "I think he's at the point where he'd do just about anything for money."

Colin tried to keep his mind on the details Sir Thomas provided rather than the lush curves of the famous soprano who would be taking to the stage at any moment. "What is it you think I can do?" he asked in a mild attempt to get to the point.

Sir Thomas finished off his champagne in a full swallow. After licking his lips, he replied, "I need you to meet with him, in his home—"

"I'm not an investigator, Thomas, you know that," Colin cut in, cocking his head to the side a little as he gazed at the man with a great deal of skepticism. "Don't you have others who can do this better?"

The older man shook his head most adamantly. "No. He would probably suspect something if we sent in one of our own; you'll just appear to be a lazy nobleman, with far too much money on his hands, who would like to buy his antique pianoforte."

Colin chuckled, incredulous. "You're joking."

"Indeed, I'm not," came the fast reply.

"I don't need a pianoforte," Colin said pleasantly, knowing such an observation was entirely moot. "I've got a perfectly good piano that of course I never play."

Sir Thomas scratched his side whiskers, a wry smile playing across his mouth as he glanced around once again to the now nearly empty foyer. "It's a good excuse, and the man will certainly sell it. He's in quite a bind financially, we believe, and the pianoforte is worth a pretty penny." He sighed. "But I also want you inside his home, to see how the man is living, to take a general count of his possessions and such. When you offer for the instrument, ask for a complete bill of sale. That's all. You can work with that, can't you?"

Of course he could work with just a bill of sale; he was a professional, after all. Still, Colin remained silent on that point, pondering the strange request from his superior.

Sir Thomas recognized his reservation and piped in jovially, "It's for the good of England, old boy."

And that settled the matter. How could he possibly say no? With an exaggerated exhale, he relented. "Give me a week or so."

Sir Thomas smiled broadly. "No problem, that. The man has a sister, as well. Had three or four Seasons already and she refuses every suitor, or so I've heard. Perhaps you can court her."

Colin snorted through a chuckle. "Not bloody likely."

The older man shook his head with feigned pity. "As the lovely Duchess of Durham only just said, you need a wife."

Following that sound advice, Sir Thomas reached up and patted his shoulder, then abruptly left him— to hunt down his own consort before she lectured him regarding the necessity of being seated on time, Colin gathered. Wives were trouble, spending all your money on frivolities, whining when you denied them luxuries, and nagging constantly about nothing of any importance. What he needed was a good mistress who did none of those things without risk of losing all she gained by the companionship. It had been ages, it seemed, since he'd bedded a woman, and the only woman he wanted right now was the beautiful and artistically brilliant Lottie English.

That thought in mind, he curbed his excitement over the evening's coming events, and turned toward the stairs just as the orchestra began to play.

Chapter 2

As always, Lottie English shined on stage. Colin sat next to Sam and Olivia in box three, the very box he'd purchased directly after hearing the famed soprano sing for the first time nearly four years ago, before she'd become the star she was today. Again tonight, she managed to engage him completely, not just with her mesmerizing performance and spectacular voice, but also by her uncanny ability to own the stage, to captivate the entire audience. He watched her now, dressed in costume, her hair, whatever its true color, hidden behind a tall, white wig, her face covered in cosmetics. Yet she still had the ability to look graceful and poised, even breathtaking, though he supposed her entire performance enraptured him. She had high cheekbones, an oval face, a small waist, and a nicely formed bosom, from what he'd noticed over the years. And she sang like an angel.

"She's magnificent," Olivia whispered to him when

Lottie's first aria concluded and the audience broke out into applause.

He beamed with a silly sense of pride through nearly every second of her performance, a satisfaction that didn't exactly make sense as she wasn't yet his to be proud of. But, God willing, and with a great deal of personal persuasion, she would be soon. Very soon.

Finally the last interval drew close, and his heart began to pound from a sudden, new surge of excitement. The time had almost arrived for him to go behind the stage to meet her, at long last, and she could hardly deny him access to her presence if he presented himself as the noble Duke of Newark. Colin rarely used his title as a ploy to get what he wanted, but he really couldn't see any other way, and shamefully, he'd grown almost desperate in his fantasies. He had to know if she stirred his blood in person as she did from afar.

He glanced to Olivia and Sam during the final scene before the break, noting with amusement how Sam could hardly keep his eyes open, which made him wonder how many gentlemen in the audience this night were reacting the same. Olivia, naturally, seemed as enthralled as he, though obviously for different reasons. Quickly, he reached over and gently squeezed her hand, begging for luck, he supposed, and she looked at him, shaking her head.

"Behave," she mouthed.

He only winked in response, then stood and silently left his box.

Colin had never been behind the stage during any production, so he wasn't at all sure what to expect.

But he fully intended to do everything in his power to remain anonymous and avoid everyone who wasn't part of the opera or theater staff. If Lottie English laughed in his face and dismissed him, he could only imagine the humiliation that might arise if someone from the audience happened to catch a glimpse of him.

The music on stage continued with intensity as he held his head high and pretended to know exactly what he was about. Quietly, he descended the stairs and swiftly made his way down the left corridor that led to the lower orchestra seating, encountering only one or two patrons outside the theater proper who hardly gave him a second glance. He had just a few seconds before applause would break out, signaling the final interval, and he wanted to be inside before anyone noticed him. Finally an overseer of sorts came into view, standing guard in front of the wooden doors that secured the backstage area, probably from people like him who would disrupt the act and its players intentionally or otherwise.

Planting his best charming smile upon his mouth, Colin strode up to the theater employee with a purposeful, regal bearing, until he stood before the scrawny young man who, up close, didn't appear to be more than twenty years of age.

"His grace, the Duke of Newark, to see Miss English, please," he stated with casual assurance, pulling down on his velvet cuffs. "I won't be but a minute."

The youth's eyes lit up fractionally in surprise as he scanned him from head to foot, assessing. "Is she expecting you?"

Predicting such a standard inquiry, Colin clasped his hands behind his back, never averting his direct gaze. "Of course. And it's important."

After only seconds of deciding it best not to tempt a confrontation with a man of his rank, the youth nodded once. "You'll only have a few minutes, your grace," he admonished, just a trace of disapproval in his tone, "before the final act begins."

"I shouldn't need more," he replied lightheartedly.

The young man moved to his side and opened the door, just enough for him to slip through, then closed it softly behind him.

Colin stood in the dark, allowing only seconds for his eyes to adjust, then made his way around various bins and large, painted scenes, ropes and pulleys, and props of all kinds, hearing the sudden cheering and applause from the audience just as he neared the small back rooms where he knew the protagonists and players would take a few minutes of rest before returning to the stage for the opera's finale.

He heard soft voices and snickering around him as the cast and crew started making their way backstage, though he acted very well as if he knew precisely what he was doing, nodding once or twice to work hands in grubby attire who glanced at him, showing only the slightest interest, or perhaps confusion, in seeing a man in formal regalia treading where he shouldn't. He knew which room belonged to Lottie, as he'd attempted to meet her here before, and he walked immediately toward it without interruption. Drawing a deep breath for confidence, and hearing not a word inside, he grasped the knob and let himself in.

Her dressing room was a bit brighter than he thought it would be, taking note of three oil lamps, lit for the interval, two on each side of the dressing table that reflected light from the long, gilt framed mirror, and one across the small room, sitting atop an old oak wardrobe.

Colin first noticed a lady's maid, adorned in costume, placing cosmetics, brushes and little bottles of who knew what on the table in front of the mirror. She glanced up when she heard him enter, staring at him, her mouth opened a bit in puzzlement.

"Are you—may I help you, sir?" she asked with wide eyes, clutching a thick brush to her breasts.

Colin smiled. "I'm here to meet Miss English."

"Oh." She hesitated, looking him up and down with assessment just as the scrawny youth had done. "Is she expecting you?"

He wanted to tell her abruptly to leave, and that his reasons for intruding were none of her business. But he supposed it was highly unusual for the famed soprano to be interrupted by strange men from the audience during a performance.

"Yes," he answered simply, looking not at her, but around the room, observing for the first time how the decorations were highly indicative of a female's touch, including a small, emerald-green velveteen settee leaning against one floral papered wall, and several dozen roses of every possible color, displayed in numerous crystal vases placed on every flat surface he could see. Apparently he wasn't Lottie's only gentleman admirer, he thought, amused and a little irked by the revelation.

He glanced back to the girl, who continued to stare at him, apparently stumped. In a fair but commanding voice, he stated, "Please excuse us, won't you?"

The girl blinked quickly, swallowing. "I—but I need to see to her needs."

Colin slowly sauntered toward her. "*I'll* see to her needs this night."

"And just what needs might those be, your grace?"

Caught off guard, Colin pivoted quickly around to face the exquisite stature and husky, sensual voice of the great Lottie English, who now stood in the opened doorway, resting her shoulder against the frame, arms interlocked across her chest, forgoing a curtsy as she gazed at him curiously.

He felt his skin prickle with gooseflesh, his face flush beneath the tightness of his collar, and he clasped his hands behind his back to keep them from shaking.

"Miss English," he acknowledged, his tone purposely low and controlled, "at long last we meet."

The great soprano watched him closely for a few long, awkward seconds. Then she straightened and stepped inside the dressing room with great effort due to the unusually wide hoops of her costume. "You may leave, Lucy Beth. I'll handle him."

Handle me? She didn't seem at all pleased by his unannounced and unexpected interruption, and the coolness in her manner took him aback, if only just a little.

Still a bit confused, the young lady's maid nevertheless did as ordered, curtsying twice. "Ma'am. Your grace." And then she scurried out the door like a rabbit on the run, closing it behind her with a thud.

Colin hardly noticed her departure as he held the candid gaze of his fantasy, standing before him for the first time. She looked positively radiant tonight, and more beautiful than he'd ever imagined. She wore a period gown of luxurious white and aqua satin, cut low across her breasts, and obviously a corset that lifted them to heights of sheer glory. Her wide eyes, a magnificent blue, were outlined in thick kohl to enhance their color and boldness on the stage, her perfectly shaped face covered in heavy white cream and dusted with powder that matched her high wig, now glittering from the golden ribbons winding through it that reflected the lamplight.

"You're staring," she remarked as she suddenly whisked past him toward her dressing table, sitting in the small, padded chair as gracefully as possible with massive hoops, pausing to consider her image in the glass.

He hadn't realized he was doing that exactly, but he wouldn't deny it. "You're a vision," he admitted soberly, moving his large form very slowly in her direction, watching with fascination as she began to brush more powder on her cheeks.

"Why are you here, your grace? Certainly you've got better things to do with your time than interrupt a performance."

"How do you know who I am?" he asked as he concentrated on his steady breathing so as not to sound totally bewitched.

One side of her painted red lips tilted up coyly as she glanced at him through the mirror. "I think everyone knows who you are."

"A fair reply," he drawled, his own sly grin etched

into his features. "But I'm more concerned with you and what *you* know about me."

"Are you," she said rather than asked. Without looking at him, she added, "I've been very much aware of you for a long time now."

She would never know how greatly those few words encouraged him.

She sighed and lowered her powder brush to open a tiny tub of bright red rouge. "You think I haven't noticed you cheering from box three after every performance I give?"

That additional comment subdued him a little, realizing for the first time that he might look nothing more than foolish to her. "I can't help myself, Miss English," he answered honestly. "You . . . entrance me."

Her smiled deepened a little as she began to paint the red onto her cheeks. "That's very interesting."

He stepped closer. "Indeed. And it appears many gentlemen are just as taken with you. Although they're undoubtedly well deserved, I've never seen so many roses in one room in my life."

Her smile faded a little, and he had to wonder if his words had annoyed her as his appearance likely had, the last thing he wanted to do now that he was finally speaking to her.

"Lottie English is a sensation," she disclosed, her voice husky and contemplative. "But none of the men who send me flowers and jewels and chocolates really knows *me* at all. They simply like what they see, or what I pretend to be." Her gaze quickly scanned his face through the mirror, then returned to her cosmetics. "They don't know me any more than you do, your grace."

Softly, he confessed, "I understand."

"Do you?" she asked lightly.

"Yes."

She shifted her attention to her bright red lips as she nimbly began reapplying the same crimson color to her mouth with tiny strokes from an outline brush.

"Is that why *you've* never sent me roses?"

Truthfully, doing such a thing had not occurred to him, and now he was quite glad it hadn't. Sending her roses would have made him just like all the other admirers she seemed to enjoy ignoring, even brushing aside as a nuisance.

Taking another few steps closer to stand behind her chair, he now peered at her through the mirror. "You're very beautiful," he asserted, his voice a deep, gruff whisper. "A token of flowers could never do you justice."

He witnessed the briefest hesitation in her lip application, but she didn't look at him. "You flatter me, sir. And yet it's true that cosmetics do wonders for a pale and ordinary face."

He frowned a little at that. "Never ordinary, dear Lottie. It's exquisite. But I meant all of you, including your voice."

She blinked, clearly unnerved by his candor, her blue eyes vibrant, striking as she stared into his through the glass. "Why are you here?"

The question, this time, held genuine interest, and the heat of her gaze coupled with the intensity in her tone pummeled him with a sudden rush of satisfaction. Smiling gently, he replied, "I want to get to know you better."

She watched him carefully, her eyelids narrowed in stark evaluation. Then she exhaled a quick breath as she lowered her lashes, turning her attention back to her table of cosmetics, reaching for a hair comb. "I hardly think you're here to ask me to dinner."

"Dinner would be lovely," he swiftly returned.

She shrugged with a sigh. "But alas, it's not to be. You can hardly court me, your grace, so what would be the point?"

The *point*? To get you in my bed, of course, he thought with exasperation. She had to know that.

Gingerly, lingeringly, he raised one hand and ran his fingertips down the side of her neck in a gentle, wispy movement, relishing the softness, aching to do more. To his relief, she neither flinched nor scolded him. She shivered instead, just minutely, and that's when Colin realized, in a moment of pure elation, how entranced she was with him.

"I think you've inquired about me, Lottie. That's how you know who I am," he said intently, his fingers tarrying at the base of her throat, his palm closing over her bare collarbone.

She almost smiled. "I have my fantasies as well, your grace," she replied, her tone raspy and deeply sensual as she gave in to the feel and closed her eyes.

Colin could hardly contain both his mental and physical reactions to her response. He grew hard from nothing more than the sound of her voice, from the sheer knowledge that he'd captured enough of her interest for her to ask about him, to show a desire in him, to express a need, ever so slightly, for his touch, to want him almost as badly as he wanted her.

Oh, yes. They would be lovers. Nothing had ever been more clear.

"Then we should share those fantasies," he murmured. "I'm looking forward to it, to our becoming . . . close friends."

Her lips lifted a fraction and she opened her eyes, looking directly into his as she closely regarded him. "So my . . . friendship is the need you said you'd help me with?"

He smiled and quietly admitted, "It will be my pleasure, and yours, I promise, to help you with *every* need. I want nothing more than to be with you."

She nodded, folding her hands in her lap. "I see." Lowering her gaze, she added in a murmur, "I can't say that I've ever been so charmed."

A sudden knock at the door startled them both, and Colin quickly lifted his palm from her neck, dropping his arm to his side.

"Yes?" Lottie said at once, her tone returned to one of confident sophistication.

The door opened a crack and a woman in full costume peered inside, fully taking note of him with her mouth open a little in surprise. "Uh . . . forgive me. Five minutes, Lottie."

"Thank you, Sadie, I'll be right out."

After only the briefest pause, the woman closed the door again.

Colin turned back to Lottie, the sensual angel of his dreams, wishing like hell he had more time. A few minutes in her presence seemed like seconds.

"So, you'll see me then?" he asked in a deep whisper. "Privately?"

She inhaled shakily, then stood, her large hoops flowing around her as she turned to look up at his face.

He met her blatant stare, capturing her gaze with his, wondering what beauty lay beneath the costume, the cosmetics, the wig, the entire facade, and eager to begin the discovery.

Very slowly, she grinned, her eyes narrowing in mischief. "You'd like that wouldn't you?" she asked slyly. "To take me to your bed, make love to me with infinite passion. To make me your own?"

Her boldness inflamed him and he sucked in a breath through his teeth. His palms itched from his enormous desire to reach out for her; perspiration broke out on the back of his neck. "I've dreamed of it for years," he whispered, revealing more of himself than he'd originally intended to share. With a quake in his voice, he added huskily, "You, and *only* you, are the center of my most private, most *intimate* fantasies."

He wanted her to know what she did to him. If he'd shocked her by revealing his erotic visions of her during his personal moments of solitary arousal, she didn't show it, which told Colin much about her experience with men.

She raised her chin a little, regarding him almost thoughtfully, her fingers toying with the string of pearls laying against her chest. "It's my understanding that men grow quickly tired of playthings," she murmured. "Perhaps I want more from a gentleman friend than his intimate devotion."

Colin swallowed from her candor, uncertain how

to respond. Then, with a vagueness that surprised him, he said, "I think we can settle that with time. And you would never be just a plaything, Lottie. I want all of you."

That seemed to take her aback as her gaze faltered. Then, to his sheer disbelief, she raised herself on her toes and placed her painted lips on his, kissing him softly, withholding an urgency beneath the surface that he could all but feel. It took everything in him not to grab her around the waist and lift her skirts, to savor every inch of her right here in her dressing room. He restrained himself, not wanting to respond too abruptly, but the moment she felt his eagerness begin to build, she slowly pulled away.

Coyly, her breathing quickened, eyes closed, she placed her palm on his chest and whispered, "I'll consider it, your grace."

And then with a lift of her skirts, gaze averted, she walked to the door and opened it.

Bursting with hope and gratification, he called out, "Lottie?"

She drew a long breath and turned back to face him, her palm resting on the door frame.

"My name is Colin."

He supposed he was hoping she'd reveal her real name as well, but she didn't. Instead, she smiled vaguely and lifted her hand to run her fingertips across the edge of her gown at her breasts.

In a low, seductive voice, she replied, "I know."

And then she was gone.

Colin dropped his body hard into the dressing chair, where she'd been sitting only moments before, stunned by her reaction, thrilled beyond anything he could have imagined, and shaking in his shoes.

She wanted him. And God, she had *kissed* him. He ran his fingers through his hair. Nothing in his fantasies had ever compared to the actual feel of her soft lips on his, teasing him, coaxing him, silently pleading for more.

Composing himself as fast as he could, he stood erect, straightening his waistcoat, then practically raced from the dressing room, ignoring the sideways glances and odd looks he garnered from the cast and crew as he walked with ease through the guarded door and out into the lighted corridor.

He reached his box and sat with confidence just as the orchestra began.

"Well?" Olivia asked impatiently, nudging him with her elbow.

He couldn't stop grinning. "Well, what?"

Suddenly she gasped. "Good heavens, you *kissed* her!"

Sam's head shot out from behind his wife's, and then after looking at him strangely for a second or two, he burst out laughing.

"What?" Colin asked again, annoyed.

Olivia snickered, then pulled off a glove by the fingers and reached up to wipe her thumb harshly across his lips. "She left a trace of herself on you, dear man," she said.

Now he understood, and he didn't care. Turning back to the stage, he replied lightly, "I'm never going to wash my mouth again."

"You're a devil," Olivia said with feigned disgust.

"Indeed," he agreed with a sigh. "But you just

watch. She'll acknowledge me before the night is through."

And she did. As the performance came to a close, the cheering began, and when the diva bowed to the crowd with roses in her arms, she glanced up to his box and smiled.

Chapter 3

Colin's week had been hell. Aside from having to dismiss a member of his staff for laziness, then tend to his books to discover a critical error his banker had made, he'd been plagued by the overwhelming urge to see Lottie again, to touch her, kiss her in passionate need, make love to her slowly with a velvet, lingering caress that left her begging for more. It had been nearly a week since that eventful night he'd introduced himself to her at last, and although he hadn't wanted to, he did actually break down and wash his mouth, even as he remembered the gentle pressing of her lips to his that incited a desire he couldn't yet manage to suppress.

He fully intended to contact her again tomorrow night, after watching another performance at the theater, and waiting all week for their next moment together had been pure agony. He really wished he knew where she lived, who she was, so he could call on her at home, but her secrets were, of course, part of her great mystery and appeal, he supposed. At this point he didn't care if she was the daughter of a rubbish collector, he still wanted nothing more than to join her delicious body with his own.

Brushing his impatience aside, he rang the bell of Earl Brixham's townhouse, located, he discovered, not three streets from his own. Immediately, the broad door opened by a dignified butler and he stated his business. He was taken at once and without question to the earl's study to await him. Upon entrance, Colin began observantly noting his surroundings, assessing what he could of the earl's standard of living.

Brixham kept his study fairly elegantly decorated, despite a lack of furnishings. The room contained two black leather wing chairs in fairly good condition facing a slightly chipped and sturdy oak desk, on top of which sat bundles of scattered paperwork and a lone inkwell. The wallpaper peeled at one of the corners, though it would hardly be noticed by a casual visitor. A coal fire softly burned in the grate to his right, its mantelpiece bare aside from the small watercolor painting of trees on a hillside that hung just above it.

Taking a moment before the earl arrived, Colin casually glanced down to the desktop, moving a paper or two and scanning the contents for anything that might appear out of order in the man's business dealings. Nothing struck him as unusual, however, except one small notation on scrap paper listing numbers that might give a clue to the man's funds. Swiftly, he stuffed it into his pocket and took a seat in one of the leather chairs just as the Earl of Brixham entered the room.

Colin noted his stature, his well-groomed appearance and casual attire in light brown, his strawberry-blond hair and freckled face, though he appeared older than he'd expected. Brixham looked to be nearly forty, and clearly a confirmed bachelor like himself.

"Good afternoon, your grace," the man said politely, walking toward him to shake his hand. With a genuine smile, he added, "I can only hope you're here to inquire about my sister?"

Colin's brows rose. "Your sister?"

Brixham's smile faded a little as he strode around his desk and sat in the wooden rocker behind it. "I was hoping—oh, never mind." He waved a palm through the air. "What can I do for you today?"

Colin eyed the earl thoughtfully, realizing at once that he seemed more than eager to send his sister packing to a new husband, probably so he could rid himself of her expense. Of course there was nothing particularly wrong with that, especially if his sister was of marrying age, though he certainly didn't intend to be the one to take the girl off his hands. Yet the acknowledgment was telling; Sir Thomas had been right about his debt.

Colin leaned back in his chair and casually regarded the man. "Actually, Brixham, I'm here to inquire about your pianoforte."

The man fairly gaped at him. "My pianoforte?"

He folded his hands in his lap. "I've heard you've got an antique, quite old, and I'd like to purchase it. For a fair sum, of course."

Brixham leaned back in his chair as well, hands folded in his lap, studying him cautiously. "I see."

Colin tipped his head to the side. "I collect antiques."

That probably sounded utterly ridiculous, but then he'd warned Sir Thomas about his lack of investigative skills, and everybody knew he didn't lie very well. But the man across from him didn't seem to witness any prevarication in his pronouncement, for he rubbed his fingers together absentmindedly and frowned.

"The pianoforte belongs to my sister," he said, his thick, reddish-blond brows pinched in thought.

That stumped him for a moment; he hadn't prepared himself for such a complication. "I see."

Suddenly Brixham leaned forward, closing his hands together on top of the paperwork on his desk. "But since she is my responsibility, I suppose it's mine to sell should I choose to." He shrugged, then laughed. "Besides, she needs to get married; let her husband buy her a piano, right?"

Colin decided he didn't like Brixham very much, or at least that part of him that cared so little about his sister's feelings. Nodding, he agreed, "Exactly. How old is she?"

He had no idea why he asked that, though he supposed he was vaguely curious.

"Nearly twenty-four," the earl fairly blurted, unable to hide his irritation. "She refuses every suitor, and I'm at the point where I'm ready to force her to take the next one or I'm tossing her out on her backside."

Colin didn't like him at all, but he covered his annoyance well. Chuckling, he remarked, "Females are a menace, are they not?"

Brixham shook his head. "You've no idea," he replied, "unless you have a sister of your own?"

Truthfully, Colin said, "I've got two, both well married by twenty and giving me more nieces and nephews than I can count."

"As every good lady should," Brixham agreed.

Suddenly Colin heard the faintest music drift in from beyond the study. "Is that her?"

Brixham nodded. "Can't get her off the thing, though I suppose once I sell it to you, she'll have to take her responsibility of choosing a husband a bit more seriously."

"Indeed," he replied, squirming a little in his chair.

"Would you like to see it?" the man asked, already standing.

"Very much," Colin replied, completely uncaring what an antique pianoforte looked like at all, though oddly desirous of meeting the poor sister.

The earl strode quickly to the door. "You can also get an idea of its sound from Charlotte's playing. Sadly, she's quite good."

Sadly? Apparently, the man seemed to think his sister spent too much time wrapped up in nonsense.

Earl Brixham led them down the dimly lit hallway, then paused in front of the last door on their right. Turning back to him, he advised, "Don't mind her if she's rude, your grace. She's not going to like this at all."

"I understand," Colin returned, his tone harsher than he'd intended.

With a strong hand on the latch, Brixham opened the door to the music room and stepped inside. Immediately the music stopped.

"I've already embroidered this morning, brother, and I'd like to play for a while."

Colin heard the soft voice before he saw her. Then he strode around her tall brother to view the stubborn, though clearly talented, Charlotte Hughes for the first time.

Instead of introduction, as he expected, she gaped at him, her mouth dropped open in surprise as she pushed her thick spectacles up the bridge of her nose to see him clearly.

"Don't be sassy with me, girl," her brother ordered through a snort. "His grace, the Duke of Newark, is here to inquire about the pianoforte."

Her face flushed pink and she bit her lip. Or rather chewed on it. Colin stood with his hands behind him, silently amused, noting her shock, taking in what he could see of her behind the instrument, her slight figure dressed in a simple day gown of cream muslin. She possessed the same coloring as her brother, though her features seemed more refined, her massively curly, thick strawberry-blond hair pulled back from her face with pins and tied with a ribbon, exposing a wide forehead, and sadly drawing attention to her spectacles, which did nothing more than hide her feminine appearance. A scattering of freckles fell across the bridge of her nose and cheeks, which, he noticed, had abruptly gone quite pale as she peered at him from across the top of her pianoforte.

"Well, don't just sit there, girl," Brixham fairly bellowed. "Either play for the man or stand up."

Her fair lashes fluttered as she realized she was staring. "Your grace," she mumbled in acknowledgment, attempting to stand, still in apparent confusion.

He bowed slightly, offering her his most engaging smile. "I'm delighted to meet you, Lady Charlotte."

She seemed quite confounded for a moment, glancing at him, and then back to her brother. "What's going on?" she asked, her voice meekly hushed.

Colin felt suddenly sorry for the girl, wishing for her sake that she could find a husband, and fast.

Her brother pulled down on his sleeves. "His grace wants to buy the pianoforte, and I intend to sell it to him. For a fair price, naturally."

"Naturally," Colin repeated.

Within seconds, Charlotte's face burned with a rush of hot color. "It's—it's not for sale."

Colin looked at her oddly, cocking his head to the side, wondering if her submissiveness and soft voice were only an act. She seemed as determined as any lady could be under such circumstances, but she didn't sound at all defiant.

"Not for sale?" her brother repeated, incredulous. "That's not your concern. Get on with you, girl, we have business to discuss."

Lips thinned in a rage she couldn't hide, she moved out from behind the object of their deliberation, and Colin couldn't help but admire her figure— lush and curvy with nicely rounded, uplifted breasts that would fill a man's hands. Although she had unruly hair and a fair, freckled face, she should be able to attract a man with her curves alone. But more to the point, he had to wonder why she continued to refuse suitors when, if he were in her shoes, he'd have jumped at the first proposal just to be rid of her brother. But then he wasn't in her shoes, and she was, after all, a female without options.

Slowly, hands on hips, she walked toward them, glaring at her brother. "You're ruining my life."

"I wouldn't have to if you'd get yourself married," the earl said through clenched teeth, trying to remain composed for the sake of his guest but ultimately failing badly.

Lady Charlotte shot a quick glance at him, and the look on her face, determined and incensed, made him pause. She seemed oddly familiar, in a manner he couldn't understand and didn't particularly want to contemplate as he grew more uncomfortable with each passing moment. The guilt he felt burned in his chest, and he had every intention of forcing Sir Thomas to give her back her damn pianoforte. Poor thing seemed to have nothing else that made her happy.

Her face pink, eyes narrowed to slits, she fisted her hands on her sides and glared at him. In a low murmur, she said thickly, "I'll never forget this, your grace."

With that, she breezed by them and took her leave, slamming the door behind her.

Earl Brixham groaned and rubbed his eyes. "See what I mean? She's incorrigible."

Colin felt his ire brimming. He needed to be done with them, and fast. "I think she's appealing, actually, and certainly talented."

The earl scoffed and waved his hand with annoyance. "She's too wrapped up in her music, is what she is."

That made him think of Lottie English, the bold seductress who made him crazy with her enchanting voice and sensual presence.

Colin cleared his throat, smoothing his hair on the

back of his head. "Why don't you take the money I'll offer you for the pianoforte and purchase her a new piano?" he suggested casually. "Perhaps then she'll take more kindly to your idea of giving her away to the next man who comes along."

Earl Brixham looked at him askance, his own impatience surfacing as his features grew tight, his body rigid. "I'll take care of Charlotte," he said brusquely. "Now, let's get down to business, shall we?"

Colin knew if he got any more personal with his feelings about the girl and her treatment, he'd be asked to leave, thus receiving no bill of sale, no signature, and alas no pianoforte.

He smiled, though he wasn't at all amused. "Of course, Brixham. Let's get down to business."

Chapter 4

Charlotte Hughes had been in love with Colin Ramsey, the marvelously handsome Duke of Newark, for three and a half years. Oh, she realized what she felt for him wasn't love in the true sense of the word, and she was quite well aware of his reputation as a rogue of the highest order. But nonetheless, he never ceased to capture her attention every time she saw him, just as he had the very first night she'd heard him yell "Brava" from box three. The man practically made love to her with his eyes every single time she took to the stage, and she'd come to count on his being there—for support, for attention, and especially for the way he practically drooled over himself when she sang. And he'd never resorted to sending her flowers.

At first it bothered her, but later she'd realized that his devotion to her and her performances went deeper than the average gentleman's. He didn't just admire her, he fairly worshiped her without begging for her affections in return, and over time she'd grown to understand his infatuation from afar, meeting it with her own. Except he didn't really know her at all, which was about to change thanks to his highly unconventional manner of confronting her at last. And during the interval no less! The man had quite the nerve, and a spark of something that went far beyond every admirer she'd ever known.

She'd been thoroughly shocked to see him standing in her dressing room at last week's performance, first hearing his voice through the door as he spoke to Lucy Beth, wondering what kind of person would be so rude as to interrupt a singer between acts. But then she quickly realized his identity even before laying eyes on him, and was able to count the blessed moments in which she gazed at his magnificently dressed and handsomely distinguished form until he noticed her.

His intensity had shaken her, though she'd done a superb job of hiding her vulnerability to him, of pretending complete composure at his suggestion of a romantic liaison between them. And she hadn't given in at all until he'd stroked her neck, so gently, with so much hidden desire exuded in the simple brushing of his fingertips against her skin. Still, she was, above all, an actress, and acting the seductress to his blatant overtures had been a complete delight, a knowledge of her sensual power as a woman. As Charlotte Hughes she would never do anything like that, say the things she said to him, act the way she had. But as Lottie, she could be what he wanted, and it pleased her enormously that he desperately wanted, it so appeared, what she offered.

Charlotte had no illusions of the man, or of the dangers of becoming his mistress. Rather Lottie didn't. But as the daughter of an earl, the sister of the living Earl of Brixham, she wouldn't think of such a thing. She'd been raised better than that, and Colin Ramsey would soon learn it. When he'd come into her home yesterday, with the intent of purchasing her prized pianoforte of all things, she'd been just as surprised by his appearance as she'd been the night he so suddenly interrupted her in her dressing room. But yesterday had been different in many ways. After her initial bewilderment at seeing the man in her music room, she was afraid he'd recognize her, thereby confronting her in front of her brother. But he hadn't. She'd been at first unsettled by that fact, then upset, then amused as she realized he fairly took no notice of her at all— except the way his gaze roved up and down her figure when she finally stood in front of him. That alone made her tingle deep inside. He admired her even as Charlotte, if for nothing else than her curves. And that was a start.

So, after a fitful night's sleep, angered in the extreme that Charles would even consider selling an antique that brought her so much pleasure, she'd decided on a few things, made a few plans. That's why she now found herself standing in front of the Duke of Newark's townhouse, very close to her own home, ready to make him an offer she felt almost certain he wouldn't refuse.

Standing tall, shoulders straightened, she held her reticule in her left hand and rang the bell, quickly glancing down her person to make certain her day gown of forest-green silk lay perfectly.

Almost at once the door opened and she faced the duke's butler, a rather old man with thick white hair and side whiskers that grazed the edges of his mouth.

She smiled politely and pulled a card from her reticule. "The Lady Charlotte Hughes to see his grace. Is he at home?"

The man grunted most unbecomingly, then moved to his side to allow her entrance.

"Please wait here," he replied gruffly.

Charlotte stood in the entryway, grinning broadly at the man's exquisite taste in expensive items—rich marble floors, solid oak paneling that had recently been oiled, lovely displays of artwork adorning the walls. A table with nothing more than a vase of fresh flowers on it rested against the wall to her left, beside which stood a single Louis Quinze chair, thickly padded in brown velvet, and an enormous crystal chandelier hung above her head that undoubtedly gave off the radiance of a thousand candles when lit. And this was only his foyer.

She swallowed a giggle. The infamous, womanizing Duke of Newark had money, the greatest catch of all.

Suddenly the butler appeared again from her right.

"This way, if you please, Lady Charlotte. His grace will see you in his study."   •

She nodded once, but said nothing as she followed the old man, her shoes making only the slightest tapping sound on the marble beneath her feet. He led her down a long hallway, bare but for various family portraits hanging on the wall.

At last she stopped when the butler did as he knocked on the door to the man's study. She drew a deep breath for confidence, squeezing her reticule with both hands to keep them from shaking. Then the butler announced her and she stepped inside the room.

Immediately, her gaze fell on him, and her heart skipped a beat from just one look at his handsome form. A simply gorgeous man, he sat at his enormous desk of solid oak, gazing down at something he was writing, the sun from the window behind his head making his dark blond hair shine brilliantly as it fell behind his ears.

He had flawless skin, as she'd been able to tell from last week's close observance by lamplight, and hazel eyes, thickly lashed and very keen. His jaw remained hard and defined, even when he smiled, which was often. He truly was a magnificent-looking man, and everything in her told her he knew it, too. Naturally, that made him susceptible to the gracious charms of the ladies. But no matter. She intended to get more from him than a few rolls between his sheets.

"The Lady Charlotte, your grace," the butler properly announced, pulling her at once from her intriguing thoughts of him.

Shoulders back, she eyed him carefully as he stood for the introduction, though he continued to gaze at his paperwork.

"Good afternoon, Lady Charlotte. Please come in and be seated."

It annoyed her a little that he only cast a swift glance in her direction and didn't even look at her person. But she took that in stride, knowing the shock to come would be entirely satisfactory.

After nodding once to the butler, he sat again as the older man quit the room and closed the door behind him.

Charlotte moved toward his desk, ever so quietly, and took a seat in the black leather chair opposite him, watching him as he concentrated on his paperwork.

"I'll be with you momentarily," he said, his voice flat with his concentrated effort.

She sat primly on the edge of her seat, meekly waiting as a good lady should, casting her first real glance around the room, richly decorated in dark greens and browns, elegantly masculine, with a grate to the right of her chair, now emitting a slow-burning fire.

At last he looked up, placing his pen in the inkwell and sitting back casually in his recently polished oak rocker to view her candidly.

Charlotte shifted her bottom a little from his scrutiny, from the intensity of his hazel eyes as he took in all of her, especially her face.

"You left your spectacles at home," he remarked with a sly, upward tilt of his lips.

She tried not to look at his mouth—the beautiful, sensual mouth she'd so boldly kissed only one week ago.

"I only need them for reading, your grace," she answered softly. "Just books and music—and of course for embroidering."

"Of course." He cocked his head to the side a little and scratched his jaw. "You're very pretty."

That caught her so completely off guard she had to blink quickly, her face undoubtedly flushing bright crimson from his sharp and verbal observance and probably coating his unfettered arrogance. But it was a compliment she couldn't take lightly. Very few men she'd ever known as the simple Charlotte Hughes had ever thought her pretty, and even fewer had mentioned it outright as he just did.

"Umm . . . Thank you kindly, your grace," she replied after only the briefest hesitation.

He seemed amused, and she liked him that way, good-natured and relaxed.

He folded his hands across his stomach, interlocking his fingers, still watching her closely.

"Why haven't you married?" he asked bluntly.

She rubbed the threading on her reticule, her heart racing as she realized he still hadn't recognized her as the infamous Lottie English, even without her glasses. That had been her hope, actually, and she fully intended to use his ignorance to her advantage.

"Haven't married?" she repeated, pretending surprise at the question.

He shrugged minutely. "Your brother said you've refused suitors, but after looking at you closely, I'm certain you've had plenty."

Closely? Though he offered her a compliment, he still didn't even know who she was. She fought hard to suppress a laugh. "I've been exceptionally busy, your grace."

"Busy?"

She gave him a slight smile. "With my music."

His brows rose. "Ah, I understand."

He didn't understand at all, which she, again, found amusing. As a typical gentleman, he no doubt assumed she had nothing to do with her time but wait to be married. She was going to positively adore this revelation.

"I suppose that's why you're here," he said, breaking into her thoughts.

"Why I'm here?" She had absolutely no idea where his mind was drifting, for *he* certainly wasn't interested in marrying the prim and awkwardly shy Lady Charlotte.

"You want your pianoforte returned to you," he lightly explained.

Now she grasped his meaning. He assumed she'd come to beg for her pianoforte. "Well, uh, yes—of course I do."

He sighed, and tapped his fingertips together in front of him. "I do think it would make a perfect dowry, in and of itself. You could sell it for quite a sum, then buy a new piano for your . . . individual playing enjoyment."

She couldn't help looking at him as if he were an idiot. Her forehead creased as she gazed at him openly, discerning at once that he realized her brother was in debt from his lazy feet to his well-oiled head of hair, and he assumed the only reason she'd called on him today was to retrieve something she so valued. He was offering her advice, poor devil, and the moments to come would be priceless.

Suddenly she stood and dropped her reticule in the chair, walking to the grate and gazing up to a magnificent oil painting of two lovely women sitting in a lush and colorful garden. Family, she decided, for the ladies looked just like him.

"Actually, your grace," she revealed, studying the portrait, "I'm here for more than just a request for my pianoforte."

She knew without glancing his way that he was taking in all of her person with shrewd speculation, and for that reason alone she'd worn her best gown, cut low across her breasts and tightly corseted, why she'd piled her unruly hair on her head with dainty elegance instead of pulling it back in a simple ribbon. She wanted him to notice her.

At last he replied, "I'm not sure what else I can do for you, Lady Charlotte, though I am willing to give you back the instrument of your desire."

The instrument of her desire. If only he knew.

Smiling, still focusing on the painting, her stomach tightly coiled in knots, she admitted in a tone of deep shyness, "You could marry me."

After several long seconds of a riveting silence, she feared he might burst out into a fit of uncontrollable laughter, and she'd prepared herself for just such a response. But to his credit, his reaction seemed a bit more staid, as if he were thinking not of what a marvelous proposal she'd offered, but of how to get her out of his townhouse, and quickly.

Smiling, she pivoted to look at him squarely, and the expression on his face was, indeed, priceless. Beyond shock, his features were contorted in absolute confusion, his brows furrowed hard, his mouth opened slightly in total stupefaction at her outrageous pronouncement.

Since he seemed so at a loss for words, she shrugged lightly and added, "You do need a wife, and I desperately need a husband. What union could possibly be more . . . agreeable?"

Finally, recovering himself, he stood very slowly, resting one hand on his hip while raking the other through his hair.

She waited, knowing he had absolutely no idea what to say to her, and likely thinking her insane.

"Uh . . . Lady Charlotte," he began, his voice controlled but suddenly gravelly. "I . . . um . . . don't need a wife any more than I need a pianoforte."

"But I can play beautifully," she returned in pure innocence, containing her joy at his delicious response.

He shook his head and rubbed his eyes with harsh fingertips. "I'm certain you can, but that's not the point."

Poor man. He really was squirming in his boots, though she had to give him credit for not attempting to throw her out in disgust. "I realize the pianoforte has nothing to do with marriage, your grace, but really, don't you think marriage would be far more . . . acceptable socially than simply taking me as your mistress?"

That struck him like a blow to the gut. His head shot up; his eyes opened wide as he stared at her aghast. "I beg your pardon?"

She fairly glided toward him, with deliberate slowness, her hands clasped behind her back as she focused on the clean, expensive carpeting at her feet, denying him the amusement, the satisfaction, in her eyes. "I'm sure you're aware, sir, how everyone speculates about your latest . . . trifle, shall we say. And to rid yourself of such unseemly gossip, I could bring some respectability back to your name. I'm the sister of an earl, an earl in some debt, as you're very much aware, and I think we could . . . help each other with our . . . mutual needs."

Lifting her lashes, she gazed up at him again, standing very close to him now, noticing how he gaped at her, his beautifully sculpted face flushed, with embarrassment she hoped, how his perfectly chiseled muscles bunched tautly beneath his expertly pressed linen shirt. He appeared nothing short of astounded at her boldness.

She waited, staring into his eyes until he answered, said something.

Abruptly he composed himself, straightening as he fisted his hands at his sides, his features hardening, his jaw tightening as he looked at her now in obvious anger at her audacity.

"I believe," he said coolly, "that you have spoken far beyond what's proper for a lady of your station. We will forget this incident, and neither of us will mention your outrageous behavior to anyone." He dropped his gaze to his desk and righted his paperwork. "I have much to do, Lady Charlotte. I'm asking you kindly to take your leave."

She instead moved closer to him, only inches away from his commanding presence, the hem of her skirt brushing his shins. "But we still have a great deal to discuss, your grace."

He stood more than half a foot taller than her, and yet she knew her outrageous behavior, as he'd so aptly called it, had disconcerted him. And she could very well sense that he'd nearly reached the point where he would call his butler to escort her out.

"Let me make this clear," he said succinctly, cutting into her thoughts with a tone of restrained but tightly wound outrage. "Beneath your prim facade and ordinary features, you are obviously a brazen little minx, the most undesirable type of female for any purpose I can imagine. I would no more ask you to clean my dusty house than marry you or take you as a mistress—"

"Oh, but I think you will," she replied as she stared at his chest, lowering her voice nearly to the depth and huskiness she portrayed to him the night she met him as Lottie. "In fact, I'm quite sure of it."

He was beyond appalled. "Do you have any idea who you're speaking to, madam?" he asked through clenched teeth.

She raised her gaze to meet his once more, offering him her best seductive smile. "I think the question should be, do you have any idea who *you're* speaking with . . . Colin?"

A sharp, static charge filled the air, sucking them into a maelstrom of heated emotions that intertwined and radiated between them. For a second, Charlotte thought he might strike her; he looked just that mad.

And then he lowered his gaze to her breasts, which she'd so carefully lifted and revealed by corset, filling her with the same heat he made her feel that eventful night in her dressing room.

Boldly, she raised one hand and placed it on his warm, exposed neck. He flinched slightly from the contact, but otherwise didn't move.

"Dear Colin," she breathed, leaning into him so that her mouth very nearly touched his chin, "would you be more responsive to my needs if I sang for you first?"

His gaze shot up sharply. And then the revelation struck him as a lightning bolt.

He staggered back, his mouth dropped open, eyes wide, features going slack with absolute astonishment as he fairly fell into his chair.

"Jesus . . ." he whispered.

She smiled and leaned to her side, her palm resting atop his paperwork on the desk, her hip perched on the edge. Raising a brow, she murmured, "I see I've shocked you."

He said nothing to that, just continued to gape at her, his eyes opened wide in a growing, shock-filled panic.

She played with the pen in his inkwell, twisting it absentmindedly between her fingers. "I'm here today because I'm hoping you still . . . um . . . need me," she added, her voice displaying only the slightest tremor of the excitement she felt.

He looked her up and down again, almost in wonder this time, taking in her hair, her bosom, the slimness of her waist, and then her face, which he peered at starkly, grazing every inch of it, stopping at last to penetrate her eyes.

"Jesus. Lottie . . ."

Abruptly, through a wave of profound satisfaction, she raised herself and stood again, walking around his desk to take a seat in the chair across from him, the husky, sensual Lottie disappearing to be replaced with her true self, the Lady Charlotte Hughes.

He continued to stare, if only to satisfy his eagerness to understand exactly how he could be so duped. She allowed him this time to gather his thoughts, to come to terms with his recent actions toward both of her personas, as she fluffed her skirts around her ankles, sitting erect once more, grasping her reticule with both hands on her lap.

At last he shook himself and cleared his throat, leaning forward again with his hands tightly clutched on top of the desk, though he couldn't hide the fact that they were shaking.

"I'm—I'm sorry. Lottie—"

"I'm more properly called Lady Charlotte, your grace," she interrupted pleasantly, "but you may call me Charlotte."

He opened his mouth to say something, then shut it abruptly, frowning slightly by her change in manner.

"Charlotte . . . I'm—I'm just—"

"Fairly speechless apparently," she said for him with a twitch of her lips. "I assumed you would be, but then I wanted you to see it for yourself rather than have me simply tell you who I am."

He wiped a palm harshly down his face, then interlocked his fingers once more. "Why?"

She shrugged, her eyes sparkling. "It was fun."

That simple answer caused his irritation to resurface. His slack features hardened again, his gaze narrowed.

Her smile vanished as well as she returned to the point of her visit. "Your grace, I've obviously come here for a purpose today, and it wasn't to embarrass you, or to beg for my pianoforte, which never should have been sold to you in the first place." She drew a long breath, watching him. "I was altogether serious about a mutual agreement between us, a marriage, legal and binding, but with . . . benefits, shall we say, for both of us."

"Both of us," he repeated, his expression flat.

She completely understood the jumble of information that had to be going through his mind at the moment, and so she just continued, undaunted.

"Indeed." She leaned forward, her eyes darkening with purpose. "I'll not play games with you, sir. I need a husband, a wealthy husband, who can afford my desire to travel abroad and build my singing career. I have no desire for marriage at all, as you very well know, just as I know you have no desire for marriage, either. And yet a simple marriage between us would satisfy exactly what we both need."

He sucked in his cheeks, perhaps to keep from laughing. "Did you say a—a *simple* marriage?"

She ignored his rhetorical question, smiling negligibly as she remained steadfast. "Just consider for a moment, your grace, that I am a titled lady with an impeccable reputation, proper in every regard, tutored by the best. I can embroider, entertain, organize a household, and play the piano for any occasion. I'll satisfy every need you have, including those of the bedroom, as you'll certainly want an heir. I will have no reservations in giving you what you deserve as the married Duke of Newark."

Amusement lit his eyes, and he relaxed against the back of his chair, studying her with his head tipped to one side.

"You seem to have thought of everything," he drawled.

Coyly, she replied, "I'm also very practical."

"Yes, that's quite apparent."

"There is one stipulation, however," she added almost too casually.

"There usually is," he interjected, placing his elbow on the armrest of his chair, his chin in his palm.

She felt warm inside suddenly, as if he were intentionally teasing to fluster her. And it was working, too, though she refused to allow him to know it.

Rigidly, with great care, she expounded, "I would like you to finance a tour for me. I want to sing, your grace, all over Europe. I can do it, and will be adored for my gift, but as the Earl of Brixham's sister, I don't now have the funds or the opportunity." She huffed. "Not to mention the fact that he'd never allow me to do what is in his mind an utterly disgraceful thing."

He thought about that for a moment, then asked lightly, "And if I . . . finance your tour, you'll give me what in return?"

She creased her brows. "I already told you. I'll provide you with a good home, a proper wife, and an heir if you so desire."

"Oh, Lady Charlotte," he whispered in a husky tremor, "if I actually go through the immense trouble of engaging myself in a *simple* marriage, I would certainly so desire."

His quick response, at once both tactless and intimate, took her aback. Her eyelashes fluttered and her mouth opened a little.

Giving her a sly grin, he stated, "But really, I can sponsor a tour for you without the legalities a marital union would require."

That hurt her a little, though she tried to ignore the feeling of being brushed aside as a lady to be courted. "You don't approve of marriage, your grace?" she prodded, her tone conveying only the hint of disbelief.

"Oh, I approve of it wholeheartedly," he replied at once, "for everybody but myself."

That stumped her. She hadn't expected him to be so against what was required of him and his duty to reproduce. "But you'll need an heir."

"Yes, so I've been told by everyone I know. Repeatedly." His smile went flat. "Still, *I'd* rather be the one to choose the lady, and the time to marry her."

It suddenly occurred to Charlotte that he might turn her and her generous offer down. Leaning forward, she reemerged as the Lottie he knew, the fantasy that had him wanting her so desperately. "Of course you would, Colin," she agreed in a sultry murmur. "I'm merely *suggesting* that we work through our options together, that the time couldn't be better for either of us. And I know how much you adore my singing, my . . . persona on the stage."

He lifted his brows a fraction, though his eyes narrowed with calculation as she altered her demeanor. "Indeed I do. But I'm not certain how that's relevant."

"You're not? What was it you said to me? That being with Lottie English was something you'd desired for years?"

His expression grew sober, his gaze piercing hers in a measure of defiance. "I think I recall saying as much."

"Then I'm here to tell you, sir, I am a properly bred lady, the sister of an earl. I would never take a lover, regardless of his appeal—or how very, *very* much I desired him. But I will fully and happily consent to being bedded by my husband."

She said that in a dark and husky whisper, her fingertips caressing the slope of her cleavage nearly imperceptibly, noting with satisfaction how his gaze lowered and lingered.

He adjusted his large, masculine body in his chair and began rocking, his palms flat on the armrests, his eyes assessing. "I suppose that is the proper thing for a lady to do," he dryly remarked.

She'd trapped him, and he knew it. There wasn't any chance on earth that Lottie English would become his mistress without the Lady Charlotte Hughes first becoming his legally married wife. And she was a perfect choice for that. His decision, then, rested on how badly he needed her physically; how much he truly wanted her as a woman.

"Do you find me appealing, Charlotte?" he asked moments later. "Do you desire me that much? Or is your act as Lottie only that—an act?"

She felt color rising up her neck and into her cheeks, but she could hardly back down after tempting him as she had. With a light shrug of one shoulder, she countered, "Does it matter?"

He laughed, though the sound carried absolutely no humor. "Yes, I believe it does. Will I be bedding a cold lady who is only performing her wifely duty, or will I have an intense love affair with the woman of my dreams?"

The woman of my dreams . . .

Charlotte squirmed in her seat, now feeling the steady heating of her blood to the roots of her hair, her heartbeat quickening. She had no idea how to answer his question in a manner that would satisfy. Instead, she asked, "I assume you want the love affair, your grace?"

He watched her for a second or two, giving nothing away, then fairly whispered, "Only if it's mutual, Lady Charlotte."

She swallowed, then allowed herself to admit what she felt deep inside. "I think, sir, that you are the most handsome man I've ever personally known, or even seen from afar."

His eyes lit with a trace of amusement, even pride, and he almost grinned.

"But then all the ladies think so," she added matter-of-factly before he could comment. "You already know that, I'm sure."

His features tightened; his shadow of a smile gradually hardened. She carried on before she lost her nerve. "I have every intention of being your lover, your grace, giving you what I can intimately, but I won't do it without marrying you first. It's your choice."

He looked irritated again, and certainly he had to be, for she was more or less baiting him, forcing him to choose between his rational needs and those desires of a baser nature.

"And one more point, sir," she said carefully, eyeing him closely.

He fairly snorted, then drawled, "I can only imagine what that might be."

She brushed over the sarcasm. "I'm a very understanding lady where men like you are concerned."

He frowned, crossing arms over his chest. "Men like me?"

She absentmindedly straightened her skirts at the knees. "Men like you who have . . . trouble remaining faithful to one lady for any length of time."

That audacious comment irked him again, but he didn't say a word to counter, only stared at her blatantly with cool, appraising eyes.

She offered him a reassuring smile. "I have no illusions about what married life will be like for us, sir, and I will remain ever practical. That is, of course, should you decide to take me up on my offer."

He rocked back, his head tilted to one side. "Of course."

After only the slightest hesitation, she asserted, "I'm an intelligent woman, and I understand that men have certain . . . instinctive needs. You may rest assured that I will always look the other way when you tire of me and choose another. I've never been, nor shall I become, a lady prone to fits of jealousy."

He didn't even blink. "That's very good to know," he returned, his tone contemplative. "And quite generous of you, Lady Charlotte."

She beamed, relaxing to her bones at his gracious understanding. "Yes, I think so. But then I plan to travel and it's more than likely we won't see much of each other, which I'm sure you'll agree is for the best."

"Is that what you think?"

"Naturally."

He studied her for a moment, once again lowering his gaze to her breasts, and she had to thank God then and there that at least she'd been blessed with a full bosom. Her voice was undoubtedly her greatest asset, but she very well knew men didn't much care about how well a lady could sing. They always, however, cared about breasts.

"And what if you take a lover, Charlotte?" he asked thoughtfully, rubbing the side of his jaw with one large palm.

That flustered her. "I beg your pardon?"

He straightened a little in his rocker. "What if I want you all to myself? Am I to let you out of my sight on a European operatic tour that gives you opportunity to take lovers in France, Italy, Spain?" He snickered and folded both hands in his lap. "Is that what you expect?"

Frankly, she'd never once thought of such a thing. The sexual act, what she knew of it, consisted of grunting men and passive wives who dutifully gave whatever pleasure their husbands needed so they could return quickly to more important obligations. Although she'd teased the Duke of Newark about becoming his lover the night they met in her dressing room, she'd never considered doing such a thing with anyone else.

"You don't have an answer?" he asked rather brusquely.

She shook her head, blinking quickly in confusion. "No, of course not. I mean—I've just—I've never thought about it."

He laughed out loud with genuine amazement. "You're telling me I'm the only man you've considered taking as a lover?"

That made her mad. "My life is my singing, your grace," she articulated, eyes flashing. "I couldn't care any less about your needs, your desires, your mistresses, nor do I care to take a . . . variety of men to my bed. So, no. I can honestly say that I have no desire for any lover but you." Yielding a bit, she added, "And only if we're properly married."

Something in her words or manner got to him. His features softened, his lips once again formed a hint of a smile, and he leaned his head against the back of his wooden rocker.

"What a priceless bargain you offer me, Charlotte."

With grace and a sweeping of her skirts, she slowly stood, her reticule clutched at her waist, facing him with marked determination. "I do hope you'll consider my proposal with care, sir. I'm very, very serious about it. I do not intend to take the marriage vows lightly, and will do my best to honor you with my utmost devotion."

He grinned wryly. "As a dutiful wife?"

For a moment Charlotte wondered if he were mocking her, then decided she didn't want to know. "Yes, exactly," she replied modestly.

After drawing a deep breath and exhaling fully, he gradually stood to meet the challenge in her gaze. But instead of simply dismissing her or bidding her good day from behind his desk, he walked swiftly around it, toward her, almost alarming her when he moved to her side, his expression one of pure satisfaction. She had no idea what to make of that.

"Your grace?" she murmured, concern edging her words.

He grinned devilishly. "I suppose you won't let me kiss you again until we're properly married?"

She stared up to his beautiful, handsome face, his knowing expression and amusement-filled eyes. "So you agree to my proposal?"

She held her breath, hopeful, with dreams of taking the stage in Milan for the first time, the applause, the thrown roses, the cheers and accolades.

"It's . . . the most enticing offer of marriage I've received from a lady, I'll say that much."

That's it? "I've offered you everything I can, your grace. It's a perfect opportunity, for both of us. We *need* each other."

His smile slowly faded, his eyes narrowed, and for a second or two she feared she'd gone too far in practically begging.

And then, instead of kissing her as she feared he'd do, hoped he'd do, he reached out and placed his palm beneath her chin, lifting her head a little as he gently brushed his thumb across her lips.

She shivered, trying to back away, but her knees bumped up against the chair in which she'd only just been sitting.

"You're quite a treasure, aren't you?" he murmured, brows furrowed as he scanned every inch of her face.

She drew in a shaky breath and he removed his thumb. "My brother thinks I'm merely trouble. But I'll try to behave myself when I'm with you, especially when we're watched by society's eye in any public forum."

His lips curved up wryly. "That's very good to know."

She waited, anxious to depart, but unable to move away from the warmth of his body so close to her own. With fortitude, she asked, "Do we have an agreement, your grace?"

"Colin," he corrected.

She acquiesced. "Do we have an agreement, Colin?"

After a moment of lingering silence, he replied, "I'll consider it, Charlotte."

She noted immediately that he'd used exactly the same words she had the night he propositioned her in the theater, certainly intentional, and not at all the answer she wanted to hear. But then it wasn't quite a rejection, either. She supposed she needed to allow him time to adjust to the idea. Marriage was, after all, a huge step for anyone.

"I—I should leave. I need to be at the theater soon in preparation for tonight's performance."

He stepped back without reluctance and formally waved his hand to let her pass. "Then don't let me keep you from your adoring admirers."

She curtsied quickly and brushed past him. At the door, she paused and glanced back.

He still stood gazing at her with his hands crossed over his chest.

"Will you be there tonight?" she asked softly.

His countenance became somber. Contemplatively, he asked, "Do you want me to be?"

It seemed like a truly genuine question, and suddenly she wanted him to know how very much she relied on him for support and adoration from afar. "I always want you there, Colin."

She could have sworn he exhaled a shaky breath, his gaze searing hers. Then he nodded once, and murmured, "We shall see, Lady Charlotte. Good afternoon."

It was a clear dismissal, and she heeded it with a fraction of a smile upon her mouth. "Good afternoon, your grace."

With a lift of her skirts, she held her chin high and walked out of his study.

Chapter 5

⟨⟨⟩⟩

Colin rapped on the door of Sir Thomas's office at the Yard, then walked in without waiting for a reply.

He wouldn't call himself angry, exactly, but the look he sported on his face and in his eyes must have displayed his agitation, for at once Sir Thomas's secretary, John Blaine, looked up from his paperwork, his expression startled.

"Is he in? I need to see him immediately," Colin remarked as he began to stride toward the closed door of his employer's inner office.

Blaine stood and pulled down on his jacket, which fit him far too tightly at the waist. "He's in, but I'd prefer to announce you first, your grace. He's been quite busy this—"

"Then do so at once," he interrupted, his tone cooler than he'd intended.

Blaine gave him a sideways glance through his large spectacles that reminded Colin of those worn by

Charlotte—plain, thick, and completely unbecoming. But where Charlotte remained a beauty underneath, this man couldn't be more unattractive, his face pulled tightly as if he were tense about life in general, his features reminding Colin of a racoon's with his large, dark eyes, rounded cheeks, small thin lips, and a flat, receding chin. But he was apparently very good at what he did, as Sir Thomas trusted him completely. And appearance hardly mattered in the competent.

Blaine knocked on the inner door, then turned the knob and peeked inside. "His grace, the Duke of Newark to see you, sir," he said mildly.

"Let him in," came the fast reply.

Before Blaine could acknowledge the response, Colin had already slipped past him, entering the inner office proper, taking only a quick note of the thin fog of tobacco smoke that enveloped the dark and musty room.

Sir Thomas had been sitting, engrossed in paperwork illuminated only by a single oil lamp on the desk, but stood and bowed his head properly as Colin took a seat in an old and creaking wooden chair across from the man.

"You set me up, my friend," Colin said a bit testily, ignoring the fact that Blaine stood behind him with the door wide open, waiting for instruction.

Sir Thomas sighed and sat heavily again, looking past him briefly. "That'll be all, John," he said to his secretary.

"And we don't wish to be disturbed," Colin added without glancing over his shoulder.

Sir Thomas almost smiled. "No, we don't wish to be disturbed."

"Very well, sir," Blaine replied matter-of-factly before closing the door behind him.

Colin never moved his eyes from the older man, his mentor, who sat across from him now, watching him in return. Sir Thomas's office—indescribably small and cramped, cluttered with stacks of paperwork and overflowing shelves of dust-covered books and odd trinkets—felt unusually stuffy and cold today, the windows closed because of a lingering drizzle and chill in the air. But Colin paid no attention aside from a passing notice. His mind stayed focused on getting to the truth.

"Well?" he prodded, keeping his gaze fixed on the man.

Sir Thomas relaxed a little and fussed with the tie at his thick neck, then perched his elbows on the wooden armrests, his fingers interlocked in front of his chest. "Actually, I'm surprised you didn't confront me at home yesterday," he said casually.

That blasé reply irritated him, and he stretched one leg out, folding his arms across his chest. "I considered it, but decided I wanted to collect my thoughts first."

"Ah. I see."

He snorted. "No, you don't." After wiping one palm harshly down his face, he added, "Do you have any idea what trouble you've caused me?"

The older man's brows rose innocently. "Trouble? You wanted to meet Lottie English. I made that possible."

Colin shook his head, closing his eyes briefly before gazing back at the man. "You could have told me her identity. As it was, you left me unprepared."

"Unprepared for what?"

"Unprepared for what? For *her,* for Christ's sake," he replied harshly.

Sir Thomas continued to watch him closely for a moment, then leaned forward, still clutching his hands together as he placed them on the desktop. "What exactly happened that's got you so riled up, Colin?"

Although Sir Thomas was technically his employer, the man also remained his inferior by title, and almost never used his Christian name. Doing so now surprised him almost as much as it made his irritation worse.

No longer able to sit still, he rose abruptly and shoved his hands in the pockets of his rain-dampened topcoat as he walked to the window, peering out to the grayness of early afternoon.

"She's cornered me," he said soberly.

Sir Thomas chuckled, and he flipped his head around to stare the man down.

"It isn't funny. The woman wants to *marry* me, for God's sake, and she's using her . . . Lottie English persona to entice me into it."

"*Entice* you?"

"Yes, entice me."

Silence reigned for a moment or two and he looked back outside, seeing nothing as the rain picked up once more, splattering the glass and blurring his vision.

Finally, Sir Thomas said, "You don't have to marry anyone not of your choosing. I'm sure I don't need to tell you that, your grace. So what's the real problem?"

Colin rubbed his eyes. "I'm not ready to encumber myself like that yet."

"Yes, you've made that perfectly clear," Sir Thomas replied. "To everybody, I should think."

He ignored the second part of that comment. "I don't want to marry someone I don't even know. Especially a plain girl who plays the piano better than I do."

"Everybody plays the piano better than you do—"

"That's not the point."

"—and she's not all that plain, either."

He grunted. "She's smart."

"Yes, she is. But what I really want to know," the older man continued, "is what happened to make you think you need to marry the girl?"

He'd assumed Sir Thomas was part of the whole blasted plan, but by the sound of the man's perplexed questioning, he was beginning to suspect the idea of a "convenient" marriage had manifested itself in Charlotte's mind alone.

He turned around to face his superior again, noting how Sir Thomas's features had changed into hard lines, his lips had thinned. He didn't look mad, exactly, just . . . irritated, as if he still had trouble grasping the gravity of the situation Colin was undoubtedly explaining badly.

Suddenly he felt drained. Pulling his arms from his topcoat, he removed it, then returned to the chair he'd sat in momentarily, tossing his coat over the wooden back before lowering his body into the seat, slumping into it this time.

"I did as you asked and paid a visit to the Earl of Brixham Friday last," he began, "and offered quite a decent sum for his pianoforte. The man agreed and sold it to me. While I was there, I had the good fortune of meeting the wily Lady Charlotte, who, as I later came to realize, recognized me as the man who met her the previous weekend when she sang upon the stage as Lottie English. Of course *I* had no idea they were one and the same person."

His voice had risen during his diatribe, and he forced himself to control his annoyance. Sir Thomas just watched him, nodding, and so he continued.

"The following day, she had the temerity to come and visit *me* with a proposition of marriage. *Marriage,* for God's sake." He shook his head. "The woman certainly has nerve."

"I think you mean, the *lady*?"

Of course he knew she was a lady. "What's your point?"

Sir Thomas sat up a little, adjusting his stout frame in the chair that looked scarcely able to support his weight. "It sounds like a very good match to me," he said with a shrug.

"*That* is certainly irrelevant," he growled.

The older man leaned back again, eyeing him speculatively. "Why did you come here, your grace, if not to get my thoughts on the matter?"

Colin stared the man down. "I want to know if her brother is indeed in debt, and a problem for which you truly need my skills." He paused, then lowered his voice to add, "Was the job you assigned me a complete fabrication, Thomas?"

It took a long moment for the man to answer, he mused, and Colin hoped he wasn't using the time to contrive a reasonable response. He needed honesty now.

Sir Thomas drew in a long breath at last, then blew

it out slowly through puffed lips. "He *is* in debt; that part is quite true." He waited, then thoughtfully conceded, "But I admit I sent you there, primarily, to give you an opportunity to meet the Lady Charlotte."

"Because you knew she was Lottie English," he stated blandly, though feeling his muscles tensing uncomfortably beneath his clothes.

Sir Thomas nodded. "Yes."

He supposed he expected more than a simple acknowledgment, and yet despite this, he'd gotten the honesty he wanted. Exasperated, he asked, "Why didn't you just tell me who she was? At least I could have been prepared for her impudent intrusion into my home."

Sir Thomas scoffed. "Nonsense. Besides, it wasn't my place, Colin. She didn't—doesn't—want anyone to know."

"And how did *you* find out?" he asked a bit sarcastically.

The man shrugged. "I'm employed by the Crown to know these things."

"That's absurd."

Sir Thomas patted his oiled hair down atop his head. "Let's just say I guessed."

Colin stood abruptly. "You know the family."

"Yes, and I knew her father quite well. I don't, however, trust her brother. He's the one who's kept her secluded and tightly under his thumb for the last three years, and he's very upset at her choice of . . . career, shall we say."

"So you thought perhaps I'd like to get her out of her unfortunate situation at home by marrying her?" he asked, aghast.

The older man's eyes narrowed. "Not in the least. But you *did* want to meet Lottie English. I arranged that for you."

"And now I look the fool," he remarked in muted embarrassment.

"I'm sure the Lady Charlotte thinks no such thing or she wouldn't have come to your home to offer herself in marriage."

Colin rubbed his eyes, his nerves on edge. "As ridiculous as that sounds, you have no idea what transpired between us the night of the opera."

After a very long pause, Sir Thomas sighed. "On the contrary, Colin. I'm quite certain I do."

The wind picked up as the rain grew heavier, now splattering the window in sheets that matched the tumultuous rush of blood through his veins.

Of course he knew. Everybody knew of his reputation with the ladies, and it irked him a little that he could be so transparent to the nobility at large, especially when he didn't exactly *try* to be blatant about his sexual escapades. Truthfully, he'd only wanted to have a little fun, to thoroughly enjoy a full bachelor life for as long as he could before duty tied him down to a sniveling wife and a house of brats. Was that so wrong?

Groaning aloud, he started pacing the little room, his hands on his hips, head down.

"I don't know what to do," he said rather weakly, words he'd likely never repeat to anyone else in the world.

Sir Thomas chuckled again. "That's the easy part. It's a perfect match socially, and you can have Miss English. My advice is to marry the girl."

"I don't want to get married," he fairly blurted. Then deciding he sounded like a child, he added formally, "I should say, I don't want to marry now. I'm not ready."

"Ready for what?"

Colin couldn't think of a response to that, and Sir Thomas evidently understood the confusion playing out in his mind.

"Your grace, if I may be so bold?"

Colin stopped pacing and stood erect, facing the man again.

"Please," he said with a casual wave of his hand.

Sir Thomas eyed him directly, his lids narrowed in assessment. "Marriage is something nobody is prepared for. Not entirely. But it's a step that must be taken eventually, especially by someone of your class. You need an heir, and it's beyond time you produced one now that your father is gone. It's your duty as a man of your station, which I'm sure has at the very least crossed your mind. Lady Charlotte can provide that—"

"Now you sound like her, ever practical."

The older man smiled in understanding. "As you said, she's smart. Frankly, I think she's considered this more clearly than you seem to be doing at the moment, and that's unusual considering how women can sometimes be so irrational."

"I'm not being irrational," he said defensively. "I'm trying to be logical. I don't even know her."

Candidly, his hands folded in front of him, Sir Thomas replied, "I don't care how long the courting process takes, one never knows his spouse until one is actually married. You could court the Lady Charlotte for months, even bed her as Lottie English, and it *still* wouldn't prepare you for marriage." Dropping his voice to just above a whisper, he concluded, "You're obviously attracted to each other. That's the first step. Now do your duty and accept her . . . proposal. Get yourself a wife and heir. The rest will come as it does."

"The rest? The trouble, you mean," he said sullenly.

Sir Thomas lifted one shoulder in shrug. "Perhaps. But there are many beneficial things that come with marriage as well. You simply have to plunge in, head first."

Colin almost smiled. "If I didn't know better, I'd say you planned this whole mess."

The man's brows rose in innocence. "Me? It's not my place to plan your future, your grace."

He snorted, reaching for his coat. "Well said, my friend."

"But Lottie English is every man's fantasy," Sir Thomas added through an exaggerated sigh, relaxing again in his chair. "I envy you."

Colin drew a long, deep breath, realizing at last that his future had altered the moment he set eyes on those luscious curves all those years ago.

He wanted her. He'd wanted her then and he could have her now—legally, willingly, and forevermore. Everything Sir Thomas said, every persuasion he offered, concluded that for him.

Jerking his coat on, he turned for the door. "So help me, you'll pay for this, Thomas," he warned, hiding a smile.

"You'll invite me to the wedding, won't you?"

Colin suppressed a sarcastic retort as he closed the door to the inner office behind him, letting that question linger as he nodded once to Blaine and headed straight for the hallway.

God, but his friends would have a good laugh over this one. The magnificent gala that had been his life was all but over, soon to be replaced by drudgery in the hands of a cunning female who wanted him for her own selfish pursuits. For everything but *him*.

Not that it mattered, he decided as he stepped out through the Yard's main doors and into the gray and gloomy afternoon, shaking off a curious wave of sadness that passed through him as a chill in the air.

Nobody really knew him anyway.

Chapter 6

![ornamental divider]

Colin stood in Earl Brixham's sparsely decorated parlor, brushing his fingers through his damp hair while he awaited the arrival of the cunning Lady Charlotte. He'd come directly here after leaving Sir Thomas, to get the offer done, he supposed, before he thought better of the lifelong consequences and changed his mind. After giving his topcoat to the butler and requesting an audience with the earl, he paced the chilly room, finally stopping to stare at the ugly bright peaches- and cherries-dotted wallpaper, hoping the lady's taste in home decor contained a bit more of a sophisticated edge. This room, though free of superfluous furnishings and useless trinkets, still fairly shrieked of bad taste within a cacophony of loud color—bright red apple, lemon yellow, and tangerine. It wasn't a parlor, it was a fruit stand display. Perhaps his soon-to-be wife had chosen this look herself, though he could hardly imagine Lottie English being gauche in anything she did.

God, what a mess. He'd already accepted her as his and he had yet to ask for her hand. Not that the question itself would matter at this point. He couldn't decide if he were elated or annoyed that she'd taken all the bluster out of the only proposal of marriage he'd likely ever offer. But then nothing in his life had run very smoothly, nor along standard expectations.

"Your grace, what a pleasant surprise."

Colin straightened his shoulders to present a regal bearing, his hands clasped behind him as the Earl of Brixham strode into the parlor in haste, his tone a combination of impatience and false humor, his gaze fixed into a hard stare. From the look of it, a call on the man today wasn't a pleasant surprise at all.

"This isn't a bad time, is it Brixham?" he asked, fighting the urge to rub his scratchy eyes and drop his weary body into the threadbare settee behind him in defeat.

"No, no, of course not," the earl blustered, waving a palm through the air before closing the parlor doors for privacy. A sudden thought gave him pause. "I hope you're not here to discuss our deal regarding the pianoforte."

"No, not at all," Colin replied without embellishment.

The earl's thick brows furrowed as he gestured toward the settee in an invitation to sit. "Then what can I do for you today, sir?"

As with their first meeting, something about the man's demeanor irritated him. Dressed in casual attire, obviously not expecting visitors for tea, he wore plain, tan trousers and an equally unobtrusive matching shirt, unbuttoned at the neck. He hadn't donned any jewelry, and yet it seemed to Colin as if he were just the type of man to do so, for any occasion. He looked and acted ordinary enough, an Englishman at ease, at home in his surroundings, though beneath his smooth disposition there seemed to lurk a certain raw tension, perhaps a general frustration caused by concern for his future if his financial situation were indeed questionable. Still, the Earl of Brixham hadn't done or said anything inappropriate or rude to him, surely nothing to garner such wariness on his part, and yet the man would soon become his brother-in-law, and Colin couldn't put his finger on one agreeable thing about him.

Doing his best to relax against the worn settee cushion, he crossed a leg over the opposite knee and interlaced his fingers in his lap. Getting right to the point, he stated, "I've come with an offer for Charlotte."

The earl didn't even respond with a glance as he neared him. "Another offer? Surely you don't think *she* possesses any antiques for your collection."

If he wasn't so annoyed at the entire situation, Colin might be amused by the earl's unsympathetic ignorance. "Doesn't she, as a lady, possess some worth?" he asked wryly.

Brixham paused beside a wingback chair, his thigh balanced against the armrest. "I beg your pardon?"

Colin shrugged lightly. "You said she needed a husband, and after careful thought, I've decided a match between the Lady Charlotte and myself would be . . . optimal. So, I'm here to offer for her hand."

It was a groundbreaking moment to be sure as Earl Brixham seemed to pale before his eyes, his mouth parting a fraction in bewilderment.

Colin waited, expression flat, actually enjoying the man's shock.

Finally Brixham swallowed, and without looking at it, grabbed the opposite armrest of the chair at his side and more or less plopped down hard on the seat. "Why Charlotte?"

"Why not?" Colin gave him a half smile. "Does it matter?"

Seconds passed in silence. Then the earl abruptly recovered from his initial daze, shaking himself and pulling down on his cuffs as he straightened in his seat and resumed a formal posture.

"I apologize, your grace. It's just that I wasn't expecting an offer of marriage, especially when you seemed so . . . unaffected by my sister at your first meeting. You clearly weren't interested in taking a wife only a week or two ago, and now . . . well . . . here you are." He chuckled, patting down on the back of his hair. "I'm surprised, that's all."

Colin forced himself from squirming in his chair, annoyed that he hadn't considered the suddenness of the proposal and how it might look to the lady's brother. On the other hand, he really didn't need to explain himself, or his actions; the man needed the financial support the union would provide and clearly wanted to free himself from the very real possibility of caring for a spinster sister until his dying breath. Colin could do that for him and they both knew it.

Tenting his fingers in front of him, he nodded as if he completely understood the earl's concern. "You're right, of course, but after considering everything in the last few days, I've decided it's time for me to do the honorable thing and marry. Meeting the Lady Charlotte has presented me with a socially accept-able and logical choice." He paused for emphasis, then added, "And I do need an heir."

Brixham eyed him thoughtfully, rubbing his chin with the tips of his fingers and thumb. "I'm perfectly willing to accept your offer, your grace," he admitted through a sigh. "But I think Charlotte will be diffi-cult to convince. It must be acknowledged that you hardly know her, and she's turned down several gen-tlemen who've attempted to court her, one or two she knew quite well from childhood."

Inexplicably, that acknowledgment irked him. "Perhaps if *I* asked her rather than having you insist on accepting my proposal, she'll be a bit more . . . agreeable?"

He'd purposely phrased that as a question so as not to insult the earl while letting the man know he would never use force or threats with Charlotte because they obviously didn't work. Brixham badly wanted to dump the burdensome Charlotte in his lap, but the man couldn't know that the lady was already his for the taking and coercion would never be an issue.

At last the earl snickered and shook his head. "Of course I can hardly deny that the match is most ex-cellent, your grace, but Charlotte can be quite a chal-lenge."

"Then I suppose she'll be my problem to handle," he replied through a sigh.

"Yes, well, she's a stubborn girl," the man contin-ued, "quite clever, even devious, when she wants something."

You have no idea.

He smiled. "I should like that sort of challenge, I think."

Brixham remained quiet for another moment or two, scratching his side whiskers, his mind clearly absorbing the details, reveling in the importance to be granted him by becoming a relation by marriage to the wealthy Duke of Newark. It didn't take him long to acquiesce.

With a soft grunt, he pushed his thick body out of the chair. "I suppose we can work out the details later in the week."

Colin knew what he was thinking and waved a palm, shaking his head minutely. "No hurry. I'm less concerned about her dowry than I am about an heir."

Brixham's features drew back into a smile of genuine relief. "Very well, your grace," he said, straightening with renewed confidence. "If you wait here, I'll get my sister."

Colin nodded once but didn't move.

It took only a moment or two before the cunning Charlotte entered the room, her features awash with a measure of quick surprise at first sight of him, then turning smug with the tiny smile that crept across her lips. She wore a simple day gown in deep blue, cut squarely across her bosom and tapering into tight stays before falling in layers of silk to the floor. She truly had a magnificent figure, and the only thought to cross his mind was to wonder how this particularly well-endowed female managed to sing so grandly wearing such a tight corset. But then that question remained highly irrelevant at the moment. He'd figure that out soon enough.

With resignation, Colin stood as required, but offered her nothing by way of expression.

"Your grace," she said softly, offering him a tiny curtsy.

"Lady Charlotte," he drawled.

Seconds of uncomfortable silence droned as she glanced from him to her brother and back again. Brixham took the cue, clearing his throat as he moved to make a gentlemanly exit. "Well then, I suppose I'll leave the two of you alone to chat." Pausing at the doors, he added, "I'll just be down the hall in my study should either of you need me."

Colin could feel the tension crackle between the lady and her brother, and he truly had to wonder at the nature of their relationship as he watched the man give his sister a sharp glance before quitting the room, closing the parlor doors behind him. She, however, seemed to take it all in stride, smiling smugly, hands clasped behind her as she kept her attention focused on him.

"I'm surprised to see you here," she said breezily.

His brows rose at her attempt at a casual air. "Are you."

It wasn't a question at all, and she obviously didn't feel the need to answer it. But after a few lingering seconds of silence, the uncomfortable anticipation of the moment overcame her. She knew precisely why he called on her, though it apparently just dawned on her that he wasn't about to make any part of their meeting easy. He crossed his arms over his chest, waiting, taking particular note of the rosy flush creeping into her cheeks. In truth, he was likely more nervous than she, though he'd never admit that to anyone, and certainly he could hide it better.

Purposely eyeing her up and down, he remarked, "You look lovely today."

He exaggerated the compliment of course, but she took it in stride, fairly challenging him with her direct gaze and rather flat expression.

"Thank you," she replied with a lift of a brow. "And may I say, sir, that you are as charming as always."

A grin threatened to escape him. "Indeed."

For several long seconds they stared at each other. Then taking a full breath for confidence, she asked bluntly, "Are you here to offer for me, your grace?"

His nerves caught fire at her forthrightness. "You're quite the presumptuous thing, aren't you?"

She actually smiled, not in the least perturbed by his irritation, casting him a sideways glance as she began to move in the direction of the settee. "I can't for a minute think of another reason you'd call on me, sir."

"Perhaps to formally turn your gracious offer down?"

She faltered briefly in her stride, her forehead creasing a fraction. She hadn't expected that response from him, and he felt an absurd satisfaction in knowing he'd taken the advantage away from her, if only briefly.

Then her mouth widened into a full grin as she continued moving slowly toward him, her gaze holding his. "Nicely put, your grace, and yet I can't help but recall the . . . enthusiasm you expressed the night we met at the opera."

"Enthusiasm?" he repeated, keeping his voice and features prosaic as she sauntered up to stand before him.

She looked up innocently. "You'd call it something else? I wouldn't."

Colin couldn't decide if her audacious resolve angered or aroused him. He studied her silently for a moment, noting her creamy, faintly freckled skin, the intelligence in her large, blue eyes that shone brightly even without the bold application of cosmetics, her high cheekbones, and the few, curling wisps of strawberry blond hair that escaped the plait woven from her crown to the middle of her back. Yes, he was very, *very* enthusiastic, though he refused to admit it to her now.

"I'd probably call it entrapment," he said at last, his gaze melding with hers in a deliberate attempt to intimidate. It didn't appear to work.

She pressed her lips together to suppress a giggle. "Nonsense. You're free to turn me down and yet you haven't because you know I offer you something not only tempting, but necessary, for both of us." Lowering her voice, she leaned toward him to slyly add, "You're as excited about the prospect as I am, though I do understand your excitement stems from a slightly different motive."

Slightly different? Their motives couldn't be more polarized. He shoved his hands in the pockets of his trousers to keep from reaching for her neck and throttling her—or drawing her close so he could caress her throat while exploring that beautiful mouth of hers again.

Quietly, he replied, "I'm excited about many things,

as I'm certain you know. I'm not, however, the least bit excited about having the choice of a wife taken from me, by anyone, regardless of the reason."

She watched him, her head tipped to one side minutely. "I suppose, in a manner of speaking, I've taken the wind from your sails, haven't I? That must be very difficult for a gentleman."

He almost snorted. "I appreciate your concern, but I think my sails are performing just fine, Charlotte."

Cheeks pinkening, she shifted from one foot to the other. "I do realize that as a man you need variety in your prospects, and your settling for one lady could become an exercise in boredom. However, as I've said before, faithfulness in marriage is not one of my concerns. We will both benefit greatly from this union, and I assure you, sir, nobody but the two of us will ever know the truth."

Her simple admission, hitting home so bluntly, shook him a bit, and he stifled a caustic response. Feeling a rising irritation within, he kneaded the tight muscles of his neck with one hard palm as he turned his back on her and strode toward a lone velveteen chair beside the cold grate, its garish, tangerine seat cushion as threadbare as the settee's. Standing behind it, he interlocked his fingers and rested his forearms on the high back, facing her again with a gnawing in his gut.

She crossed her arms defensively just under her breasts, seemingly unaware how it pushed her cleavage up and out provocatively.

"In my experience, variety can be highly overrated, my Lady Charlotte," he murmured seconds later, eyeing her up and down with deliberate slowness. "Your generosity in this matter is no doubt unmatched, but really, why would I want to stray with Lottie English warming my sheets every night?"

His daring question flustered her. Her face flushed with warmth anew as she followed his gaze to her bosom, then spun on her heels at once, walking toward the far window to stare outside at a garden totally hidden by the blur of the cold, persisting rain.

Another long silence ensued, though he took her embarrassment and the uneasy strain between them in stride. He intended to remain formidable in his approach, to let her know without any doubt that although he might be giving in to her desire for a convenient marriage, he would remain the dominant presence in their relationship, that even under the spell of her Lottie English persona he would not be made a fool. Still, even watching her now, catching her off guard by his unexpected arrival and bold, lascivious comment, he couldn't shrug her prettiness aside, nor ignore her cleverness, sophistication, and radiant sexual appeal, all held modestly in check beneath the guise of a gently bred lady.

Oh, yes. She would please him for a long time to come.

Feigning defeat, he swallowed his trepidation and announced, "Very well, my lady. I suppose it appears that I have no choice but to ask you formally to become my wife."

He knew immediately, by her rigid posture and the fact that she didn't cast him even the slightest glance, that he hadn't offered her the most flattering proposal. Yet what could she expect after coercing him? Flowers and a ring on bended knee? Groaning at his own ineptitude, he squeezed the back of the chair and added softly, "Would you kindly do me the honor of marrying me, Charlotte?"

It was the best he could do under the circumstances, and they both knew she had no intention of denying him.

After several long, tense seconds, she leaned her head back a little and very faintly sighed. He waited for a reply, knowing what her answer would be and yet keenly aware of how dry his mouth had become as the time ticked by in maddening silence.

Finally, she turned to face him again, clasping her hands behind her, standing tall and unintimidated, her features calm and unreadable.

"I would be most honored to accept your proposal of marriage, your grace," she said somewhat breathlessly.

An unanticipated mixture of apprehension and unbridled lust washed over him and he straightened, realizing he'd been tightly clutching the back of the chair. Collecting himself, he nodded once, unsure if more were required of him in response to her answer, then deciding it didn't matter. She did nothing but watch him, thoughts hidden, and after another moment or two he elected to just carry on and get the terms of their agreement out in the open, so to speak, to avoid any misunderstanding on her part as to the conditions of their marriage that was now a certainty with her acceptance.

After rubbing the chair's velvety back with his palms, he moved away from it, clasping his hands behind him as he first stared at the grate, then turned to face her fully from across the room.

"Now that our . . . betrothal is settled," he announced matter-of-factly, "there are a few minor details we need to discuss."

"Of course," she replied. "I shall be happy to plan the wedding, though I would like to marry as soon as possible."

"So would I," he agreed, catching himself before he told her his reasons differed markedly from hers. "And I'm certain you'll plan a lovely wedding, though that's not what I meant."

She frowned just enough for him to realize she never expected him to make demands or that he might come to the marriage with his own stipulations, and such knowledge of her ignorance encouraged him. The thought of regaining an advantage over her made him hold back a grin of total satisfaction.

"Very well, your grace," she yielded with a slight tip of her head. "I suppose I should expect you to have concerns."

He did smile at that, strictly for her benefit. "Concerns, no. Requirements, yes."

She bit her lip hesitantly, standing as regally as possible in front of the window, one hand still behind her, the other now nervously tinkering with a golden chain at her throat. "I already told you I will be a most appropriate wife, in every manner possible. I can't imagine what other requirements there might be." Suddenly, a look of horror crossed her features. "You don't expect me to quit—"

"I will never stop you from performing, Charlotte. You needn't worry about that."

She slumped minutely, her relief palpable.

He waited, allowing her curiosity to build, anticipating the coming moment immensely. Finally, he shrugged and said, "No, I'm talking about bedroom requirements. We need to discuss those before we become . . . intimate."

She actually gasped, jaw dropping, her eyes growing wide in offense.

Colin remained outwardly unmoved by her surprise, inwardly delighted by her embarrassment as he noticed her cheeks color with another magnificent flush.

"We do not need to discuss any such thing," she countered in quiet defiance. "I believe I already told you I'll provide you an heir. There's nothing more to say in that regard, your grace."

Colin began a slow saunter toward her, hands still behind him, brows slightly furrowed, his mouth hinting at a frown. "It's not that simple. Of course I expect you to provide me an heir in exchange for the trouble that comes with the binding ties of matrimony, but there's more involved than just bedding you until you carry."

She blinked, pulling back a little as he neared her, apparently dumbfounded as her fingers and thumb now rubbed the chain between them fiercely.

He held her stunned gaze with candor in his own, lowering his voice to continue. "Though I have every intention of claiming you as mine on our wedding night, I have no intention of getting you with child at that time. I'm not expecting an heir immediately, nor do I want one that quickly."

She lowered her hand from her neck and hugged herself, looking him up and down in stark bewilderment. "That's—that's not even logical, sir. A man of your position needs a son and I need—" Drawing a full breath, she raised her chin a fraction and said with forced confidence, "We have an agreement."

"Ah, yes. The agreement." He folded his arms across his chest as he towered over her, holding her beautifully stunned gaze. "Let me explain my position on that, Lady Charlotte. I will fund a tour for you, but only on my terms, and at a time of my choosing."

She gaped at him.

"For my trouble," he continued, "I expect a bit of selfish time with you before you carry my child, then hand him to a nanny and a house full of servants to raise while you leave for the Continent on a wave of good riddance, your piano in tow. Until then, you may continue singing here, in London as you do now, and I will continue to support you and your endeavor wholeheartedly, as long as you are home every night to warm my sheets." Smiling wryly, he leaned very close to her to murmur, "I want what I bargained for, Charlotte, and that's you, in my bed, taking care of *my* personal desires before I allow you to carry on with yours."

Blushing furiously now, anger replacing her chagrin, she narrowed her eyes and glared at him. "So, I'm to remain your plaything until you grow tired of me? How convenient for you."

He tried not to show surprise at the question that had, frankly, never crossed his mind. And he had to give her credit for retrieving her nerve and standing her ground in what had to be a most uncomfortable discussion for a lady.

"I don't believe I said that," he replied, "though I seem to recall it *was* part of your argument when trying to convince me that marriage between us would be a good thing."

She hesitated, then brushed over that bit of honesty. "And just how, pray tell, do you expect to keep me in your bed and childless at the same time, sir?"

Colin righted himself as he rubbed his jaw with a palm, uncertain whether she intended to rile him with such a ridiculous question, or if she truly lacked imagination concerning the sexual act. "Would you like me to explain it to you here?" he asked, his tone low and challenging.

"Absolutely not," she seethed, glancing quickly to the door as she took a step away from him.

She dug her fingers into her upper arms, no doubt to keep herself from punching him.

"What I *do* expect, Lady Charlotte, is loyalty, devotion, and compliance from you during our most intimate interludes together," he reassured her softly. "And for that, I will give you everything you've ever wanted, in time."

For a long moment she didn't move, didn't back down, and didn't speak. Colin knew perfectly well that he wasn't being at all unreasonable, and she knew it, too, which likely explained her reluctance to argue with him further. He recognized the conflicts that guided her as she struggled to find words to agree with him, or at the very least acknowledge his demands. But he now felt certain she wouldn't refuse him any of them.

"It's getting late and I need to leave," he said, his tone deep and contemplative.

She visibly relaxed. "Of course, your grace. I will be in touch with you regarding the wedding preparations and members of your family who—"

He cut her off by reaching out and grabbing her around the waist, yanking her forcefully against him as he brought his mouth down hard upon hers.

Too stunned to react, for seconds she just languished in his arms, her body pressed into his, her lips unresponsive to his tender urging. Then a tiny whimper escaped her as she faltered and slowly succumbed to his embrace, her arms encircling his neck and pulling him closer. He cupped her head with one palm, the small of her back with the other, and deepened the kiss, the heat and feel of her voluptuous form igniting a flame of desire deep within that he hadn't at all expected. He reveled in her response, thoroughly savoring the taste of her delicious lips for countless long, glorious moments, his tongue invading her moist depth at last, only briefly, before his senses returned and he began to pull back, gradually releasing her with the greatest reluctance.

A charged moment of mutual shock followed, her breathing as irregular as his, her palms clinging to his shoulders. Then trembling, she drew her hands away and stepped toward the window, turning her side to him, her eyes tightly closed as she covered her mouth with her fingertips.

Colin straightened and gritted his teeth, willing his heartbeat to slow, confused and even frustrated at his own behavior. He never presumed to kiss her with any trace of passion. His intent, though only transiently considered, was to leave a small, required peck of affection on her cheek as he took his leave.

Now she'd aroused him, through no fault of her own, and the only thing he could think of was pulling her on to the settee and kissing her again—on her breasts, her thighs, between her legs. He had to get out of there.

"Plan the wedding quickly," he ordered in a fast breath, his throat raw.

She didn't acknowledge him.

With a harsh brush of his fingers through his hair, he stepped past her and quickly strode out of the parlor.

Chapter 7

Charlotte sat on her white, satin-covered vanity chair in her beautiful new withdrawing room, staring into the gilt-framed mirror at her reflection while her longtime lady's maid, Yvette, silently brushed her thick, curly hair.

She still looked remarkably composed, she decided, her skin flushing with dewy color from the excitement of the last week, her eyes sparkling, their color deepened by the shiny white satin of her night robe, made especially for tonight. It had been a harrowing day, the wedding of the season, and though exhaustion permeated her to the core, sleepiness eluded her. That was probably a good thing since her new husband of only a few hours waited in the bedroom adjoining hers, and he'd made it perfectly clear he had no intention of retiring for a while.

She'd seen him just three times since his proposal six weeks ago, and all three occasions were formal and dull. Oh, he had been unbelievably handsome and attentive enough, but the events themselves occurred only because society at large required they must, especially to the gossips.

But as she finally walked down the aisle toward the altar to become his wife, her stomach coiled in tight knots at first sight of him. In all of her life, she'd never known a man as handsome as the Duke of Newark, and today he looked marvelous, his dark blond hair combed off his face to reveal the hard planes in masculine detail, his eyes sharply intense as they scrutinized her from the top of her tiara to the hem of her beautiful gown. He'd worn black on white silk, his clothes tailor-made for the event, and she supposed everyone in attendance noticed how she stared at him with pure admiration in her gaze from the start of the service until the final moments when he brushed a brief, warm kiss on her lips to seal their destiny. Truly, it had been a grand wedding, and the only snag in the event was all the while knowing she'd coerced him into being there.

Still, he'd been an excellent and attentive companion throughout the day, remaining at her side during the reception and delicious dinner following, even spending a good deal of time talking to Charles, who seemed pleased beyond words that his sister had married so well, as if the match were his own choosing. She simply took that in stride, knowing she was finally out of her brother's clutches and could do as she liked without listening to him constantly criticize her for her thoughts and decisions.

In those few hours, she'd gleaned a bit more of her husband's personality as well, meeting his closest friends and enjoying them at once. She especially enjoyed their wives, Vivian, Duchess of Trent, and Olivia, Duchess of Durham, both lovely women in their own right, and both immediately kind to her, giving her new insight into the workings of her husband's mind, and especially his apparently well-known sense of humor. She had yet to experience it for herself, but then she'd gotten to know him under somewhat trying circumstances. In due time she expected to grow to appreciate him, his disposition, and whatever he did to occupy his time. At least that was her hope.

For now, she had to give him high marks for allowing her full reign of his home and servants, even redecorating her bedroom suite for her arrival. She wouldn't have known that, of course, if it weren't for his housekeeper, Trudy, a middle-aged, buxom widow with four grown children and a mightily stern temperament. She'd only been in his employ for the better part of three months now, but the woman took it upon herself to make sure she understood that he'd fairly gutted her room of all furniture and adornments, then had it repapered in lilacs and lace to match new white lace curtains, purchased a large wardrobe, a canopied bed, and a small, white velvet sofa for the bedroom proper, all matching the vanity, at which she now sat, in her connected withdrawing room, its wood painted white and splashed with inlaid gold. To complete the look and add warmth, thick lavender rugs were placed generously across most of the polished wooden floor. She admired it at first sight, and couldn't wait to lower herself onto her new bed and pull the floral quilt up over her shoulders for a good week of sleep. But that would have to wait.

Suddenly the door behind her creaked open, and her thoughts returned once more to the present when she realized her new husband had entered her bed chamber unannounced. She inspected him for a moment through the mirror, noting how handsome he still looked even after such a tiring day, his face bathed in lamplight, his expression unreadable as he glanced first to her, then to Yvette, who had stopped brushing her hair in mid-stroke at his entrance.

"You may leave us now," he said brusquely.

"Yes, sir," Yvette returned with a curtsy. Then she laid the hairbrush on the vanity and quickly made her departure through the hallway exit, closing the door behind her.

Charlotte sat perfectly still, her eyes on him, caught a little off guard by his intrusion and even slightly embarrassed that he'd allow her maid to see him enter her room through their private, connecting door as if he couldn't wait to take her in marital consummation. He still wore his wedding clothes, though he'd removed everything but his trousers and shirt, unbuttoned to a "V" at the neck, hinting at soft curls that grew upon the broadness of his chest just beneath the fine, silk fabric. The sight made her toes tingle even as she swallowed hard in an attempt to quash her nervousness.

"I still need a bit of time, your grace," she said, hoping to sound haughty, securing her satin robe at her chest with a lightly closed fist.

He didn't respond to her comment, and he didn't give the room a second glance. For a moment he just studied her face, her long, softly brushed hair as it draped over her shoulders, and the base of her throat where she clutched her robe, his eyes narrowing in some sort of thoughtful contemplation. Then a slow smile crept across his handsome mouth as he brought his hands out from behind his back.

"For you, my darling wife," he replied at length, his voice low and husky as he began to saunter in her direction.

Charlotte remained rooted to her chair, her uncertainty growing with each passing second as she lowered her gaze to the shimmery gold box tied with a red satin ribbon he held out in one large palm.

"A gift?" she asked, confused and attempting to crack the tension that threatened to envelop the room.

"Indeed." Dropping his tone to a dark murmur, he added, "Something I had made specially for you, Charlotte."

Her mouth went dry and she hesitated, unsure what she could possibly say when understanding his motives totally eluded her. He stood over her now, still smiling, though seemingly more thoughtful than amused, close enough for her to feel the warmth of his body and experience the lingering scent of his unique cologne.

Grasping the edge of her vanity with both palms to steady her trembling hands, she slowly raised herself to better face him at his level, then tightly laced her fingers in front of her.

"Are you going to take it?" he asked, holding the box between them.

Her lashes fluttered as she glanced down, her first

thought being that it looked too small to carry fur or linens, and too large for jewelry.

He chuckled. "Open it, Charlotte."

For untold reasons, she felt her stomach tightening into knots, her pulse begin to race, but she could no longer deny his insistence. Without comment, she took the box from his outstretched hand and slowly loosened the ribbon. He watched her; she could feel his gaze on her face, and he no doubt noticed her slightly trembling hands.

The satin tie came off easily and he took it from her. Lifting the top of the box to reveal silk wrapping in deep red, she wasted no time in spreading it aside to expose the item of his enthusiasm.

At first glance, it appalled her, not only by what it appeared to be, but by the fact that he actually gave it to her as a gift. Then she reached into the box, lifted it by a thin string of lace with one finger, and couldn't decide whether to laugh hysterically or slap his face for his utter indecency.

Made of brilliant scarlet and pitch-black satin, this . . . thing he wanted her to wear on her wedding night wouldn't cover her torso, much less her legs, arms, and chest. Something resembling a corset, it had no sleeves or straps to hold it in place on the shoulders, but sheer, black lace over red satin stays that undoubtedly stuck to the ribs and presumably lifted the breasts to unimaginable heights.

The bodice, if one could call it that, opened and closed with four tiny, satin-covered buttons hooked into small black lace loops just under the bustline and down to about an inch below the navel, where the satin fabric parted to expose a female's most private area. There appeared to be nothing else to the obscene bit of clothing, and as she turned it around, she noticed how the satin back skimmed the top of the buttocks, there replaced by sheer, black lace that flowed to the knees in a wispy frill. To top off such an outrageous outfit, beneath the corset in the box, he'd placed slip-on shoes with enormously high heels—four inches at least—their toes covered with red feathers.

No, she wasn't appalled, she was speechless. The mere thought of a *lady* owning such a thing . . . She looked back into his eyes and snickered.

He didn't enjoy her amusement. If anything, he stared at her even more intently, lust revealed in his gaze, and slowly her laughter faded as her heartbeat quickened from a growing revelation.

"You—" She glanced once more to the little piece of nothing in her hand, then back into his eyes. "You *really* can't expect me to *wear* this, your grace." It wasn't a question, but a statement, and she hoped she sounded forceful.

He took a step closer and placed the box on the vanity. "I wouldn't have given it to you if I didn't expect to see you in it."

She dropped it back into the box as if it scalded her fingers, deciding to argue with reason. "Forgive my reluctance, sir, but I can't possibly sleep in such a thing. I'll freeze."

He chuckled, reaching for her chin which he raised a bit so she couldn't help but look into his eyes. "You won't freeze, and you won't be sleeping in it, darling wife," he whispered in a husky timbre. "I expect you to tempt me in it, make love to me in it. That's what it was made for."

Her eyes flashed with shock—and a growing fear. "No."

Instead of arguing with her further, he reached down and lightly grasped the sash at her waist, pulling it open before she even sensed his action.

"What are you doing?" she asked, taking a step back, clutching the top of her robe again as she held it tightly closed at the neck.

He smirked. "Undressing you."

Her eyes widened in horror. "Absolutely not."

Straightening a little, he crossed his arms over his chest and gazed at her candidly. "Then you have five minutes, Charlotte. Five minutes to put the corset on and come to me, or . . ."

She looked him up and down furiously. "Or what?"

He shrugged. "That will be at my discretion as your husband." Then he turned and walked to the adjoining door. Without looking back at her, he added, "I'll be waiting for you."

She wanted to scream as he clicked the latch shut, leaving her alone for five whole minutes before he . . . what? She couldn't think about that. Just as she knew deep inside she had no right to deny him anything, not if she wanted him to support her in her dream.

Deflated, she glanced down to the corset and slippers in the box.

Dear God, help me get through this night.

"I married a brute," she whispered, fingering the

lace. Then with a deep breath for confidence, she slowly began to remove her robe.

Colin stared at the flicker in the grate, sipping a brandy, barely able to control his intensifying desire as he waited for her. It had been at least ten minutes since he'd left her bedroom and he knew she took more time than he'd allotted her simply to antagonize him. Or defy him.

She hesitated in embracing the inevitable as her finest wifely duty. He acknowledged that. But even as he understood her apprehension, he also reminded himself that making love to Lottie English would be the most memorable experience of his life, and the *only* reason he found himself here now, anticipating the night to follow, craving the sensual pleasure he would soon share with the woman he'd been aching to bed for years, who now belonged to him by law.

It had been hard to suppress his need for her today, knowing what the night would bring for both of them. The week had been long and tediously eventful, and she'd played her part perfectly as the soon-to-be Duchess of Newark, always regal yet demure, gracious yet unassuming, and ever the lady.

Theirs was the wedding of the season, naturally, and she looked remarkably glamorous, radiant even, surprising him because for the first time since he'd met the Earl of Brixham's sister, she appeared as close as he'd ever seen her to the stunning image of Charlotte and Lottie combined. Still, he didn't think anyone recognized her as the famous opera singer; nobody in attendance would ever expect the new Duchess of Newark to be the seductive coloratura who made her living on the stage. Only Sam and Will, his two closest friends, had learned the truth from him after the formal wedding announcement had been made, and they'd never tell anyone save their wives. And he *had* to tell them, because his sudden agreement to a marriage of convenience would strike them as completely out of character when he'd gone for so long postponing, even ignoring, his marital duty.

Colin glanced at his clock on the mantel again. Half past midnight. It had been almost twenty minutes since he'd left her and his patience was beginning to thin. He bunched his shoulders, then loosened them and stretched his neck to ease the raw tension within, deciding he would give her two more minutes, then march into her room and seduce her there, details be damned—

The click of the latch jarred him and he flipped his head around to stare at their adjoining door, his blood suddenly heating his veins.

She'd dimmed the light in her withdrawing room so that he saw only darkness beyond, couldn't hear anything louder than his own quick breathing and the soft crackling of the fire at his side. And then very slowly, from the shadow, she stepped into his bed chamber.

At the first sight of her he felt a trace of irritation that she remained covered by her robe, fastened tightly at her waist. Then a rush of lust as he had never felt before flooded his entire body when he glanced at her feet to see the feathered slippers he'd given her adorning them, peeking out from beneath the chaste silk wrap.

She'd donned his corset, hidden purposely as a manner of seduction, and just considering the pleasure he would have in removing it to view her intimately nearly knocked him to his knees.

It's really going to happen . . .

"Jesus," he whispered as he placed his brandy snifter on the mantel with an unsteady hand, never taking his eyes off the vision.

She seemed to falter as she moved a bit farther inside, her discomfiture apparent as her gaze quickly skimmed his large bed, its dark blue sheets, blankets, and coverlet that he'd lowered for easy entry; the candles he'd arranged for atmosphere, now glowing from atop the night stands on either side of the oak headboard; his leather settee and book-covered end table just behind him. Then at last she captured his gaze and held it.

Colin swallowed, standing tall and inhaling deeply to control his actions and, if honest with himself, his mixed emotions. She looked beautiful, he decided, her curly hair flowing long and thick over one shoulder and down her back to her waist, brushed away from her face that now shone luminously in the dim, flickering light. Brows creased gently, she bit her bottom lip and tugged at the edges of her robe, pulling them tighter at her neck.

"Your grace," she murmured, her voice hoarse and low.

He smiled faintly. "You're a vision."

She shifted from one foot to the other. "I'm—I'm sorry it took me so long."

"You are well worth the wait," he said reassuringly.

Her lashes fluttered and she glanced around again nervously. "You have a lovely room, sir. Very masculine. And I haven't yet told you how much I appreciate the feminine decor and new furnishings in my bed chamber as well."

He couldn't decide if she were serious or stalling to make him crazy, but he wasn't about to discuss room decorations now. "Come here, Charlotte," he ordered softly.

After only a second's pause, she raised her chin a fraction and moved toward him, her high-heeled slippers making a muted clacking noise on the wooden floor.

He began to unbutton his shirt, keeping his gaze on her, knowing he couldn't ask her to undress him their first time; it would be awkward for her since they'd never been together. But that would come later.

She stopped in front of him, only a foot away, glancing to the fire at her left.

"Isn't it a bit warm, sir?"

He frowned, suppressing a chuckle. "I hope so."

She looked into his eyes, then glanced down to his fingers as he pulled the bottom of his shirt from his trousers and began to remove it.

Hugging herself tightly, she whispered, "Perhaps I should lie down on the bed."

"The bed?" he repeated. "No, my darling, Lottie. I want you here, for now."

Her brows creased faintly and she took a step away from him. He reacted by reaching out and grabbing the tied sash at her waist, easily tugging her against him.

She gasped in surprise, but before she could speak, he brought his mouth down hard on hers.

Colin could hardly contain the passion within as it threatened to explode from just the slightest feel of her lips pressed to his. He deepened the kiss immediately, encouraging her to follow his lead as he brought one hand around to cup her head, lacing his fingers through her soft hair. Lifting her hands, she gingerly rested them on his shoulders as she started kissing him back, moving her mouth against his in growing abandonment.

Her compliance ignited him. Of all the women he'd known in his thirty-six years, desire had never felt like *this*, and he relished it, savoring each second as she gradually succumbed to the fire.

With a muffled groan from low in his throat, he pulled the satin sash at her waist until it loosened a bit and her robe fell open for him. For the tiniest slip of a second, he thought she might reach down instinctively to close it again so he quickly moved his lips to brush them across her cheek and neck, to gently tug her earlobe in an effort to make her pulse race, her skin tingle—to make her forget the details and succumb to the hunger.

She closed her eyes, leaning her head back to give him access, losing all reason as she moaned very softly and pressed herself against his warm, delicate touch, her hips grazing the firmness of his erection just enough to push him closer toward a blissful insanity.

Her hot fingertips kneaded his shoulders and he inhaled sharply though his teeth, deciding he couldn't wait a moment longer to disrobe her and view her intimately.

"Let me see you," he urged in a raspy murmur, pulling back just far enough to lightly grasp the edges of the silk at her neck.

Her lashes fluttered up and she gazed into his eyes. "Wha—what?"

"Take the robe off, Charlotte," he repeated, resting a thumb on her very moist mouth. "I want to see you."

Embarrassment—or something like it—sent a shiver of uncertainty through her and she shot a fast glance to the enormous bed, then lowered her gaze to the floor. He watched her, hoping she'd remove her clothes herself, tease him with his gift, and after several long seconds of standing motionless before him, she gave him his wish by inhaling deeply and raising her hands to push the soft white satin over her shoulders and arms, letting it fall to the floor.

Colin's breath caught in his chest and he staggered back a foot or so to view her fully by firelight.

She was stunning—a seductive goddess barely concealed by a red satin corset and sheer black lace.

She kept her eyes closed, fisting her hands at her sides, and he had to wonder why she appeared so unsettled when he obviously desired her so much.

"You are more beautiful than my dreams of you, Lottie," he whispered huskily, his mouth going dry.

She shook her head minutely, but he ignored the reason for such a reaction as he took ardent note of her near-perfect form, from her thick, silky hair that flowed over her shoulders and down her back, to the tips of her toes, which peeked out from under the feathers on her shoes.

His gaze settled momentarily on her exquisite breasts, firm and round, her nipples, taut from arousal, only vaguely discernable through the sheer black lace. Then with deliberate slowness, he followed the line of the corset where it tapered in at her waist before ending just below her navel, parting to the sides to offer him a luscious view of the triangle of light, curling hair that enticed him from between her firm, long legs.

"God, you're perfect," he breathed, his throat tight with need.

She still hadn't opened her eyes, just silently trembled in front of him. Colin quickly unbuttoned his trousers and pushed them to the floor. Then he reached for her once more and pulled her against his nude body.

She gasped, but before she could protest or struggle, he captured her mouth again in a masterful, unrelenting kiss, coaxing her to abandonment, clutching her tightly so she couldn't back away. She struggled for only a moment or two, then gradually succumbed again when he traced the tip of his tongue across her top lip, then delved deeply inside.

Her fast breathing fused with his as he took in the exquisite feel of her beneath the very provocative corset that grazed his sensitive skin, his erection boldly pressed into the satin that covered her belly. He cupped her head again with one hand while lowering the other to her lace-covered bottom, caressing her through it, letting his own fingers tingle from the sensation.

She wrapped her arms around his neck and began

to kiss him back fervently, boldly daring him with a flick of her tongue on his, letting out a low moan when his hand reached under the lace and touched her directly at the crease of her thigh.

Colin didn't think he'd ever felt such sudden, overwhelming lust for a woman in his entire life. He was, at long last, making love to the intoxicating woman who charged his fantasies, in his own bedroom, as her husband. She would never have another, and he would be the envy of all. The heady thought of being able to take her every night like this, appeasing his desire, nearly drove him to enter her now, standing, to relieve the ache that curled up tighter and tighter inside his body with each passing second.

Keeping his mouth locked with hers, he reached down and grabbed her behind one knee, swiftly lifting her leg so that it rested on his hip.

She abruptly pulled away from his kiss. "What are you doing?" she asked, her voice gravelly, face flushed with dewy warmth.

Colin moved his lips to her neck, ignoring her question by instead letting her know exactly what he was about, through touch, by feel.

He gently sucked her soft, heated skin, and she instinctively lifted her head to allow him better access, her breath quickening again, a whimper escaping her. He nuzzled the silky valleys of her throat, drew his tongue across her jawline, lightly sucked her earlobe. Then without warning, he reached under her raised thigh and moved his fingers to the sensitive, innermost softness between her legs, first just grazing the curls with the tips, then growing bolder, moving deeper between the folds to touch her cleft, finding an abundance of her intimate moisture that slid through his fingers like warm honey.

She moaned—and he nearly climaxed.

"Jesus, Lottie . . ." he said through a fast, pained breath. "I can't wait."

"Please . . ."

He knew what she wanted, and he needed to give it to her *now*, before he completely embarrassed himself by coming too early and spilling himself on her bright, red satin corset.

In one smooth action, he lifted her, one arm at her waist, the other under the knee still resting at his hip, carrying her backwards until his calves brushed up against the seat of the settee behind him. He reclaimed her mouth in a heated kiss, doing nothing more until he felt her start to yield again to the passion. Then, clinging to her leg and firmly holding the back of her head so that she couldn't break the contact of his lips against hers, he lowered the two of them as one onto the soft leather.

Startled, she gave a muffled shriek when she landed on his lap, then tried to jerk away from him when her hot, wet cleft touched the tip of his erection.

He held her tightly, fighting for his own control, refusing to let her go as he deepened their kiss, flicking his tongue across hers, grabbing it, sucking it until she whimpered.

She gripped his shoulders so tightly she pinched the skin, only making him hotter, more desperate to be inside of her.

Her wetness smothered him; her lace-covered nipples teased his chest. Releasing her leg, he shifted his weight so that she straddled him, then he placed a palm on her breast, caressing for seconds, flicking his thumb across the nipple, then squeezing it gently, the lace scratching him exquisitely. She squirmed again; a low moan escaped her throat, and he didn't think he could take the wait any longer.

In a reckless surrender, he grabbed her hips with both hands, pushing her up just enough to release his erection from beneath its warm heaven. Then he took the base of it in one hand as he finally broke their kiss.

He gazed at her beautiful face, noting her tightly shut eyes, relishing in her heavy breathing, the spark of desire she exuded as she licked her lips.

He gazed down the front of her, clothed by only a small piece of satin and lace, her intimate curls teasing the sensitive skin at the tip of his engorged member.

"I have to be—inside you, Lottie—" he said in a broken murmur, placing himself against her cleft, clenching his teeth in a painfully delicious effort to stay his release. He waited for several unending, agonizing moments—for her to say something, do something. She tensed her body as a tremble passed through her, but otherwise she held steady, eyes squeezed shut, biting down on her lower lip. He couldn't take any more.

He began to guide himself up into her, pulling her hips down to meet his urgency. Immediately he felt a certain unfamiliar tightness, the barrier of her virginity, and for a second or two it disconcerted him. Then she gasped, whimpered, clung to him with her nails digging into his shoulders, and he was lost.

He came with such force, such intense pleasure, that he thrust up hard inside of her—once, twice, a hundred times. She cried out, attempting to pull away, but he held fast to her hips, clutching them with both hands, his head thrown back, his body bathed in perspiration as he drove himself into her, wanting her to experience the fullness of her own orgasm before he slowed his pace and dared loosen his grip.

She shuddered and he reached behind her, splayed his palm across her spine, and drew her against him, cradling her on his lap, his face in her hair, taking in the feel of her curves, the scent of her skin, while his breathing slowed, his heartbeat calmed.

He held her for a long time, and she didn't make any attempt to move, or speak. She simply melted into him, reveling in the stillness, the closeness between them, as he did.

Finally, he felt himself sliding out of her, and with great reluctance, he placed his palms back on her hips, gently this time, and lifted her up to stand in front of him, noting with some humor that she still wore the ridiculous, high-heeled slippers he'd purchased for her.

"Let's go to bed," he whispered huskily as he rose beside her, a wave of sleepiness overcoming him.

Inhaling shakily, she turned to find her robe.

"Leave it," he said, grabbing her hand. He pulled her along with him to his bed and she followed without comment, lying down on the cool sheets at his side after kicking off her shoes.

Colin drew the blankets over them. Then snuggling into her, his face in her warm neck, his hand crossing over her corseted chest to cling to her lace-covered breast, he drifted off into a blissful, peaceful slumber.

Chapter 8

Carlotte sat in Colin's study, on the cushion-covered bench seat in front of her beloved pianoforte, staring at the keys through the thin veil of light streaming in from a street lamp outside. The room smelled faintly of tobacco, leather, and polished oak, distinctly masculine scents that irritated her because they spoke of him. She had to wonder if he put her pianoforte in his private study on purpose because he wanted her to be reminded of him every time she played.

It had to be nearly dawn, and yet she didn't feel a bit tired. She felt restless, unable to sleep after what he'd done to her this night. He hadn't stirred when she gingerly climbed out of his bed, and she prayed he'd stay that way for hours, dozing heavily, unaware of her absence. It shouldn't be too difficult for him, she decided, as he'd clearly exhausted himself with her willing body, a thought that once more sent a tremor of shame coursing through her.

She no longer wore the indecent, scratchy, tight-fitting . . . *costume* he'd purchased for her. She'd practically ripped it from her body the moment she left his sleeping side, replacing it with her beautiful, hand-stitched nightgown and robe she'd so carefully selected for comfort and enticement on her wedding night.

My wedding night.

She didn't know if she should laugh or cry at the absurdity of her current situation. Her head pounded, and she still felt the ache between her legs from a pain she had never anticipated. Why she thought a marital bedding would be a pleasant experience was beyond her imagination. Perhaps if love were involved in the union there would be a better . . . connection. She didn't know. He seemed to enjoy himself, but she never wanted to go through such intimacy with her new husband again. At this point she didn't even care about giving him an heir. She'd rather stay in England and perform than have to relive last night's embarrassment anytime soon.

Blinking quickly to hold back tears of frustration, she reached out and placed a finger on middle C, then C and E, then the chord C, E, G, letting the notes quietly resonate. Always had her music soothed her nerves, and she wished it wasn't the dead of night so she could actually play and sing to the rooftop.

"What are you doing in here?"

Startled at the unexpected interruption, she drew her hands from the keys and glanced over her shoulder, catching sight of him at the doorway, his figure in shadow. She swiftly turned back to the pianoforte, folding her hands primly in her lap, breathing deeply because as angry as she was right now, as confused as she felt, the sight of him still managed to heat the blood in her veins and she'd be appalled if he noticed.

"Charlotte?" he asked again. "Why are you sitting in here in the middle of the night?"

She supposed she had to answer him. Closing her eyes, she leaned her head back a little. "I couldn't sleep," she replied, her voice sounding hoarse and distant to her ears.

After a long moment of silence, she heard a creak of the floorboards and his footsteps on the scattered rugs, and then seconds later, he lit a lamp on his desk. She lifted her lashes again to a brightened room, though she kept her gaze focused on the keyboard until he strode to her side and she couldn't help but notice him.

He wore only his trousers, hands stuffed into the pockets, his marvelous chest naked for her view as if he had no shame at all. And as much as she wanted to slap herself for feeling a nervous heat permeate her cheeks, her only clear thought was how perfectly stunning he was to look at, his hair mussed, his sleepy eyes keenly fixed on her.

"I don't suppose you came down here to practice at half past four in the morning," he said, leaning his hip on the edge of the keys, his tone colored with amusement.

She sat straighter on the bench and did her best to ignore his stare—and the warmth emanating from his muscled form. Reaching for a stack of music to her left, she began to sift through it. "As I said, your grace,

I couldn't sleep. Since I'm still new to your home, I couldn't think of any other place to go."

He remained quiet for a moment or two, then after drawing a long breath and letting it out loudly, he sat on the bench beside her without any warning at all. She scooted over to give him room, realizing perfectly well that he wouldn't budge even if she begged him to leave. Her only hope was that he'd grow tired of boring, brittle conversation and return to his bed on his own.

"Play something," he said.

She could feel his eyes fairly caressing her face, which made her squirm inside, feel hot all over. But she didn't dare look at him directly. Instead, she vowed to keep her manner wearisome.

"I really don't want to wake the staff—"

"Oh, damn the staff," he cut in, reaching up to brush her hair off her shoulder. "I want to hear you play. For me."

She tried not to cringe from the intimate manner in which he spoke, from the way his fingers grazed her neck and made her skin tingle. "I think I'd rather go to bed now, sir," she countered, attempting to stand.

He quickly grabbed her wrist to hold her down. "What's wrong, Charlotte? Why did you leave me?"

Tightening her jaw for strength, resolute in her bearing, she finally turned to glare at him. "Honestly?"

"Honestly," he replied, tipping his head to the side a fraction in curiosity.

She couldn't stop her confession now. The wound had been opened. "I was a bit—no, I was *thoroughly* uncomfortable trying to fall asleep wearing a scratchy corset, sir."

He blinked in surprise, eyeing her up and down as if noticing for the first time that she'd changed her attire. Then his gaze returned to her face as a slow, crooked smile spread across his mouth.

"I was hoping to bed you again, Charlotte," he said mischievously, "but men tend to get . . . sleepy after such vigorous lovemaking. I wouldn't have slept for very long, though, before the feel of you next to me stirred me back to life."

Her forehead creased as she shook her head in amazement. "Are you insane, sir? Or just an idiot?"

For moments he did nothing. Then very, very gradually, he drew away from her, releasing her wrist, his features hardening before her eyes.

"I beg your pardon?" he charged in a husky whisper.

She snickered caustically, unwilling to look away from the stony planes of his handsome face. "Firstly, what we did wasn't anywhere near the bed. Secondly, I'm quite sure there was no love involved since you could hardly contain yourself long enough to remember who you were with."

Her bitterness, her forthright acknowledgment, absolutely stunned him—so much so he sucked in a breath through his teeth and jerked back as if scorched by her vehemence.

"Do not tell me you didn't enjoy yourself, madam," he said, his tone grave. "I felt every inch of your luscious body respond to my touch."

A fresh wave of heat suffused her cheeks again but she resisted the urge to avert her gaze from his intimidating stare. Instead, quietly furious, she fisted her hands in her lap and leaned toward him to continue her tirade.

"Respond to your touch?" she seethed in a whisper. "You didn't *touch* me, sir, you used my body and humiliated me for your own lustful intentions. I was willing to give myself to you as your wife, but you made me wear an absurd costume and ridiculous shoes, then called me by my *stage* name while you yanked me down on top of you to take me *sitting*." Tears filled her eyes and she decided not to fight them at this point. "You *hurt* me, sir, without considering my feelings or the fact that I had never been intimate with a man, and I still feel the pain from what amounted to nothing more than a callous . . . acquisition of your right. If that was lovemaking, I can only hope that you left me with your child tonight so that I will never have to be *touched* by you again."

He gaped at her, speechless, his face growing deathly pale even in the dimness of lamplight. Unable to stand his company a moment longer, she stood abruptly and rounded the piano bench, backing away from him as she moved toward the door, her anger overflowing.

"You couldn't wait to have a lusty time with my body in the most selfish way imaginable, and yet you still haven't even asked me to call you Colin."

That said, she turned on her heel and walked out of his study, chin high, back rigid, leaving him alone on her piano bench to wallow in his thoughts.

She could only pray he'd feel as miserable now as she did.

* * *

Colin reclined on the settee in his bedroom, one leg stretched out on the floor, the other hitched up over the armrest, a half-empty whisky bottle in his hand, which he dangled over the edge of the seat while he stared blankly at the ceiling. Dawn had broken at last, and yet he didn't feel like moving, like talking to anyone, like working, or even rising to bathe.

For a long time he'd tried to think of something practical, household matters or work, things he needed to do for Sir Thomas, swallowing his expensive liquor with zeal and gazing at nothing in particular. It hadn't worked. He simply couldn't help but relive his night with his new wife, the crazy eroticism that had overtaken him, the way she'd responded to the striking desire between them, reacted to every stroke, every shared kiss and the touch of his lips on her skin. She *had* responded physically, he knew that as any man would, but it had never entered his mind that she hadn't enjoyed him, or the act itself. Somehow she'd fooled him . . . or he had been blind.

Now quite drunk, feeling pitifully wounded, even embarrassed, he let himself consider and reflect on every moment of their interlude together, how she'd returned his kisses with passion as her wetness coated his fingers, how she'd complied with his order to wear what had to be an uncomfortable outfit in every way, especially for a virgin. And he knew she was a virgin. Logically he'd known as much before his wedding to the Lady Charlotte Hughes, though the line between Charlotte and the exotic, sensual Lottie seemed to blur with him, a fact Charlotte threw back in his face when she accused him of calling her by her stage name.

While it was true that he'd wanted to bed his wife to make their union legal, he hadn't really considered the ramifications of doing so as if he were making love to the woman of his dreams. What he wanted more than anything was to take Lottie in a whirlwind of lust and passion, hot breaths and moans, to make her come over and over before she satisfied his raging sexual hunger. He'd wanted to be her greatest lover, and instead he'd hurt her because he'd been not her greatest, but her first.

Suddenly, through a wave of nausea, he heard the faintest musical notes drifting up to his bed chamber from his study below. She played magnificently, a minuet he only vaguely recalled.

Colin closed his eyes and raised the bottle to his mouth again, taking a long, full swallow, feeling the burn in his gut and strangely delighting in it.

Had he been stupid in imagining a full week in bed with her, the two of them laughing, touching, stroking, lying together in a pleasure-filled embrace? After last night she wanted nothing to do with him, and never in his life had he been brought to his knees by a vision so beautiful, then hit over the head with insult at his lovemaking abilities. He was Colin Ramsey, the noble Duke of Newark, admired by every female in the land, married to a well-respected lady of the peerage. He knew how to treat a woman, and Charlotte should have anticipated grand lovemaking by someone with his reputation, even, he realized, if society had exaggerated that reputation just a little. Yet she said he'd left her in pain, a thought that not only cut him to the core, but filled him with a certain, rare humiliation.

Now, lying flat on his back in his bedroom, still wearing his wedding trousers and a loosely opened shirt, he listened to her play to the beat of his pounding head. And the more she played, the more it annoyed him that his wife of less than twenty-four hours had brushed him aside after only one night and returned to *her* passion at the pianoforte. Ridiculous, and he'd be the fool of London if anyone learned how fully in charge of him she'd become in one day. He wasn't about to let her win this battle.

With resolve, he attempted to sit up on the settee, the room spinning suddenly at his effort. After allowing his rolling stomach to calm, he slowly stood, still clinging to his half-empty bottle.

What the hell. He swallowed deeply again, then wiped a palm down his face before walking unsteadily toward the hallway. He took two or three deep breaths to balance himself, then staggered down the stairs in bare feet, following the sound of the music until he reached the door of his study, cracked just enough for him to watch her and listen for a moment before he fully opened it.

She didn't hear him, wasn't aware of his intrusion, which gave him ample time to consider how he might begin a discussion. She'd plaited her long hair, twisting it up atop her head, and now wore a modest morning gown in light green, its wide skirts flowing over the piano bench, its puffed sleeves stroking her ear lobes with each fast movement of her nimble fingers.

Head splitting, he leaned his unsteady form against the door frame and crossed his arms over his chest, his open whisky bottle clutched in one palm.

"Beautiful," he said just loud enough for her to hear.

Startled, her fingers fairly flew off the keys and she whirled around to view him, her luscious mouth dropped open.

He offered her a crooked grin, but said nothing for a moment, enjoying her surprise.

Removing her spectacles, she looked him up and down, noting, he supposed, that he carried the bottle and still wore his clothes from the night before, though her eyes lingered on his chest, reassuring him that she certainly enjoyed his body, at least on a conventional level.

"I like it when you look at me," he drawled very softly, his eyes narrowing as he focused on her face.

Her features went flat as she sat up straighter on the piano bench, placing her hands in her lap. "You're drunk, sir."

He nodded faintly. "Indeed, I am, madam." He watched her for reaction to his honesty, but she cleverly hid her feelings behind an expression of simple irritation.

"I'll be leaving in a few minutes," she declared in a haughty tone. "I've scheduled a lesson with my vocal tutor, and then I'll need to be at the theater by noon. We're beginning rehearsals for *The Bohemian Girl* today."

Colin stood erect again and started to saunter toward her. "You're very busy for a newly married lady," he replied, scratching the day-old growth of beard on his cheek.

She huffed. "Unlike you, I have a profession—"

"Unlike me?" he cut in, trying like hell not to slur his words. "You think I don't have work to do?"

"Actually, I've no idea what you do with your time, sir," she shot back.

"Indeed you don't," he replied just as quickly, offering nothing more.

Confusion crossed her brow for a slice of a second at his obvious evasiveness, though he noted with pleasure how she couldn't stop staring at his exposed chest. Then suddenly, as if catching herself and realizing where her attention lay, her cheeks flushed with color and she turned away. Gracefully standing, she folded her spectacles and dropped them into a side pocket on her gown, then lifted a pile of music sheets, shuffling them into a tidy stack, effectively dismissing him.

Colin felt like crawling out of his skin, aching to grab her around the waist and yank her against his body so she couldn't help but give him her undivided attention. But that would only make her angry, less willing to disclose her thoughts with candor.

Swiftly moving very near her, one leg between the bench and the instrument, her gown blanketing his shin, he leaned around to put his face in front of hers. She didn't even react, just continued ignoring the fact that he was even in the room.

"I'll leave you alone to go about your business, Charlotte," he said in a gruff murmur. "But you must answer one question for me first."

She sighed, exasperated, then placed her hands on her hips and turned to him. "What is it, your grace?"

He waited for a moment, blinking in an attempt

to hold her irritated gaze, trying to organize his thoughts through the fog in his aching head, to calm another wave of queasiness. He hadn't been this intoxicated in ages and the effects of the alcohol were beginning to catch up with him. He didn't have long before he lost his stomach and embarrassed himself in front of her all over again.

Inhaling deeply, he reached out and took one of her hands in his. To her credit she didn't immediately try to pull away; she just watched him wearily.

"I want to know," he whispered very slowly, "if you were satisfied last night."

She tipped her head to the side minutely and glanced down his body again, taking particular note of the bottle dangling at his side.

"If you can't remember last night, your grace, then all the better. I'm trying to forget the incident myself."

The *incident*? That comment certainly spurred his agitation, as was no doubt her intent. "My memory is fine, madam," he countered in a low drawl, "which makes your answer all the more important. I remember how you felt on me, but I was rather engaged in my own . . . satisfaction. I want to hear, from your lips, if you received yours."

Her eyes narrowed slightly and she tried nonchalantly to free her hand from his grasp to no avail.

"I refuse to discuss the intimacy that occurred between us, sir, especially when I can hardly understand your words which, at the moment, lack enunciation," she charged. "Now, if you please—"

"Were you satisfied, Charlotte? That's all I want to know, and then I'll let you go."

She shook her head, totally baffled. "Your question makes no sense. The entire affair was completely unsatisfactory as a marital bedding, especially wearing that ridiculous outfit. You obviously seem to remember *that* part and I believe we've been over this." She huffed and stood straighter, looking him up and down for a final time. "You are highly inebriated and would do best by returning to your bed and getting a decent night's sleep. Now."

Naturally, in such a state of drunkenness, he couldn't react very quickly when she suddenly jerked her hand out of his and stepped back far enough to put the piano bench between them, clinging to the music she held against her chest as if it might protect her.

"It's time for me to leave," she maintained, "so if you'll excuse me—"

"No."

Her mouth dropped open a fraction. "I beg your pardon?"

He lost his balance briefly, caught himself, then braced his hip against the pianoforte once more in a concerted effort to remain standing. Doing his best to focus on her face, he slurred, "I said no, or at least not yet."

His command took her aback. He watched her eyes widen, then narrow to slits as she stared at him, fuming, knowing fully well that as his wife she didn't dare challenge his authority.

Colin rubbed his own tired eyes, thinking. Something about her answer troubled him, and because of the blasted whisky and incessant pounding in his temples, he found it exceedingly difficult to understand why. He needed another swallow from his bottle but refrained from taking it, certain she'd grow more disgusted if he gulped it in front of her.

She continued to stare at him with an anger he could actually feel, her lips thinned, her gaze markedly defiant, waiting for direction as a good wife should. And suddenly, as if hit in the head with falling bricks, it occurred to him that she might not really understand what he'd asked, that she might not be even vaguely aware of the pleasures of the bedroom. She might be totally ignorant of—

"Did you climax, Charlotte?" he asked in a husky timbre.

For a moment or two she looked confused, squeezing her music hard against her chest. Then a certain shock overwhelmed her and she gasped, hot color flooding her cheeks, a look that pleased him enormously. He decided to move closer, stepping away from the pianoforte and rounding the bench toward her, careful in his stride so he wouldn't fall.

"You know what it is to climax, don't you?" he drawled as a statement rather than a question, noting how she continued to stare at him with wide, dazed eyes, her green gown accenting the rosy tint in her skin, the reddish highlights in her hair. "I want to know if you climaxed when I was inside of you, last night. See . . . I thought you did, and that you thoroughly enjoyed it. Am I mistaken?"

She swallowed, then seemed to recover herself as she stiffened before him. "This conversation is appalling, sir," she whispered. "I refuse—"

He grabbed her upper arm, yanking her against him, and she immediately attempted to break free.

"Let me go," she hissed through clenched teeth.

He held on tightly, gazing down at her beautifully flushed face. "Answer me."

"When your drunken stupor is finished, perhaps you'll recall that I hated what you did to me. It was shocking, uncomfortable, and humiliating in every way. *Nothing* about it was enjoyable."

Colin dropped her arm as if she'd scalded him, staggering back a foot or so, reaching out to clutch the mantelpiece on his left as the room began to spin. She swept past him at once, holding her music with one hand, her skirts with the other, her head held high.

"Charlotte?" he called out as she reached the door.

She paused without looking over her shoulder at him. "What is it?" she enunciated angrily.

"I'd like you to call me Colin from this moment on," he said in a dark murmur, realizing he likely slurred every one of his words but deciding he no longer cared. "Especially during the intimate times we'll share together in future."

For several long, silent seconds she did nothing. Then without comment, or even an infuriated glance in his direction, she walked out of his study, chin high, as if she had so many more important things to do.

He stood there for a long time, feeling disillusioned like he never had before, still clutching his whisky bottle, which he finally placed upon the mantel.

"I am a goddamned idiot," he admitted aloud to no one. Then closing his parted shirt in case he spotted servants on his way, he staggered back to his bed chamber, emptied his stomach, and crawled between his sheets.

Chapter 9

Charlotte had great difficulty concentrating on the tedious lecture given the cast of the latest production of Balfe's *The Bohemian Girl* that would premier at the Royal Italian Opera House in Covent Garden next fall. She knew from the players that it would no doubt be a magnificent run—if they could get Adamo Porano, one of Italy's finest tenors, to stop complaining about everything, including, even, the quality of food provided them at rehearsals. But then their theater manager, Edward Hibbert, had courted the famous Porano, hoping that by giving the man the lead he would also be able to court Balfe himself, wooing Great Britain's most famous modern composer from the Continent, where he remained dedicated to finishing the four-act French version of *La Bohemienne*, scheduled to premier next year in Rouen. And if Balfe arrived, the theater might be graced with Queen Victoria as well, which would mean splendid sales and increased income and exposure for all.

Charlotte had her doubts about being an integral part of something so grand, though secretly she'd give everything she had in the world to meet Balfe. If granting Porano's every wish made that possible, she'd hire an Italian chef and feed him herself. Funny how thoughts of the great Balfe, even now and in a professional, operatic setting, led to thoughts of her husband, a nobleman with more money and connections to the elite than anyone she knew. Perhaps if she begged him, he'd arrange an introduction, even take her to Rouen to meet the man. But then the gracious, generous Duke of Newark would probably require another bedding in a brand-new corset in exchange for the favor, a notion that made her shudder inside.

"You're not paying attention," Sadie whispered from her left.

Charlotte offered her friend and fellow soprano a wry grin, sitting up a little in an attempt to concentrate on Walter Barrington-Graham, their director, as he scolded them for musical notes bungled or forgotten or both when they sang through the second act.

She'd been given the lead soprano role of Arline, her first time with the part, though because she'd sung the music for years, none of the arias were new to her. Being chastised by Barrington-Graham wasn't new to her, either, so in an attempt to keep from yawning through his tirade, she opened her fan and began swishing it slowly back and forth in front of her chest.

They'd all taken seats on the stage in the now-empty opera house, where they would meet almost every day for the next two months, preparing, practicing, and readying themselves for opening night. Rehearsals would last several hours each day, starting with just one pianist and the music, followed by placement on the stage, culminating in dress rehearsals with costumes and cosmetics and full orchestra, led by the famous French conductor, Adrien Beaufort. In the meantime, she would be subject to Barrington-Graham's daily reprimands and insistence that if they performed as poorly in front of an audience, the government would reinstate banishment to Australia and he'd be the first to go, his head hanging in disgrace. A notion beyond the ridiculous, but then this was drama.

Charlotte couldn't help but groan, sinking a little lower in her chair again as Adamo began to argue with both the director and the pianist in pure Italian fashion. The backstage hands had been hammering and stomping around on the platform, sewing and creating the scenery, talking and laughing and dropping things, apparently interrupting Adamo so much that he found it necessary to complain about the pandemonium hurting his concentration and causing him to blunder his notes. Charlotte found that rather amusing since he'd been in theater for some twenty-five years and would most assuredly be able to practice above a little loud set building. But then he was the star.

Sadie tapped her own fan impatiently on her lap, and Charlotte's thoughts couldn't help but stray again to things besides rehearsal, to Colin. It had been a week since her wedding night fiasco, and since that time she'd only seen him briefly, usually in passing or at meals. He'd apparently decided to respect her wishes to leave her alone, which was fine with her, and frankly, she hoped he'd never again mention the drunken, humiliating discussion they'd shared in his study. What a nightmare. In some manner, she'd been surprised that her husband hadn't expected more from her in bed each night, though perhaps he still remained embarrassed by his actions toward her a week ago.

Her self-imposed celibacy wouldn't last. She'd started her monthly yesterday, more or less depressing her because she really was hoping, after careful consideration of the horrible bedding on her wedding night, that she'd gotten with child. At least then her duty to him would be over. Yet she also realized what would happen if she carried. The London Gossip Society, as she liked to call the busybodies, would know that Lottie English was either loose, or married, or she would have to hide it and pretend several months of illness. Any of these options could hurt her career badly, a risk she wasn't ready to take.

Still, she was now the Duchess of Newark, with a husband to control her, and the constraint in which she now found herself meant she needed to keep her secret identity more than ever and play her part well. That meant coming to the theater as she had before, dressed in unassuming, practical clothing that wouldn't garner notice, her hair meticulously kept in a conservative style. It meant no glamour. But then, on opening night and for a month or two thereafter, she would be the glamourous Lottie English, made up for the adoring public. She would be the star.

"Lottie!"

The interruption jerked her out of her musings

and she sat up straighter, smiling at Mr. Barrington-Graham, who'd apparently been talking to her without her awareness. "I beg your pardon, Walter?"

"Please take your place stage left," the tall, rather gaunt man directed with exasperation, patting down the sparse strings of hair on his oiled head. "I would like you and Mr. Porano to sing the duet again, and *this* time I shall clap the beat *loudly.*" He grunted, then waved his arm through the air. "The rest of you . . . *out!*"

Charlotte rolled her eyes and Sadie snickered, gently squeezing her hand in response before she stood and, along with the rest of the dispersing cast, made her way backstage toward the exits. They'd been rehearsing act two all day, but secretly she realized Walter trusted her to help Porano stay on task with his practice, and so the duet it was. Again. After that, it would be a stuffy and hot ride home, a lukewarm bath, light supper, and bed. She couldn't wait.

Porano moved his thick figure center stage, scratching his curly, black beard as he studied his sheet music. She lifted her skirts and moved to stage left as ordered. Walter probably wanted them separated, Porano closer to the piano, so that the Italian could hear the music from his right, her singing from his left, with Walter clapping from just in front of the orchestra station.

The crew had cleared the chairs so that nothing remained on stage but them. Once Mr. Quintin, their regular pianist, acknowledged his readiness from the keyboard, Walter began clapping the tempo, then raised his hand to direct.

The melody began.

Knees slightly bent, shoulders back, music held at arm's length, Charlotte stood erect to lift her diaphragm, drew a full breath through her nose—and then came a startling commotion.

First a screech, then shouting from the rafters. She quickly glanced up.

"Lottie, *move!*"

Somewhere through a slice of panic, her husband's voice registered and she bolted forward as a beam of wood swung down from above. Walter grabbed her upper arm and yanked her, but not before the corner of the beam slammed into the back of her thigh, knocking her over to fall flat on her belly near the edge of the stage.

Suddenly cast members and crew surrounded her, jostling her, speaking to her. Her heart thudded in her breast; her mouth went dry and she couldn't find her voice if she tried.

"Lottie! Oh, my God, Lottie, are you hurt?" Sadie asked as she pushed through the small group to kneel beside her, her own words shaky with alarm.

Charlotte attempted to recover herself as Walter took charge.

"Back away, everyone, back away," he said in a commanding, concerned voice. "Please give her air."

They all started speaking at once, and even as the shock began to wear off, she couldn't help thinking of Colin, sitting in the back of the theater, his voice shouting to her in warning, probably just in time to save her life. In her confusion, she couldn't decide if she should be grateful for his interference or angry that he surreptitiously kept track of her whereabouts. But for a moment, it didn't matter. Suddenly he knelt beside her, wrapping a strong arm around her shoulders as he helped lift her to a sitting position.

"Are you hurt?" he asked, his voice low and matter-of-fact.

She raised a trembling palm to cover her mouth, shaking her head as her initial daze turned to disbelief. "It hit me—it hit me in the leg."

He looked into her eyes pointedly and asked again, "Are you hurt?"

"No," she whispered. "I—I don't think—" She winced as she attempted to move her leg. The dull ache in her thigh had turned to shooting pain and she sucked in a breath through her teeth. "Perhaps a little, but—it's getting better."

Colin's lids narrowed as he continued to watch her skeptically. "Can you stand?"

She nodded, clutching his arms as he gently pulled her to her feet. Clinging to him, she placed her weight first on her uninjured leg, then the other, from tiptoe to heel as the pain began to dissipate. "I'm fine," she said, her tone forcefully bright.

"Your grace?" Sadie said from behind him.

Colin turned and took a cup from her.

"It's brandy," she offered, patting Charlotte on the arm.

"Drink this," he said, sniffing it first, then lifting the glass to her lips.

She did as ordered without argument, taking several sips of the burning liquid that warmed her tongue and slid down her throat.

The crowd began to disperse, talking among themselves. Two brawny stage hands lifted the beam and carried it backstage; Adamo burst into one of his typical Italian diatribes, his hands in the air as he walked away; Edward Hibbert, the theater manager, pulled Walter aside, engaging him in deep discussion. She felt better, in control of her emotions again, and she concentrated on her breathing, keeping herself steady. She didn't dare look at her injury here, for she'd have to lift her skirts far too high for decency, but she knew she wasn't bleeding. It wasn't that kind of wound, though she'd likely suffer a nasty bruise come morning. That being said, she supposed she was grateful for it. If the beam had hit her in the head, she'd be dead already.

Finally Colin stood back from her and Charlotte noticed immediately how people instinctively moved away from his commanding presence, several minor cast members and costumers staring at him in awe, then curtsying or nodding in acknowledgment. Even now, she knew they were all questioning his reason for being at their closed rehearsal, his immediate response to the mishap, that they would whisper for days about his reaction and obvious concern for her person. And although none of them knew the Duke of Newark personally, they knew of his reputation, everyone did, and speculation would soon turn to rumor. Her only hope was that her fellow cast members would be gracious enough not to ask any delicate questions regarding his reasons for attending her at the theater day after day.

"Your grace," she said, forcing a pleasant smile on her lips, "thank you for your help, but I do think I'm fine now. Really."

He raked his fingers through his hair, staring down

at her through narrowed eyes. "My driver will take you home."

It was a strong statement, catching them all by surprise, including her. She usually took public transportation so no one would be the wiser. Yet she could never argue with him here, in front of everyone. And nobody else would dare question a nobleman, either, though this spectacular turn of events would be the talk of the theater once they left—especially among the women.

After assurances to Walter, Sadie, and even Porano that she felt much better and would be just fine, Colin gestured and said, "This way, Miss English."

As she limped her way toward the backstage door, his hand firmly on her elbow, Charlotte glanced over her shoulder for one last look at several of the workers standing around the spot where she had been spared certain serious injury, all of them studying the rafters, mumbling among themselves.

And then without another word, she found herself stepping into one of her husband's decorated carriages for a quiet trip home.

The ride back to his townhouse proved slow and hot, the streets crowded and the air inside his coach stagnant, making a usually short trip long, unsteady, and uncomfortable.

Charlotte sat across from him, staring blankly out the small window she'd cracked in the hope of a comforting breeze that never ensued, her forehead creased in deep thought, her skin pale even in the heat that she occasionally attempted to ward off by waving her fan. He hadn't said much to her since they'd left the theater, and she didn't appear to feel like talking, which he supposed was understandable considering the events of the last hour. Still, she had to be badly shaken, and as her husband and protector, he supposed it was his duty to demand answers to a few delicate questions regarding an accident that, after considerable consideration, seemed highly suspicious. He'd heard the hammering, heard a crack, shouting, and a commotion in the rafters, and instinct had made him call out. It was the only time in three hours that she had been standing alone, without other cast members near her, and the entire episode seemed . . . planned. Or extraordinarily accidental. But maybe he just felt the suspicion in his gut.

Shifting his large frame on the hot leather seat, he pushed up his shirt sleeves in an attempt to stay cool, then decided it was time to broach the subject with her.

"May I be blunt with you, Charlotte?" he asked, his tone a bit more "mother hen" than he had hoped.

She blinked and turned to face him. "Pardon me?"

He tendered her a reassuring smile. "I don't think what happened on the stage today was an accident."

For a long moment she just stared at him, a certain turmoil crossing her features that he could read like a book. Then she shook out her skirts and looked away once more.

"Of course it was an accident," she countered through an exhale. "Accidents happen at the theater all the time, your grace—"

"Not deliberate accidents," he cut in, irritated that

she refused to either acknowledge the issue as important, or didn't want to confess her doubts to him.

"Accidents, by definition, cannot be deliberate," she informed him through a sigh, folding her hands in her lap. "But more to the point, you can't possibly think someone deliberately tried to hurt me."

Raising his brows, he replied, "Can't I?"

"Such a thought is ludicrous," she chided.

Shrugging, he pushed for detail. "You don't think there might be one or two people in the production who are jealous of your success? Who might have something to gain if you're . . . disabled in some manner?"

She squirmed a little on the seat. "My goodness, it's so hot today—"

"Charlotte, stop avoiding the issue and talk to me."

Her gaze shot back to his face, eyes narrowing as her expression went flat. "You'd like to talk? Then answer this, sir: Why were *you* there?"

For a slice of a second, it crossed his mind that she might actually consider him to blame for the ordeal, as he'd been the one to call out to her first with a warning just barely heeded, that he was the only person in the theater at the time who really had no business being there, and the one person she found herself distrusting. And yet he had trouble believing she would doubt him to such an extent. More likely it angered her that he'd been watching her every move without her knowledge or consent.

"I was there because I admire the theater," he answered matter-of-factly. "And now that . . . well, now that my *wife* is the star soprano of the next production of Balfe's most famous opera, I just thought I'd wander in to view for myself what you do each day when you're away from me."

She blew a stray lock of curly hair off her cheek. "You shouldn't have been there."

He smiled. "I don't think there's anyone alive who would deny me."

That didn't seem to faze her. She continued to eye him candidly, lids narrowed in speculation, head tipped to one side. "Don't you have anything more important to do with your time, sir?"

He wanted to know her more, trust her better, before he revealed exactly what he did for the Crown. So instead of revelation, he casually replied, "Not really. I have wonderful employees who manage my estate, leaving me all the time in the world to entertain myself by watching you."

One side of her lips twitched up and she glanced away again, obviously deciding not to comment. Colin took that to mean she had very little regard for him and his apparent laziness. He didn't mind. Eventually, she'd learn the truth and he'd relish the look on her face when she did.

He tried to stretch out a bit, his legs cramped and uncomfortable in their confinement. They were still several streets away from his townhouse, and moving slowly, occasionally stopping for pedestrians and hired hacks, giving time for the sounds and smells of the busy city to drift in through cracked windows and assault the senses.

"You sang beautifully today, as always," he said, attempting a different approach to garner information since they had the privacy and weren't going anywhere fast.

Peering outside, she admitted, "I know the music well, but I still have trouble blending the higher octave in act two with Mr. Porano. He blames me for the inability to get it perfect, but we all know it's really his problem with the tempo—"

"Mr. Porano has problems with the tempo?" he cut in, amused.

She glanced at him askance, her luscious mouth open a little. Then she snapped it shut and huffed, "Oh, never mind. I'm sure it's all very tedious to you."

He waited for a moment, then countered, "Not really. I'm aware of the great Italian tenor and his antics. Remember, Charlotte, I'm a proud opera aficionado."

She shook her head gently, her lips curving into a half smile as she realized he teased her. "The man is a very talented buffoon, but of course you didn't hear that from me, sir."

Colin grinned, enjoying their easy banter. "A buffoon, eh? And the other performers?"

She reopened her fan and began waving it slowly, absentmindedly. "I've sung with most of the others before, so I know their abilities and the manner in which they interpret music."

"I see." Of course he didn't really care in the least what the others were about, their talent or lack thereof, but discussing it gave him the opportunity to learn who among them might have reason to resent his wife, or dislike her enough to want to do her harm.

"So tell me who they are," he pressed, wiping his perspiring neck with his palm.

"Who they are?"

"Your fellow cast mates." He shrugged. "Who's playing which part?"

For a second or two she gazed at him dubiously, as if she were going to ask him why on earth he cared, then obviously decided against it by proceeding without question.

"Well," she began through a fast exhale, "Porano plays Thaddeus, the leading man, though it's my opinion that he's too old for the part—an insignificant little issue that doesn't seem to matter much in opera. Anne Balstone, a magnificent contralto, by the way, plays the Queen of the Gypsies. I've only been on the stage with her once, but she's a lovely person, if a bit conceited."

"Aren't they all?" he asked with droll humor.

She gave him a crooked smile in return. "That's mostly an act. In my experience, many talented singers, even those who are famous, are quite insecure."

"Are you?"

"Ha! Of course not."

Colin observed her closely for a moment, enjoying their rapport, quite taken with the honest smile on her face. She really was a lovely woman, even dressed in a modest, light brown day gown, her hair piled without flair atop her head. But he didn't want to stifle the moment by changing the conversation to something more intimate.

"Go on," he urged with a wave of one hand. "Who else is in the cast?"

She pursed her lips and rubbed her nose with a finger. "I play Arline, as you know, the leading soprano. Buda, Arline's attendant, is played by Sadie Piaget, a young French soprano who's been with me on the English stage for nearly three years. Unfortunately, Buda isn't a singing part in this opera, so she also has singing parts in the chorus. She's probably the only person in the cast who I'd actually call a friend." She tapped her fan against her fingers, thinking. "Then there's Raul Calvello, another Italian, a bass, but he's performed on the English stage for nearly thirty-five years and more or less counts himself an Englishman. He's a rather quiet gentleman, very nice."

"I've met him," Colin replied. "A bit odd was my thought. Never married and spends his free time gardening in the country."

Her brows rose in surprise. "You do know him." She smiled again. "I like him; he's never demanding, never intimidating."

And obviously plants his roses on both sides of the fence, Colin knew, though he would never mention that to her.

"Of course there are the smaller parts," she continued, "played by singers from all over England, including Stanton Lloyd, who plays Chief of the Gypsies, and John Marks, who plays Raul's nephew."

"And an opera wouldn't be complete without musicians, stage hands, a director, conductor, theater manager . . ." he added with a roll of his wrist.

"Very true," she agreed, "though not everybody is present at every rehearsal. In fact, we all won't be together until we begin dress rehearsals several weeks from now. Until then, we share the theater at different times."

He leaned forward on the coach seat, sweating from the blasted heat, though noting thankfully that they were almost home. He wanted to get to the heart of the discussion again before they arrived and she disappeared for the evening, leaving him alone once again with his thoughts and unabated desire.

"So tell me," he said, lowering his voice as he rubbed his palms together in front of him, "just who among those you mentioned would gain from hurting you, or forcing you out of the opera by any means?"

She pulled back in returned annoyance. "*Nobody*, sir. That's why I've tried to stress to you that this . . . incident that happened to me today was nothing more than an *accident*."

There was far more to the incident than she admitted. She knew it—he could feel it to his bones. "What about Sadie? Would she have your part if you left the production? Wouldn't that make her the star?"

She actually chuckled. "Sadie? Sadie and I are friends."

"That's not an answer to my question."

"No, I suppose it's not," she returned sedately. After pausing a second or two to collect her thoughts, she explained. "If I were to become . . . indisposed, shall we say, another well-known soprano would be brought in from Ireland or the Continent to play Arline—one who's probably already sung the part— or they would close production entirely. Sadie, quite frankly, doesn't have the experience, nor a famous name behind her, to sing the lead with Porano or bring in the necessary money needed to pay the cast, much less the entire orchestra and crew. If she were given the lead, the opera house would certainly lose financially, and if that happened, rumors of every sort would begin. At its worst, from that moment forward, the best singers would decline invitations thinking they might never be paid, or worse, that they may sing with someone unknown in the lead, or to empty boxes; patrons would see no point in purchasing seats, and in the end, the Royal Italian Opera House would lose its standing as one of the finest theaters in Great Britain, if not Europe." She relaxed in her stays a little. "And believe me, sir, everybody who is part of the production knows this."

He couldn't help but grin. "You're telling me that you alone are responsible for the success of England's best opera house?"

She shifted her feet on the floorboards. "That's not what I said, nor what I meant, and you know it."

"I do," he remarked nonchalantly, "because you're absolutely right. If you were to become indisposed, as you put it, I would give up my box. Why would I want to attend the opera without Lottie English on the stage?"

That made her hesitate, her brows furrowing with uncertainty. "Are you trying to charm me, your grace?"

He reclined deeper into the seat cushion. "I usually don't have to try. I'm always charming."

She shook her head, smiling crookedly in feigned disgust, then once again turned her attention outside.

He waited for a moment, eyeing her speculatively, then soberly asked, "Aren't you the slightest bit angry about this?"

"What I'm angry about, sir," she replied quickly,

without even a glance in his direction, "is that everybody at the theater today will now believe you and I are lovers—"

"But since we're not lovers at the present time, you won't be lying when you correct them," he cut in sardonically, hoping, in part, to drive that fact home.

It apparently worked. She fidgeted a little, adjusting her shoulders, tapping the tip of her fan on her fingertips.

"Speculation will still run rampant," she said seconds later.

"But your reputation is safe," he replied. "Operatic stars all over the world have lovers, Charlotte, and they're usually admired for it."

She gave him a thoughtful glance. "I understand this is my chosen profession, but in the end I'm still a lady."

He nodded. "Yes you are. A married lady. Should anyone discover your identity, they'll also assume you're married to your lover."

She continued to gaze at him for several long moments, taking in all of his facial features. Then she closed her eyes and leaned her head back against the seat cushion, a grin of satisfaction twisting her lips. "Little do they know."

That flippant comment made him mad. She was his wife but she certainly wasn't his lover, and if she had it her way, they'd never be together intimately again. Colin had no intention of allowing that to happen.

Swiftly, he raised his body and moved to her side of the coach, squeezing in beside her, pinning her as he sat on her wide skirts.

Her eyes flew open and she gaped at him. "What on earth are you doing?"

With resolve, he grasped her cheeks with both hands and drew her lips against his.

She didn't fight him. In fact, to his sheer delight, after her initial surprise faded, she began to respond to his unexpected touch, kissing him back with fervor, wrapping her arms around his neck and drawing him close.

It quickly became a steamy, heated kiss that made him hard with need. She moaned, clutching his shoulders through his shirt; he grasped her tongue with his, sucking, quickly losing control. His breathing grew fast, as did hers, and in the sweltering coach, he fought the urge to strip them both and make passionate love on the leather seat. God, he'd give her anything if she would only touch him where he ached!

He pulled back a little and began a trail of hot, wet kisses down her neck. She leaned her head back, clinging to him as she silently begged for more. He lowered his hand from her cheek and placed it on her chest, just above the neckline of her dress. She didn't seem to notice.

He drew his tongue across her jawline in a trail of fire and she whimpered, caught up in a blissful torment that matched his own. Perspiration broke out all over his body, his erection strained against the tightness of his trousers, and just as he ventured lower with his hand, cupping a well-concealed breast and squeezing it gently, the coach came to an abrupt halt in front of his townhouse.

Startled, she stilled in his arms.

"Stop it. *Stop it*," she gasped in a whisper, turning her face away from his.

Reeling, Colin inhaled a shaky breath, his hand lingering on her breast until she reached up and removed it for him as if it scalded her.

Suddenly their driver opened the door and she jerked as far away from him as she could get, pushing her palms against his shoulders with all of her strength.

He reacted quickly. In one smooth move he leaned around her and grabbed the handle, yanked it from his driver's grasp and slammed the door shut.

"We're not through," he murmured huskily, gripping her chin with his free hand.

"You're insane, sir," she whispered, her confusion, even frustration, apparent in her impassioned eyes.

He placed his fingers softly on her lips. "You're making me that way, Charlotte. I need you, and you know it."

She blinked quickly several times, then swallowed and righted herself, brushing his fingers aside. "We're making a spectacle of ourselves and rumors among servants—"

"I don't care about the servants," he interjected, his jaw tight. "We're married, my darling, and it pains me not to act that way, in and out of the bedroom, especially when I know from your response to my kisses that you need me just as much."

The flush in her cheeks deepened. "You know what I need you for," was all she could think of to say.

He almost laughed. "Yes, I do, and I want to hear you say it."

She struggled, but he held her down.

"Say it," he repeated in a low, intense murmur.

"Say what?" she seethed. "Say that I need you financially? I do. Now let me go."

"You need me physically, as well," he persisted, tracing her bottom lip with his thumb.

Furiously she slapped at his hand.

He didn't budge. "Admit that, at least."

"Don't be ridiculous," she spat.

"Tell me," he said very slowly, his intent to show her nearly exceeded by his desire to make her believe. "Tell me that you know there's passion between us, that you're attracted to me, and that you need me physically."

She glanced to the door, then back into his eyes. "And if I refuse?"

"I'll make love to you right here, right now."

Her expression turned to one of horror. "You wouldn't."

"And you would let me. I know that for a fact," he breathed, gliding his hand down her neck to her chest.

Suddenly, to his great shock, tears filled her eyes. "I'm not stupid, Colin," she whispered with a tremble in her voice. "You don't want me. You want the infamous, sensual Lottie English, the fantasy you met backstage during a performance. You always have. Now let me go."

It was a truly deciding moment for him. He blinked, his gut twisting even as she rendered him speechless. And during those few brief seconds of bewilderment and inaction, she slipped beneath his arm, grabbed the handle, and pushed the door open.

With a marvelous dignity, she offered her hand to the driver, who stood waiting next to the coach, expressionless.

"I think I'll retire early," she called over her shoulder. "Good night, your grace."

Colin didn't even acknowledge the man as he stepped from his coach and followed her silently inside, noting to himself that for the first time in his life, a woman, and her emotions, had shaken him deeply.

Chapter 10

Dinner had been routine and rather uneventful despite the awkward tension pervading the air. Although they'd only finished eating dessert a few minutes ago, Colin couldn't even recall the main dish. Roasted hens, he thought. Or was it duckling?

As he'd done since their kiss in his coach three long weeks ago, he'd spent the entire evening concentrating only on his wife, dressed in peach silk, her glorious hair piled loosely on her head, her cheeks flushed with color as she laughed and sliced her poultry and chatted easily with his two friends' wives, Vivian and Olivia, as if he weren't even in the room. She'd hardly paid any attention to the other men, either, as the three ladies had been in deep discussion about female trivialities like perfume, seamstresses, and the latest fashion, topics about which he couldn't care any less and frankly knew nothing.

Will and Sam had lightened his mood somewhat by recounting some of their boyhood antics, but he knew they wondered at his absent mind. He was usually the jovial one in any conversation, and yet tonight he'd been rather withdrawn, wallowing in his own internal irritations and musings, considering, for the first time, how lovely Charlotte looked by candlelight.

"So, brandy in the study, gentlemen?" Sam said from across the table, interrupting his thoughts.

Colin glanced up from what was left of his raspberries and cream, offering a smile he didn't feel at all. "Excellent idea."

"Yes, please go," Vivian insisted with a wave of her hand. "The three of you are boring us terribly."

"We're boring *you*?" Will responded in feigned consternation, standing with ease as he placed his napkin on the table. "I've heard all I believe I'll ever need to know about perfume tonight."

Sam rose as well. "It's hardly exciting, is it?"

Colin twisted his wineglass stem in his fingers. "Perhaps your perfumer of a wife can find a scent of the heart for mine, Samson. My darling Lottie should wear a fragrance both warm and exotic."

His obvious sarcasm certainly stumped them all into silence. Everybody in the dining room turned to look at him, with various expressions of uncomfortable bewilderment, including Charlotte, who, after only a few short seconds, blushed deeply and glanced at her lap. It was enough to temper his irritation.

After downing the remainder of his wine, he stood abruptly and offered a slight bow. "Excuse us then, ladies?"

"Absolutely," Olivia remarked almost haughtily.

Sam chuckled under his breath, which made him

all the more annoyed, but without another word, the three of them walked from the dining room and wordlessly made their way to his study. Once inside, Colin headed straight for his oak sideboard, having to shuffle around the pianoforte to reach it.

"This is old," Will said from behind him, stopping in front of the keys. "Is it hers?"

"Of course it's hers," he answered gruffly. "Have you heard *me* play?"

"Not lately, thankfully."

Colin grunted. "In case you're wondering, yes, she plays beautifully, as every good wife should."

"Ah," Sam piped in as he took a seat in one of the winged leather chairs. "Is she a good wife?"

"The question of the ages," Colin said, pouring the amber liquid into three snifters from a crystal decanter. "What exactly *is* a good wife?"

Will chuckled, walked to his side to take his drink, then moved around the pianoforte to stand with his back to the cold grate. "You're asking this already and you've only just married? I'm still trying to figure out what makes a good husband."

"Before she leaves you?" Sam asked lightheartedly.

"Indeed," Will replied. "I'm too old to go looking for another female to make me crazy with her whims."

Colin only half-listened to their banter as he carried the two remaining snifters in his hand, offering one to Sam before he walked around the desk and sat heavily in his rocker. The silence lingered for another moment, and he raised one leg and rested his ankle on the edge of the desktop. He knew they were curious about his marriage, his absentmindedness this evening, most likely because he'd been adamantly opposed to finding himself in such a restraining state for nearly thirty-five years. Naturally, they didn't disappoint.

"So, is she making you crazy with her whims?" Sam pried with raised brows, swirling his snifter in his hand. "Or is it everything you thought it would be?"

"Both." Colin took a sip of his brandy, then grinned wryly to murmur, "And more."

"More?" Sam stretched his feet out and crossed an ankle over the other. "That bad, eh?"

"Did I say that?" he rejoined, irritated again but trying like hell not to show it in front of his friends.

Will placed his arm lengthwise across the mantel. "Judging by tonight, I'd say things . . . probably haven't gone quite by the plan."

He grinned sardonically and raised his snifter in a mock toast. "That, my friends, is the secret to marriage. There *is* no plan."

"Yes, but . . . uh . . ."—Sam cleared his throat—"you're the only man I've ever known who has never failed once in charming the ladies. You certainly had no plan to do so tonight."

Confused, he rubbed his eyes with his fingertips. "I don't follow."

"Meaning," Sam explained, "that although you couldn't seem to take your eyes off of her, your wife hardly acknowledged you, and you've been married for less than a month. So, instead of trying to flirt with her or tease her to get her attention, you were sarcastic and glum, which is completely unlike you." He shrugged, then added, "Will and I have never been charming, but you? Something is amiss."

Colin's first thought was to tell them both everything was perfectly perfect in his married life, and more importantly, it wasn't any of their damn business how he and his wife got on. But their good-natured concern gave him pause. True, he could brush the whole thing aside by lying, or offer a vague explanation in hopes of satisfying their curiosity, and yet they were his closest friends, here now, indirectly asking him if they could help. Discussing one's intimate affairs with friends wasn't exactly done, but it wasn't unheard of either. He wasn't sure he could talk about such things without humiliating himself, though a little humiliation might be worth it in the end if they could offer advice on how to handle a wife—both when she purposely kept things from him, and especially during private moments. In that regard, he could only assume his friends' wives weren't as unresponsive as his own since Vivian had delivered Will a son and Olivia carried Sam's child even now. He supposed it was worth a try.

Growing exceedingly uncomfortable, Colin rubbed his palm across the back of his neck, then lowered his leg and sat forward, placing his forearms on the desktop, turning his snifter in front of him by the stem as he gazed at it contemplatively.

"I admit my marriage to the famous soprano has been a bit more . . . complicated than I'd first expected," he revealed at last, his voice tight. To his relief, neither of them laughed.

"Marriage is always complicated in the beginning," Will replied quietly. "Especially in your case where you married someone you didn't really know."

"And of course it takes time before one is truly comfortable in any marriage," Sam added.

Frustrated because they offered nothing but standard comments he could get from a discussion with one of his sisters, Colin harshly raked his fingers through his hair. "Thank you for your simplistic answers gentlemen, but you have no idea what I'm talking about."

Sam grinned. "You don't think we've suffered like you have?"

Colin suddenly downed his brandy in two swallows, then abruptly stood, walked around his desk, and began to pace the carpet in front of the pianoforte.

"No," he maintained with false humor, "I don't think either of you have suffered like I have."

Will took a sip from his snifter. "What really is the problem?"

Colin stopped in his stride, studying the floor. "It's difficult to explain."

"Oh, my God," Sam murmured.

His head jerked up. "What?"

"You're in need of a mistress *already*?"

Startled by the question, he actually laughed. "Are you out of your mind? Nothing would be more complicated than that. Especially before Charlotte and I—"

Dead silence reigned supreme for a moment. Then, with genuine concern, Will murmured, "The problem is Charlotte?"

Colin closed his eyes, pinched the bridge of his

nose, and swallowed his pride. "The problem is that I might have . . . made a mistake with her."

"A mistake?" the two other men repeated in unison.

God, they were getting nowhere. Dropping his voice to avoid rumors by eavesdropping servants, he stood erect, his hands clasped behind him, and said, "She's angry at me because she didn't—she didn't care for the bedding on our wedding night."

Nothing had ever stunned his two friends more, of that he was certain. They gaped at him, both with furrowed brows, Sam gently shaking his head as if his statement of ineptitude in bed throughly confused the man.

He supposed the whole thing was rather funny coming from him, as he had such a marred, or rather, a deliciously sinful reputation in society regarding his sexual prowess and methods of seduction. If his bedroom troubles were known, he'd be ruined in a manner he didn't want to contemplate. Not that it would matter now.

Suddenly, he started chuckling, which seemed to bring the others out of their stupor. Then they were all laughing, not at his expense, but because they, as the marvelous friends they'd always been, completely understood what an oddity this had to be for him.

"Jesus," Sam said, "you're not joking, are you?"

Good humor fading, he shook his head in a form of self-disgust. "I'm afraid not. And I don't know what to do about it."

They all became quiet again after his breath of honesty, the house silent around them, the ladies no doubt continuing to discuss the fashions of the day, or Olivia's impending birth, or just everyday gossip, whatever that might be. And here he was in the middle of his study, tired and under stress from weeks of pent-up desire, requesting help from his closest friends regarding the seduction of his wife. He'd never experienced a more peculiar moment in his life.

"Well," Will said after a loud exhale, moving away from the fireplace to take a seat in the second wing chair, making himself comfortable as he stretched his legs out and crossed an ankle over the other.

"Well, indeed," he repeated. His body now charged, he began to pace in front of the pianoforte.

"Sit down, Colin, you're making me nervous," Sam directed with a wave of his hand.

Immediately, he dropped his body onto the padded piano bench, leaned forward and placed his elbows on his knees, his palms clasped together in front of him. He stared at the floor, feeling an uncomfortable flush creeping up his neck. How the hell was he supposed to discuss such a thing?

Will cleared his throat. "Perhaps you should start at the beginning. You are asking us for advice, are you not?"

Colin smirked and glanced up without raising his head. "I certainly wouldn't ask anyone else."

Sam scratched the back of his neck. "Without . . . uh . . . too much detail, what exactly went wrong?"

He briefly closed his eyes, his memory of the night as fresh in his mind as if it had happened only an hour ago. He still recalled the wave of intense desire that raced through him when he saw her nude for the first time, wrapped seductively in a bit of lace and satin that hid nothing. He supposed he should start there.

"Everything was fine at the wedding, and the dinner following," he began quietly, his gaze darting from one to the other. "But as she prepared herself for the night, I gave her a specially made gift that I more or less coerced her into wearing for me. When she came to me, she was . . . amazing. Beautiful. But the following morning she was very angry and told me she never wanted to be bedded again." At least by me, he thought, though he kept that to himself.

For seconds nobody offered a comment, or even moved. Then Sam rubbed his jaw with his fingers, his expression growing contemplative. "Explain the gift."

He swallowed. "It was . . . something like a corset, made of red satin and black lace, with matching shoes."

Will chuckled again. "What in God's name were you thinking, my friend?"

"He wasn't," Sam answered for him, stifling his own laugh with a palm down his face.

Colin felt his gut wrench. "I admit it was a forward thing to do, maybe even the wrong thing to do. But I had just been married to Lottie English."

"No," Sam countered, "you had just been married to the Lady Charlotte Hughes."

Irritated, Colin clutched his hands together. "Yes, but Charlotte *is* Lottie."

"No, she's not. The reserved lady we had dinner with this evening is lovely in her own right, but she's definitely not the same lush woman I saw at the opera," Sam chided, now sounding just as annoyed.

"Lottie is a fantasy for every man; Charlotte is yours, a noblewoman who went to you, her husband, a virgin on your wedding night."

He grimaced. "You don't understand. I *know* they're different personas, but you can't assume they're different personalities. I married the most sensual, exciting woman—"

"When she's on the stage," Will interjected. "*Acting.*"

"Which you no doubt made her feel with such a gift—like an actress, there to perform for you on your wedding night," Sam said, his voice colored with amusement and a trace of disgust. "No wonder she wants nothing to do with you." After a lingering pause, he added softly, "Consider this Colin: Do you really want her to *act* for you in bed? Because that's probably what she thinks."

His head shot up as those intently spoken words struck him hard. Both men stared at him dubiously, as if he might actually admit he desired Charlotte for just that purpose. In a sudden flood of understanding, her words came back to haunt him: . . . *you made me wear an absurd costume and ridiculous shoes, then called me by my stage name . . . You don't want me. You want the infamous, sensual Lottie English . . .*

Slowly, clarity washing over him, Colin sat upright, inhaling a long, deep breath as he lowered his gaze to the plush rug at his feet.

Such a notion had never occurred to him until just this moment. Yes, obvious to everyone, he'd absolutely wanted the fantasy that had enticed him for three years, just as they all—including Charlotte—knew it was the reason he'd married the woman in the first place. That was never in doubt. But he never wanted or expected her to *act* with him, to play a part she didn't feel. An act in bed would be false lovemaking, and false lovemaking required nothing from the heart. In the end, with no heart, there would be no real intimacy, and certainly no joy. It took the full impact of that thought to realize just how much he had wronged his wife.

"No, of course that's not what I want," he replied at last, leaning back against the unprotected keyboard that clanged ugly notes of disharmony. Seconds later, he glanced up and murmured, "I was stupid."

"Perhaps not stupid, but definitely unthinking," Sam corrected. "The corset had to have shocked her."

Or scared her.

"And she probably didn't understand at all what you wanted from her," Will piped in.

She didn't have a chance.

"So what do you suggest I do now?" he mumbled, feeling utterly deflated.

Will snorted. "Why don't you seduce her? It's what you should have done in the first place."

He ran the fingers of one hand through his hair. "I'm certain that sounds easy enough to the two of you, but I obviously failed with her the first time, and doing so now seems hopeless."

He regretted saying that almost at once. He was the one among them who had never had trouble seducing a woman in his life, the one who could charm them all, and he knew absolutely that they were thinking the same thing.

A long and uncomfortable silence ensued, an awkward measure Colin was certain he would never forget should he live a hundred years. He'd never done anything more difficult—admit to his friends that his new wife, attraction for him aside, didn't want him as a man. The humiliation he felt at that moment was palpable.

Finally, Sam expelled a slow breath and said frankly, "The problem is yours, of course. But my suggestion would be to use her innocence to your advantage. Don't expect her to be experienced, Colin, because she obviously isn't. You've made one mistake, but she's still your wife, and still yours to bed. Start again from the beginning. Expect her to know nothing and *show* her."

"When she's not the least interested?" he countered caustically.

"You're not thinking this through," Will added, his voice low and decisive. "There's no doubt that the lady admires you and feels an attraction. Use that to your advantage as well. Give her what she desires, not what she expects. Seduce her when she doesn't see it coming. And for God's sake, move *slowly*."

Slowly. He was ready to crawl out of his skin with sexual need, his wife in the next room night after night, but these were surely words of wisdom where women were concerned. Will and Sam, both already married, knew this. His true problem, as he saw it, was that he'd never really had to work at seducing a woman before. Women either wanted him or they didn't, and in his experience, his charm rarely failed. That Charlotte would be his first real challenge proved to be the ultimate irony. He'd have to be more charming than she was clever if a slow seduction were to succeed, but if it did, the rewards would be grand.

Subdued, one problem considered, Colin stood again and moved to the window behind his desk. He crossed his arms over his chest and rested his shoulder against the pane, seeing nothing as the sky had gone black and silence prevailed beyond—no moon, no wind, rain, or even stars. Just stillness. The calm before the storm.

"There's something else," he said quietly. Turning to face them once more, he disclosed, "She was nearly killed at the theater three weeks ago."

"What?"

That from Will who sat forward in earnest. Sam just remained motionless in his chair, his expression contemplative.

Colin pulled out the rocker behind his desk and sat heavily, leaning back as far as he could and folding his hands in his lap. "A beam from the rafters fell while she stood alone on the stage, missing her head by inches only because I called out to her in time for her to move. She more or less brushed the incident aside, insisting it was a simple accident. But I made some discreet inquiries of my own and this isn't the first time something like this has happened to her at that theater. She's either lying to herself, or she's lying to me for reasons unknown. Either way, I'm starting to think she's in trouble."

No one said a word for a minute or two as they absorbed his rather disturbing disclosure. Finally, Sam asked, "Do you think these . . . mishaps have anything to do with you?"

He shrugged. "That's a question I can't answer. I can't get close enough to her to find out."

"Why ever not?" Will asked. "Regardless of her lack of interest in the bedroom, she's still your wife."

Lack of interest in the bedroom. Hearing that again made him want to hit something. Instead, he smiled wryly and pushed himself up from his rocker. "Need a refill, gentlemen? I do."

Sam shook his head; Will held out his snifter for him to take as he walked by. He strode quickly to the sideboard and poured the amber liquid for both of them, giving himself more than he should, but deciding he didn't give a damn if he woke with a headache.

"I can protect her here at home," he said at last, turning to face the men with both drinks in his hands. "Doing so at the theater is more difficult. I make her nervous, I think, and frankly my appearance, day by day, would look . . . out of place, shall we say. Even odd. Everyone will wonder what the devil I'm doing there." Sarcastically, he added, "Everyone except the great Porano who apparently thinks only of himself."

Sam adjusted his frame in his chair. "The great who?"

Colin shook his head and moved away from the sideboard. "Never mind."

"You could always tell them, or better yet, let them assume you're pursuing Lottie English romantically," Will suggested, taking his snifter. "Not a soul knows the two of you are married. Imagine the possibilities."

"Imagine the rumors," he said. He took a full swallow of his brandy, then lowered his body once again into his rocker. "And although that would be a marvelous excuse to stay close to her, I don't think Charlotte would appreciate my interference with her work."

"If you really believe she's in danger, perhaps you should alert the authorities," Sam suggested.

Shaking his head, he replied grimly, "I can't. I've thought of that, but I don't have proof of a plot to harm her, just . . . a feeling in the gut. And I, apparently, am the only one concerned about it."

"Here's another thought," Will maintained, his eyes narrowed as he concentrated on the brandy he swirled very slowly in his snifter. "There must be other women at the theater on whom you could . . . focus your attention."

"Now, there's a brilliant idea," he returned wryly, finishing off his own drink in two large swallows. "Let my wife think my former reputation is intact by charming someone else."

"Wait a minute," Sam interjected, his mouth breaking into a crooked smile as he glanced from one to the other. "That's not a bad idea, Colin. *Are* there other young women at the theater on a daily basis?"

He grunted. "Of course there are. I suppose."

"Then think about it," Sam continued. "Charlotte can hardly avoid you completely if you're there with the pretense of wooing someone else, and it would save her from having to reveal her relationship with you to anyone who might be overly curious." He grinned. "And, intentions aside, you might find her to be a bit jealous of you placing your affections elsewhere."

Colin was dubious. He really wasn't at all interested in wooing another female at the moment, but he did find himself warming to the idea of making his wife jealous. It might get her into his bed faster than a slow seduction alone. Then again, it might not. It was altogether possible she wouldn't care in the least. He would have to be very cautious in his approach. Still, there was one thing that bothered him about it.

"The country, as a whole, knows I'm married to the Lady Charlotte, the Earl of Brixham's respectable sister," he said, irritated again for no reason at all. "If I'm too blatant about it, word will certainly spread through society that I'm being unfaithful."

Sam blinked. "And that bothers *you*?"

The question, asked honestly, made him mad. "Of course it bothers me. I'm not a cad, for Christ's sake."

"Then don't be blatant about it," Will remarked with a lift of a shoulder. "If you're careful, whatever you do with whom will only be speculation. Rumor with no factual basis. In the end, only you and Charlotte will know the truth, and that's really all that matters."

Colin rubbed his eyes. His head hurt, both from the alcohol he'd drunk, and thinking so hard while under its influence. He needed sleep.

At last Sam glanced at the wall clock and stood. "It's nearly midnight and I'm exhausted."

"You're exhausted?" Colin replied through a weak smile.

Sam ran his fingers through his hair. "One day,

when you get your wife with child, you'll understand. But I do need to get Olivia home."

Will finished off his brandy and stood as well. "We should be on our way, too. We're leaving for Cornwall next week and I'm sure there's something Vivian needs to pack."

Colin pushed his body out of the rocker for a final time and stretched. "It's amazing how domesticated you two have become. Quite sad, actually."

"Domestication has its advantages," Sam acknowledged as the three of them walked to the study door. "And honestly, it's far better, in every way, than living alone."

Alone. With my wife in the next room.

The advice given tonight—all of it—would be well taken. He'd truly had enough of the confusion, self-doubt, and tiptoeing around her whims. He was a married man, with a wife to protect and a body that craved her attention. It was time to make some decisions.

It was time for him to act.

Chapter 11

~~~

Charlotte sat at her dressing table, wearing her practical cotton nightgown, staring at her face in the mirror, noting that her cheeks still flushed with color from the effects of too much wine. Yvette had just taken her leave for the night, with instructions not to disturb her until eight if she didn't wake up on her own. Utterly exhausted from a four-hour rehearsal at the theater, then dinner and entertaining with Colin's friends, she couldn't wait to crawl between the sheets for a long, restful sleep.

She hadn't seen her husband since he'd left to have brandy with the gentlemen, and that was perfectly fine with her. The uncomfortable static charge between them whenever they were near each other caused her certain distress and kept her from concentrating on more important matters. Indeed, she'd been fully aware that he spent the entire dinner staring at her, just as she'd been unnaturally aware of him as a man. Well, perhaps that wasn't the right word. One knew it was only *natural* for her, as a woman, to respond to his masculinity, his powerful physique and incredibly handsome face. What they shared was nothing more than an awkward physical attraction that would no doubt fade over time. Until then, she would need to keep her wits about her and stay as far removed from his presence as possible. Work, it seemed, was the answer to that, though even when she worked, her mind often strayed to him.

His kiss three weeks ago in the coach still lingered—in her mind, on her lips—and she recalled it constantly, much to her chagrin. He had cast a spell on her, and what made her angry at herself was the knowledge that he didn't even have to be in the room for her to want him to kiss her all over again. Everywhere.

She shivered and lifted her hairbrush off the vanity, twisting it in her fingers before she began pulling it through her thick hair.

She knew the "accidents" at the theater were intentional, meant not to harm her, but to scare her. She also knew why, though after thinking about it for some time now, she still couldn't determine who among her friends and colleagues could possibly be in collusion with her brother. And Charles had to be the one behind it. Although not aware of the Handel score she owned, he was the one person who wanted her to quit the theater to save his name from disgrace should her identity ever become common knowledge among his peers. But he couldn't be acting alone as he would never—aside from opening night—lower himself to show his face in such a place. Someone was helping him, and the only thing she felt certain of was that it probably wasn't Porano; the tenor didn't have time to think of anything but his own fame, and probably wouldn't care anyway.

Colin would come to her aid if she asked for his assistance, but she wasn't ready to do that. She still didn't know him all that well, didn't know if she could trust him to keep her secret, or if he might attempt to sell the only piece of property she alone possessed—the piece that could render her independent for the rest of her life—simply because he now technically owned it through marriage. He clearly didn't need the money its sale would bring, but she remained uncertain of his intentions where she was concerned, in every aspect of their married life, and that was enough to give her pause.

"You have beautiful hair."

Startled, Charlotte let out a short gasp at the sound of his husky voice from their adjoining doorway. "I'm just on my way to bed, sir," she said, placing her hairbrush on her vanity.

He offered her a sly smile, and she watched him through the mirror as he began to saunter toward her.

"Did you enjoy yourself tonight?" he asked with a casual air.

Her heart started beating hard. "Of course, your grace. Your friends are lovely people."

He nodded as if he expected such an answer, standing behind her now, gazing down to her reflection, his features mildly contemplative as he took in all of her through the glass. Reaching out, he lifted a few strands of her hair, lacing them through his fingers. Charlotte's eyes widened negligibly with sudden concern over his intentions, though she remained very still, concentrating on her composure, afraid of raising his ire should she jerk away from his grasp.

At last he released the silky strands and placed his palms on her shoulders, gazing at her face once more through the mirror.

The touch of his skin felt hot, even through her nightdress, but she didn't move.

"You know," he murmured softly, his head tipped fractionally to the side, "I remember asking you to call me Colin the day after our wedding, and yet I still haven't heard you do so in casual conversation."

How could she possibly reply to such a statement? Apologize? Honestly, she couldn't now remember if she'd ever called him by his given name or not, but his unusual manner and unexpected presence in her bedroom was beginning to intimidate her. And although she wasn't exactly afraid of his closeness, with his hands firmly on her and the look of thoughtfulness on his face, she'd never felt so vulnerable in her life.

"Actually, Colin, I'm very tired—"

"Stand up, Charlotte," he interrupted with gentle insistence.

With a blink, she repeated, "Stand up?"

His eyes narrowed on her face and he almost smiled. "You are off to bed, are you not?"

She could feel her pulse racing through her veins. "I am, but—"

"Then stand up." He removed his hands from her shoulders and took a step back. "Right here."

She couldn't very well deny him such a simple, seemingly innocent request, and she could think of no reason to stall. Bracing herself with her arms on the vanity, she dared not look away from his intense gaze through the mirror as she did his bidding and slowly rose to meet his level.

In one smooth action, he pulled her vanity chair out from behind her and took its place with his powerful body, essentially pinning her without touching. Her mouth went dry and she couldn't move.

"What are you doing?" she whispered.

Without explanation, he stooped down a bit so that he could place himself cheek to cheek, his eyes still locked with hers through the glass. Then, once again, he grasped her shoulders very lightly over her nightdress and began a gentle massage with his fingers.

"Close your eyes," he insisted huskily, his lips only an inch from her ear.

In a state of near-panic, she swallowed, "Your grace—"

"Close your eyes, Charlotte," he repeated with a little more force. "Just relax."

How on earth could she possibly relax? He held her spellbound, practically a captive in his embrace. Yet, she also knew instinctively that if she brushed him aside, or lashed out at him angrily, he'd let her go. At the very least, she trusted him that much.

Drawing a deep inhale for confidence, she did as he asked, lowering her lashes, feeling his warm breath on her skin, inhaling the faintest scent of cologne and brandy, noting how the ends of his dark blond hair tickled her jawline and made her shiver inside.

He began to increase the pressure of his hands on her shoulders, moving them subtly outward to her upper arms and then back again, faintly massaging the length of her neck, then gradually pushing his fingers forward to leave feather soft caresses on her collarbone just under the edges of her nightgown. She couldn't help herself. It felt divine, and without clear thought, she leaned back a little closer to his chest.

"Why are you doing this?" she asked in a whisper.

"Shh . . . No questions," he replied in a husky timbre. "I'm going to leave you in a moment, but I want to show you something first."

Charlotte eased ever closer to him so that she fairly leaned against his large, firm chest. She had no idea on earth what he could possibly show her, even less of a sense of his intentions, but at this point, she didn't think it mattered. His evasiveness, coupled with the expert kneading of her tight muscles, made her maddeningly hot all over.

Moments later, he said softly, "I'm going to give you my first direct order as your husband, Charlotte."

Her legs suddenly felt weak beneath her and she teetered on the brink of giving in to him, allowing her entire body to relax into his. It took every bit of strength she possessed to keep her composure.

"My order," he continued without waiting for reply, "is that while I show you this one small thing, you will stand here without moving or speaking, and keep your eyes closed. Nod your head if you understand."

Understand? The tiniest part of her still wished to push him away, run to her bed and hide under the covers. But she couldn't seem to give herself over to doing the logical thing while he caressed her shoulders and arms, drew his thumbs across her shoulder blades, left feathery trails on her throat with his fingertips. In the end, she acquiesced and nodded minutely.

Immediately, his breathing quickened and he ran the tip of his nose along the length of her ear, pausing to faintly run his lips across her lobe. She trembled, succumbing to a liquid fire in her belly, inhaling a shaky breath, knowing he probably felt her response to his touch but deciding at once that she didn't care. At last he pulled her closer so that she rested lightly against his hard, broad chest, the heat from his body radiating through their clothes to warm her back. Gradually, he traced his fingertips up and down her arms until she felt gooseflesh appear, never touching her indecently, but making her long for . . . something not quite within reach. Whatever his intentions, she could no longer fight such an utterly delicious effort on his part, though with every breath she fought the urge to moan and turn to him in surrender. Instead, unable to stop herself, she simply rested her head against his shoulder, relishing the way his warmth and strength enveloped her.

"One more minute," he breathed against her neck, "and then I'll leave you."

Leave her? She didn't want him to leave, she wanted him to caress her like this for hours.

For another moment or two he continued to caress her arms, then finally paused all movement and whispered, "Now open your eyes . . ."

It took her a second or two to respond to his command, and then, very slowly, she lifted her lashes to meet his gaze through the mirror in front of them.

She looked at herself, noting the flush in her cheeks, her parted, moist lips, her pulse beating rapidly in her throat. But as she shifted her attention to him, her breathing faltered and she swallowed with an incredible sense of awe. Never before had she witnessed such intensity from a man, such dark determination in his hardened jaw, such desire in his eyes. And she had done this to him—without doing anything.

"You really are a beautiful woman, Charlotte," he said, his voice low and tight, his cheek to her temple.

She couldn't reply. Her throat ached and her body felt hot and shaky.

He sensed her weakness. With a twitch of his lips, he wrapped his arms around her to hug her close, brushing his lips against her hairline at her forehead. Then with one arm just under her breasts, he lowered the other to her hips and pulled her bottom against him.

She inhaled sharply when she felt his rigid desire for her. But as much as she wanted to escape him, she couldn't. He mesmerized her.

"Touching you, being so close to you, *thinking* of you does this to me, Charlotte," he whispered in her ear once more, never moving his gaze from hers. "And I think about you every minute of every day."

Her eyes widened to round pools of incredulity; his narrowed as he then boldly raised his hand and covered one breast with his palm, over her nightgown, and left it still, tempting, waiting.

"Colin . . ." she breathed.

He inhaled shakily, and then as she watched him lower his head to skim her cheek with his lips, he reached inside of her nightdress and placed his palm over her bare nipple.

Unable to resist him, she whimpered softly from the exquisite touch and clutched his arms with her hands, suddenly afraid her knees would give way beneath her.

"Do you like this?" he asked, his eyes capturing hers again through the mirror.

Nodding negligibly, she whispered, "Yes . . ."

He ran his fingertips across her nipple, once, twice, and she licked her lips and pushed herself into his hand as a surge of need swept through her. He noticed it as he watched her, caressed her, his eyes lit with fire. And then, very slowly, he released her.

Brushing his lips to her ear a final time, he whispered, "Good night, sweet wife."

With that he backed away, leaving her to the chill in her room as he turned and walked through their adjoining door, closing it softly behind him.

Chapter 12

❧

Charlotte sat rigidly across from her husband in the hackney coach he'd hired for her morning ride to rehearsal, sifting through sheets of music for something to do to keep from looking at him, or engaging him in conversation.

He'd been watching her silently for the better part of an hour now, pretending drowsiness, his hands folded in his lap, body relaxed as if he hadn't a care in the world. She, however, couldn't seem to calm her racing heartbeat, her nervousness, the tingle she felt deep inside whenever she recalled what he'd done to her last night. Admittedly, it wasn't much as far as touching goes, but whatever his goal, his endeavor had been effective. The result had been wholly unpleasant, both in how he made her feel before leaving her alone in frustration at her weakness, and in not knowing if he'd attempt such boldness again. If he did, she was afraid she might not be able to resist.

Frankly, the event still lingered in her mind as if

he had only just touched her. But he'd done more than that. He'd numbed her, confused her, and yes, even alarmed her when she later stopped to consider how he'd managed to arouse feelings in her she didn't understand simply by rubbing her shoulders, breathing softly in her ear. She should be angry that he'd awakened that kind of desire in her, but she wasn't, probably because he really hadn't done anything improper. Aside from the fact that they were legally married and he had the right by law to approach her in any way he chose, he didn't exactly have to force her into submission. But the memory that had kept her awake most of the night, the memory that, oddly enough, both embarrassed and thrilled her, was the feel of his desire, pushed so intimately against her, that she alone had roused in *him* by doing absolutely nothing. For some inexplicable reason she just couldn't drive that from her mind, and the thrilling part, she supposed, was knowing she possessed some sort of sexual . . . power over him. She only wished she knew how to use it to her advantage.

"What are you thinking?"

She jumped at the interruption, startled, and for a second, concerned that he could actually read her mind. Mentally shaking herself of that ridiculous notion, she replied, "Of act three."

He grinned at her through slitted eyes. "That's surprising. You've been staring at the same page for ten minutes."

She ignored that and began shuffling the pages of music in her lap.

"Did you sleep well?" he asked moments later.

Her heart started beating fast in her chest. What did

he expect her to say? Without looking at him, she said blandly, "I had a very good night's rest, thank you."

"That's quite a lot of music you brought," he remarked very casually.

She shrugged her tight shoulders. "It's a long coach ride to the theater."

"Ah." He waited, then asked, "And you need all of that today?"

She glanced up briefly, deciding that since he seemed determined to have a conversation, there was likely no way to avoid it. At least the topic of music would keep it neutral.

Sighing, she said, "No, most of this isn't necessary for today, but I store a great many pieces in my dressing room and go through them frequently, exchanging them from time to time with those I keep at home." She held up a few pages with both hands. "They're mostly works for practice."

"Works for practice?" he repeated with a slight lift of his brows.

He didn't sound all that interested, though she had to admit he wasn't exactly brushing the topic aside, either.

"This," she explained, lifting one small, bound book, "is a *vocalise*, or series of pieces made up of various scales and arpeggios, some intricate tunes, usually sung a capella with a pianist for guidance. All singers must warm the vocal cords daily."

"I see," he replied. "I never knew singing could be so complicated."

She smirked, caught up in his amusement. "Singing is easy. Music can be complicated. Putting the two of them together is almost always either frustrating, or immensely rewarding. Sometimes both."

"As with Mr. Porano's tempo problem?"

She knew he was teasing her, but surprisingly, she actually enjoyed it. Smiling, she nodded once. "Exactly, though to be fair, all singers have problems, minor or major, with which they must deal."

"And what is your problem?"

"I'm not only the exception," she said through an exaggerated sigh, "I'm the leading soprano. Thus, I have no problem."

He grinned. "You're also very humble."

She shrugged and turned her attention back to her music. "One should always strive to do one's best. I strive to be the most humble person I know."

That made him laugh. Seconds later, he asked, "So where are your spectacles?"

She glanced up. "I beg your pardon?"

He motioned toward her with the back of his hand. "Your spectacles. You're not wearing them and yet you told me you need them for reading music."

The truth was, she felt rather unattractive with the large frames attached to her face, and with an acknowledgment to her vanity, she didn't like wearing them anywhere near her husband. But she would never tell him that.

"I suppose I forgot them," she replied without elaboration, looking down to the sheets on her lap again.

"Your mind has probably just been elsewhere this morning," he said through a false sigh. "Distraction happens to the best of us, especially after such a late night."

Her body went still as her cheeks flooded with

heat, but she didn't dare raise her gaze to meet his. He'd said that on purpose, to fluster her, and she refused to give him the satisfaction of knowing his tactic had worked. She just didn't bother to answer, and thankfully, he didn't push her for response.

They sat quietly together for a few minutes longer, until their coach, meandering through traffic, made the final turn on the road to the theater.

Charlotte began to gather her sheets of music into a pile. "So, what are your plans today, sir?" she asked brightly, glad to be leaving the close confines of his presence.

He inhaled deeply and sat up straighter in his seat. "I'm not sure."

She frowned minutely, feeling a bit anxious from his evasiveness. "You can't possibly stay with me all the time, sir. Don't you have estate matters with which you need concern yourself?"

He shook his head. "No."

Charlotte couldn't decide if he was teasing her again or trying to make her mad.

Annoyed, she made a great fuss of putting her music sheets into a tidy stack, then folding her hands on top of it in her lap.

"Then perhaps you should find a cause to occupy your time, your grace," she maintained. "I simply can't be bothered by your presence at rehearsal day after day."

Seconds of awkward silence passed before he murmured, "My presence bothers you, Charlotte?"

He'd asked that in such a manner that she almost chided herself for making such a callous remark. But then, perhaps honesty was in order.

"I didn't mean to be rude, your grace," she admitted, feeling a little deflated. "But the truth is, you make me . . . nervous. I don't know why. And really, my work can't possibly be that interesting to you."

He actually smiled. "Your work doesn't interest me at all."

She squirmed a little in her seat. "*I* am not a cause, your grace."

He tipped his head to the side as his gaze traveled over her face. At last, he asked quietly, "Did you think about me after I left you last night?"

She felt heat rising up her neck and into her cheeks again. "That has nothing to do with our discussion."

"Oh, I'm certain it does," he countered knowingly.

She pressed her lips together with irritation. "Will you stop being so evasive? I've asked you repeatedly what you do with your time, where you go, why you're so interested in me and my whereabouts, and instead of giving me answers, you've decided to start following me." She huffed, and without clear thought, added, "Perhaps you need a mistress, sir."

She'd blurted that out before thinking, and immediately she wished she could take it back.

Obviously surprised, his brows shot up. "Is that what you'd like, Charlotte? For me to take a mistress?" He rubbed his shoe up and down along her skirt-covered calf as he lowered his voice to confess, "Somehow, I don't think so. Besides, I wouldn't dream of it after the marvelous few minutes we shared last night when we were both so aroused. For now, I don't need anyone but you."

Startled by his candor, her mouth dropped open a

little as her entire body seemed to melt like warm butter. He must have enjoyed her astonishment, for he suddenly leaned forward and whispered, "We're here, my darling. Shall I follow you inside?"

Charlotte couldn't have reacted faster. Fairly jumping from her seat, she unlatched the handle and opened the door before their driver had even stepped down to offer help.

Colin didn't think he'd ever had a more enjoyable ride in a hired hack in his life. Initially, he'd wanted to take one of his own smaller coaches for the comfort, but Charlotte had persuaded him otherwise. She had reasons to be concerned, he supposed, as many would see them arriving and wonder at their relationship. He didn't give a damn what people thought, but he knew it would disturb her and so he'd acquiesced. After last night, when he'd so cleverly manipulated her into an aching need left unsatisfied, he supposed he owed her something. It had been a perfectly arousing few minutes together, and a first for him, which probably made it all the more erotic.

It had taken him a long time to fall asleep after leaving her. He'd stared at the ceiling, recalling her reaction to just a light touch here and there, the way her nipple hardened and she moaned when he brushed his fingers against it. But what surprised him most was how *he'd* reacted. He'd never left a woman wanting more, if he recalled. Always, if he worked at a seduction, at least they got the ultimate pleasure from it. But Charlotte was different. The ultimate pleasure he got from her, for now, was the challenge. And he was enjoying it immensely.

Now, after their warm and somewhat bumpy ride to the theater, he followed her inside the backstage entrance of the opera house, watching her hips sway gently with each step, thinking that if he continued to dwell on her hips and nipples, he'd no doubt be bothered by an erection all damn day. And the gown she wore didn't help at all. Although she'd donned a plain olive-green work dress with short, puffed sleeves and a high neckline, which didn't usually make for tempting fare, Charlotte managed to look splendid. Regardless of the fabric and style, nothing could hide her marvelous figure. At least that gave him something to look at when she wouldn't let him touch, he supposed.

The theater felt warm when they entered, and Colin pulled at his neckline, loosening his tie. The smell of fresh paint assaulted his senses, and already he heard singing, probably Porano, as the notes reverberated through the building while someone clapped in time to the music. Charlotte more or less ignored him, but he followed her anyway, toward her dressing room, he assumed. They were behind the stage, but the curtains were drawn, making it impossible to see anything more than a couple of feet in front of his face, though she knew exactly where to go.

"Is he getting the tempo right this morning?" he asked.

"Shhh," she replied without turning around. "He hears everything."

"Except for rhythm, apparently."

She actually chuckled at that, and it occurred to him that the only place he'd heard her laugh was on the stage. Now it warmed him within to think she found humor in something he'd said. He only wished he could have seen her face.

"Who else is here this early?" he asked as they neared her private room, fairly centered at the back of the theater.

"Just a few of the stage hands; they're working on scenery today," she replied as she turned the handle and opened the door. "Anne and Sadie will be here shortly, and—"

She stopped short and gasped. Colin quickly moved up behind her, his own eyes widening at the scene before them.

Illuminated by only a trace amount of window light, the two of them stared at a paper mess, sheets of Charlotte's music that had been pulled from boxes and drawers to be strewn across the floor.

At first sight, Colin thought the room had been fully ransacked, though after a moment of careful observation, he quickly changed his mind. The large wardrobe remained closed, and none of the cosmetic bottles and brushes atop the vanity had been disturbed. This was a deliberate attempt to either destroy sheets of music, or look for something, a warning of some kind left in the disarray.

Although she hadn't yet said a word, Charlotte seemed calm—too calm, in his opinion, as if finding her dressing room vandalized was something she might have expected. At the very least, she didn't seem at all surprised.

Immediately, Colin took action. Grasping her wrist, he moved her forward and out of the way so that he could enter completely and shut the door behind them.

"What are you doing?" she insisted, turning to him with a look of irritation on her face.

"Keep your voice down," he ordered in a whisper. Then, "Does it lock?"

She frowned. "The door?"

"*Yes*, the door. Does it lock?"

Shaking her wrist loose, she said, "I think so, but I never lock it. I don't have a key if that's what you mean."

After raking his fingers through his hair, he walked quickly to the wardrobe, careful to avoid the scattered sheets on the floor, and opened both doors, scanning the contents, making certain they were alone. Then he turned back to her and placed his hands on his hips. "What is going on, Charlotte?"

She took a step back in defense. "I have no idea—"

"Yes, you do," he charged, his tone low and firm. "If you didn't, you'd be shaken by this. As it is now, you don't even seem surprised."

She faltered, her expression going blank as she clutched the music she'd brought with her against her chest like a shield.

"No more evasiveness," he said, his gaze locked with hers. "Tell me what you're hiding."

His insistence made her mad. He could see it in her flattened lips, her pinkening cheeks. She'd been caught, and she knew it.

"I want the truth," he continued, starting a slow saunter toward her. "Now."

Flustered, she wiped a palm across her forehead and looked away, as if she couldn't decide where to start. He waited, walking past her to stand once more in front of the closed door, preventing her untimely departure should she try to avoid him. With that, she moved away from him and walked to her vanity, then placed the sheets she still had clutched in one arm gently on top of it.

After a few silent seconds, she inhaled deeply and stood erect, her hands clasped behind her, and faced him fully.

"I have something someone wants," she said hesitantly.

He cocked his head to the side a little and crossed his arms over his chest. "What is it? Music?"

"Yes," she replied at once.

He'd been more or less sarcastic with his question, assuming, naturally, that music wasn't worth stealing or risking a life for, but he could tell simply by looking at her across a darkened room that she spoke the truth.

Taking a step toward her, he asked, "What kind of music would someone go to such great extremes to acquire?"

She looked at him oddly. "Music worth a lot of money, your grace."

"Of course," he replied, his mouth curving into a sly smile. "Very expensive music."

She drew her hands forward and crossed her arms over her breasts defensively as he approached. But her gaze never wavered.

"I didn't say it was expensive, sir, I said it was worth a lot of money."

He paused, glancing around, then said, "Well they obviously didn't find it, or you'd be a bit more distraught."

She almost smiled. "It's not here."

He leaned toward her and enunciated, "Where is it?"

"Hidden."

Standing directly in front of her now, his anger roused, he leaned over so that his face nearly touched hers. "Charlotte, darling, tell me what the devil is going on. Now."

The intensity in his quiet tone made her blink. Then in one smooth action, she plopped her bottom down in the vanity chair behind her, ignoring her twisted and bunched skirts.

He waited, saying nothing, knowing the moment of truth was at hand.

"Can I trust you, Colin?" she asked in a deep murmur.

Perplexed, his brows furrowed minutely. "I'm not sure how to answer that."

She fidgeted in the chair, wringing her hands together in her lap. "Before I can tell you anything, I need to know that I can trust you."

He leaned to his side and rested his shoulder on the gilt-framed mirror, his arms crossed over his chest, his frank gaze locked with hers. "If you're asking me to trust what you say, then I will. If, instead, you're asking me to trust your judgement, I don't honestly know, Charlotte. Up to this point, you haven't made it easy."

It was the most candid answer he could give her, and even with its vagueness, the words seemed to have the desired effect.

"My first vocal tutor was the great baritone Sir Randolph Hillman. I began my singing career when I was only eleven years old, and he trained me as if I were the best. I was fatherless, as well, and over the years we grew very close, as would a proud father of his talented daughter."

Although not surprised, it occurred to Colin how small the world was when learning her vocal coach of many years was a man he'd known, had spoken to on occasion at social events, and had even seen many times on the stage. But he didn't want to discuss it now when he needed her to get to the point. "Go on," he said after a moment's pause.

She inhaled a deep breath and relaxed into her stays, resting the full of her body against the back of the small vanity chair, her gaze lowered.

"When I turned seventeen, my brother, who was my guardian at that point, decided it was time for me to stop my singing nonsense and put my efforts into finding a husband. As you might expect, I didn't take to the idea all that well. I wanted time before I had to give up my dream of the stage, but Charles was quite impatient. He more or less forced me to stop my tutoring sessions with Sir Randolph, regardless of my feelings."

"That had to be difficult for you," Colin interjected, his tone sincere.

She gave him a vague smile. "It was. But I was also very determined," she continued. "It was about this same time that Sir Randolph succumbed to years of a weakened heart and fell ill. As my luck would have it, Charles felt sorry enough for me he allowed me to visit. After all, my brother assumed I couldn't spend my time practicing my 'singing nonsense' when the man was bedridden."

Colin continued to watch her, rather engrossed and

trying not to smile from her sarcasm. She really became dramatic, and quite adorable, when she was irritated.

"I only got to see him twice in the long week he lay abed," she continued, subdued. "The first time he made me promise I would never stop singing. I made him that promise, but I didn't mention the fact that I couldn't, of course, afford any kind of tour, or sing on the stage as a leading soprano. My brother would never allow it, would never fund it, even if he could, and he was insistent that I marry well, settle down, and have children to better occupy my time." She grinned crookedly. "But Sir Randolph knew this."

"Because you'd told him," Colin remarked.

"No, because Charles told him," she corrected with a lift of her brows. "And because my brother is so insensitive, the day before he died—the last time I saw the great baritone—Sir Randolph gave me something that would make my dreams come true, if I ever had the nerve to leave Charles and actually begin a music career."

Colin scratched the hairline at his neck, a little confused. "Sir Randolph gave you priceless music?"

Charlotte leaned toward him, her eyes shining, a smile of genuine excitement gently tugging at her lips. "Exactly. Charles made Sir Randolph so angry, he gave me the one thing that would assure I could sing professionally, if that was my choice, for the rest of my life."

"What music is so valuable it would finance you for years?" he asked. He grinned slyly to add, "I'm aching to know."

Her features turned serious once more as she replied, "What I'm about to tell you stays between us, Colin. Is that clear?"

He shrugged lightly. "If you have secrets, Charlotte, I will do my best to keep them—provided it doesn't put you in danger."

For a second or two she stared at him skeptically, as if trying to decide if his answer was fair enough. But he wouldn't budge on this, and she knew it.

Leaning forward, she placed her elbows on her thighs and clasped her palms together in front of her. In a barely heard whisper, she announced, "Sir Randolph gave me an original piece, never published, by the great George Frideric Handel."

Colin just stared at her, at first dazed, then growing cold with understanding as the meaning of her words began to sink in. The look on his face must have been as priceless as the music she claimed to own, for she suddenly started giggling, covering her mouth to keep it silent.

After a long moment of speechlessness, he mumbled, "You're not joking, are you?"

She dropped her hand and pulled back, appalled. "Of course I'm not joking. Just look at this mess."

He glanced at the floor as he ran his fingers through his hair. "If it's not here, where is it?" he asked, his throat dry.

She gazed at him curiously, her head tilted to one side, and replied, "It's safe."

Recovering himself, he pulled away from the mirror and took a step toward her, his nerves catching fire. "Safe? That's not an answer, Charlotte. I want to see it."

"It's not here," she reiterated flatly.

"Yes, you've made that clear," he returned as patiently as he could. "But I still want to see it. I *need* to see it. Where is it?"

For several long, lingering, silent seconds, she held back, biting down on her bottom lip in obvious doubt as he studied her.

"If you trust me," he said softly, "you have to trust me completely, Charlotte."

At last, she swallowed and said, "Frankly, because we're married, I'm a little afraid—"

"I have no intention of selling it," he interjected with a sudden understanding of her fear. "But I might be able to help you if you trust me."

She glanced once to her reflection in the mirror at her side, then lowered her lashes to her lap. "It's at home."

He blinked. "At home? At *our* home?"

She nodded.

He closed his eyes and raised his arms, interlacing his fingers behind his head.

Jesus. He'd been living under the same roof as an original Handel, probably since they'd married, and he had yet to have a look at it because she didn't trust him not to sell it. At that moment, in a rush of sheer frustration, Colin wished he'd told her of his profession when they'd met. If she only knew what he could do . . .

"Have you had the piece authenticated?" he asked gruffly as the thought suddenly occurred to him.

"I don't have to," she replied a bit defensively.

He dropped his arms, and chuckled as he looked

at her again. "You don't have to?" He shook his head. "Charlotte, it may be worth nothing. It may be a forgery—"

"Then tell me, sir," she cut in, irritated, "why would someone keep trying to steal it?"

Before he could respond, a sharp burst of female laughter floated in from beyond the dressing room door, startling them both.

"Sadie and Anne are here," she whispered. "They'll be looking for me."

He didn't care. His mind was still on the precious, priceless piece now sitting somewhere in his home. "We need to get it, lock it in a vault." He sighed within. "And I suppose you won't tell me where to look so I can return and get it myself."

"Absolutely not. Besides, you'll never find it, never know where to look, even if I told you," she said, standing to meet his gaze and smoothing her skirts. "And I obviously can't leave now. Everyone would question my absence."

"Including the person who did this," he speculated, drawing conclusions as his mind began to organize a plan. Abruptly, he said, "Help me clean this up."

Without argument, she stooped down and started collecting the scattered music. "What are you thinking?"

"I'm thinking we need to keep this a secret for the time being," Colin said as he began to help gather the scattered paper. "The person who did this is trying to scare you, Charlotte, or he or she would have been far more discreet, wouldn't have left a mess for you to clean."

She glanced up and frowned. "But that makes no

sense. Why try to frighten me? Why would someone want me to *know* that they want to steal my
work?"

His eyes narrowed in thought as he placed the remaining sheets into a loose stack. "I don't know. How
many people know you own it?"

"I didn't think anyone knew," she murmured. "I
haven't told anyone aside from you, today."

"Then Sir Randolph must have mentioned it to
someone," he maintained.

"Impossible," she insisted again, standing along-
side him and surveying the dressing room. "According to him, nobody even knew he owned it, and he
made me promise not to tell a soul until I was ready
to make it public and sell it myself."

Colin grasped her elbow and turned her to face
him. "*Somebody* knows, Charlotte."

He watched her brows furrow in confusion, but
she just shook her head, perplexed.

Seconds later, he added, "I really do need to see
the music."

"You will," she replied, annoyed at his insistence,
"though I have no idea what you think you'll discover."

You're right. You have no idea . . .

With a grin, he released her elbow and handed her
his pile of music, which she added to her own. Then
she walked to the wardrobe and opened one side of
it, placing all the music on a shelf within before closing the door tightly.

Colin watched her as she turned back to him, her
lovely eyes sparkling, her expression only slightly
troubled by all that had just happened between them,

and he found himself caught up in an intense rush of excitement he hadn't felt in ages.

"I need to get to work," she said, smoothing her sleeves down with her palms. "We can discuss this later."

Suddenly, another thought occurred to him, one that first bewildered, then made him stagger back a foot or two to block her exit from the door.

She stopped in front of him. "What are you doing?"

He eyed her strangely, a half-smile on his lips as a shred of clarity pulsed through him and understanding dawned. "You didn't have to marry me, did you, Charlotte?"

His whispered words, and probably the look of mischief on his face seemed to catch her off guard. She wavered and took a step back, looking him up and down. "What are you talking about?"

He couldn't help himself as a wide, satisfied grin graced his mouth. "I think you know."

"Know what?" she asked with exasperation.

He slowly shook his head. "You could have brought the music to the public's attention at any time, sold it, and lived comfortably for the rest of your life, *touring* on stage anywhere in the world. Instead, you came to me." He reached out and ran a finger down her neck and across her shoulder, making her shiver. "Why is that?"

For a moment she looked startled. Then, much to his surprise, she smiled wickedly and leaned toward him just as Lottie would do.

"Because I knew you wanted me, Colin," she answered seductively, a palm to his chest. "I didn't *have* to sell it."

Colin's pulse began to race from her transformation into the seductive woman he thought he was getting when he married her. But he could no longer match her humor. He couldn't tell if she teased him or actually admitted she'd explicitly used him with her sexual charms, but the admission left him cold nonetheless.

"So you instead sold yourself to me," he said quietly. "I'm not sure if I should feel flattered or insulted."

She noticed the change in his demeanor, the rawness laced through his words, and it suddenly dawned on her that she'd offended him. Gradually, her grin faded, her eyes widened, and she withdrew her hand as she took a step back. "I didn't mean—"

"Yes, you did," he interjected in a whisper. "But at least you're being honest."

She licked her lips and shook her head once or twice, her cheeks pinkened with embarrassment. Purposely expressionless, Colin took the cue, reached behind him, and opened the door.

"Your fame awaits you, Lottie."

That seemed to render her speechless. Seconds later, without another word, she brushed past him, and left the dressing room.

Chapter 13

〜〜∞〜〜

Charlotte had never had to act so well in her life. She was furious, really furious with him—and confused and uncomfortable and angry with herself for experiencing such unrefined feelings and then expressing them aloud. But she couldn't, in any way, let him know what a mess he'd made of her emotions, which was turning out to be the most difficult thing she'd ever done.

The first hour at rehearsal had gone rather well considering the events that took place earlier in her dressing room. Nobody at the theater seemed suspicious to her, or treated her differently than they did every other day. Most were actors by profession, of course, but at least one person had to know she'd found her dressing room vandalized and hadn't said a word about it to anyone.

But after she and Porano sang their first duet, and the cast took a five-minute break, she decided to look for Colin. She felt rather subdued about how he'd reacted to their last verbal exchange, and she wanted to apologize, although truthfully, she *had* been honest. But the moment she found him, behind the stage in a darkened corner, practically head to head in quiet conversation with Sadie, making amends vanished from her mind.

Unsettled, and taken aback by their closeness, she'd watched them quietly from the shadows a good distance away, which made it impossible to hear their conversation. But as the minutes progressed, she found herself growing more and more annoyed, even concerned, because she didn't know if she could trust him to stay silent about the Handel piece. Then she heard him laugh softly at something her friend had said, Sadie smiling and touching his arm in response, and in a matter of seconds she became completely incensed, concluding that she just couldn't trust him, period. Colin Ramsey, always the charmer.

Initially, she decided to ignore them, forget the entire incident, and return to the stage to begin the second hour of rehearsal, knowing Sadie would have to be available as well and their little rendezvous would end of necessity. But as the day wore on, her imagination took over, her anger grew, and by the time they left for the day, she could hardly speak to her husband civilly. During the coach ride home, which again seemed overly long and miserably hot, she feigned exhaustion so she wouldn't have to converse with him, and for the most part he managed to leave her alone with her thoughts. That only seemed to make matters worse for her, she decided, because it gave her time to ponder the entire episode.

It wasn't as if he'd done anything *wrong*, exactly;

flirting seemed a natural thing for many people and he and Sadie *were* both discreet and decently clothed. But by the time they reached home, she'd become infuriated again, of course by the entire incident, but even more in herself because she couldn't, in any way, say anything to him about it without sounding like a shrew. Especially after suggesting he take a mistress just that morning.

So now, as they entered the townhouse, she wanted nothing more than to take a bath, eat supper in her room, and go to bed. He, however, would hear nothing of that, as he'd waited all day to see the treasure.

"It's in your study," she said curtly at his demand, walking in front of him down the hall, carrying the day's music she'd brought home inside the linen bag in her hand.

"In the pianoforte, I assume?" he replied.

"How clever you are, your grace," she said, trying not to make her words sound too sarcastic.

"I am," he agreed, "and I would have looked there first if I'd come home earlier." He paused, then leaned over to whisper in her ear, "After I went through your stocking drawer."

She couldn't decide whether to slap him or laugh at such an outrageous comment. Instead, with a quick, stern glance over her shoulder, she ignored it altogether.

Without another word, he followed her into the study, then closed the door behind them and waited for her to move first to the pianoforte.

She took her time intentionally, forcing him to wait to view the masterwork. He seemed patient enough, however, and when she plopped her music bag in one of the wing leather chairs in front of his desk and turned to face him, his look of amusement made her nerves catch fire. The cad.

"Is there a problem?" he asked, wide-eyed.

"Of course not," she answered at once. "I'm starved, and was thinking of eating first."

His brows rose and he mouthed, "Absolutely not."

Chin high and a smirk on her lips, she walked to her old and cherished instrument and inhaled a full breath. Then with skillful hands, she lifted the top just enough to see a few dusty strings in the darkness, and reached inside.

Her fingers touched it at once, exactly where she'd hidden it the day she moved into the townhouse.

Very carefully, she grasped one corner of the protective envelope, gently lifted it, then pulled it out slowly before she lowered the top of the pianoforte once more.

"Wouldn't it affect your playing in there?" he asked, moving toward her.

She held the envelope flat in one palm and turned to hand her husband the prize. "No, I had it laying on its side in the crack, not on the strings." She shrugged minutely. "And really, what better place to keep it where nobody would think to look?"

"Where else, indeed," he remarked, gazing at it for several seconds, his expression growing serious, thoughtful. Then, cautiously, he reached for it.

"As you can see, it's quite well protected," she said, following him as he carried it toward his desk. "I've kept it bound in paper inside the envelope. There was no other way I knew to care for it, though I've tried my best to keep it away from the elements and with other music."

"Until the mishaps began, I assume," he replied, pulling his rocker out with one hand and sitting.

She followed suit as she returned to the wing chair opposite him, dropped her music bag to the floor, and lowered her body into it.

She watched him, rather impressed by his meticulous examination, noting his furrowed brows, the intensity in his gaze as he turned the envelope over slowly in his hands.

"Should I lock the door?" she asked after a moment, glancing over her shoulder.

"It's not necessary," he answered a bit absent-mindedly.

That made her nervous. "But what about the servants? They might interrupt, and if they knew—"

"I don't have problems like that with my staff, Charlotte," he said with a fast look into her eyes before turning his attention back to the envelope.

The more she learned of her new husband and his personality, the more he confused her. She found him charming and jovial, as everyone did apparently, but also carefree with his servants and his time, worried about nothing when he held something absolutely priceless in his hands that he had *yet* to open because he studied it with an intensity she'd never seen in him before. Except, perhaps, when he looked at her in that . . . corset costume.

She fidgeted. "I assure you, sir, the envelope is not worth anything. It's been opened before."

He smiled a little. "I look at everything."

She decided not to argue.

"How was rehearsal?" he asked seconds later.

Bewildered by his mundane attitude when he'd been so desperate to see the incredible treasure all day, she had no idea how to answer. If he didn't open it soon, she would claw at the paper herself.

"Hmm?" he said, giving her another quick glance when she didn't respond. "Rehearsal?"

"Rehearsal was . . . fine," she replied, fighting to keep her exasperation intact. Then, "Shall I order *tea*, your grace? What is taking you so *long*?"

"Are you that anxious to leave my company, Charlotte?"

She smoothed her skirts for something to do. "That's not the point. You know I'm anxious to hide the music again."

He actually chuckled, then sat up a little and placed the tip of his thumb under the flap. "I'm taking my time so I don't damage anything. The older the work, the more easily it can crumble from any movement at all. Even," he added, "tucked inside a very ordinary, inexpensive envelope."

She wanted to question his knowledge, but decided against it since he was very likely correct and she really didn't feel like arguing—or listening to an amateur lecture her on the delicate aging of musical scores.

Finally, with the envelope flap raised, he pushed the corners open just slightly and peered inside.

"I suppose you saw me talking with Sadie today," he stated quite casually.

Shocked, her mouth dropped open a little as she felt her face grow hot. "I—I don't think so, your grace. I was quite busy today."

He didn't even look at her. "I thought you did," he said, reaching inside the envelope at last.

She swallowed hard and ignored the comment, and the quick beating of her heart.

With one finger and thumb, he gingerly started withdrawing the treasure from the envelope, moving slower than molasses in winter, she mused.

As it was wrapped in newspaper, it took him a minute or more to pull it out completely and lay it on his desktop. With that, he tossed the envelope on the floor beside him. To her surprise, instead of spreading the paper to reveal the work, he pushed his rocker back a foot or two and opened one of the drawers on his left, hunting for something she couldn't see.

She tried peering over the desk to no avail. "What are you doing?"

"Looking for the right tools," he replied, distracted.

That puzzled her. "Tools? What tools?"

"You'll see. I'm being careful, Charlotte," he intimated, his voice reassuring.

She could hardly argue the attempt, she supposed, and so she just continued to watch him, waiting, her concern growing that with each passing minute someone would enter and see what a treasure they possessed. Such a notion was probably ridiculous, however, since, to the untrained eye, it would appear as if they were simply looking at a newspaper or music. Still, it made her nervous when her future lay so open and exposed.

He sat up again, and in his hands he held a rather

large magnifying glass and a pair of what appeared to be oddly shaped tweezers, like something a surgeon might use, which he then placed on the desktop beside the newspaper.

Charlotte sat forward once more, her bottom now perched on the edge of her chair, her intrigue growing with a renewed excitement. Although she didn't view it often, she never got tired of looking at the priceless music signed by a genius. Truly a wonder.

"Aren't you a bit interested to know what Sadie and I discussed?" he asked casually.

First she didn't understand him. Then meaning dawned and her stomach coiled into knots. He had to have seen her watching them at the theater, or knew she was there, else why would he keep trying to aggravate her with talk of Sadie? At a time like this? What flustered her the most was his apparent notion that she might be jealous and that he had the skill to bring it to the surface. He obviously had little faith in her ability to act.

She sighed loudly. "I'm far more interested in knowing why you would have such tools in your desk drawer."

"We all have our little secrets, don't we?" he acknowledged with a quick glance into her eyes.

She ignored that.

He returned to his work, his expression tight now with concentration as he lifted the tweezers and began using them to very gently pull the newspaper back inch by inch, corner by corner, until the musical piece underneath began to appear.

Charlotte leaned over the desk, giddy again at the sight of it. "Isn't it magnificent?"

He didn't reply. The score, in reality an unfinished but nearly complete violin sonata in A minor, included several pages, yellowed with age. With grave concentration, Colin lifted his magnifying glass with his free hand and began closely scanning the border, then the handwriting, followed by each note, bar, and measure on the first page, then the next, until he reached the last, lifting each page at the corner with his tweezers. He then turned the entire work over and examined the paper on the back, its edges and creases. Finally, he returned to the signature, his eyes, through the glass, nearly touching the composition as he traced each curve from first letter to last.

Charlotte watched him in utter fascination. As long as she'd known him, she'd never seen him so centered on anything, moving so slowly and with such concentration. Frankly, she had no idea what to think of her charming, lazy nobleman of a husband who suddenly seemed more like a . . . what? An authenticator? Could one do that as a hobby?

She waited until he placed the magnifier and tweezers down to the side of the music and sat back before she dared speak. But the look on his face told her everything.

"You think it's real, don't you?" she whispered excitedly.

"I think it's a masterpiece, yes," he returned softly, smiling. "The age of the paper is correct—it's at least one hundred years old. The ink has sufficiently faded, bled into the paper, and looks to be the right age as well. But I'll need to check Handel's signature to know conclusively."

"Conclusively?" she repeated, eyes wide. "You sound like a professional."

"I am a professional," he replied with a trace of arrogance.

"A professional at . . . what, exactly?"

"Have you played the music?" he asked, as if that had suddenly occurred to him.

She laughed, eyes sparkling. "Of course I've played it. Carefully."

He nodded, amused. "Did it *sound* like Handel's work? You're the music professional."

Just hearing him use that term to describe her filled her with an odd sense of calm coupled with pure satisfaction. She could hardly keep from beaming. "I believe so. It's not very long, but it's very much like his other works for the violin."

He leaned back in his rocker and folded his hands over his stomach, gazing at her speculatively.

"Put your hair down, Charlotte."

"My—" She shook her head minutely. "I beg your pardon?"

"You have beautiful hair," he said with a lift of a shoulder, "and I want to see it down."

Perplexed, she scoffed and sat back a little in her seat. "I don't think this is the appropriate time, sir."

He tapped his fingers together. "I have some secrets of my own, but I won't tell you any of them unless you take your hair down for me. Right now."

Aghast, she simply stared at him, more intrigued by his confession of secrets than shocked by the manner in which he wanted to reveal them.

Tilting her head to the side, she narrowed her eyes and asked, "It depends on the value of the secrets. And how many you're hiding."

He laughed, then leaned forward to rest his wrists on the edge of the desk. "They're *enormous* secrets."

She watched him candidly for a moment. "Do these *enormous* secrets have anything to do with your tools?"

"Maybe," he replied casually. "But you'll never know if you refuse my request."

In a manner, he was teasing her, and oddly enough, she quite enjoyed the interaction. But she absolutely could not resist such a temptation, and he knew it, too. Through an exaggerated sigh, she raised her arms and began pulling each pin from her unruly hair, dropping them into her music bag on the floor at her side. With the last one out, she shook her head a little to let her massive strawberry-blond curls fall loosely about her shoulders and down her back.

He reclined in his rocker again, resting an elbow on the arm, his chin on his fist, staring at her most intently, his gaze traveling over every inch of her hair and face and torso.

Charlotte squirmed a little in her seat, trying to remain composed. "Well?"

His mouth turned up slyly. "The first secret, darling wife, is that I *am* a professional."

"And what is it, sir, that you do professionally?" she asked, unable to hide the captivation in her voice.

He waited for a moment, rocking back and forth minutely.

"You really are quite breathtaking with your hair loose," he admitted quietly.

She suddenly felt hot all over, sensing a strange turn in conversation—a turn, of which she wanted no part.

Smiling blandly, she replied, "And you are a very handsome man, your grace. Now, what does a handsome man like you do professionally?"

His eyes narrowed and he tapped his fingertips against his chin, his lips curled in wry amusement. "I do illegal things professionally."

She stilled, riveted, her smile fading.

"Do you like that secret?" he asked seconds later, his voice low and husky.

Her heart started beating wildly again in her chest. "I—I'm not sure," she acknowledged after a harsh swallow.

He watched her, all humor removed from his features. Then abruptly, he stood and began walking around his desk, toward her.

"Stand up, Charlotte," he ordered as he moved to her side.

She looked up at his face. "Why?"

He smirked. "Because I told you to."

Her body felt like lead of a sudden, but after only a moment's hesitation, she managed to gradually raise herself up to meet his gaze.

"Do you want to hear another secret?" he asked, placing his palm at the base of her throat.

She felt the warmth of his skin against hers, the strength in his fingers, and her eyes grew large as a fearful thought occurred to her. "If you kill people professionally, I don't want to know."

He actually laughed. "No, I've never killed a soul, though a couple of women have tempted me."

She stiffened and he felt it.

"I meant my sisters, Charlotte."

"Oh," she muttered, fairly captured now by the remarkable intensity in his eyes, the heat of his body so close to her own.

Suddenly, he leaned forward and brushed his lips against her jawline. She sucked in a sharp breath, then leaned back a little and instinctively lowered her lashes as he trailed very slight kisses down her neck.

"I suppose you'd like me to tell you another secret," he whispered.

Reeling, she had no idea what to say.

"Would you?"

She felt her legs weakening, and, afraid she might fall, she reached up and clutched his sleeves over his arms. "No. I—I want you to tell me what you do that's illegal."

He drew the tip of his nose up the side of her neck until it touched her earlobe, then murmured, "I want to . . . But . . ."

"But?"

"But not now . . ."

Ready to shove him away in frustration, Charlotte thought she might actually faint when at that moment, he moved his head around and placed his lips on hers, just barely touching, and then invited her into the kiss with slow, soft pecks until he finally captured her mouth completely.

She fought him with control as long as she could, her mind racing, trying to understand why he would kiss her now, here. And then all reason evaporated as he drew his tongue across her top lip and pushed his fingers through her thick curls to draw her against him.

On instinct, she wrapped her arms around his neck and held him tightly, kissing him back as she cradled his head with both hands. He worked his numbing magic on her, inflaming her from the inside out, his tongue darting into her mouth to tease and taste and suck as his own breathing grew fast and hard. And then just as suddenly as he began the glorious assault on her body, he released her, pulling gradually away, caressing her cheek with his palm as he did so.

Trembling, it took her ages before she could open her eyes to the depth of his, her mind now a whirl-wind of turmoil and questions, her body heated and aching for something more. He continued to watch her, but his breathing had quickened, his eyes looked glazed, and her first coherent thought was that *she* had affected him this way.

They stood like that for a moment, gazing into each other's eyes, and then he reached up with one hand and closed it over her covered breast with his large palm.

Her breath caught in her chest; she couldn't move.

"I want to tell you all my secrets," he disclosed in a husky timbre, "but I have to trust you first."

She blinked quickly several times, feeling the rage of heat between her legs, unable to respond. Then he drew his second hand up and placed it over her other breast, holding it still for seconds before he drew his thumbs across her nipples, back and forth.

She whimpered, mesmerized, clutching his arms again to keep from falling.

"Can I trust you, Charlotte?" he whispered, his breathing now shaky, his jaw tight.

She felt like melting. "Yes . . ."

He closed his eyes and dropped his forehead to hers, gently massaging her breasts with both hands as if he cherished them.

"Colin . . ." she breathed.

And with that, he drew his lips across her brow and released her, stepping away as he took her hands from his arms and kissed each one on the knuckles.

Charlotte closed her eyes again, shaken, and not just because he'd touched her. There had been no groping in his caress, just an intimacy between them that hadn't been there before, and that she couldn't begin to describe. And she wanted more of it.

"I have lots of things to tell you, and we have some decisions to make," he murmured.

She nodded.

"But I'm hungry, you're hungry, and we need to hide the Handel again," he added, squeezing her hands gently before letting them go.

Disconcerted, she raised her lashes and pulled away from him, searching for her music at her feet. "Thank you, your grace," she said, her voice sounding thick and scratchy to her ears.

"I'll put the composition in my safe, behind my desk," he said. "But it will be in here and you may see it at any time."

Wiping her palm across her forehead to push her curling hair aside, Charlotte righted herself and managed a weak smile, forcing herself to look at him once more.

He'd crossed his arms over his chest, his face still

flushed from an obvious passion, but his eyes were lit with amusement. Suddenly, she was desperate to get away from him and into the confines of her own private bed chamber.

"I—I'm tired, sir," she asserted, trying to keep her tone matter-of-fact. "I think I'll retire and have dinner brought to me."

For a moment or two he said nothing. Then the relaxed humor he'd shared with her fled his face and he turned away. "As you wish, madam."

Charlotte felt an immediate sense of wrongness about the entire situation, as if she'd started seducing *him* and then quit with the tease. But then he made her feel that way, she decided. He had started the kiss.

Drawing a deep breath for confidence, she said, "When are you going to tell me?"

He glanced up briefly. "Tell you what?"

Clutching her music bag in her hand, she bit her lip, then replied, "What you do professionally."

He almost grinned. She could see a twitch of his mouth even as he looked now at the Handel score, lightly folding the newspaper back over it with his tweezers.

"Soon," he maintained vaguely.

That's it? Soon? Confounded and confused, Charlotte concluded that he had no intention of revealing anything more about him now or he would do so. She also knew he was irritated with her for wanting to leave his company after the . . . engaging time they'd just shared. There was really nothing more for her to say.

And so, dignity intact, she excused herself and left him at his work, alone in his study to hide her treasure, wondering if he realized that her doing so was the first great sign that she trusted him.

Chapter 14

✦────◦◦────✦

Gripped by his own determination, Colin waited until he heard Yvette leave Charlotte's room for a final time, then stood at their adjoining door for another moment or two to give her time to settle before he surprised her with a nighttime visit.

It had been four long hours since they'd been together in his study, since he had stared at the absolutely priceless treasure she possessed. Under any other circumstance, he would have spent those few hours alone following her departure to contemplate the score's originality, giddy with an excitement only a former thief and forger could feel, ready to begin a copy if for no other reason than to know he could make a solid and undetectable reproduction. If he'd kissed any other woman as he kissed his wife, he could have left her without a second thought to pore through music scores to verify the signature. But strangely, between the night they'd married and this afternoon, something had changed in him. In the last few hours he'd thought of nothing but her—her thick and gorgeous head of hair, her sharp, beautiful blue eyes, the way her voice turned husky when he aroused her, and especially her stunning, perfectly curved body that he wanted to see nude again—and again and again and again. It had been a remarkable thing, he decided, that a woman could make him think of her more than a project, but Charlotte had managed to do it without even trying, and without purposely changing into her Lottie English persona that forever managed to make him hard with need. In the last four hours his thoughts had dwelled on his renewed desire for her, his wife, and finding some way to get her to respond to him sexually. Her satisfaction in bed had become his primary focus.

Pressing his forehead to their adjoining door, he squeezed his eyes shut and took a deep breath to calm his nerves before he entered. Then with resolve, he righted himself once more, turned the knob, and walked into her room.

The night was dark, with no moon to speak of, and she'd already dimmed the light on her bedside table. It took him a second or two for his eyes to adjust, though he immediately noticed her shapely form outlined in shadow on the bed to his right, heard the rustle of her sheets as she realized he'd entered.

"Colin?"

"Charlotte, could I have a word with you?" he asked evenly.

"Of course, come in," she replied after only a momentary hesitation, sitting up a little from under the covers.

"You can leave the lamp off; I won't be a minute," he lied as he slowly walked toward the bed.

He'd purposely left his door open a crack so there was just enough light from his room to see what he was doing, and what little there was allowed him to find his way easily and sit near the foot of the bed on the side where she lay.

"What is it?" she asked hesitantly.

He brought his knee up and rested the side of it on the mattress, then leaned back on one hand, watching her in the near darkness. "I just thought of something, an idea, actually, regarding the Handel sonata."

"An idea about it?"

"Mmm . . . more like a way to use it."

She sat up a little. "Go on."

She sounded more alert and he smiled to himself, noting a shade of intrigue in her voice and realizing this would wake her up enough for his seduction attempt.

"My idea," he continued, "is to make a copy of the Handel composition. A perfect duplicate."

She turned on her side and lifted her head to rest it on her hand, her elbow braced on her pillow. "I don't understand. Make a copy for what?"

He grinned. "To expose the person, or individuals, trying to steal the original."

Silence lingered for a moment, and he could almost hear the possibilities rumbling in her head.

Finally, she said, "You think to lay a trap."

He nodded once. "Exactly."

She stretched out beneath the sheets and her legs bumped against his arm, though she didn't seem to notice.

"Do you think you can find someone who can copy such a piece?" she asked.

He relaxed into the mattress, leaning over so that her shins were more or less locked beneath the crux of his arm as he rested his own head in his hand.

"I can," he disclosed, his tone low.

She sighed. "It's an interesting notion, but I can't imagine anyone who would be able to do so with the skill enough to fool someone who really knows Handel's works, or even music in general. And we'd have to expect the person trying to steal it knows his music." She paused, thinking, then added, "You'd have to find an expert, and I'm sure it would cost a fortune. I'm not sure I would be able to trust anyone else with it, either."

She didn't understand, and an immense pleasure in revealing himself right now sliced through him.

"I meant, dear wife, that *I* can do it. I can make a replication."

He expected her to be shocked or puzzled into silence. Instead, she laughed.

"Colin, darling," she purred with great exaggeration, "is this one of your little secrets?"

He didn't know whether to feel smug or irritated by her apparent lack of faith. But then she really had no idea where his true talents lay and what he could do with them. She also had no clue what he did with his time, as she'd said so often, which made this moment something he'd remember for a long time.

Nonchalantly, he began running his fingertips over

the coverlet, along the length of her shin, with just enough pressure she had to notice. "I told you I had a few secrets. Forgery is one of them."

He felt her try to tug her leg up, but he held it too firmly and she abandoned the attempt.

Skeptically, she remarked, "And what if I told you that's a little difficult to believe?"

"I'd say you don't trust me not to lie to you yet."

That comment seemed to hit her, on more than one level. She stirred a little on her pillow, and with the minimal light filtering in from his bedroom lamp, he could see the slow widening of her eyes, the tilting of her head.

"You're not joking, are you?" she murmured in whisper.

He inhaled deeply and shook his head. "No, I'm not joking, Charlotte. I've never lied to you, and the truth is, I'm a forger. By profession."

She sucked in air through her teeth. "That's . . . absurd, but—"

"But you believe it, don't you?" he finished for her. "You saw the way I took care with the composition, the unusual tools I used to authenticate it, the time and manner in which I reviewed the paper, the signature. It's what I do for a living."

"A *living*?" she returned at once. "You're a titled gentleman with a wealthy estate, sir. I rather believe you were pretending to authenticate it simply to impress me."

He fought the urge to laugh. "Impress you? Darling, I don't need to pretend anything to impress you."

"Ridiculous," she scoffed.

He rubbed her kneecap with his thumb. "But again, I speak the truth."

That silenced her for a moment or two, and she jerked her leg away from him with annoyance. Still, he could positively feel her quick mind churning with ideas, and he let her take her time in processing the information before he delved into his past.

"Then—so this is the illegal secret you kept from me," she charged, her tone turning somber and flat with distaste. "You forge documents."

He pressed his palm to the bed and sat up, inching closer with his body, his hip next to hers, hoping she wouldn't notice, or at the very least, pull away from him. "I do. And I'm very, very good at it."

"And for *whom* do you do this illegal forgery?" she asked with extreme emphasis. "There can't possibly be that many people who would need your expert, or professional, services."

Colin thought about that for a moment. He'd come into her room tonight expecting to tell her everything, to gain her acceptance, her trust, even her admiration. But something about her reaction made him pause. She'd certainly kept secrets of her own during their short marriage, and had been quite unwilling to confess them even as he discovered them himself. Keeping one of his own secrets from her now, perhaps the most important secret, might actually be the prudent thing to do, though admittedly he wasn't sure why he felt that way. True, he was, indeed, a forger by profession, and he didn't want her to think she'd married a nefarious liar and criminal. But for some completely irrational reason, it suddenly occurred to him that he wanted her to want him, to like him, to desire him for the man he was now, a man with a faulty past and good intentions, not for the champion he'd become for their government. For the first time in his life, he wanted a woman to care for him beyond his charm, his mystery, and the revelation shocked him.

Dropping his voice to a near whisper, he said, "Charlotte, you asked me once what I do with my time. The fact is, my time is my own, and it has been since I returned from university."

That got her attention. She sat up a little more, intrigued without trying to hide it.

He grinned slyly. "I have an advanced degree in chemistry."

"I beg your pardon?"

"Chemistry," he repeated. Shrugging, he added, "As a child, I had a keen interest in explosives."

She gasped, then giggled, and her reaction made him chuckle. "It's not as frightening as it sounds. It's probably more accurate to say I enjoyed the composition of gunpowder."

Amazement slicing through her voice, she repeated, "Enjoyed gunpowder . . ."

"Yes, and . . . other interesting substances that one could mix to create a loud bang."

She was speechless for a moment. Then she shook herself and ran her fingers through her hair. "I'm—I don't understand. What does a fascination with gunpowder have to do with forgery?"

"Ah, yes. Forgery." He leaned over, resting his head on his hand again, this time with his chest closing over her hips, barely touching. "It didn't start out that way, of course. I make it all sound rather grand, but in actuality, I studied basic chemistry in the beginning, probably because it was the only thing that held my interest as a child. Later, at Cambridge, I began an extensive study into the chemistry of substances like paint, paper, ink, and so forth, because I had the very good fortune of working for and with a German scholar called Rolf Nuerenberg, who had spent his entire career transcribing ancient Persian documents."

Very carefully, he reached out and placed his palm on the side of her hip, on top of the sheet, and to his good fortune, she didn't even notice.

"I had no idea you were such an interesting, gifted man, your grace," she returned, her tone carrying a whiff of humor.

"And very smart, Charlotte," he added as he stared into her darkened eyes.

She sighed and relaxed into her pillows again. "I knew that about you the first night we met."

His brows rose. "Really."

She smiled at him. "I refuse to elaborate."

"A shame, that," he said, teasing.

"Yes," was her vague reply.

He couldn't help but grin as he lifted his palm from her hip and reached out for her hand, covering it with his own at first, then lightly caressing her fingers.

"When I returned home from my studies, I was very bored," he revealed, his voice low. "My family expected me to carry on with my duties as the heir to my estate, move my way into court, support causes, be socially active and marry a titled lady. In other words, no more gunpowder, no more chemistry, no more fascinating work on ancient documents. To me, nothing could have been more mundane."

He heard her exhale a long, slow breath in understanding, and it occurred to him at that moment how very much their lives paralleled each other's—duty first, and abandoned dreams.

Rubbing her knuckles, he said, "When I was nearly twenty-five, I was arrested for attempting to produce counterfeit currency."

He felt her entire body tense beside him, though she didn't attempt to pull away. He continued before she could comment.

"Of course I knew it was wrong, and I didn't need the money. I never wanted to do it for the money. I wanted the challenge, the excitement. I simply wanted to see if I could do it, if what I produced could be accepted as real."

"This is unbelievable," she whispered.

He nodded. "Indeed it is, but it's the truth."

"I married a criminal . . ."

"I was never convicted of a crime, Charlotte," he replied gravely.

"And yet you committed one."

"No," he insisted. "I never cheated anyone and I never actually sold counterfeit money. I was more or less in the planning stage, working on the process, when I was caught." He gave her a moment or two to digest that, then said, "Three things kept me out of prison. The first, I'm embarrassed to admit, is my title. I also swore before a judge that I would never do it again and at the same time offered my willingness to help others with my expertise whenever I could. My plea was accepted and the rumors of my arrest were silenced. The only thing I was ever truly guilty of was stupidity. In the last ten years I've done nothing but try to right every one of my wrongs, and to this day, I believe I've succeeded."

For a long time, it seemed, she simply stared at him in the darkness, totally unaware of how close he was to her, of how he gently caressed her hand, her fingers and knuckles.

"So you can duplicate money, musical scores . . . what else?" she asked at last, her tone cool and calculating.

"Actually, the Handel sonata will be my first for music."

"That's not the point," she said, dismayed.

He sobered a little. "I know. The truth is, I have a special . . . gift, shall we say, for noticing and creating detail. I can analyze handwriting, forge documents, and over time I've learned my craft. I can tell by careful examination if something is an original or a copy."

She waited for a moment, watching him as if she might discern lies from his features in the darkness.

"I don't suppose you need a hobby now, do you?" she asserted at last.

He couldn't decide if she were serious or trying to lighten the mood. Finally, he replied, "What I *need* is your trust, Charlotte, in what I say and what I do."

She drew in a shaky breath. "And if I don't?"

He hadn't expected her to challenge him. But without hesitation, he replied, "Then we can never, truly, be married."

She stilled, her hand going limp in his, and with that, he made his move.

Leaning over, he placed his face only an inch from hers, their dark eyes locked, and he whispered, "Trust me, Charlotte. I'd rather be married . . ."

She had no time to react. In one smooth action, he captured her mouth with his in a searing kiss, giving her a taste of the passion she stirred within him.

Charlotte had never felt so charged with complex emotions in all of her life. And when he closed over her to finally place his lips on hers, she didn't know how to respond. But the touch of his lips to hers started a marvelous, heated tingle that rolled in waves through her body.

She let him kiss her even as her intellect fought against it. He felt so warm, tasted faintly of brandy, and made no move to force her into anything other than a sweet caress of his mouth against hers.

She closed her eyes as his kiss grew slightly more passionate, all clear thought of his confession gradually evaporating as she began to succumb to his blissful insistence. He remained fully clothed, the sheet and blanket between them, allowing her to relax and revel in the feel of him at her side, hovering over her, stroking her fingers with his own.

A heady power enveloped her and she raised her free hand to his neck, resting it softly against him, feeling his fast pulse under his hot skin.

"Charlotte," he whispered against her lips, "do you trust me?"

She felt an unusual stirring in her heart, not from

his words, but from the hope in his voice, the eagerness to hear her affirm what he so desperately wanted.

He drew his lips across her cheek, placing soft pecks at her jawline, and reason vanished.

Ignoring the remaining tug of doubt, she replied, "I do . . ."

He groaned, and with it took her mouth again with a sudden, urgent need. She responded in kind, allowing him access as she hadn't before, giving in to the feel of him, the yearning he exposed within her that she couldn't now deny.

His tongue brushed her top lip, then plunged deeply into her mouth, searching, stroking, finding as his breathing grew uneven and quick.

Without warning, he grasped her fingers, which he'd been stroking, and with them lifted her hand above her head, resting it on the pillow before letting it loose. He then reached for the palm at his neck and did the same, raising it above her before he clasped both of her wrists with his strong left palm and held them secure.

Uncertain of his intentions, she squirmed a little beneath the sheet, but he only steadied her, taking her to further heights of unreality with each stroke of his lips, each shaky breath, each plundering kiss.

Her head reeled with wonder anew; her body ached for a completion she refused to consider. And in that second in time, his desire unrelenting, she released her failing inhibitions with the trust she had promised.

He released her mouth and ran his tongue along her jawline until he reached her ear, sucking the lobe. She whimpered, lifting the top of her head to allow him better access. He gladly accepted, moving lower as he kissed his way down her neck to the top of her chest, where her nightgown lay buttoned. With quick expertise, he raised his right hand and unfastened the top three or four, then pushed the cotton aside to expose the tops of her breasts.

Charlotte couldn't deny him if she tried. Her mind screamed for him to stop; her body ached for more, and when he nuzzled his head between the soft flesh, she arched her back with increasing need, silently begging for more.

He responded in kind, brushing his lips back and forth across her nipple then rolling his tongue across it, his hot breath igniting her skin as he finally closed his mouth over the hard, aroused tip and began to gently suck.

She gasped from the instant rush of pleasure, whimpered again, and somewhere in the back of her mind, she realized he'd moved the sheet aside and pushed her nightgown up as she felt his palm caressing her bare leg from ankle to knee. She drew her feet together instinctively when he reached the inside of her thigh, but it only seemed to make him more determined. He lightly stroked the soft skin with his thumb and fingers, forcing delicate, little moans from the back of her throat as he nuzzled her breasts, ran his lips across her nipples, then kissed them gingerly before drawing one into his mouth once more.

In a final endeavor to recover her sanity, she tried to ease her hands out from his grasp, but he held them fast against the pillow, securing her in his embrace. And then, as sudden as it was shocking, she felt his heated palm inch up between her legs until he found the hidden treasure of a raging desire.

She jerked against him, twisting her hips in an attempt to free herself.

"Trust me, Charlotte," he pleaded, his lips once more brushing hers, his voice low and raw, his body tense.

She shook her head minutely in quick denial, squeezing her eyes tightly shut, feeling her heart race, his fingers lightly teasing the soft hair between her thighs.

"Trust me . . ."

With that last urgent whisper of need, he captured her mouth again in a deep, searing kiss—and she relented.

She stilled as he began to stroke her, gently at first, holding her wrists down, his tongue searching for hers. She felt nothing but the heat from his hard body, the warmth of his breath on her cheeks that mingled with her own, a tightness coiling up within her that silently begged for more.

He moaned as she did, caught up in the fever, quickening his pace as his fingers pressed harder against her, stroking, caressing, bringing her closer to the edge of a blissful torment. Her wetness coated him, her body rocked into his, and with a gasp, she felt him slide a finger inside of her.

Lost in a new and wondrous delirium, Charlotte clutched his hand on the pillow as she kissed him back with abandon, arching her hips in time to each masterful stroke. He moved his finger in and out of her, his thumb teasing the nub of her pleasure, unyielding in his effort as she balanced at the brink of glorious insanity.

And then it struck her hard. She cried out, through wave after wave of intense pleasure, feeling his finger inside her with each pulse of fulfillment that swept through her body. He covered her mouth with his to muffle her long moan of exquisite abandonment, made all the more gratifying as she heard his own groan of satisfaction curl up from deep in his throat.

He continued caressing her softly, slowing his pace as the seconds passed, until at last he removed his finger and then his hand from between her legs, allowing her body to calm, her breathing to quiet and return to normal. Finally, he drew his mouth away and lowered his forehead to rest lightly on hers, releasing the pressure on her wrists little by little.

They remained unmoving for several lingering moments, not a word spoken. Charlotte felt the tension in his body, noted his own erratic breathing, and realized by instinct that he tried to control himself. For a fleeting second she became fearful that he might quickly remove his clothes and enter her to relieve his own desire. Instead, he lowered his lips to her lashes, kissing them lightly as he raised the hand that only moments ago had caressed her intimately and covered her breasts again with her nightgown.

"At long last I know what you feel like when you climax," he whispered with a brush of his lips to her ear. "I'll never make that mistake again." Then in one smooth movement, he stood and walked to their adjoining door. "Sleep well, my darling wife . . ."

Charlotte never opened her eyes. Confounded by what had just happened between them, emotions she couldn't understand flooded her, and as she heard the door click shut, she turned on her side and allowed the tears to flow.

Chapter 15

C harlotte had never been so conflicted with emotion in all of her life. To say last night's strange turn of events at the surprise visit from her husband confused her would be an understatement of huge proportion. He'd not only shared some of the most intimate details of his past, details he knew would shock her, he'd then done things to her body that even now, hours later, made her hot all over even as it made her shiver with the most intense desire to do it again. And the most amazing part about the entire episode was that even after recalling each blissful second of what they had done, she felt no shame in it at all.

She'd only seen Colin for breakfast this early Sunday morning, then had gone to church with him as the Duchess of Newark, dressed in a conservative gown of lilac silk with cream-colored flounces, her hair wrapped up on her head and under a matching hat covered with lilac lace. She felt rather pretty for a change, though he'd said very little to her aside from casual dialogue. At Mass he acted just as pleasant and charming as usual, ignoring the stares of wishful infatuation from all the young girls, for her sake she supposed, but more or less treating her as if nothing between them had changed, or even happened for that matter. Frankly, she had no idea how to take his indifference, which was why she now found herself walking to the Duchess of Durham's townhouse only two streets away to partake of afternoon tea with the Frenchwoman.

Olivia Carlisle had invited her twice before, and both times she'd had to make excuses because she'd been occupied at the theater. But this was Sunday, and with her husband home working on the Handel, she decided she wanted a good discussion with another female.

Charlotte rang the bell, then presented her card to the butler, who invited her in at once with a flat smile and a formal announcement that her grace was indeed at home and waiting for her in the parlor.

She took note of the scent of berries in the air, the warm decorations in French Provincial furnishings accented in white and gold as she followed the tall, aging man around a white circular staircase covered with teal carpeting that blended with the Persian accent rugs scattered across the main floor. At the back of the airy entryway, he paused in front of French double doors and rapped twice with his knuckles on the glass, then entered after an acknowledgment from within.

"Madam, may I present the Duchess of Newark," he said, very stately, moving to his side to allow her to enter.

"Charlotte, I'm so glad you could come today!" Olivia expressed in lightly accented English, rising with effort from a large blue velveteen sofa at the center of the room.

Charlotte smiled, feeling a bit overwhelmed in the presence of such a beautiful woman. "Please don't stand on my account," she insisted, removing her bonnet and smoothing her hair. "I'm just happy to be here."

Into her confinement, Olivia's pregnancy had begun to show, and yet she still looked remarkably stunning in a modest day gown of silver and sapphire that fairly equaled the color of her eyes and accented her dark hair now curled and piled on top of her head. The parlor, spacious and scented as well, matched the decor of the foyer in colors of white, deep blue, and gold, providing a lovely backdrop for the Frenchwoman to entertain guests.

Charlotte walked toward the sofa as Olivia moved out from behind the tea table, reaching for her hands and planting a kiss on both cheeks. Then she looked at her butler, who waited patiently for instruction by the door.

"We'll have tea, James—oh, and what's left of the chocolate cake Elsie made yesterday," she said in an airy voice, her French accent only barely perceptible.

The elderly man nodded. "Madam." And with that he quit the parlor, closing the French doors behind him.

"So, tell me," Olivia began, still holding her hands as she pulled her toward the sofa, "how does it feel to be married to that handsome devil?"

Charlotte laughed as she lowered her body onto the cushion. Olivia released her hands and sat beside her, both women smoothing their skirts as if readying themselves for deep discussion.

"Well?" Olivia pressed, her eyes wide and flashing with keen interest.

She couldn't help but grin; the Frenchwoman's excitement was truly contagious. "He is a devil," she replied, anxious to delve into the personal issues that plagued her, though uncertain how to go about doing so.

As if reading her thoughts, Olivia cocked her head to the side a little, her lids narrowing. "So what are you *not* telling me?"

She pulled back a little. "Nothing," she insisted a bit too quickly. "Nothing really. Colin is . . ."

"A devil," Olivia repeated, her smile gradually fading as she sensed a serious turn in the conversation. "But he really is a good man. Sam trusts him implicitly."

Charlotte relaxed into the sofa, ignoring the slight pinching of her stays. "I know. Of course he's a good man. Honestly, he's a good provider and a lady couldn't ask for a better husband."

The Frenchwoman laughed, tossing her head back. "A good *provider?*" She reached for one of her hands and squeezed it gently. "Charlotte, what on earth are you not telling me?"

A knock at the door interrupted them and Olivia groaned. "Come in, James."

Her butler did as ordered immediately, entering the parlor with a silver tray resting on his palm as he carried it to the tea table, placing it on top without even a clink of china. Expertly, he lifted a sterling pot and poured two china cups three-quarters full of sweet-smelling jasmine tea.

"Would you care for cake now, madam?" he asked, removing lace napkins from atop the two plates and laying them to the side.

The chocolate confection looked scrumptious, and yet Charlotte felt minutely relieved when Olivia voiced her own thoughts.

"We'll wait, James, and cut it ourselves. That will be all."

He nodded once, and with a formal turn, quit the parlor again, closing the French doors behind him.

Olivia eyed her candidly, refreshments forgotten. "Now. Explain yourself, dear Charlotte."

Somewhat unnerved by the delicate topic, she decided to plunge into the heart of the matter, to get it out quickly before she changed her mind.

Rubbing her palms together in her lap, she acknowledged the obvious. "I suppose I am a bit . . . troubled by our marital relationship," she murmured.

Forehead creased in thought, Olivia relaxed against the plush sofa back, crossing her arms over her breasts. "I'm sure it must be difficult when two people marry before they get to know each other very well."

She managed a soft smile. "That's very true," she replied. "But with Colin . . . It's more than that, actually."

The Frenchwoman's brows rose, but she remained silent, allowing her to continue at her own pace.

Exhaling a fast breath, she asked, "May I be honest with you?"

"Of course," Olivia returned at once, surprised.

Drawing courage from within, she said, "Actually, I may need your advice."

"My advice?"

"I—I'm rather confused about Colin . . . romantically," she fairly whispered, feeling a flush creep up her neck but purposely ignoring it.

Olivia's jaw dropped as her brows pinched tightly in disbelief. "Colin—*romantically?*"

Charlotte kept her chin high, though truth be told the conversation thoroughly embarrassed her. "I'm sorry, perhaps it's inappropriate—"

"No, no, *no*," Olivia interrupted, reaching for her arm and patting it tenderly. "Of course it's not inappropriate. We're both married ladies, and becoming good friends, I hope. It's just—" She shook her head. "It's just that I'm so surprised to hear such a thing from the wife of a man who prides himself on his . . . charm, shall we say."

The side of her mouth tipped up as relief coursed through her. "Yes, exactly," she agreed. "He's very charming, quick witted and undeniably handsome, but . . ."

"But?" Olivia pressed, sitting back again and hooking her elbow over the sofa back.

Charlotte patted the hair at the back of her neck. "But I don't think he finds me interesting at all."

Olivia tossed her head back and laughed wholeheartedly. "Darling Charlotte, you cannot be serious," she stated seconds later, her eyes sparkling mischievously. "The man is completely infatuated with you."

In a rather strange way, she felt both encouraged

and almost smug to know her feelings in this matter would be validated once she told the Frenchwoman everything. Or almost everything.

"He's not infatuated with me, Olivia," she revealed in a low voice. "He's infatuated with Lottie English, and perhaps even with, in some measure, her fame."

Olivia gazed at her for a long moment, then gradually lowered her arm from the sofa back and leaned toward the refreshment table, her expression contemplative.

"Cream and sugar?"

"Only cream, please," she replied, watching the woman pour with dainty fingers, then lift the white china cup and saucer to hand to her.

"Now that I'm carrying, I can't seem to get enough sweets," Olivia professed as she stirred two large teaspoons full of sugar into her own cup before lifting it and settling back into the sofa.

Charlotte waited, sipping her lukewarm beverage, wondering for a second or two if the woman would comment on her last disclosure. She wasn't yet ready to change the subject to babies and happy families.

"Explain something to me, Charlotte," Olivia requested after a sip of her tea, her tone pensive. "Who do *you* think you are?"

That question took her completely aback. "I beg your pardon?"

Olivia smiled knowingly as she returned her cup and saucer to the table. "How do you define yourself? Are you Lottie English, the sensual, glamorous soprano from the stage, or are you the proper Duchess of Newark?"

She considered the question for a moment. "I'm

not sure exactly how to answer that," she replied honestly. "When I'm on the stage, I'm Lottie. Here, now, having tea in your parlor, I am obviously Charlotte."

Olivia studied her through narrowed eyes. "So you think Colin is infatuated with your persona on the stage, but not the least bit interested in the lady he married?"

The line of questions made her increasingly uncomfortable, though she didn't know why. In point of fact, she wasn't exactly certain how to define such a thing to the striking woman who sat beside her.

Olivia sighed and folded her hands in her lap. "Charlotte, when I first met my husband, he maintained a very clear dislike of Frenchwomen, for several complex reasons I don't really need to address here. But for a long time he remained rather . . . untrusting with me because I have always defined myself as both French *and* English. This simply made no sense to him." She smiled. "Until we grew to love each other, he would get quite irritated with me whenever I mentioned the fact that I am both."

Charlotte took a sip of her tea. "I see."

"No, actually, I don't believe you do," Olivia countered frankly. "You're describing yourself to me as two completely different people—Charlotte the proper lady, and Lottie, the gifted, singing enchantress. And by separating the two, you've come to the conclusion that your husband won't adore you for who you are as the complete woman."

She wanted to squirm in her stays, feeling suddenly hot all over, uneasy and not quite sure she wanted to discuss this anymore.

Olivia gave her a crooked smile. "Are you in love with Colin?"

She blinked quickly several times. "In love?"

"Mmm-hmm?"

She attempted to place her teacup and saucer back on the silver tray gingerly, but it rattled anyway. "I'm sure my husband and I haven't been together long enough to know such a thing," she replied as evenly as she could, avoiding the woman's gaze as she smoothed her skirts.

Olivia would not be daunted. "Charlotte, darling," she said through a small chuckle, reaching for her hand again and squeezing it gently, "one can fall in love very fast, sometimes almost at once. You either are or are not in love with your husband."

In truth, Charlotte had never given love a second thought, but doing so now, by direct confrontation, unsettled her to the core.

"Is that how it was with you and your husband?" she asked as pleasantly as possible.

Olivia shook her head. "Not exactly, but then we're not discussing me. But I will say this: if you were in love with Colin, you would know it, and you could answer the question easily enough."

Discouraged, she said, "Honestly, Olivia, I've not given love any thought. I married the man for . . . other reasons, the most important of which is to support my pursuit of opera on the Continent, and he knows this. What concerns me, and why I wished to speak with you about it today, is that Colin, I believe, is infatuated with Lottie English, *thinks* I'm Lottie English, and wants to have a love affair with *her.*" She shook her head. "I'm just not sure what to do about it."

"And this bothers you because, if I understand you correctly, you don't think you're that person," the Frenchwoman stated rather than asked.

She groaned within and rubbed her palms across her cheeks. "It's not that simple," she replied, trying to succinctly reveal something she couldn't even quite explain to herself.

Olivia smiled again in understanding. "It's not that simple because it's very clear, in my mind, Charlotte, that you have romantic feelings for your husband and you think he wants nothing to do with the noble and proper lady you were raised to be." She clucked her tongue. "It sounds as if you are hoping he'll fall in love with *only* that part of you, and I'm not certain it's possible."

Befuddled and agitated by a discussion that seemed to be going nowhere, Charlotte could no longer sit. Rising abruptly, one palm on her hip, one on her forehead, she crossed the thick Persian carpet to stand in front of a long east-facing window, gazing down to a small rose garden, flowers of all colors in full bloom.

A strained silence ensued, giving her time to consider her next most private disclosure. She needed to get to the heart of the issue in her mind, since she didn't know anyone else she could trust to help her understand. Softly, she murmured, "I think he expects me to *be* Lottie when we're intimate."

She closed her eyes, waiting for Olivia to laugh, or deny it outright, she supposed, though all she heard from behind her was a long exhale and a creak of the sofa.

Deciding to ignore the heat in her cheeks, she turned to bravely face the beautiful Frenchwoman again, careful to keep her chin high, body erect lest the Duchess of Durham know how truly embarrassed she was to reveal such secrets of the bedroom.

Olivia had adjusted herself so that she could view her standing at the window, but she didn't appear at all shocked. Her features remained neutral, though her forehead had creased minutely into a frown. Finally, she patted the seat beside her. "Come back and sit, and don't be ashamed to discuss such a thing, either," she said in understanding. "As I said, we're both married ladies and quite clearly this bothers you." She raised her brows to add, "It would bother me, too."

For a second or two, Charlotte didn't move. Then she did as ordered, deciding Olivia might just sympathize with the situation after all.

Following another adjustment of her skirts around her ankles, she folded her hands in her lap. "I'm sorry if this is too delicate—"

"Oh, nonsense," Olivia chided with a wave of her hand. "Let's have some cake and muddle through it."

Unable to hide a smile, she said, "Thank you, but I really shouldn't. My waistline will grow too large for my costumes."

Olivia briefly eyed her askance, then cut two pieces anyway. "There is one thing Colin has mentioned to Sam about you," she disclosed, placing a slice of gooey chocolate on a china plate. "He thinks you have a marvelous feminine form. In fact, he's quite in awe of the beauty of your body. I wouldn't worry too much about a little bit of cake."

Charlotte coughed and ran her fingers across her

upper lip, completely startled by such a heady compliment, especially spoken aloud.

"He . . . um . . . said this to your husband?" she asked in reply.

Olivia laughed again, handing her a generous portion. "On more than one occasion, I assume." She reached for her own plate, then paused, holding it out in mid-air. "Sam seems to think he's mad for you."

"For Lottie," she corrected, feeling an uncomfortable tightening in her stomach.

"Oh, I see," the other woman acknowledged at once, slicing into her cake. She placed the bite in her mouth, chewing as she rolled her eyes.

Charlotte just stared at the rich chocolate confection on her plate, having absolutely no appetite at the moment.

"So," Olivia continued after swallowing and licking her lips, "explain to me how you change forms at home."

She gazed at the Frenchwoman, puzzled. "I beg your pardon?"

Olivia flipped a hand in her direction. "Your marvelous figure. If he's so enamored of it as Lottie, how do you change back into his wife when you retire each evening?"

She couldn't decide if the Duchess of Durham teased her or simply tried to confuse the issue, though Charlotte clearly comprehended her intent.

"My figure is not *me*," she asserted, probably too curtly.

Olivia smiled. "I know." She lowered her fork to her plate and leaned forward, eyeing her intently. "But you do understand my point. Charlotte, you are both personalities wrapped into one person, just as I am both French and English. You can't change who you are, even when you're on stage. Think of it that way. Charlotte was born with a gifted voice and takes the stage just as Lottie is sitting here in my parlor, eating—or shall I say *not* eating—my chocolate cake." She sat up a little, raised her fork again, and sliced another bite. "You are a mixture of all these wonderful qualities, Lottie." She brightened as if totally satisfied by her argument. "In fact, I'd rather call you Lottie. It suits you, and I imagine Colin feels exactly the same."

Charlotte had never been spoken to so boldly in her life, by anyone, and it dazed her a little. Apparently Olivia realized how she'd take such a statement, for the woman simply continued eating her cake with gusto, wiping the china plate clean with her fork, then licking it free of icing before placing both back on the tea table.

"You really should try a bite," she said after daintily patting her lips with her linen napkin. "It's delicious."

Charlotte lowered her gaze and stared at the chocolate, unseeing as she tried to come to terms with all the Frenchwoman had said. Then, voice edgy, she murmured, "He bought me a corset to wear on our wedding night. Or rather, he bought Lottie a . . . costume resembling a corset." Feeling utterly mortified, she added in a whisper, "To complete his fantasy."

Olivia remained silent for a moment or two, then relaxed against the sofa back again, her hands in her lap. "I don't understand."

Charlotte inhaled deeply, attempting to find a

confidence she didn't feel at all, then raised her gaze to look the Frenchwoman squarely in the eye. She couldn't change the subject now, even if she wanted to. She'd come too far for that, and frankly needed answers.

"On our wedding night he came to me with a gift. I stupidly thought it would be something practical, or thoughtful, or . . . I don't know." She shook her head. "Instead, I opened the present to find this . . . costume— a red satin, black lace corset that covered nothing, a little piece of apparel I imagine might be worn by a dancer on the French stage, or the like. Beneath it in the box were matching shoes that had heels so high I could hardly walk. He insisted I wear the ridiculous thing, and I did, because . . . because I wanted to please him, I suppose." She swallowed, then added in whisper, "He wanted to make love to the woman in the corset, which would have to be his perception of Lottie, not me. *I* would never dream of wearing such a thing on my wedding night."

For a long time Olivia said nothing, just watched her, her brows furrowed a little. Charlotte grew rather afraid the woman might laugh again, or tell her flatly that gentlemen of all nature and classes purchase such things, forced their wives to wear such outrageous outfits.

Finally, the Duchess of Durham began to slowly shake her head. "Unbelievable," she mumbled. "Even intelligent gentlemen can be such stupid creatures when desire comes into play. His action only fed into your doubts, didn't it, Lottie? Good heavens, what on earth was he thinking?"

She couldn't begin to describe the rush of relief

that washed over her at that moment. Realizing she'd been holding her breath, she let it out loudly through her teeth and sagged into her stays. "I'm so glad you see it from my perspective. It's obvious he was thinking I was Lottie, the person from the stage who wears costumes and—"

"No, absolutely not," Olivia cut in with a firm shake of her head. "That's not what I meant at all. Perhaps that's what he expected, and it's very likely his fantasy is to make love to you while you're wearing such a thing. But *he* knows you're one and the same person, of that I have no doubt."

God, they were back to this point. Charlotte felt like screaming. Olivia must have seen the frustration in her face, for at that moment, she reached over and took her hand again, this time cupping it between both of her own.

"You are Lottie, who is just one part of Charlotte," she said with absolute sincerity. "Never doubt that Colin knows this. He admires you for your talent, for your appearance, and probably for your intelligence and humor and all the things that are attractive about you." She squeezed her hand and continued. "I suspect what you need to know is if he feels that way about you intimately. Am I right?"

Truthfully, Charlotte had never before thought about it in such a way. Yet, as she considered it now, she supposed her doubts centered around lovemaking, and the way he made her feel, the manner in which he touched her and brought her to such delicious heights of—

Shaking herself of such a lascivious memory, she said, "I'm just not sure *what* he wants from me."

Olivia smiled again in understanding. "He wants a wife, Lottie. He wants a companion, a seductress in the bedroom. On top of everything, he probably wants you to fall in love with him for who *he* is."

That comment made her stomach twist in knots. "He's never mentioned love. I don't think he thinks about that."

"Ha! Gentlemen never do, not directly at least." She shrugged. "Honestly, I don't think they recognize it until it strikes them in the face, usually from learning that we're one step away from leaving them."

Charlotte actually giggled. The more she knew of Olivia, the friendlier the two of them became, the more she adored her.

Slyly, the Frenchwoman asked, "Do you want him to fall in love with you?"

She felt perspiration break out on her neck, between her breasts, and she swallowed. "I—I haven't thought about it."

"Of course you have, all women do," Olivia replied at once. "And it's always better to love your husband, and be loved by him, than for either of you to find it elsewhere."

Love, love, *love*. The French were always talking of *love*. And yet there was probably much truth in her words, Charlotte decided after a few seconds of consideration. She had just never thought about it in regard to her own complex feelings for her husband.

"I just want him to be . . . pleased with me," she admitted, hoping her voice didn't make her sound as discomfited as she felt.

"Pleased with you?" Olivia repeated, eyes wide.

"Then you must first forget the silly notion that you are not Lottie English."

Charlotte groaned inside.

"And then," the woman continued before she could argue, "if you truly want to please your husband, be the seductress in bed that he adores when you bring that part of your personality out on the stage. And yes, that means wearing the costume he gave you and letting him *know* you want to please him."

Her mouth dropped open a little. "I'm not sure I—"

"Of course you can," the Frenchwoman interjected, reading her thoughts. Then she grinned crookedly. "I suspect you are already a good wife as the Duchess of Newark. Now you must take direction of Lottie, and let Colin know you can successfully combine the two parts of *you* into the lover he wants, perhaps becoming the one lady he can love completely, and cherish always."

Charlotte couldn't deny the depth of satisfaction she felt as such an idea began to take shape in her mind. She wouldn't say the notion confused or overwhelmed her, either, as she understood everything Olivia suggested, and knew rather instinctively how to go about seducing him. She just wasn't certain if she could bring herself to play a seductress for him in the privacy of the bedroom. But would it actually be an act? Not, she supposed, if she stopped trying so desperately hard to draw a line between Lottie of the stage and the part of herself she presented to the outside world. She'd pretended to be two people for so long now it had become natural for her, but in truth, the seductress had to be inside of her, part of her, just as her singing was.

Her greatest confusion, she decided, really rested with the delicate emotion of love. Her parents had never been in love, although they'd had as decent a marriage as anyone in the nobility could ever expect. She'd never had the time to think about love, really, and now, suddenly, it had been thrust to center stage in her relationship with her husband.

Did she love Colin? She didn't think so, and she felt quite certain he didn't love her apart from the lust he felt for Lottie. In that regard, she supposed she also lusted after him, though just the notion distressed her. Ladies did not lust. Still, after last night's remarkable interlude, she absolutely knew that she wanted him to bed her again, which complicated everything. Becoming closer, more intimate with each other could prove disastrous for her ambition and desire to work abroad. And what if she became pregnant? She'd told him she'd give him an heir, but after the fiasco of their wedding night, she'd changed her mind. He'd told her before their wedding that he wanted her to remain childless for a while, and yet he'd left his seed inside of her during their first time together. At this point the only thing about which she could be absolutely certain was that when it came to Colin and her as a couple, nothing was certain; clearly, neither of them knew what they wanted from each other.

With a sigh, Charlotte ran a palm across her forehead, feeling the heated flush of her skin, realizing she probably looked as mortified by the entire conversation thus far as she felt. But she couldn't leave yet, not when Olivia had been so cheerful and understanding of her complex problem. And so, with resolve, she reached for the slice of cake she'd been offered, planted a sunny smile on her face, and changed the subject to Olivia's forthcoming baby—a much safer and thoroughly welcome topic that had nothing whatsoever to do with her.

Chapter 16

Charlotte stared at her reflection in the mirror, her heart racing with the knowledge that in just a few minutes, she would be attempting the seduction of her husband.

She had little doubt that he would want her, or at least that was her hope, especially after taking the time to don the corset he'd given her on their wedding night. But now, eyeing herself objectively, she did have to give him credit for having something fashioned that fit her perfectly. Yes, it was tight, scratchy, and not very comfortable, but it made her body look quite seductive, barely concealing her breasts with lace, outlining her curves, which, she supposed, was the entire point of the outfit.

They'd taken dinner together in the dining room, though she'd been too nervous to eat much. He didn't seem to notice, however, as he'd been engrossed in his own food. She'd retired after the meal, taking a long, relaxing bath in the rose-scented oil Olivia had given her. Then she'd brushed her hair to a sheen and waited a good forty-five minutes before she heard him enter his own room just a short time ago. That's when she finally squeezed herself into the corset and applied only a touch of rouge to her cheeks for an appealing flush. And now the time had come to startle the man.

Shoulders back, pulse racing, stomach tight with apprehension, she donned her white silk robe and loosely tied the sash, deciding to forego wearing the ridiculous shoes. It would make his surprise all the more palpable when she removed her covering for his view.

With a deep breath and a long exhale, she shook her hair loose and walked quietly to the adjoining door. Without knocking, she turned the handle and silently opened it.

All but one light on the night stand had been dimmed, and it took her a second or two to find him, as he wasn't on the bed. And then as her eyes adjusted, she caught sight of him, sprawled nude as the day he was born across his small sofa, his head perched on the armrest, eyes closed, a brandy in his left hand, his right laying on top of his most private area, his thumb brushing back and forth across the tip of his—

She gasped and her palm flew to her mouth. But to her horror, he'd heard her. He sat up abruptly and glanced in her direction, confusion crossing his shadowed brow.

"Charlotte?"

She couldn't move. *God help me . . .*

"I was just thinking about you," he admitted in a low, husky murmur.

She couldn't close her eyes, couldn't avert her gaze. The fascination at seeing him like this—nude and muscular and strong—caused a quick rush of heat to flow through her.

She swallowed, and lowered her hand from her mouth. "I'm sorry," she breathed, backing up a step.

Slowly, he stood, without any shame whatsoever, and her eyes couldn't help but wander down to the most powerful, intimate part of him, now long and stiff with arousal, surrounded by thick dark curls and hard, chiseled thighs.

For a second she thought she might faint.

"Why are you here?" he asked, his voice deep and speculative.

Play the part.

Shaking herself of as much trepidation as possible, she replied, "I wanted to bring you a gift."

He placed his hands on his hips, facing her fully, and it took all that was in her to drag her gaze up to his face.

"What gift would that be?" he asked with a trace of amusement.

God, had he no shame? He had to know how embarrassed she felt to find him like this, doing . . . what? She shivered just to envision it.

"Come here," he whispered as he began to saunter toward her.

She hesitated, but the appeal of his physical form coupled with his unique blend of humor and caring became far too ardent of a pull for her to deny. She could feel her heart pounding in her temples, a dangerous sense of her own need building within, but she knew without doubt that she could be what, or who, he wanted.

"Do you desire me, Colin?" she asked in a deep, husky tone.

The amusement faded from his face; his eyes narrowed. "Why are you here, Charlotte?" he asked again, this time with dark intensity and even a trace of suspicion.

"I'm here to give you Lottie," she revealed as she began to move toward him.

He stopped walking in mid-stride, his hard gaze traveling from her face to her bare feet, then back again, his expression one of pure calculation.

Charlotte realized at once that he didn't trust her intent. And with that sudden thought, she instantly, and recklessly, became the Lottie English of his dreams, the Lottie that was *her,* no longer hesitant in approaching him.

Smiling provocatively, she reached down and began to slowly untie the sash at her waist, noting how his gaze fell to her hands briefly before he raised it back to capture hers again. His jaw tightened; the muscles in his chest bunched as all remaining humor escaped him, replaced by a fresh surge of sexual hunger. She felt it. Just as she felt awash with a new appreciation of her power over him. And it was at that moment that all lingering doubts and trepidation evaporated.

Pulling the tie apart, she allowed her silk wrap to open as she continued to close the distance between them. His gaze remained locked with hers until she reached up with both hands and lifted the silk from her shoulders, allowing it to fall in a feather-soft heap to the floor.

He didn't move, but she heard him suck in a sharp breath at the sight of her in his specially made corset.

"Do you want me, Colin?" she breathed, nearing him at last, focusing on his beautifully masculine features, his tightened lips, knowing his erection stood between them as the only barrier to her touch. "Answer me," she insisted in a husky whisper, her mouth curled into what she hoped was a tempting smile.

His nostrils flared, his lids fell heavy over his eyes. And then he murmured, "Yes."

Confidence growing, she reached out and placed her palm on the hot skin of his chest. "How much?"

She felt him stiffen, and with that she began to draw a line with one finger down his stomach to his navel.

In a flash of a second, he startled her by grabbing a handful of lace at the top of her corset, between her breasts, and yanking her hard against him.

She gasped and clutched his shoulders as he lowered his face to within inches of hers.

"What game are you playing with me, Charlotte?" he asked, his tone coarse and hard.

She blinked. "I'm not playing any game."

"Do you have any idea what you're doing to me? How you make me feel? How you look in this?" He shook his head negligibly as he glanced down at her figure. "I don't need you to tease me if you're not here because you want to be."

The strain in his voice took her aback, and it

immediately dawned on her that she was a very real weakness in him, that he refused to be baited if she had no desire of her own to give him pleasure. That he was vulnerable.

Trembling inside, she replied, "You *made* me want you, Colin. I want you to make me feel like you did last night. I want to be your wife, your lover, and the only mistress you'll ever need to satisfy you."

For a long, tense moment, he said nothing, barely breathed as he peered into her eyes, searching for falsehoods imbedded in her honest claim of longing.

Then his cheek twitched. "The mistress you tempted me with the night we met?"

She melted inside, and with a determination she didn't know she possessed, she moved her hand between them and grazed the hot flesh of his engorged member with her fingertips, making him flinch.

"The woman you desire from me now," she replied in a silky murmur.

He swallowed hard as his gaze roved over her face. And then he grasped the back of her head with one hand and crushed his lips to hers so hard she cried out, stunned.

He was everywhere on her at once, one hand at her breast, pinching her nipples over the lace, tongue exploring, searching, sucking as he lowered his palm from her head to her bare bottom, massaging her there for seconds before pulling her forcefully against his hips.

His erection seared her between her thighs, and a marvelous new surge of longing sliced through her, causing her to whimper, to wrap her arms around his neck and hold him tightly.

In one smooth action, he lifted her off her feet and carried her, still joined at the mouth, to the edge of the bed. Dropping her quickly, he fell on top of her, bracing himself with his hand on the mattress to keep from crushing her with his weight.

He kissed her hard and long, one leg between hers as he fumbled only a moment with the buttons on the corset before giving up and ripping them apart with one strong hand. She inhaled sharply when he lowered his head to her breasts, sucking one nipple, then the other in a frenzy.

"Touch me again, Charlotte," he said, his voice muffled, pained. "It felt so good."

The delight she felt in arousing him so thoroughly pushed all hesitation from her mind. Reaching down between them, she closed her hand over him, whimpering from a new and exciting touch, relishing in the feel of his desire, brushing her thumb across the tip as she'd seen him do so erotically to himself.

"Oh, Jesus," he whispered, jerking his hips back a little as he moved his mouth to her neck.

His passion inflamed her, her erratic breathing mingled with his, and just as suddenly as she began to instinctively stroke his hard flesh, he reached down and pulled her hand away.

"Not yet," he said, his voice raw with need. "You'll make me come too soon."

"I want to please you," she murmured, lifting her hips to meet his.

He groaned, pulling back a little. "God, sweetheart, everything about you pleases me."

The sincerity in his voice made her crazy for him, made her desperate for him, as Charlotte, as Lottie—

"I want to touch you there," she said breathlessly. "I want—I want to feel you climax, Colin."

He stilled above her, inhaling an unsteady breath, and she closed her eyes, afraid she might have gone too far. Ladies never said—

"God, Charlotte," he whispered, cutting into her thoughts, "you are a dream come true . . ."

She raised her lashes, and the look of pure, untamed lust he emitted from his startled gaze, meant only for her, flooded her with an intensity that struck her hard.

He briefly touched her lips with the pad of his thumb, and then lowered his hand and placed it between her legs. She whimpered, her eyes widening as he began to stroke her. He watched her, his gaze melding with hers as he ran his fingers along her cleft, taking her nearer to the edge.

And then he lowered his head and began to kiss her chest, her breasts, her stomach. She clutched the coverlet with both hands, lifting her hips again impulsively, matching the rhythm of his expert caress—until she felt his lips brush against the mound of coarse, curly hair at the junction of her thighs.

Startled, she sat up on her elbows and looked down at him when he rested his body between her legs. Then he suddenly placed his mouth where his hand had been.

"Colin—"

He ignored her shock as he started teasing the nub of her desire with his tongue. She watched him, her initial fascination soon replaced by a rush of pleasure she could never have imagined, quickly taking her to the edge once more.

He pursued her satisfaction, moving faster, harder, and she lost herself in the feel, leaning her head back, moaning, pushing her hips instinctively against his hard mouth, gasping when he drove his tongue into her, then back out again, pacing himself, driving her to the brink of insanity.

She relaxed against the mattress again, clutching the coverlet with tight fists, pushing against him, needing, wanting. Desperate. And then she felt that wondrous explosion of pleasure. Body shuddering, she gasped for air, allowing herself to experience every tingling wave of sensation that roared through her, given her with the expertise of his mouth, the caress of his strong hands.

Before she could reach for him, he released her, moving up and over her once more, staring at her through dark eyes glazed with hunger. She felt his hardness between her legs, and she braced herself for his entrance, welcomed it.

"Touch me now, sweetheart. Make me come," he pleaded in a husky, choked murmur, lifting his hips over hers.

She did as he asked without question, reaching for him without restraint, holding his gaze as her hand closed over his rigid erection. He groaned as the heat of her skin seared his own hard flesh, and she felt him jerk minutely in her hand, his emanating need for release forcing a low whimper of satisfaction from her throat. He sucked in air through his teeth when she brushed her thumb along the tip, and for a second or two she hesitated, unsure what to do next.

Then as if reading her mind, he began to move his

hips as he towered over her, watching her through glazed eyes, his features taut, jaw tense. The stroking came naturally as he moved, teaching her without words, his head rolling back as he neared his own crest of pleasure.

She stared at his face, mesmerized by the beauty of him, swept up again in the passion of the moment.

"God, Charlotte," he breathed, squeezing his eyes shut. "Oh, yes, make me come . . ."

She'd never felt more powerful in her life, caught up in the wonder of him, feeling his strength in her palm, so touched by his need for her, so ready to watch him climax.

"Colin . . ." she said through a soft moan.

He opened his eyes again and looked at her. "Faster, Lottie," he begged, teeth clenched, breathing erratic. "Oh, God, stroke me—"

Suddenly she felt him twitch.

"Oh, God—oh, God, Charlotte—"

And then he jerked into her hand fast, twice, three times, moaning deeply, breathing through his teeth, the sticky fluid that pulsed from him spilling over her thumb and fingers and down onto her belly.

Charlotte knew immediately that she'd never experienced anything so intense in her life. She licked her lips, closed her eyes to the feel, stroking him softly until at last he pulled back and slipped out of her hand.

He fell onto the bed beside her and drew her close to him, holding her head against his chest until his breathing slowed, his body relaxed.

Charlotte closed her eyes and fairly buried her

body into the side of his as a smile tugged at the corners of her mouth, feeling confident she had finally made her peace with Lottie.

Colin lay awake for a long time, on his back with only a sheet to cover his naked body, both hands stuffed up under his pillow as he stared at the darkened ceiling, seeing nothing, too edgy to sleep. Charlotte snored faintly beside him, something about which he'd later get profound joy in teasing her. She'd dozed off after he'd insisted she stay with him for the entire night, and just thinking of her horror at such a suggestion made him grin in the darkness. She had come to him as the temptress every man alive had fantasized about bedding, and yet the notion of sleeping an entire night beside her husband mortified her. His wife—such a complex creature.

Tonight had been the most erotic of his life. Never, ever, had he imagined that sex within marriage could be so . . . unpredictable, so lush and charged with a palpable erotic energy. So utterly perfect. Charlotte had become the Lottie English he'd dreamed of taking intimately, of teaching and making his own for years, but she had also been much more than that. The fact that he alone possessed her and she would never have another lover in her life filled him with a contentment he couldn't begin to describe.

True, he'd been quite shocked when he caught her watching him from the doorway, and he'd very nearly climaxed the moment he saw her. He'd been aroused and thinking of her, envisioning her touch, needing her desperately. But it was her own desire that unraveled him. Of all the women he'd been with in his life, not one of them had stroked him to climax, and his wife had *asked* him to let her. After tasting the delicious sweetness that flowed from her, feeling her experience her own orgasm, he'd been desperate to enter her and come deep inside. But that tiny part of him that had needed Lottie for so many years had held him back long enough to see if she'd touch him, and to his complete gratification, she'd done it without reservation. Before she fell asleep she asked him if she'd done it correctly, and he'd laughed. Not from the question, but because she had absolutely no idea how much her openness, her enjoyment in bed meant to him.

Their love life would be grand. Of that, he had no doubt. Charlotte was more than a wife, more than a mistress. She was his partner in bed, and he would give her everything she could ever desire. After tonight, he knew he'd never need another woman, would never need anything more.

With that knowledge in mind, peacefulness enveloping him, Colin finally closed his eyes and allowed the comfort of sleep to take him.

Chapter 17

⟨∞⟩

Charlotte felt surprisingly refreshed this morning after such a fitful night's sleep in his bed. She rose early, bathed, and dressed in a modest day gown of lavender chiffon—probably the best she'd ever worn to the theater for rehearsal—hoping that Colin might notice and comment on her attire, or better, remark upon the way she looked in it. Unfortunately, she didn't see Colin at all this morning as Betsy, their new housekeeper, informed her he was working in his study and had asked not to be disturbed. She suspected he was well into copying the Handel piece, though since she'd never actually seen him at work, and had yet to view his progress, she had no idea how far along he was in the process or if he'd even managed to make a convincing forgery up to this point. But she could hardly concentrate on that now when she centered her thoughts on the events of last night, what he did to her body, her emotions. It subdued her a little when he didn't meet her for breakfast, or choose to ride in with her this morning. But no matter. Her work would likely come easier today as she'd be able to better concentrate on her performance with him not there to distract her. Although she tried not to think about it, her body still tingled from the memory of his touch, his delicious kisses, the expert way he made her . . .

She shivered even in the warm sunshine as she opened the backstage door to the theater. Making her way toward her dressing room, she couldn't help but feel a keen embarrassment from lingering thoughts of last night—not so much by her boldness in going to him, but because in the end she had touched him so shockingly, in a manner that he had thoroughly enjoyed, even begged for. The constant musings made her suddenly recall their meeting in her brother's home before they were married when he emphasized in no uncertain terms that he wanted to keep her from getting with child until he'd gotten enough of her physically. Of course he hadn't said it quite that way, but just remembering his insistence that fateful day helped her to understand exactly why he'd not wanted to leave her with the possibility of getting with child last night. Then again, she would be the first to admit that she didn't know anything, really, about the male mind and how their logic worked, though to her, it did make sense.

"You're here early."

Charlotte paused in her stride and turned to see a smiling Sadie walking toward her own dressing room from the opposite direction.

"I am, aren't I?" she replied good-naturedly. Hugging the day's music to her chest, she offered a smile in return. "I think Walter is getting annoyed at me for being distracted every day."

Sadie laughed lightly as she adjusted the pins that held her long mahogany braid to the back of her head. "No, he's not," she replied in slightly accented French. "He can't chastise you too much or you might threaten to leave him for the Continent. Then where would we find ourselves?"

"With you as lead soprano, I suppose," Charlotte returned at once, knowing that probably wasn't true but choosing to compliment her.

"Ha! I would never follow in your footsteps, Lottie," Sadie teased, dropping her arms to her sides.

Her smile faded a little as she wondered if the Frenchwoman had deliberately said *would* never instead of *could* never, or if she'd only gotten the meaning wrong due to her less than perfect knowledge of English. But she quickly shook such a thought from her mind. Her husband had made her doubt her friend when there was no reason to do so.

"But," Sadie added with a cunning grin, "he was looking for you earlier."

Charlotte sagged a little into her stays. "Why? I just got here," she said, exasperated.

Sadie shrugged, clasping her hands in front of her. "I have no idea, but he wasn't angry, if that makes you feel any better."

Charlotte grumbled within and opened her dressing room door. "I'll find him in a moment."

"Where is your handsome duke today?"

She whirled around, astonished that Sadie had mentioned Colin to her, and that the woman actually seemed to assume they were involved in something together, perhaps even romantically. For a slice of a second she had no idea how to respond. Then, playing her best part yet, she sighed and revealed nothing. "I have no idea."

"Ah. I see," Sadie said knowingly, placing her hands on her hips. Then with a quick glance over her shoulder, she added mischievously, "You know he married a noblewoman."

Charlotte could feel her cheeks burning, but she gracefully ignored it, clutching the music in her arms like a barrier. "Really? I thought I'd heard as much."

"And I'm sure you know that man will trifle with anyone," Sadie added, her lips tilted into a crooked grin as she looked her up and down. "He seems to like you."

She couldn't decide if her friend was warning her to beware of the rake, or suggesting she have a romantic affair with him if she wasn't doing so already. But the fact that other cast members seemed to think she was involved clandestinely with the Duke of Newark rather unnerved her.

"There you are," Anne cut in, fairly waltzing up to the two of them from behind the stage curtain to their left.

Charlotte exhaled deeply in relief. "Good morning," she said cheerfully.

"And to you, as well," the woman answered, patting her olive-green day gown at her abundant hips while she gazed at her from head to foot. "My goodness, don't you look pretty today, Lottie."

She'd completely forgotten she'd worn a day gown in chiffon rather than her usual work clothes made of linen in colors that struck the onlooker as practical rather than comely. She'd also dressed her hair in a loose pile on top of her head rather than an unbecoming knot at her nape. Apparently Anne had noticed, and possibly Sadie had, too, which may have been why she'd brought Colin up in conversation in the first place.

"Thank you," she replied with a nod.

"Goodness, I hadn't even noticed," Sadie said, taking part of the chiffon from her skirt into her fingers. "You could almost pass as a noblewoman yourself in such a gown."

Anne laughed. "Indeed. And your English is just as good. But I suppose that's what comes from having a good ear."

"Think the queen herself will invite me to tea?" Charlotte mocked with a curtsy.

Now both women chuckled, then Anne remarked, "Well, *my lady,* before that happens you'd better see the director. Walter is looking for you."

Joking aside, she maintained, "Yes, I heard, and I suppose I'd better see what he wants before he turns red and hunts me down."

Sadie moved to the older woman's side, linking her arm through hers. "Come, Anne," she said with feigned impertinence, "*we're* obviously not needed."

"Thankfully," Anne added with a wink. " 'Tis truly a bonus when one is *not* the star of the opera. See you on the stage, Lottie."

With that, the two women walked away arm in arm, Sadie whispering and Anne laughing at whatever she'd said.

Charlotte sagged into her corset, knowing they teased her but feeling unsettled just the same. They couldn't possibly know her identity, and yet dressing in better clothing had obviously been a mistake, certainly a lesson learned.

Quickly, she walked into her dressing room to leave her music on the seat of her vanity chair, then she righted herself, smoothed her skirts, and headed for the director's office on the second floor.

She paused at the closed door when she came to it, hearing male voices raised in anger, immediately recognizing Porano's. She could only imagine him waving arms dramatically since he sounded upset. She could not, however, distinguish what they might be discussing.

Standing erect with confidence, she knocked twice and walked into Walter's office when she heard his gruff call to enter.

As always, the small, windowless room remained spotless. A perfectionist beyond description, Charlotte could only wonder what the man's wife of twenty-five years thought of a husband who filed everything from production notes and costume receipts to the weekly grooming schedule of his terrier, Coco, who followed him everywhere, even to the theater.

Charlotte noticed the dog first, who perked up from her quilted blanket in the corner of the room and waddled toward her for attention.

"Coco, you darling," she said, kneeling to pet the dog's very clean and recently brushed coat.

Coco licked her hands, nipped at her fingers, and she scratched her behind her ears while looking up at Porano.

She could tell immediately that their discussion had been less than affable. Porano's nose and rounded cheeks flushed scarlet, though he'd managed to clamp his mouth down hard at her entrance. Walter seemed contrite, rubbing his oiled hair incessantly as he gazed at her from behind his polished and bare desk.

"You wanted to see me, Walter?" she said, still petting Coco while the dog tried but failed to jump into her lap.

Porano turned his back on her, gazing at the files Walter kept stacked and dust-free on the shelf to her left, his hands clasped behind him.

Barrington-Graham cleared his throat as he smoothed his black- and white-striped cravat. "I received a letter yesterday from the director of *La Scala,* in Milan," he disclosed, his tone oddly mollified. "The . . . uh . . . Italians have heard of your magnificent talent, Lottie, and are requesting your response."

Very slowly, Charlotte stood again, glancing from Porano's back to her director, her interest aroused. "My response to what, exactly?" she asked when he offered no more.

Walter's thin face seemed gaunt in the bright lamplight, his forehead and lips crinkled with what appeared to be concern.

"Actually," he explained, lifting a finger to pull at his ridiculously tight collar, "they'd like you to come to Italy, with Adamo, and sing at *La Scala* with him, for the whole of next year, perhaps longer."

It took her a long moment to actually understand what her director meant by such a stunning announcement. Then she felt her heart stop beating, her knees grow weak, as meaning sunk in.

"I—*La Scala* wants me?" she mumbled, her voice shaky.

"As their leading soprano." Barrington-Graham tried to smile. "Italy wants you, Lottie. And as much as I despise the notion of losing you for a season or more, I must inform you of the interest."

Charlotte desperately needed to sit, to gather her thoughts and come to terms with such incredible, such . . . fabulous news. But suddenly, as if this were all about him, Porano threw his hands in the air and walked to the only chair in the room in front of Walter's desk, fairly dumping his large frame into it, exasperated.

Barrington-Graham didn't appear to even notice the uncivilized error of decorum, instead plopping his own skinny backside down in the chair behind the desk as if winded.

Charlotte just stood there, gazing from one to the other, the shock on her face likely noticed as her mouth remained open with a totally unladylike speechlessness.

"They like you. They *want* you," Porano exclaimed in heavily accented English, breaking the silence at last.

At that moment, Charlotte came to the conclusion that Adamo was none too happy with the news, and her first clear thought was to wonder how he learned about it before she did. But that hardly mattered. Standing in her director's office, her heart now pounding wildly, she began to realize what exactly this unbelievable opportunity meant to her, to her future.

The director of *La Scala,* Milan's grand opera house, had offered her a chance to sing in Italy. She'd only seen drawings of the building, of the stage, but it was large enough to sit thousands, she suspected. It remained one of the greatest in the world, and would be the first step toward the attainment of her dream.

Barrington-Graham apparently noticed her initial shock, and he offered her a tentative smile.

"It's a marvelous offer, Lottie," he said quietly, ignoring Porano altogether. "But I will expect you to finish your engagement in *The Bohemian Girl,* as will Adamo." He leaned forward, placing his forearms on his desk, lacing his fingers together in front of him. "The theater can't afford to lose you—you know that—before next season."

Charlotte hardly noticed as Coco began yapping, then pulling at the hem of her delicate chiffon skirt with her teeth, vying for attention again. Reaching down, she absentmindedly picked the terrier up and began petting her.

Italy. God help her, but this was the chance of a lifetime. "I . . . I have to accept such a generous offer," she said moments later, her mouth dry.

Adamo shook his head and then dropped it, staring at his lap.

"Do you have a problem sharing the stage with me in Milan, Mr. Porano?" she asked flatly, her wits returning to her as his childishness grew ever more pronounced.

Adamo glanced over his shoulder. "Of course not," he snapped back, his voice gruff.

Charlotte actually appreciated his reaction, as it wasn't altogether unexpected. The tenor was, and would always be in his mind, Italy's greatest star. To share the stage at *La Scala* with an invited English singer, regardless of gender, would in a manner take away from his glory. Still, she mused, he also had to know what their pairing could do for his own career on the Continent, if he chose to manage it properly.

Giddy with a growing exhilaration, she purposely dismissed all negative and disconcerting conjecture. She had been offered a gift, and she would take it.

"Of course I'll be here for the entire season, Walter," she acknowledged, trying to sound matter-of-fact about something that was, to him more than anyone, a business decision. "But you know as well as I that I can hardly refuse an offer like this from one of the greatest houses in Europe."

Adamo sank lower into his seat. Barrington-Graham nodded once with acceptance, his expression grim.

"Then congratulations are in order, I suppose," he declared, subdued. "Coco and I will miss you."

And I'll miss Coco. "Thank you, sir," she replied, starting to shake inside. "And now, shall I get back to practice?"

Walter waved a hand in dismissal. "Yes, do. I'll be downstairs momentarily. Oh, and Lottie?"

"Yes?"

"Let's not mention this to anyone for the time being," he added. "I don't want the rest of the cast concerned about their work next season without you here to draw in the patronage."

That tempered her a little. "Of course, Walter. I won't say a word about it until you do."

Porano didn't even look at her as she lowered the dog to the floor, then opened the door behind her and slipped outside, closing it softly with a marvelous grin on her face as she heard Coco start her relentless yapping again.

Italy. Her dream had come true.

It wasn't until she climbed down the stairs to the foyer and walked through the curtain toward the stage that she began to consider just how difficult it was going to be to tell Colin.

Chapter 18

Colin sat in the dark recesses of the theater, in the last row of seats, listening to the men in the cast sing their parts, assuming he'd have to endure the ladies' numbers as well when this particular torture ended. Then, according to Charlotte, they would all do a complete run-through of the entire third act, during which, under different circumstances, he would probably sleep. Today, however, he'd get to watch his wife perform, something that made him immensely, even curiously, proud.

She had been his passionate lover for three weeks now, and truthfully he had enjoyed every single moment of watching her squirm beneath the sheets, learning what he liked, and witnessing the enjoyment she received from pleasing him. And she certainly pleased him. Likewise, he had given her everything she could have asked for in bed, sometimes before she even thought of it, surprising her, delighting her, and having such a damn good time in her company it seemed like a fantasy. A very, very good fantasy, at that.

Still, even with their newfound physical pleasure, something bothered him about it that he couldn't quite define, or ignore. Something between them was missing, and after careful consideration these last few days, he'd come to the conclusion it had to be Charlotte's reluctance to accept him, as her husband, before her fame and her desire to sing abroad. True to his word, he'd done his best not to get her with child, and she seemed to enjoy the fact that they could be intimate without him having to be inside of her. But now the idea of her leaving to tour the continent didn't much appeal to him. He supposed he'd been stupid enough to assume he'd tire of her as he had other lovers, but he and Lottie were different together. The longer they were married, the more he wanted her by his side, and not just in his bed. If he got her pregnant, would she stay for the baby? Giving him an heir had been her card to play in exchange for his so-called financial sponsorship, and yet in the last few weeks he'd truly begun to question his own idiocy in thinking he could easily let her go. He wasn't sure he could do that now at all.

Her sudden appearance on the stage at that moment brought his thoughts to the present. Even without costume, wearing a rather conservative day gown and no cosmetics, she still managed to dazzle him. He never tired of hearing her sing, as the center of a major production, or at home in the privacy of his study. Sometimes even just the sound of her voice running scales made him pause, close his eyes, and imagine the beauty of such a gift. Now she and Porano appeared ready to sing a duet, as the men cleared the stage and the women had yet to appear.

Colin yawned. It wasn't as if he'd grown bored coming to her rehearsals, but listening to the same music over and over each day, while knowing one or more people in the cast wanted her priceless musical score and would do anything to get it, made him increasingly agitated and tired of waiting for answers.

For the last three weeks, as he worked in the evening on the forgery, by day he had been carefully watching and listening and getting acquainted with those at the theater. And he'd been able to all but eliminate everyone but a few who worked closest with Charlotte.

First, he'd come to the conclusion, after a great deal of thought, that the person responsible for dropping the beam, and of course the other unfortunate "accidents," wasn't actually trying to injure her permanently, or kill her, or rid her of the lead role, but was simply attempting to get her out of the way because the Handel piece was thought to be here at the theater. With Lottie gone for a few days because of an injury, her dressing room, and all the boxes of old and dusty music it contained, would be free to investigate. The only flaw in that reasoning was the fact that she could very well take the score with her, though the more he thought about that, the more it seemed unlikely. She couldn't just shuffle it back and forth due to its age and delicate condition. Whoever wanted the masterpiece would know this. And because she'd never been followed to and from home, that he knew of, whether to his townhouse or Brixham's, and that neither he nor her brother had been victims of robbery, the culprit had to think the music was, indeed, somewhere in this building. It was, for the time being, a logical assumption, although whoever had vandalized her dressing room hadn't obviously found the piece in question, leading to even greater concern over the treasure's whereabouts. It was also quite possible that the would-be thief hadn't intended to leave the unimportant music scattered on her floor at all but had been nearly interrupted, by Charlotte or someone else, and needed to leave her dressing room quickly without putting everything back as it was.

During these past several weeks, using the excuse that he was a patron of the arts and therefore wanted to attend rehearsals to be certain where his monetary gift would be used, he'd become better acquainted with both the director and theater manager. Naturally everybody assumed Lottie was his mistress, or would be soon, and although the theater crew and cast basically ignored his presence, they were also all aware that he had married the shy sister of the Earl of Brixham. Everybody who read society pages or kept up with the idiosyncrasies of the peerage knew that. But he didn't think anyone here had drawn the conclusion that Lottie and the Duchess of Newark were one and the same, which, he supposed, happened to be the first time his rakish reputation could be put to good use.

So, after considerable conjecture, he'd all but eliminated the orchestra players, lesser cast members, and backstage hands as the would-be thief. Those who worked on the sets and costumes probably wouldn't know a priceless Handel from a recent copy of the national anthem. The cast members with small singing parts hadn't been at the theater the day the beam fell, nor had they yet arrived for the day—the few who were scheduled to sing—when he and Charlotte found her dressing room vandalized. The same applied to the orchestra as only the pianist had been available, and he nearly always remained on stage. True, neither Anne nor Sadie sang grand parts in the production, but Sadie in particular always seemed to be lurking, out in the open or behind the scenes, as if she had nowhere else to be. Just as he generally did, he mused.

The key to the puzzle, he concluded, was Charlotte's assurance that she had told no one she owned such a treasure, including even her brother. The Earl of Brixham had no contact with the theater, cast, or management for fear of ruining his reputation by giving Lottie's identity away, and as far as he knew, hadn't even been in contact with Charlotte since their wedding day.

In his final analysis, Colin came to the conclusion that the person responsible had to be one of four people: The director, Walter Barrington-Graham; Anne Balstone; Sadie Piaget; and the theater manager, Edward Hibbert.

Hibbert didn't often attend rehearsals, and after quietly inquiring at the Home Office, he'd learned the theater itself was in good financial condition. It was also very true that if Lottie English left the production, the opera house would be out of a great deal of money. Therefore, it would be to Hibbert's great advantage to keep her healthy and performing. He wasn't a musician, either, and although the man worked with the musically talented, he might not be as savvy when it came to a priceless manuscript and how and where to go about selling it. At least not by himself.

Barrington-Graham, he decided, seemed unlikely as well, simply because of his position at the theater. From what he'd learned, the man was held in fairly high esteem by colleagues, society, and even the peerage due to his longtime association with London opera and the arts. The only thing remotely suspicious about the man was his rather secretive private life, though that in itself could mean nothing. He'd been married for more than two decades, his wife a quiet woman who bred terriers for show. Little was known about his finances. He undoubtedly made a decent salary, and he'd never been reported to be in debt, though he would certainly know where and how to sell a valuable musical score, both legitimately and illegally. The trouble with this theory, Colin mused, was the director's ability to move about the theater unnoticed. *Everyone* noticed him, and he remained more often than not on stage during practices. If Barrington-Graham were indeed involved, he very likely had to have someone helping him, someone he could trust to keep his or her mouth shut in the years to come.

That left Anne and Sadie. Both would know the value of an original Handel score, and both could certainly use the money it would bring to travel and sing abroad. Anne, however, was married, and well into middle age. The advantage in that was her ability to stand up to a man, even her director at the theater, use her experience to pressure him, or comfortably

deny him. Sadie, on the other hand, was young, un-
married, beautiful, sensual, and French. And in Colin's considerable experience with women, he knew
without question that sexual expertise always won
over matronly demands. In his best estimate, Sadie
was probably, in some manner, involved.

He could also be absolutely wrong about everything.

Colin rubbed his eyes. Charlotte and Porano were
deep into practice, the rest of the cast either lounging
in the audience chairs or backstage and out of view.
There wouldn't be any better time, he supposed, to
begin a plan of action, to start investigating Sadie, the
person whose involvement seemed most reasonable.
He hadn't said a word of any of this to Charlotte
because the only way he could think of to approach
the Frenchwoman was to pretend to romance her.
The greatest surprise to him was in realizing how
very little he wanted to do such a thing, even in pretense, now that he had Charlotte to warm his bed.
He grinned to himself at the thought. If Sam and
Will knew he lacked interest in other ladies, the joking would never end.

Standing, and without being noticed, Colin turned
and moved with ease through the curtain behind
him, then walked quickly down to the backstage entrance. Sadie hadn't been sitting in the audience area,
and as Lottie still sang with Porano, he felt confident
he'd find her behind the scenes, in her dressing room
or somewhere nearby.

Almost immediately, he heard faint female laughter from behind the huge black drapes that separated
them from the stage proper. Although rather dark,

he knew at once that the voices were those of Anne, Sadie, and one of the girls who worked on costuming called Alice Newman. But being just sixteen or so, and from a family of modest means, he was sure that she was no threat at all to Charlotte.

The three of them stood just next to Lottie's dressing room, its door closed. Since they hadn't yet seen him, he paused for a moment, rolling up the sleeves of his linen shirt to his forearms. He then raked his fingers through his hair twice and straightened with confidence to confront them.

Anne noticed him first as he strode toward them, her plump face turning from one of joviality to a look of surprise at her first sight of him, all conversation coming to an abrupt halt. She curtsied as the others turned and did the same.

"Ladies," he drawled, sauntering up to stand before them.

"Your grace," they all murmured collectively.

He smiled and crossed his arms over his chest. "I hope I'm not interrupting anything important."

"No, no, of course not," Anne replied, suddenly flustered. She brushed the back of her hand across her high brow and glanced first to Sadie, then the other woman, whose youth and meekness kept her from looking at anything but the floor.

"The production is coming along well, is it not?" he asked casually.

"Indeed, it is," Anne agreed with a nod. "We are very fortunate to have the great Italian Porano to play Thaddeus."

"But of course Lottie is the star," Sadie added, looking him squarely in the eye.

He grinned, holding her gaze. "Yes, but I thought you were just as dazzling when you sang yesterday."

She stared at him curiously, her brows slightly furrowed. An awkward moment passed, for all but him, then Anne exhaled a long breath.

"Well," she said, brushing her palms down her skirt, "Alice was just about to fit me in costume. Will you excuse us, your grace?"

She certainly timed that well, he mused. "Please don't let me keep you, Mrs. Balstone. Miss Newman."

Sadie said nothing, though he felt her eyes on him as the two other ladies curtsied, turned, and walked toward the left side of the stage and into the darkness.

He heard Charlotte singing again, alone this time, and so he glanced back to Sadie and smiled wryly. "I suppose we're all alone."

"So it seems," she fairly purred in thickly accented English, looking him up and down with her hands clasped behind her.

God, sometimes he wished he wasn't so right about women.

He took a step closer and leaned his shoulder on the doorframe of his wife's dressing room. "And why aren't you on stage, Miss Piaget?" he asked warmly, his voice low.

She shook her head, grinning. "Please, your grace, last time we spoke, I asked you to call me Sadie."

She had to be referring to the time Charlotte saw them together, since he hadn't spoken to her privately before or since. Although he teased his wife about it, their discussion at the time had nothing to do with anything but trivialities. And she certainly hadn't asked him to call her by her Christian name. That he would have remembered.

"Of course, Sadie," he murmured. "And I'd like you to call me Colin."

She beamed and nodded once. "Colin."

"It's rather dark and quiet here, isn't it?" he remarked as he glanced around the backstage area.

"Everyone is very busy elsewhere, I suppose," she said with a shrug.

Nobody was busy, he knew, but that was beside the point. "Ah. And when do you sing again?"

"Not for a little while," she replied with a sigh. "I'm not needed until we begin rehearsing the next act."

"Oh, I see."

She waited for a moment, eyeing him cautiously. Then she moved close enough to him that her skirts brushed his legs. "You have a wife at home, do you not?"

Colin lifted a shoulder negligibly, playing the disinterested husband well, he thought. "I do, but she is very busy with her charities and helping the Duchess of Durham prepare for her baby." He sighed. "I'm afraid I don't see her very much."

"So you are not in love with her?"

Colin blinked, suddenly flustered by the notion that had not, as yet, occurred to him. "What is love?" he countered with another shrug, forcing himself to keep his mind on the present task.

Sadie tipped her head to the side. "That is a shame," she murmured. "If you loved her you would know."

"I suppose so," he agreed, shuffling a foot back and forth on the wooden floor.

"And now you and Lottie are lovers?" she asked, her voice soft and cunning.

Colin grinned, a little surprised that she asked so bluntly. "It wouldn't be gentlemanly of me to say," he whispered with a wink, trying to decide if the woman knew Lottie and his wife were one and the same. At this point, he simply couldn't tell.

She laughed softly, tossing her head back as if he'd completely flattered her.

"Then you keep very good secrets, sir," she teased, slyly touching her elbow to his chest. "I know her very well, and she's never been so *enamored* of anyone. She's spoken of you and your handsome, charming manner for years."

His first thought was how she'd accentuated the word *enamored*, as if he needed to be reminded she was French. But that quickly vanished when he actually considered her point. The notion of Charlotte being crazy about him for years struck him in a manner he couldn't describe if he chose to. He grew completely warm inside, immensely pleased with himself, though he would never, in a million years, tell that to anyone.

"Has she now," he replied, rubbing the back of his neck as if the praise embarrassed him.

"I happen to agree," she fairly purred. "You are very handsome and charming, Colin. I've thought so since the first time we met."

He couldn't care any less what Sadie thought of him. True, she was a beautiful Frenchwoman, sensual and no doubt experienced in bed. But where six months ago he would have pursued her without question or restraint, considering doing so now seemed childish and silly. It suddenly occurred to him how much he really did adore being married to Charlotte, and how much honesty and trust within that marriage mattered to him.

"And you are very lovely," he replied, trying not to sound as unaffected by her as he felt.

Sadie sighed with exaggeration, gazing into his eyes as she leaned back against the wall. "Perhaps you'll tire of Lottie."

He contained a laugh of absurdity. "Perhaps," he said huskily. "But I thought you were good friends."

Sadie rolled her eyes, and the idea that she was far less of a friend than Charlotte made her out to be irritated him.

"We are friends," she agreed, "but when she leaves for Italy, I will still be here. Lonely."

Colin stilled, his features going flat. "Leaves for Italy?"

She blinked in feigned surprise. "Oh, my goodness, you didn't know? She is to accompany Monsieur Porano to Milan when *The Bohemian Girl* closes. She's been invited to sing at *La Scala* next season."

His chest burned as if it suddenly caught fire, his gut wrenched, but he did his best not to show his astonishment, his anger.

"She didn't tell me," he said, trying to sound dejected rather than infuriated.

Sadie offered him an understanding smile. "Perhaps she cares less for you than you thought."

That comment hit so close to home Colin's first

reaction was to slam his fist into her dressing room door, though with noble dignity he restrained himself. He simply couldn't believe anything this Frenchwoman said as fact without confirmation. And he knew, just *knew*, that Charlotte cared for him enough to discuss such an enormous opportunity with him before she accepted it wholeheartedly.

"Perhaps she does," he repeated, though his voice sounded tight to his ears. "When did you learn of this marvelous offer she received?"

He had no idea why he asked that, but the look on her face told him everything.

She frowned as she toyed with the chain at her neck. "I suppose we've known for several days, perhaps a week now."

He nodded, though for the first time in his life he felt utterly betrayed by a woman. His body broke out into a cold sweat as his mind began to boil with complex emotions he'd never before felt as one—frustration, hurt, bewilderment, fury.

His wife planned to leave him, had known about it for a week, and she hadn't said a word to him. What did that say about their marriage and newly discovered love affair? That she cared more for opera than the two of them? Really, he'd known all along that she did. He just wasn't prepared to admit it to himself after all they'd so recently discovered about each other, all they'd shared.

Sadie reached out and placed her hand flat on his chest. "I see you are surprised, Colin."

He shrugged. "There will be other lovers in my life," he murmured, trying not to look or sound as heartsick as he felt.

"I hope so," she whispered. And then, before he considered her intentions, she leaned over and wrapped her arm around his neck, pulling his head down to meet her waiting lips.

She kissed him fiercely with an expert tongue, her palms planted on his cheeks. Stunned, Colin didn't react for several seconds. Then he placed his hands on her shoulders and gave in to the pretense.

Lottie, Lottie, Lottie . . . I can't lose you now . . .

He supposed Sadie was a fine kisser, eager and clearly experienced. But he could think of nothing but his wife, her lush body, her sweet laugh and gorgeous blue eyes, her innocence in bed and outside of it. She was the only woman who mattered to him now, and as quickly as Sadie lifted his hand and placed it on her breast, he released her and took a step back.

"We can't do this here, not now, sweetheart," he murmured, glancing briefly over his shoulder as he clasped his hands behind him.

She actually pouted and he almost snorted in distaste.

"Lottie will be looking for me soon," he explained in an effort to appease her.

"Of course I understand," she replied, her voice edgy with irritation even as she feigned sweetness. "But you know you can always find me here, willing to help you in your time of need."

Colin sensed that she'd grown bored with him for now as she shook her gown out and smiled flatly, ready to dismiss him as if he were her plaything.

He inched closer again and ran a finger down her upper arm. "I'm so glad. I can always use female . . . companionship, Sadie." Lowering his voice to a grave whisper, he said, "But there is another reason I'm pursuing Lottie English."

Her brows rose with renewed interest. "Indeed."

"I've heard she possesses a rare piece of music," he said, holding her gaze. "I'd like to find it."

Colin watched her intently for any response. He'd used the word "find" instead of "see" because he hoped Sadie would infer that he wanted it for himself, without Lottie's knowledge.

Slowly, the Frenchwoman's expression went from curious to blank—the first honest response he'd gotten from her, he decided. Then she frowned negligibly and shook her head.

"I'm sure I don't know anything about rare music," she replied quietly, lifting her hand back to the chain around her neck and rubbing it nervously. "Why do *you* want to find it?"

That question told him much. She hadn't asked what kind of music, who composed it, its sentimental value, age, or monetary worth, nor had she brushed it off easily as if she hadn't a clue and didn't really care. Instead, she asked him about his interest in finding the piece. Again, he could be completely wrong about her involvement in the plot to steal the score, but even the little doubt he'd held until now began to fade.

In a low murmur, he said, "Perhaps it's best to say I'm intrigued? As an admirer of music and the theater, you understand."

She laughed softly, glancing up and down his body. "I never realized you were so secretive and had such . . . devious reasons for your daily visitations, Colin."

"Do you know where it is?" he prodded good-naturedly, attempting to stay on topic.

She bit her bottom lip, eyeing him cautiously for a moment. "I have no idea, but if I hear anything about rare music, I will tell you first."

He reached out and ran his thumb down the side of her neck. "I would be most appreciative."

She took his hand and squeezed his fingers. "Then I will try very hard."

Suddenly she released him, straightened, and took a step away. "And now, I will leave you to look for Lottie, your grace."

With a formal curtsy, she turned on her heel and gracefully walked away.

Colin remained unmoved for seconds, listening to Porano sing. Then he turned a little and pressed his back into Charlotte's dressing room door—and saw her standing ten feet away, arms to her sides, gazing at him as if he'd just slapped her.

Goddammit all to hell.

She began walking toward him, and he noticed at once, even in the darkness, that her face had gone pale.

"Lottie—"

"I'm very busy right now, Colin," she interrupted in a low, shaky voice, attempting to whisk by him and enter her dressing room.

He grabbed her by the shoulders before she could open the door, stopping her in her tracks. "What's wrong?" he asked gravely. "Did you see me with Sadie?"

For seconds she said nothing. Then she looked up into his eyes, her features neutral, smiling sweetly.

"I'm sure I don't know what you're talking about, but what you do with your free time is your business."

Not wanting them observed in argument, he reached over and opened the door, then fairly shoved her into the room, closing it quickly behind him.

"What are you doing?" she asked, provoked by his gall.

He blocked her exit, his hands on his hips. "*She* kissed *me*, Charlotte."

"She—" Her eyes grew wide as she blinked several times. Then her mouth dropped open and she began backing away from him.

It took him only seconds to realize she hadn't seen Sadie's aggressive contact with him at all. He groaned and rubbed his eyes. God, what a nightmare.

"Charlotte—"

"I need to get back to the stage," she whispered.

Irrationally, that made him mad. "She knows about the music."

Recovering her composure, she scoffed. "I'm sure you're mistaken."

"No. I'm not," he insisted, keeping his voice hushed.

Her eyes flashed angrily. "And you thought by kissing her you could gain that kind of information?" she asked through a hiss. "There isn't a woman alive who wouldn't like to be kissed by you, sir."

He didn't know whether to gloat or be appalled.

"*She* kissed *me*," he repeated. "I played along in an effort to gain her trust."

"Her trust?" She shook her head. "So I suppose you didn't enjoy it," she said sarcastically.

He groaned. "You're missing the point."

"Oh, no. I think I understand the point all too well," she shot back. "I realize I'm the one who told you to take a mistress at your leisure. The only thing I'm angry about is that you've chosen to seduce a personal friend of mine."

He took two steps toward her and grabbed her by the shoulders, yanking her against him.

"Let me go!" she seethed in a whisper.

He ignored that. "First, she is not your friend if she's part of the scheme to harm you and steal your music," he murmured succinctly, staring into her hurt-filled eyes. "Second, she is not your friend if she openly kisses your lover, and she knows we're lovers."

She glared at him. "What did you do to encourage her, Colin?"

He had no answer for that, and she knew it. Everybody in England knew he was the country's most celebrated rake, even if it wasn't actually so. But as far as he could recall, he'd never hated, really hated, his reputation more than he did right now.

"Charlotte," he started again, clutching her shoulders, "I'm trying to find the truth, and Sadie knows something. I'm sure of it." He drew a deep breath, deciding it was time to reveal what was in his heart. "But more importantly, what matters the most to me is you. I don't want anyone but you in my bed. What we share when we make love—"

Her laugh of disgust cut him short. "We don't share anything in bed, Colin. Just bodies. And you're very, very good at sharing yours. Now let me go."

Colin had never felt so stung by a comment in his entire life. Utterly shocked, he dropped his arms to his sides and she immediately brushed by him, opened the door, and walked out.

Chapter 19

Their ride home had to be the most tense and uncomfortable they'd ever shared. Charlotte decided to ignore him as if he weren't even in her presence, and he hadn't bothered with an attempt to engage her in conversation, no doubt sensing the immense displeasure emanating from both her rigid form and avoiding gaze. Unfortunately, the time alone with him gave her ample opportunity to revel in her miserable thoughts.

It had to be one of the worst weeks of her life. After days of rejoicing in the offer to sing in Italy, trying to decide the best way to inform her husband and beg for his permission and good wishes, her well-ordered world had collapsed seconds after learning her husband had been kissed by one of her closest friends. Oddly, she believed Colin when he said Sadie had initiated it, though with his reputation, she didn't doubt he enjoyed it, which, she supposed, saddened her most of all.

Part of her just wanted to cry, the other part scream, though she refused to do either with him sitting across from her in close confines, his eyes shut, body relaxed, arms folded over his belly as if he hadn't a care in the world. At this point, she couldn't wait to retire to her room and crawl into bed where she could punch her aggravation into her pillow.

What made her angriest at herself was not knowing if she hated him or loved him. She did, however, realize that the man was far more complex than she had ever imagined, and she liked that about him very, very much. She'd married an illegal forger, a criminal, a funny and charming rake, and what amused her most was the keen realization of just how much she enjoyed him because of, or aside from, these flaws. So what did that make her other than stupid? Yet even if she remained blindly involved with him, never could she deny how he made her laugh with witty conversation, made her tingle at the mere sight of him, and yes, made her come alive in bed. Simply put, he fascinated her, and the more she considered his goodness, the guiltier she felt for saying they shared nothing but bodies when they made love. That was wrong of her, whether she felt that way or not, because she could see from his expression the second it came out of her mouth that she had hurt him.

Still, she'd meant it, though it hadn't occurred to her until today that something *was* missing when they were together intimately. She had to assume he'd done the same things in bed with other women, which meant that nothing they shared made her special to him. That's what hurt *her* most of all, especially after seeing him so closely chatting with Sadie.

Now, as the coach stopped at the townhouse, she had to consider how to tell Colin of her offer to sing abroad, knowing fully well the circumstances had changed. He hadn't spoken to her since they'd left the theater, and she rather assumed he was angry about her last comment to him. But she wanted to get everything out in the open, to let him know he'd no longer need to sponsor her financially in Europe, at least for her engagement in Milan. Then again, maybe he didn't care what she did after their confrontation this afternoon. In any case, she had no intention of bringing the subject up tonight.

The two of them remained silent until they entered the house, then before she could bid him good evening and take her leave, he grabbed her hand and began pulling her toward his study.

"There are some things we need to discuss, Charlotte," he said without explanation.

She grumbled. "Not now, Colin. I'm tired—"

"I'm tired, too," he cut in, refusing to let her go. "I'm tired of the secrets between us. It's time to get them all out in the open." He glanced over his shoulder, a tiny smirk on his mouth. "Wouldn't you agree?"

She couldn't possibly fight his grip, much less his determination, and so she gave him a flat smile and replied, "Of course. I'm always agreeable. Lead the way, sir."

He shot her another fast look, though he didn't release her as they walked down the hall. But instead of stopping at his study where they always went for conversation, he continued past the drawing room and into the dining room already set with china and linens for the evening meal, guiding her through the swinging door that led to the kitchen.

Three servants and their housekeeper, Betsy, worked dutifully inside, preparing a dinner of roast beef with onion, by the smell of it. They all took quick notice of her and her husband, curtsying appropriately before returning to their duties, apparently not the least surprised to see the Duke of Newark walking past them, clutching his wife's hand.

A bit bewildered by his silent sense of purpose, she grew completely surprised when he moved directly toward the scullery under the back stairway that led to the second-floor bedrooms.

"What are you doing?" she asked while he opened the creaking door with his free hand.

He said nothing as he ushered her inside the dark, cramped area, the scent of cleaning solvents and flour assaulting her senses. He quickly moved around her, finally dropping her hand so he could push aside a tall shelf that held a few pots and pans, revealing a second door, unnoticed by her at first, secured with a large, sturdy lock.

A whirlwind of intrigue suddenly replaced her annoyance when he reached up onto the shelf and removed a key from inside a large saucepan. He inserted it into the lock, turned it until she heard a click, then removed the key and dropped it back into the pan. That done, he unlatched the door and pushed it open.

The distinct musty odor mixed with tobacco struck her at once. Without saying a word, he reached for her hand again, gently this time, and guided her into a room bathed in total darkness.

"Colin?" she whispered.

"Just a minute."

Slightly unnerved, she stood where she was as he disappeared into the blackness. Seconds later he lit a lamp and she gasped, taking a step back, her eyes opening wide as she gazed around the room, absolutely incredulous.

Perhaps only twenty square feet in size, she stood inside a windowless alcove hideaway. Row after row of books, stacks of paper, manuscripts, and newspapers, most of them very old by the looks of their yellowed edges, lined three of the four walls, from floor to ceiling. Against the wall to her right, he'd erected three long, wooden shelves, piling them to the edges with glass jars and corked bottles filled to various levels with fluids of every color from clear to black, stacks of paint brushes, charcoal, metal plates of all sizes and shapes, and a basket full of tools similar to the two he used the day he first saw the Handel score. Directly across from her, on the opposite wall, stood a very thin, wooden ladder braced against stacked books, leading to a hinged door latched on the ceiling. To her left she noticed a tall reading lamp and one lone rocker, exactly like the one in his study, and at the center of the room, on a relatively high wooden table, sat two additional lamps, one of which he'd lit upon their entrance.

"Close the door," he said, placing a palm flat on the table as he watched her with some amusement.

Gradually, her curiosity overcame her astonishment, and she did as he asked, pushing the door all the way shut so they remained alone in the silence. Then, crossing her arms over her breasts she began to walk toward him, her eyes immediately focused on the table.

A wooden box, bolted near the far edge, contained three paint brushes of various sizes, and three jars of tightly sealed ink, placed into cleverly cut holes in the wood to prevent accidental spills. And in the center lay the Handel piece she'd given him, opened to the third page.

"This is the copy, Charlotte," he said quietly. "The original is in my safe. I bring it here only when I'm working."

She swallowed, giving him a quick glance before gazing back to the magnificent forgery. If he hadn't mentioned it, she would have scolded him for allowing her masterpiece to sit in the open next to jars of ink, tightly sealed and secured or not. But then he was a professional, and as she stared down at his copy, she couldn't help but be in awe of his talent. It truly looked original.

"You're very good," she mumbled, her mind instantly filled with questions.

He grunted. "No, I'm better than good. I'm the best in England, perhaps even the best in all of Europe."

She straightened, eyeing him from the other side of the table, a wry smile planted on her mouth. "The best at what? Forgery?"

He crossed his arms over his chest. "Yes."

She gave a soft little laugh, shaking her head in confusion. "You seem quite certain of yourself, though I'm not sure *forgery* is something to be proud of, Colin."

His expression remained quite serious as he cocked

his head to the side a bit, evaluating her. "Sit down, Charlotte," he quietly ordered.

She frowned. "Why?"

"Because I want you to," he replied, hoisting himself up onto the side of the table, one foot still on the floor, the other dangling over the edge.

Charlotte began to sense an overwhelming gravity in his manner, and the notion that he seemed about to reveal some enormous secret made her walk to the rocker and sit, her hands folded in her lap and not a thought given to straightening her skirts.

After a long moment of silence, she expelled an exasperated breath. "How long are you going to make me wait?"

He smiled minutely, then replied, "I'm gathering my thoughts."

She raised her brows and leaned back in the chair. "Really? You've never had trouble expressing yourself before."

"You looked beautiful on stage today," he murmured, watching her closely. "Sang brilliantly."

His change of topic stumped her. "Thank you."

"And," he continued, "I'm very sorry about what happened at the theater."

She felt her face flush as her heart sank. "I don't want to talk about it," she returned evenly.

"We'll, we're going to talk about it because I need your trust, Charlotte," he countered, his voice low and husky. "Can I trust you?"

Flustered, she had no idea how to gauge the workings of his mind. "What is this place?"

"Can I trust you?" he repeated.

His frank gaze and reflective manner seemed

strangely foreign coming from him, though the combination mesmerized her.

"Yes, you can trust me," she said, subdued. "I've said as much the other times you've asked."

He inhaled deeply and ran his fingers through his hair. "That's because trust is important in marriage. Especially in *my* marriage."

She almost grinned. "You're that special?"

He smiled. "I'm that specia*lized.*"

She shook her head. "I'm sorry, Colin, but I don't understand."

After only a brief hesitation, he said, "You've asked me, on numerous occasions, what I do with my time. Well, this is it." He gestured around the room with his head. "This is my workshop."

She frowned. "I could have guessed that much."

He softened a little, clasping his hands together between his spread legs. "I'm employed by the government."

She blinked. "I beg your pardon?"

A very slow and beautiful grin graced his face, warming her within.

"When I was arrested years ago," he explained, "I was given the opportunity to meet with Sir Thomas Kilborne, who is now my superior. He thought my work remarkable and offered me a deal I could not refuse. I told you the reasons I never went to prison, except for one: that I agreed to put my talents to good use for the Crown, for which I would be, and have been, handsomely paid."

She gaped at him, her heartbeat quickening with every word of his disclosure.

"And so, ten years ago," he continued, "I began

working with the branch of government that deals with forgers, forgery, and counterfeiting. Frankly, when I started, I was skeptical regarding the amount of work I'd be given, but I quickly learned there would always be plenty to do." He grinned again, slyly. "It's amazing, Charlotte, how many forgers there are in the world—some professional, most amateurs, and very bad ones at that, and of course an ample number sponsored by their countries' governments."

"This is unbelievable . . ." she breathed.

He shrugged. "Not really. I can forge anything, including money, papers, ancient or recent documents, and signatures. I can also detect a forgery, and that's generally what my employer needs and requires of me." He gestured to the papers on the shelf to his right. "In those stacks are the signatures of nearly every dignitary in the civilized world today, and of course I add and delete them as they change. I also have access to signatures or handwriting samples from important people through the ages—from ancient Greek philosophers to Constantine, Shakespeare, Napoleon, Roman and Chinese emperors, American presidents, and of course our own monarchy. They're owned by the government and kept in a tightly secured area, sealed within a vault, to which I have unconditional admittance when needed." He slumped a little. "The only thing I can't forge is creative art, though I can expose clever copies by analyzing the paper or background on which it's painted or drawn, and of course the signature of the artist. But the expert copy of art remains in the exclusive control of the artistically gifted, I'm afraid. I can't paint to save my soul."

Charlotte just sat there, thoroughly dumbstruck. Never in her life would she have expected her notably lazy, socially engaging, rogue of a husband, who had spent the last few weeks following her around at the theater as if he had nothing more exciting to do, to be employed by the British government, accomplishing work so specialized and secretive he hadn't even revealed it to her until now, months after their wedding. Regardless of his wayward past, he now had to be widely held in high esteem given his expertise, and as she considered the respect he no doubt garnered from distinguished government officials, she grew strangely elated and extraordinarily proud of him as a man.

After taking a few long moments to collect herself and organize her thoughts and feelings, she mumbled, "I'm—speechless."

"That's so unlike you, my darling Lottie," he teased.

She brushed off the comment. "How many people know?"

He cocked his head to the side. "Well, let's see. A select few at the Home Office, mostly those who work in the field of counterfeiting and forgery. Will and Sam know, because they're my closest friends and supported me unconditionally after my arrest. Their wives know as well, though I've never discussed it with the ladies, and of course they've never been in this room. And all of my staff know."

She blinked. "Your staff? You trust this information with your staff and you didn't tell me until now?"

He laughed. "Are you jealous, Charlotte?"

Eyes sparkling, she replied deviously, "I'm sure there's nothing you've done that would make me jealous, my darling Colin."

His gaze narrowed considerably and he leaned over to rest his palm on the tabletop. "I adore it when you call me darling," he murmured huskily.

"I don't think I've ever called you darling," she replied at once, adjusting her body in the rocker.

"Then you should more often, my darling Lottie."

She closed her eyes briefly in annoyance. "Colin—"

"My staff know because they're employed by the government as well," he carried on, his voice light with lingering amusement. "I need them to be completely trustworthy so I can come and go as I please, free of worry that someone from outside the government will find this room and expose me or my work, or some of these priceless items."

"You're joking," she argued through a laugh.

His lips turned down as he shook his head. "No, I'm not joking. You've noticed I have new servants from time to time?" He scratched his temple. "Frequently, actually. That's because they rotate to other places of employment for the Crown. With every second or third project assigned to me, I also receive an entirely new staff in my home. That way those working here won't know what secretive items I've worked on before, or after, in case any of them hear it discussed or see it. It's safer for them, I suppose."

Brows furrowed, she remarked, "You're a spy?"

He grinned. "Not at all. And I'm not a detective, either. I'm a forger. That's it."

It all sounded so wild, so exotic to her as she gazed

around the room again, taking note of everything anew in light of his confession.

"Where does that ladder lead?" she asked, pointing with her forehead.

He glanced over his shoulder. "That leads to my bed chamber on the second floor, though I don't think I've ever used it. I suppose I consider it as a method of escape should I need it."

"Oh." She felt totally dumbfounded—and thoroughly riveted.

"Now," he continued, dropping his leg to the floor as he raised himself up to stand beside the table, his hip resting on the edge, "Since we're discussing secrets, do you have one or two you'd like to share with me?"

Charlotte looked at him again, this time absorbing all of him in a brand new light, taking note of the rolled-up sleeves that revealed his muscular arms, his taut chest, and the hard planes of his face that would make any woman swoon. A truly spectacular man, she mused. And after his revelation today, in his incredible, hidden workroom, she realized for the first time how very much she admired him, and didn't want to leave him. Or lose him.

Drawing a deep breath for confidence, she said softly, "I'm not sure I have any. At least nothing that can match . . . this secret confession of yours."

"Oh?" His brows rose minutely as he began to walk slowly toward her. "Sadie mentioned that you'd been offered a marvelous opportunity to sing in Milan."

Her mouth opened a little in surprise. "That's impossible."

"Impossible? Are you telling me she was mistaken?"

He paused in his stride when he reached the end of the table, about two feet in front of her. Looking up at the doubt on his face made her uneasy.

"No—I mean, yes, I spoke with Mr. Barrington-Graham about it a few days ago, but I'm surprised she knew."

"Surprised she knew?"

"Yes, surprised she knew," she repeated. "Porano knows about it as well; he was in the office when Walter informed me, but I was told to keep it to myself for now, until he's ready to inform the cast. Why Sadie is aware of the offer is anybody's guess, although I suppose it's possible Porano told her, or she heard it as rumor and assumed. She shouldn't know a thing about it, though."

"But she does," he countered. "And what's more, she made it sound as if it's common knowledge at the theater. She was certainly happy to inform me."

Suddenly irritated, she asked, "Did she tell you before or after your kiss?"

Colin blinked, startled, and she smiled smugly to herself.

Then he gave her a slow grin and said slyly, "Before she kissed me, I think."

She could feel her face getting hot. "And how, pray tell, did she kiss, your grace?"

"My darling, Lottie," he drawled, "she kisses nothing like you do. But that isn't the point."

"Then what *is* the point?" she asked sarcastically.

He studied her, his eyes narrowing once again in

grave speculation. "The point is that other people knew of your plans for days and I, as your husband, did not. Why is that?"

Exasperated, she flopped her hands in the air. "Because I've been trying to think of a way to tell you about it without you flatly denying me before the words were even out of my mouth."

He pulled back a little, brows furrowed. "Why would you think I'd deny you this grand opportunity without . . . consideration? Discussion?"

She looked at him as if he were daft. "Because you haven't tired of me in bed, apparently. Nor have I given you an heir, per our agreement."

For a long time, it seemed, he didn't say a word, though his jaw had hardened and his shoulders appeared to bunch beneath the fine linen of his shirt. But his sharp gaze never strayed from hers.

Finally, he murmured, "Do you honestly believe there's nothing between us beyond what we had when we married?"

Agitated, she fairly jumped out of the rocker, skirting by him to stand on the other side of the workroom, staring down at the rows of paints and chemicals.

"Why do you insist on making this difficult?" she asked.

He was silent for a moment, then replied, "What am I making difficult, exactly?"

God, did he really not understand, or was he just trying to make her say it?

Whirling around, she placed her hands on her hips and glared at him. "Do you intend to take her as your mistress?"

Head tipped to the side a little, he looked at her strangely, and slightly amused. "Sadie?"

"Yes. Or . . . someone else."

He shrugged. "I hadn't planned to, no."

That's it? She wanted to scream in frustration. She closed her eyes momentarily and inhaled deeply. It was time for total honesty.

"Colin, are you in love with anyone?" she asked, eyeing him candidly once more.

Very, very slowly, the gentle smile on his face faded as his features grew serious once more. "What are you asking me, Charlotte?"

She swallowed with the immediate coiling in her belly, but she couldn't drop her gaze from the starkness of his. "Do you intend to have a love affair with anyone else while we're married?"

Seconds ticked by in deadly silence. Then he raised his chin a little and exhaled a full breath. "Not if you give me everything I want," he revealed softly.

She shifted from one foot to the other. "What, exactly, do you want from me, Colin?"

The heat from his eyes seared through her, making her suddenly weak at the knees, and horribly afraid of his answer.

"I want you to stay here, in England, with me," he murmured gravely. "I don't want you leaving me to go to Italy. Not now. Not until we have a chance to be together for a while." He clenched his jaw, then added huskily, "I need you, Charlotte."

"To satisfy you in bed," she replied.

He shook his head. "For everything."

She'd never expected such a blunt admission from him, and something inside of her melted, wanted, hoped for all he could give in return. She assumed they were discussing sex, but their discussion had suddenly become more than that, much more. And he felt it, too.

A sharp tension sparked between them, instantly charging the air. Then he straightened and started moving toward her, staring at her intently.

"And now that I've told you," he articulated, his tone dark and quiet, "it's your turn. What exactly do you want from me?"

She started trembling and reached behind her with both hands, grasping the shelf with tight fingers. "Honestly, I don't know."

He shook his head very slowly. "I don't believe you."

He towered over her now, effectively securing her from all movement, peering into her eyes as if waiting for her to voice some incredible truth, even vital information. But Charlotte refused to be intimidated.

"I *don't* know, sir," she said thickly. "I—the logical and headstrong part of me wants you to just take a mistress, find love and passion elsewhere, and leave me alone to travel, to sing, to be content, and fulfill my dreams—"

"And the other part?" he cut in sharply.

She bit down hard, her eyes no doubt expressing the twisted confusion and longing she felt inside. At last, she inhaled a shaky breath and replied, "The emotional and *irrational* part of me wants you to call me Lottie every day, to . . . stay by my side and never leave me, wherever I am, so that I'm not only content, but also happy. I want you to tell me I'm more exciting, more beautiful, and . . . that I kiss better than Sadie."

His expression went blank with absolute incredulity.

She closed her eyes and wiped a palm across her forehead. "I know that's stupid."

He lifted her chin with a finger and she couldn't help but raise her lashes, unable to avoid his intense scrutiny.

Almost smiling, his gaze skimmed her face, her lips. Then he murmured, "I've never known anyone who kisses as perfectly as you do, Charlotte, and I've never known anyone more beautiful. You're an amazing woman, deserving of everything you've ever dreamed about. All you need to do is ask."

Tears filled her eyes, though she never looked away from his mesmerizing face. With mounting determination, she whispered fiercely, "I want what's *missing*."

In that flash of an instant, everything changed between them. He stilled for a timeless moment, his breathing nearly stopped, his gaze melding with hers. Then, very slowly, he lowered it to her mouth and placed his thumb on her lips, swallowing hard as he made contact.

Charlotte couldn't move, couldn't take her eyes off his face even as she blinked away tears. Her body still trembled, and he certainly felt it, for as he raised his gaze back to capture hers once more, he cupped her chin in his palm, and leaned over to kiss the wetness from her lashes.

She sighed and wrapped her arms around his neck. With her surrender, he lowered his lips to hers, and in one fast action, lifted her up into his arms and carried her from the workroom.

Chapter 20

He carried her through the scullery and out into the kitchen, breaking from their kiss only long enough to tell Betsy to lock the workroom door.

He didn't care what his servants thought; he didn't care about anything but her—her lush lips teasing his, her soft breasts crushed against his chest, her arms around his neck, clinging to him as if she were afraid he'd let her go.

I want what's missing . . .

Her desperate and softly spoken wish had been the key that unlocked the deepest chambers of his heart, exposing his fear of all the uncertainties they shared. He'd wanted Lottie English for so long that having her in his bed had been enough. But now his desire went beyond that. He wanted to be his wife's greatest passion, and to give her everything in return.

Swiftly, and with little effort, he carried her up

the stairs and into his bed chamber, pausing only long enough to close the door with a firm push of his foot.

"Colin—"

"Shhh . . ." he whispered against her cheek. "I'm going to make love to you, Lottie."

"It's still daytime," she said hesitantly.

He brushed his lips against hers as he gently lowered her to the floor at the edge of the bed. "It's the perfect time. Now turn around."

She did as he bid without question. Quickly, with nimble fingers, he unbuttoned her gown, then slipped his hands inside the soft fabric and pushed it over her shoulders. She slipped her arms out of the sleeves and pulled the bodice over her breasts as he went to work untying her corset. In less than a minute he had undressed her, and as she stood in a puddle of silk and petticoats, he grazed her bare back with his palms, her neck with his lips, eliciting a shiver.

"Take your hair down," he murmured as he began to unfasten the buttons on his shirt.

Raising her arms, she silently unpinned her braids from atop her head, then ran her fingers through them, pulling her hair loose, then shaking her curls free. She kept her back to him, facing the bed, as he finally pulled off the remainder of his clothes and tossed them aside.

Standing hard and erect, he stepped forward and pressed his body into hers. She gasped when she felt his chest against her shoulder blades, his rigid erection pressed into the curve of her lower back. He brushed her hair aside and kissed her neck again, ran his lips along the edge of her ear, then wrapped his arms around her to cup her breasts and lightly knead them.

"I want to give you what's missing," he whispered.

A tiny whimper escaped her throat. She leaned her head back to rest on his chest as she covered his hands with her own, lightly stroking his knuckles with her fingertips.

Her nipples stood out tautly against his palms as he caressed them, and a tremor of excitement surged through his groin. Grasping her thumb with his own, he slowly began to draw their right hands together down her belly, caressing her warm, silky skin with every inch, pressing lower until he reached her intimate mound of hair, then threading their fingers through the softness until she instinctively spread her legs apart ever so slightly, giving him greater access.

He left gentle kisses across her shoulder, brushed his lips back and forth along warm skin as he kneaded her breast with his left hand and held steady with the other between her thighs. Then he released his hold of her thumb and closed his right palm over hers, pressing her fingers into the folds of her cleft.

"Let me feel you touch yourself," he whispered, his warm breath making gooseflesh rise as his lips traced a line down her neck.

He sensed her hesitation, but with a gentle pinching of her nipple and the movement of his own fingers over hers, she released her final inhibitions and began to stroke herself, using him for guidance.

Colin closed his eyes to relish the feel of her arousing herself as he held her against him, urging her ever deeper into the moist recesses of her femininity.

Her wetness coated them both as she began to make small circles over the tiny nub of her pleasure. He followed her lead, then backed up enough to allow his engorged erection to fall into the crease of her bottom before pressing into her again and resting his lips on her neck.

Her breathing grew rapid, as did his, and when she finally began to moan and gently move her hips in rhythm, when she stopped caressing his knuckles at her breast to concentrate on the feel of their fingers intermingled between her legs, he sensed her impending release. Taking her hand again, he slowly pulled her away, easing the pleasure building at the center of her, making her whimper in blissful agony.

He felt her tremble as he lifted her hand, turned it over her shoulder, and brought two of her wet fingers to his mouth, drawing them in, sucking as his own moan escaped him.

Her breath caught in her chest; she tightened her grip on the hand he still held at her breast, and an urgency he hadn't felt before ripped through him as he suddenly neared his own climax from only her scent, her taste, her arousal, and endless desire to please him.

That thought in mind, he could no longer stand the wait to take her. In one swift action, he let her go, moved around her and yanked the coverlet and sheets down to the foot of the bed. Then, placing his hands on her hips, he silently urged her face down onto the mattress. She complied, spreading her legs a little, resting her cheek against the sheet, her eyes closed, face flushed as her beautiful hair splayed out behind her over the pillow.

He marveled at the graceful splendor of her backside, her delicate, perfect curves and smooth, glowing skin, the slightly defined muscles of her legs and arms. Then he briefly knelt at the edge of the bed and placed his face between her thighs, inhaling her scent, then drawing his tongue once, very slowly, up her cleft.

She gasped and he felt her tense. Quickly, he climbed onto the bed and gingerly turned her over to face him at last.

She kept her eyes closed, licking her lips as she stretched out beneath him across the sheet.

"Look at me," he murmured, his voice low and tight.

Her lashes flickered up and she gazed at him with longing, with need and acceptance and tenderness. Then she reached up and covered his jaw with her palm. "Colin . . ."

He inhaled a shaky breath, mesmerized by her willingness to give him everything he wanted, his eyes roving over her face to take in every feature before capturing her gaze with his once more.

"Lottie, my beautiful duchess," he whispered, placing a hand on her breast and stroking her nipple.

She blinked quickly, the depth of her unspoken feelings for him radiating from her to envelop them both, and at that split second in time, he knew that everything between them hadn't only changed, it had changed forever. He knew exactly what was missing, and that instantaneous burst of realization struck him profoundly.

Swallowing harshly, he clenched his jaw, holding her vivid gaze, caressing her marvelous body. Then he took her hand from his face and placed it at the center of his chest.

"Give your soul to me, Lottie," he breathed, "and I will give you the world."

For seconds she just stared at him. Then her eyes filled with tears and before he could begin to unravel his own confounding emotions, he leaned over to take her mouth with his.

He kissed her with a passion spent in years of pent-up longing, caressing her lips with his own, then plunging deep to invade her with his tongue.

She wrapped her arms around his neck, pushing her fingers lightly through his hair, holding him close. He draped one leg over hers, pressing his erection into her hip, feeling a sudden urgency to enter her and stay there always.

She moaned softly against his mouth when his hand found her breast, kneading it, stroking her nipple with his fingers. Desire raged anew, for both of them, and the time had come to end the stay of exquisite release.

Pulling his lips from hers, he reached down and hooked his hand under her knee, raising it a little, then finding her hot, wet center with his fingers as he began to stroke her, moving deeper, closer to heaven with each tingling caress.

She moaned again and closed her eyes to the rising need, biting her bottom lip as she instinctively lifted her hips to meet his rhythmic touch.

Colin sensed the nearness of her climax and quickly moved his fingers from the hidden treasure that awaited him and centered himself between her parted legs. He lowered his head and kissed a nipple, then glided his tongue across the waiting peak before pulling it into his mouth to gently suck.

She squirmed beneath him, her breathing erratic and fast. Lifting her leg by the crook in her knee once more, he raised himself up on his free hand, and placed his erection at the center of her.

She felt it, and opened her eyes to gaze into his.

Colin clenched his jaw tightly, and with one smooth action, pushed himself deeply into her tight, hot sheath. She tensed from the pressure, then gradually relaxed as he held himself very still, watching her.

She clutched his shoulders with tight fingers, then whispered, "You feel wonderful . . ."

Colin groaned from her honesty, marveling in her beauty, her surrendered desire for him. It was a defining moment for them, he knew, connecting in the most intimate way possible, relishing a newfound sense of fulfillment.

He moved his hand from her knee and placed his fingers between their bodies, lifting himself just enough to allow him to stroke her, bringing her once more to the edge of bliss.

He watched her as the urgency built inside, holding himself steady, his thoughts centered on her alone with the concern that he might lose himself first.

She never moved her gaze. Eyes dark and glazed with passion, she began to whimper and push her hips against him as she neared her crest. He increased the pace of his fingers, his eagerness to feel her come almost overwhelming him.

Then her nails dug into his skin and her eyes widened. Colin held himself still, mesmerized by the sight of her at the brink of climax. And then she jerked into him once, twice, her head falling back as she squeezed her lids shut, moaning over and over in sweet agony.

He didn't move. Just watching her come, feeling her shatter with pleasure beneath him as the muscles inside of her stroked him over and over, made him lose the battle, took him to the point of no return.

He grasped her chin and brought his mouth down hard on hers, stifling the low grown of satisfaction that poured forth from deep in his chest. She kissed him back wildly as he pulled himself out once, then plunged deeply inside again as his climax struck him hard, as wave after wave of an incredible, intense taste of heaven coursed through him and he spilled himself inside of her.

Charlotte stirred and stretched out beneath the sheets, her mind a blur for a minute or two until the events of the last few hours came rushing back when her leg brushed against his and she felt him beside her.

Smiling, she snuggled down deeper into the covers.

She would remember this night forever—the way he aroused her, the way he looked at her with utter longing, and especially the emotions he exuded from feelings for her that went far deeper than he'd ever before shown, and no doubt experienced. Of course his feelings were conjecture on her part; he hadn't actually expressed them verbally. But she wasn't stupid, either. It was fairly obvious that if he wasn't in love with her yet, his feelings strayed very, very close to the emotion. At least she preferred to think so, even with his own doubts about their relationship. For now, at least, she remained content and remarkably happy.

She felt him stir beside her in the darkness and she turned on her side, draping one leg over his.

He reached out and pulled her close to him, tucking her into his chest.

"You snore," he said sleepily.

She suppressed a giggle. "I know."

He grunted. "And you didn't tell me?"

"Why would I tell you such a thing, your grace?" She nuzzled her nose into his neck. "You might not have married me."

He adjusted his head on the pillow, gazing down at her, though in shadow, she felt more than saw him looking at her.

"Would you like to know a secret, my darling wife?" he asked, sounding amused.

"Hmmm . . . Of course. You keep the best secrets."

He started drawing the fingers of his free hand up and down her thigh. "I'd decided to marry you as soon as you left my study the day you came to me with your incredible and rather uh . . . brazen offer."

She grinned and left a light kiss on his jaw. "That's not much of a secret, Colin. I think you would have kicked puppies for the chance to marry Lottie English."

He chuckled, and the low sound reverberated through his chest.

"Not true. Bedding Lottie would have been easy. Marriage, on the other hand, is a trickier prospect, but I knew the moment you so unconventionally proposed, I would accept. I just needed a bit of convincing." He nuzzled the top of her head. "And just so you're aware of the goodness of my character, I've never kicked a puppy."

She grinned, teasing the smattering of hair on his chest with her fingers. "That's not how it seemed to me. You were quite irritated to be put in such a position. I realized that when you finally came to my brother's home to offer for me."

He groaned. "That's because a gentleman prefers to do the proposing. You put me in a very unmanly position."

She thought about that for a moment, then asked, "So why on earth did you accept such an . . . unrefined proposal if not for the chance to bed Lottie? I guarantee you, sir, I would not have been easy to seduce."

He turned a little so that he could look into her eyes in the darkness. "Oh, no? I believe you would have been marvelously easy to seduce, sweetheart," he teased. "But I chose marriage because, dear Charlotte, you are remarkable in every respect."

He moved his arm out from under her so they could lie side by side, facing each other with their heads on the pillow.

"Why didn't you marry before?" she asked softly, a question that hadn't, until now, crossed her mind. "It's not as if you didn't have prospects, I'm sure."

He sighed and reached down under the covers to lift her leg at the knee, pulling it over his hip so that his thigh caressed her between her legs.

"You're certainly full of questions," he said softly. Without light on his face, she couldn't be sure if he was amused or intentionally trying to be vague.

"So it's a secret you're not willing to share?" she prodded.

"Lottie, Lottie, Lottie . . ." he said through a sigh. "Do you really want to know?"

Now he had her completely intrigued. "Of course," she answered, probably too eagerly. "You know how much I adore your secrets."

"You really are quite enchanting when you want something," he mused, reaching up to brush stray hair from her cheeks.

"Thank you for the compliment, my handsome duke." She took his hand and kissed his fingers. "Now tell me why a man of your station, who finds it so easy to charm the ladies, has been reluctant to marry all these years?"

"I was waiting for you," he answered, amusement lacing his words.

Somehow she knew he'd say that and it warmed her even as her intrigue grew. "Naturally I'm flattered, your grace, but that answer is just too simple and convenient."

He was quiet for a long moment, studying her in near-blackness. She waited, grazing his shin with her toes.

Finally, he inhaled a deep breath and murmured, "The truth is, my father married my mother at the age of twenty-two. She loved him deeply, but by the age of twenty-five, he'd had enough of her, and chose to bed anything wearing a skirt. I just . . . didn't want to be like him."

Charlotte felt her heart swell with tenderness, not from his disclosure, but by the gentleness in his voice, the honesty he conveyed about something that had obviously affected his childhood.

"Your father didn't love your mother?" she asked softly.

He shrugged a shoulder negligibly and replied, "I don't know, but I don't think love had anything to do with his lust for other women."

She didn't know how to take that answer exactly. "My parents married by arrangement," she revealed quietly. "I don't think they were ever in love, but I don't think either one was unfaithful."

"Charlotte, I don't think that's something you could ever be sure of," he replied, his voice subdued. "Most people are discreet with their affairs. My father flaunted his."

A shade of anger had seeped into his tone, and the last thing she wanted to do right now, while they remained centered on each other physically and emotionally, was bring up memories that would make him uncomfortable.

She turned on her back and stared at the ceiling. "Perhaps that's the secret to a good marriage," she maintained. "If you never expect too much, your heart can never be broken."

She could feel him staring at her as a lingering silence followed. Then he raised up on his elbow and gazed down at her to get her attention, quiet until she looked into his eyes.

"There is no secret," he whispered gruffly. "Some people are happy, some are not. I don't think love has much to do with it."

With a suddenly sinking heart, she replied, "So you don't believe love in marriage matters?"

Even in near-blackness, she noticed a trace of a smile at the corners of his mouth.

"That's not exactly what I said." He lifted his hand and brushed the curls off her forehead with his fingers. "From my observance, there are people who marry for everything but love and remain faithful their entire lives. I don't know why. Then there are those who marry *for* love who stray after only a short time together. Why that happens is anybody's guess, though I don't believe there is any guarantee of faithfulness just because two people have vowed before God to remain so."

Although she understood, even believed, what he said, something in his cynical attitude still cut her deeply. For the first time since they'd married, Charlotte wanted desperately to know how he felt about her, if he would stray, remain faithful, love her. But she couldn't ask him. Not now.

"So, what does all this have to do with you waiting to marry?" she asked hesitantly.

He watched her for a moment or two, then ran the back of his hand across her cheek.

"I don't think this is the best time to discuss it," he said gently.

She refused to let him end the conversation there. "Tell me, Colin," she insisted, her tone hinting at the depth of her concern.

He exhaled a long breath as he placed his palm on her chest, just above her breasts, and began stroking her collarbone with his thumb.

"You know very well of my reputation for romancing the ladies," he said rather than asked, his voice overflowing with reluctance.

She actually smiled in the darkness. "Yes, Colin, I know."

He waited, gathering his thoughts, then revealed in a husky murmur, "Much of what is said through the chain of gossips is highly exaggerated. However, I think I just—I think I wanted to rid myself of as much desire for variety as I could before I settled down with one lady." He dropped his voice to a whisper. "The truth is, I didn't want to hurt my wife as my father had hurt my mother."

Charlotte felt a wonderful peace settle inside her. He'd chosen his words carefully, she realized, in some chivalrous manner of protecting her from the vulgarities related to his bedding others before her. But she'd understood him completely. She worked in the theater day after day, where lust and indecencies were ever present and accepted as part of daily life. She fully recognized how passion could dominate men.

Still, she couldn't deny the tinge of jealousy that shot through her as he acknowledged his former indiscretions. But then, as even he had said, his reputation had always preceded him. More important to her, however, was his conveyance that he didn't intend to cause the pain in their marriage that had so overshadowed his parents'.

She reached out to touch his face, unsure what she could possibly say.

He kissed her palm. "Just remember, my past has nothing to do with us, Charlotte."

She smiled and countered softly, "It has everything to do with us. But you should know that with each revealing secret you share with me, I grow ever more thankful that you married me."

He inhaled a shaky breath. Then with a quickness that defied the action, he hoisted her on top of him, one palm on her bare bottom, caressing her lightly, the other brushing her curly hair from her face.

"Beautiful Lottie," he whispered, his eyes melding into hers. "There is no woman on earth more perfect for me than you."

She wanted to cry, from his words, the sincerity flowing through his words. Instead, she leaned over and placed her lips on his, drowning out everything but the moment.

Chapter 21

Colin entered Charlotte's dressing room unnoticed, then closed the door very softly behind him, his now-completed forgery tucked into the long sock covering his right leg. Quickly, he walked to the wardrobe closet and opened it, looking for one of the boxes of music that could be easily opened, leading to an easy discovery.

He selected the first of the four boxes he noticed at waist level and pulled it out. He then placed it on the floor, knelt beside it, and lifted the lid.

The contents revealed two rows of various kinds of vocal music, from sheets to books, all rather dusty, some old, though at first look, none of it appeared to be organized by any logical means.

After a fast glance over his shoulder to verify once more that he was alone, and hearing nothing beyond the closed door that might signal an interruption, he lifted his trouser leg to the knee, carefully lowered his sock, and pulled out all six pages of his first forged musical masterpiece. That done, he dropped the music on top of the others until he once again straightened his sock and trousers, then took the sheets and righted them, making sure they were placed in order.

Knowing time remained valuable, he immediately chose what Charlotte had described as a *vocalise,* a book of vocal exercises, and opened it to the third page before placing the forgery inside. Certain that it would be both hidden and yet easy to find if one were determined, he then returned the book to the box, this time standing it upright with a stack of loose music so that about a half an inch of the forged paper stuck out noticeably from the book itself, though blended with the other sheets in its vicinity.

He then stood, pulled out another box, and switched the two in the wardrobe so that the box containing the forgery would be second from the top, less obvious to anyone searching to steal it.

A sudden knock startled him into action. As fast as he closed the wardrobe doors, the one at the entrance to the dressing room opened and Sadie stuck her head inside.

"Lottie?" she called out, her face covered in cosmetics in preparation for their final dress rehearsal before opening night. Then her painted brows rose in surprise. "Your grace?"

Heart pounding, Colin planted a grin on his face and tried to look sheepish. "Anne Balstone came to get her a few minutes ago," he said. "I think the director wanted to see her at once."

"Oh . . . of course. I forgot he was looking for her," she replied with a satisfied smile as she entered the room and closed the door behind her. "I thought she would be here dressing."

He didn't believe that for a minute, mostly from instinct. She'd found exactly who she wanted, though he played along with her desire to confront him with Lottie clearly otherwise engaged.

"I see you're ready for rehearsal to begin," he remarked with a nod to her attire.

She glanced down her body, her palms deliberately smoothing her servant girl costume at her waist. "Yes, well, I'm confident with my part and anxious to get the production under way." She began to sashay toward him, her hands on her hips. "What are *you* doing in here, your grace?"

Colin hadn't expected to discuss the music with her until later, perhaps not until opening night, after he'd figured out exactly how to introduce the topic without sounding obvious. But her sudden appearance provided him an excellent opportunity—as long as his wife didn't walk in and discover them.

"Just . . . waiting for Lottie to return," he replied, scratching the back of his neck as she approached him.

"I think you were looking for her rare music instead," she counted coyly, her painted lips tipped up at one end.

He chuckled, dropping his hands to his sides. "You're a very clever woman."

"Can I help?" she offered, standing very close to him now.

Although it would be a prime opportunity to find out how much Sadie knew, he nonetheless hesitated, again concerned that Charlotte would walk in and he'd be stumped for words. The scene would no doubt confuse his wife since having Sadie look for the music with him wasn't part of their plan.

"Don't worry," the Frenchwoman fairly purred, evidently reading his thoughts. "Lottie and Mr. Barrington-Graham will be in deep discussion until rehearsal begins. We have some time."

"You can't be certain of that," he replied, purposely glancing to the door.

She laughed softly. "Yes, I can. Because she has also been invited to sing in Florence, and he'll want to discuss her impending departure for Italy. The particulars have become more complex."

That startling information caught him off guard, troubling him deeply, and he frowned. "Are you sure?"

She looked insulted. "Of course I'm sure."

"How is it that you know of these invitations before she does?"

She nonchalantly rubbed her breasts against his chest, gazing into his eyes with raw appreciation. "I look and I listen, Colin. Trust me when I tell you that I know everything that happens in this theater."

He didn't doubt that at all, but more to the point, if Sadie's information was indeed correct, Charlotte would be even more tempted to travel abroad and he wasn't certain she could ever let such an opportunity slip through her fingers.

Tugging his thoughts back to the gravity of the moment, he ignored Sadie's sexual overtures and replied huskily, "Then we do, indeed, have a bit of time to search."

Just as she looked ready to draw him into another

long kiss, he turned around and opened the wardrobe
door. She sighed, but apparently decided to forgo an
embrace for a possible fortune. That was, of course,
if she actually had outside information about the music and would likewise know a priceless masterpiece
if she saw it, and Colin still contended that she did,
and would.

"I've already checked the first box," he said, lifting the one on top to give her access to the next. "I
didn't see anything important, though I'm not sure
what valuable music looks like."

She reached for the second box and pulled it out
easily. "I will certainly recognize rare music if it's
here," she replied confidently.

He didn't offer comment as she placed the box
containing the forgery on the floor, knelt before it,
and quickly lifted the lid.

He'd hid it well, he decided, but as he didn't want
to lead her, he began sifting through the music still
laying flat, allowing her the opportunity to start with
the stack he'd left standing.

They searched for a minute or two, he pretending
to be entirely ignorant, she completely engrossed in
her effort.

"How do you know she hid it in her dressing
room?" she asked without looking at him.

He lifted his shoulders negligibly. "I don't. But I
heard she possesses priceless music, and my guess is
she'll want to sell it before she travels abroad. And
what better place to store it than with other music?"

"You don't think she would keep it at home?"

"It's possible, I suppose." He paused for effect,
then replied, "But it would make more sense to hide

it more or less in the open, where nobody would suspect."

"I see," she muttered as she finally neared the book of vocal practice. "A thief would never think to look with the music she uses every day."

"Yes, exactly."

"And she is here every day, so it is always with her," she added.

"Right again," he returned as gentle praise.

She glanced up and grinned at him. "You still haven't told me how you came to learn of this rare music."

He sat on the ground as if discouraged with his own progress, watching her. "I heard she received it as a parting gift from a vocal instructor years ago."

Sadie stilled for the slightest second, then returned to her assessment the music at her fingertips, amusement fading from her features as she neared the *vocalise*.

"Heard that from whom?"

He had to think quickly. "From a drunken peer at a very lucky game of cards."

She shot him a quick, sideways glance, her forehead creased. "A member of the peerage?"

"Indeed, though I don't now recall his name."

"I see." At last she pulled the book out from the stack. "What do you plan to do with the music if you find it, Colin?"

His gut tightened the moment she opened it to the third page and began to skim the forgery.

"I don't know, Sadie," he replied as evenly as he could. "Maybe keep it for my personal collection. Maybe sell it. What would you do?"

Cautiously, she turned the pages one by one. "I . . . would probably sell it, depending on the value." She looked up into his face, her eyes sparkling mischievously. "If one could easily sell something deemed priceless."

His heart nearly stopped beating as she studied him with a calculating expression.

And then suddenly he had his answer as she abruptly closed the music book and replaced it, reaching for another.

Clever girl. "I'm sure it can be sold," he argued, his mouth unnaturally dry. He groaned for effect. "I just wish I knew precisely what I was looking for."

She patted his thigh, then caressed it. "Not to worry, Colin. If it's here, I'll know it."

For another few moments she continued scrutinizing the remainder of the music in the box, then finally replaced it all into a neat stack and sat back on her heels.

"Unfortunately, I don't see anything in this box that strikes me as rare or priceless," she remarked through a sigh.

"Are you certain you'd know if you saw it?" he asked once more, giving her a final time for truth.

She looked into his eyes and smiled. "If it's very old, or composed by a master, then yes." Leaning toward him, she whispered, "I'm very good at what I do, Colin."

He grinned slyly. "I've no doubt, Sadie."

Thankfully, the sound of female voices on the other side of the door startled them in to action. Colin jumped to his feet and lifted the box, stacking it quickly, then stepping back as Sadie closed the wardrobe door.

Charlotte knew Colin waited for her in her dressing room, and since she hadn't seen Sadie since she left Walter's office, she suspected the woman was with him.

She trusted her husband wholeheartedly, and yet she couldn't deny the slight edge of doubt and even jealousy she felt just knowing they were together and alone. She could only hope he'd had the time to hide the forgery, and if not, that he hadn't undressed for the woman she no longer considered a friend. But she didn't think that likely. Not after the magical way he made love to her.

Nearing her dressing room door, she greeted Anne and two other ladies in the cast, pausing only long enough to let them know Walter was on his way and rehearsal would begin shortly, then turned the handle and walked in.

The sight of her husband huddled so closely to Sadie disturbed her momentarily, though she managed to act as if seeing them together meant nothing. Sadie looked contrite, but Colin admired her up and down as if undressing her with his eyes, a thought she found amusing since she wore costuming, heavy cosmetics, and a wig.

"Your grace," she said with a slight curtsy. "Sadie."

She left the door ajar and slowly walked inside. "What are you doing in here?" she asked pleasantly, hoping her husband would have an answer for the question.

Sadie stepped in front of him. "I was just looking

for you, Lottie, to let you know we're on in less than ten minutes." She glanced over her shoulder. "His grace and I were just chatting about music."

"Music?" She raised her arms to adjust her wig as she walked to her vanity. "I hope I'm not interrupting."

"Of course not, Lottie love," Colin replied, his voice laced with amusement. "You look spectacular, as always."

Charlotte peered at him through the mirror, fighting a grin and using as much strength as possible to keep from blurting that he really, really couldn't act very well.

"Thank you, sir," she said blandly, lighting the lamp next to her cosmetic case.

An awkward moment passed. Then Sadie cleared her throat.

"Well, I think I'll be on my way," she said breezily, fairly waltzing toward the door. "See you on the stage, Lottie."

"I'll be there shortly," she replied, gazing at her face in the mirror.

As soon as the door clicked shut from the Frenchwoman's departure, she whirled around to face him. "What happened?" she whispered, moving to his side.

He grinned. "She knows. She saw it and didn't say a word of its worth."

Hands on hips, she eyed him skeptically. "You don't suppose she knew it was a forgery, do you?"

He looked at her aghast. Then he grinned again as he reached out and grabbed the yoke of her costume, yanking her against him.

"You saw it," he teased. "Did *you* think it looked original?"

She wrapped her arm around his neck. "You have a point, my darling, and if I thought it looked original, she surely did, too. But why on earth did you show it to her now?"

Colin dropped his hands to her waist, scanning her entire face. "Your cosmetics have transformed you into the bewitching minx."

She laughed softly, then scolded him. "Answer my question, you insufferable man."

He shrugged a shoulder negligibly. "I'd just hidden it when she walked in unannounced and asked me what I was doing." He kissed the tip of her nose, then added, "I'm afraid I had to improvise."

She pulled back a little, her expression growing serious once more. "But even if she now knows, it's quite possible she's not working with anyone and you've just given away a secret treasure she'll simply want to steal herself."

"I've already considered that."

Raising her brows with skepticism, she asked, "You have?"

"I have indeed, and that's why I'm going to take it out again."

"What?"

He smiled again. "Well, actually, I'm not going to take it out, I'm simply going to move it for now."

Charlotte shook her head, confused. "What would be the point in that?"

"The point, sweetheart," he explained, lowering his voice to a near whisper, "is that I pretended to have no idea what kind of music it was, and so she doesn't, right now, suspect me—or rather, she won't know if she can trust what I've said. I'm going to remove the forgery, so if by some chance she comes back to look for it, she'll discover it missing, which will only mean, to her, that I have it."

"And then what?" she asked, her own excitement at this new development thriving. "Confront her?"

He pulled her closer so that her breasts crushed up against his chest. "Blackmail her, and find out who's behind this."

She fairly gaped at him. "Blackmail her?"

"Tell her I'll give it to her for a price." He ran his fingers up her spine. "That should shake the leaves from the tree."

The sound of orchestral music abruptly interrupted their dialogue.

"They're beginning to warm up the instruments," she said, withdrawing from his embrace. "I need to be on the stage before I'm missed—"

He grabbed her arm, effectively cutting her off.

"One more thing," he murmured, his grin fading a little as he gazed into her eyes. "I heard you've been offered the chance to sing in Florence as well."

She blinked, startled and confused for a second or two—until she realized Sadie must have informed him of her meeting with Walter. With a sinking feeling in the pit of her stomach, she gently pried her arm from his clutches and he let her go.

Frustrated, she said, "Why does she know of these things before I do?"

His eyes narrowed as his body tensed. "That's what concerns you?" he asked quietly, crossing his arms over his chest.

She felt his sudden shift in mood and knew at once that he wasn't all too happy with the news. Turning away from him, she walked back to her vanity, gazing down to the disorganized mess of creams and color-filled jars.

"I just learned about it, Colin," she replied matter-of-factly. "And yes, that concerns me. How does *she* know?"

He inhaled deeply and leaned to his side, resting his shoulder against the wardrobe door. "I don't know, Charlotte. Maybe she's having an intimate affair with Barrington-Graham. Maybe he's the man who's really after your Handel masterwork. Maybe she simply eavesdrops because she's a dishonest person at heart."

"I just can't believe any of that," she replied with a shake of her head. "I've worked with her for three years, Colin, and I've never known her to be deceitful." She tossed her hand in the air. "Except where you are concerned, and her . . . attraction to you."

He remained silent for a long moment, though she could positively feel his eyes on her, sense his uncertainty. Then she heard him begin to move toward her, and just as she lifted her lashes again, he wrapped his arms around her from behind, lightly kissed her neck, and captured her gaze in the mirror.

"She also knew about the music, of that I'm sure," he said with conviction, his tone low. "She studied two or three pages and then put it back where I'd hidden it. Whoever she's working with will soon hear of the discovery and then we'll know."

She nodded, wrapping her arms around him as he clung to her. "I need to go. We open tomorrow night and this performance is vital. And I don't want Sadie to suspect anything unusual."

He inhaled deeply once more, yet he didn't drop his arms. "You still haven't told me about Florence."

She swallowed, staring into his beautiful eyes through the glass. "The director of the *Teatro della Pergola* heard about my engagement in Milan, and he contacted Edward Hibbert. Walter told me of the offer only a little while ago, but I don't know the particulars yet. I'll learn more tomorrow evening when I speak to Edward about the offer in detail."

"I see," he replied. They stared silently at each other for a moment, then she turned and briefly kissed him.

"What are you going to do about Sadie?" she asked, pulling away from him.

He ran his fingers through his hair. "I'm going to leave her an anonymous note telling her I have the music and want to meet with the person in charge tomorrow night. I have no doubt they'll contact me."

She frowned. "Anonymous?"

He shrugged and smiled. "Just to keep her guessing."

Touching his cheek with her palm, her gaze scanned every inch of his face. "Thank you, Colin. For everything."

His features grew serious as he gazed at her intently. But before he could reply, she lifted her skirts and walked from her dressing room.

Colin stared at his handwritten note.

I have the Handel masterpiece. I want to meet the person you're working for during the second interval, opening night, in your dressing room. Bring no one else. Have him there or you'll never see the work again.

He left the page unsigned, then folded it and wrote her name on the front, leaving it unsealed. With the entire cast and chorus singing on the stage, he paused for a moment outside Charlotte's dressing room to make sure he wouldn't be seen, then swiftly moved to his right, passing two smaller rooms before coming to Sadie's. After a quick glance around him to make certain nobody could see or place him there, he then knelt down and shoved the paper under the small crack at the floor. That done, he once again stood and promptly made his way past the large black curtain and out into the audience area to watch their final performance before opening night.

Their plan of attack had begun.

Chapter 22

The entire theater was abuzz with exhilaration, the chatter and laughter loud as the cast and crew of London's revival of Balfe's *The Bohemian Girl* arrived at the theater for opening night.

Charlotte had been in her dressing room for an hour now, fairly oblivious to the excitement around her as notes, vases, and bouquets of flowers began arriving from well-wishers, dignitaries, and members of the aristocracy who'd watched her performances for years and planned to be in the audience tonight.

She'd come early today because she wanted to meet with Walter and Edward Hibbert to learn the details about her extended offer to sing in Italy. And just as she'd anticipated, it was a marvelous proposition in every respect, which was why she now found herself sitting at her vanity, in full costume, staring at her reflection with the deepest sense of sadness and an immense feeling of regret, hardly aware of her lady's maid, Lucy Beth, standing behind her putting the final pins in her wig.

Never in her life had she imagined so great an opportunity to come her way, and one fully paid by the Italian theaters that requested her. Singing on the stages in Milan and Florence would no doubt bring her growing fame across Europe, an aspiration she'd embraced for as long as she could remember. But even after her marriage to Colin, she never thought leaving him would be so hard.

In all her life, she'd never dreamed that her love of music and the theater might be less than her love for a husband, but perhaps that, in itself, was why—her dreams had never been about Colin specifically. She'd been raised knowing she'd have to marry, simply because of her station, and yet marriage to her had meant the kind her parents had—confinement not freedom, losing opportunities rather than gaining them, duty instead of joy. If her life had actually turned out that way, opera would always remain her greatest love. But it hadn't. She'd wed a most intriguing, unusual, intelligent, honorable, talented man who made her come alive in bed and trusted her with his most delicate secrets. He admired her, enjoyed her company, and frankly, the opportunity to be with such a man had replaced the music as the greatest gift imaginable.

But was he truly in love with her? That question had plagued her for the last few days, so much so that she'd had trouble concentrating on anything else. She suspected that he did, but could a man with such a colorful past ever love one woman wholeheartedly?

And if he did love her, would he admit it to her before she left to embark on a fabulous career?

As Lucy Beth continued to comb and pin her wig, Charlotte closed her eyes, hearing the faintest music begin from the orchestra as they warmed the instruments for the impending opening of the production, due to start in less than an hour. She'd slept restlessly last night, not only from the anticipation of going on stage before the London elite again, but from the knowledge that she would at last know who had gone to so much trouble to steal her precious manuscript. She only hoped the confrontation with those involved would progress as Colin assumed it would, and learning the truth wouldn't distress her so much the final act would suffer.

But she would give her best tonight, as she always did, with the added comfort of knowing her husband, the man she loved, would be there watching and waiting and protecting her, as he had since the day all those months ago when she'd married him.

A knock at the door brought her thoughts back to the moment as she opened her eyes again and sat up properly. Before she could summon a reply, in walked her husband, dashing and regal in his expertly tailored evening suit of black on white, with silk-trimmed collar and revers, his frilled shirt and double-breasted waistcoat fitting snugly across his expansive chest. Charlotte didn't think she'd ever seen him look as powerful and aristocratic as he did now. The marvelously handsome Duke of Newark simply took her breath away.

Lucy Beth's mouth opened a little in surprise as

she turned and curtsied with her comb and pins in hand. Charlotte smiled at his reflection in the mirror.

"Your grace," she said pleasantly.

He nodded once to them. "Please, don't let me interrupt."

"We were just finishing. Thank you, Lucy Beth, that will be all, I think."

"Yes, Miss English," the girl replied meekly, curtsying one final time before laying the comb and pins on the vanity, then fairly rushing out of the dressing room.

Colin closed the door behind her, then turned back to meet her gaze.

"You look beautiful, my darling Lottie," he said, slowly walking toward her.

She gave a short laugh and stood. "Dressed as a servant girl whose face is covered in cosmetics?"

Shrugging, he walked toward her. "Your curves are fabulous in anything you wear, and the color on your eyes and lips dazzles me, especially from afar."

She grinned dryly. "And the wig?"

"The wig is atrocious," he replied. "Nobody on earth has hair more beautiful than yours."

She nodded once. "You flatter me, sir."

He stood in front of her now, gazing down and into her eyes, his expression growing serious.

"Are you nervous?" he asked softly.

He referred to their plan, so soon to begin if Sadie and her accomplices succumbed to the lure he'd left for her yesterday. Truthfully, she worried about him, but she didn't want him to know that. Instead, she replied, "Not really, though I'm feeling a little anxious for the opera to begin."

"Have you seen Sadie yet today?"

She shook her head. "I'm rather glad I haven't. I don't know if I can act well enough to pretend I know nothing."

He didn't have an answer to that apparently, as he just continued to watch her, eyes narrowed in contemplation, which she fully understood. There still remained a tension between them from their discussion of Florence yesterday, and he was no doubt waiting to hear the details.

At last he broached the subject. "You spoke to Barrington-Graham and Hibbert, didn't you?"

"I did," she answered without prevarication. "The entire trip abroad would be a wonderful opportunity for me, and they know it, but they're not happy about the situation. Walter would have to look for another leading soprano for next season, and Edward is worried about the financial difficulties the theater might suffer—"

He cut her off by wrapping his arms around her and placing a quick and gentle kiss on her mouth. "We don't need to discuss this now," he whispered against her lips.

She nodded and pulled back a little. "I—I still need you to know . . ."

"Need me to know what?" he pressed after a moment, his gaze stark, jaw hard.

She drew in a shaky breath and murmured, "I'm not sure I want to go anymore."

For a timeless moment he just held her, watched her intently. Then he whispered, "Why?"

Charlotte knew it would come to this, her desire for fame and recognition to be replaced by the love of her husband, if he could admit it. If he asked her to stay because he loved her, she would.

"I don't want to leave you, Colin."

She could positively feel him relax against her. "You don't have to."

"You could come with me," she suggested softly.

His eyes narrowed and very slowly he released his grip and backed away from her. "As what, Charlotte? As who?" he asked. "Our priorities and desires have changed since we married. I no longer want you to leave. I think I've been more than clear in that respect."

She straightened her shoulders and faced him defiantly. Then with the fullness of the sincerity in her heart, she replied, "Yes, Colin, you have. And yet, has it not occurred to you that you can accompany me as my husband?"

The moment she uttered the words, she wished she could take them back. Although he'd never said as much, she realized fully that exposing Lottie English as the Duchess of Newark could irreparably stain his reputation as a nobleman. If that were the case, she might be forced to quit the stage forever, and she knew in her heart he would never forgive himself if she were made to choose between them.

Charlotte reached out and placed her palm on his chest. "You have my soul, Colin. You asked for it and I've given it to you." With tears stinging her eyes, she whispered, "Now do as you promised and give me the world."

He shook his head minutely, his brows furrowing in confusion. Then clarity seemed to wash over him as his expression went flat and he stilled before her.

"What do you want from me, Charlotte, permission to go?" he breathed in a husky timbre. "What is it you want me to say?"

Squeezing her fist over the ruffles of his shirt, and with great intensity, she replied, "You know what I'm asking. Give me the world, and I'll *stay*."

He clenched his jaw; his gaze pierced hers.

She waited, granting him time, but he didn't utter a sound. Either he didn't understand what she wanted, what she *needed* to hear from him, or he refused to express it for reasons unknown. But she would never coerce him, or embarrass him, into admitting he loved her. That would be for him to discover on his own. If he did it in time.

Very slowly, she dropped her hand from his chest, lowered her lashes, and without another word, walked to the door and out of her dressing room.

Opening night at the Royal Italian Opera House in Covent Garden was an extravaganza to behold, a night of magic, lights and glamour, of laughter and romance. Yet Colin was oblivious to it all, restless with worry, and thinking of nothing but her last great passionate plea.

Give me the world and I'll stay . . .

He knew what he wanted him to say to her; he wasn't an ignorant man. But he also knew that if he confessed to being in love with her, she would not only stay, she could forever regret leaving behind what he dreadfully feared she loved more.

He refused to entertain the possibility that she would ever leave him, and he would gladly travel with her to the ends of the earth if she asked. But he would have to know in his heart that she loved him more than any great passion in her life. Not just hear her admit it, but know it, *feel* it.

Tonight would be the climax of months of preparation, for her at the theater, and for them as they confronted those who wanted her priceless manuscript, and his anticipation of the two events only continued to build as he entered the central foyer of the opera house.

He hardly noticed the ladies dressed in silks and satins and jewels, only briefly acknowledged members of the gentry as he made his way toward his box. He'd asked Sir Thomas to be here tonight as well, giving him the details of the impending confrontation, though he doubted anyone would be arrested. His goal remained in simply getting to the truth, and if Sir Thomas could help, all the better.

As the audience filled, Colin took his seat in his box. He peered down at the glamour of the aristocracy filling the seats below and across from him, watching, though he knew the unfolding of events would take place behind the stage later. Of course that would only happen if everything worked as it should. He had no idea if Sadie had even received the note, though he could only assume she had, and was now more nervous for the encounter to come than for the opening act.

At last the orchestra leader entered to great fanfare and applause. He quickly took his place before his players, then lifted his hands with his baton as the audience grew silent and the production began.

From attending the day-after-day rehearsals, Colin

knew the music and the action well, and realized his wife would not appear until act two. But the first act was rather short, allowing for Porano to garner the attention he wanted, as the stately tenor took his place on the stage.

Sadie appeared, as Buda, and he watched her closely from his box, though he couldn't tell from his seat if she were nervous or distracted. She sang like a professional in the chorus, but her only solo role in this production called for speaking. In his opinion, however, she would never, even with maturity and under different circumstances, sing with the ability and talent of his wife.

Colin remained in his box through the whole of the first interval, keeping an eye on the audience, though seeing nothing out of the ordinary. When the second act began, he sat forward in his seat, his opera glasses at the ready as Charlotte took the stage.

The amazing Lottie English received a round of enthusiastic applause at her appearance, perhaps even more enthusiastic than Porano received at his entrance. Then she began to sing brilliantly, the opera unfolding, and he sat back, totally enthralled by the performance.

Colin had never been so proud of anyone his entire life. She shined on stage, beautiful in form and voice, and his reaction equaled that of her audience. He had married an incredible woman, and listening to her now, watching her perform, left him with the most amazing sense of awe, even peace.

Colin didn't think he'd ever been in love until now.

He had pursued women near and far, made love to them on occasion, but he'd never been given the gift of someone so precious. Someone who belonged to him alone. If he'd felt love for anyone before tonight, it paled by comparison, never amounting to the soul-searing breath of joy he felt at this moment.

But even as he smiled at her with a profound sense of contentment, it was her first solo that captured his attention as it hadn't during the many times he'd heard her sing it before. He sat forward, listening raptly to the words as she performed one of Balfe's great arias.

> *I dreamt that I dwelt in marble halls,*
> *With vassals and serfs at my side,*
> *And of all who assembled within those walls,*
> *That I was the hope and the pride.*
> *I had riches too great to count, could boast*
> *Of a high ancestral name;*
> *But I also dreamt, which pleas'd me most,*
> *That you lov'd me still the same . . .*

Colin swallowed with emotion as the words, sung by his enchanting, beautiful, loving wife, struck him hard. She had become Arlene, the Bohemian girl who vaguely remembered she'd been born in the aristocracy, dreamed of it. Just as Charlotte had dreamed of being her real self in the world of Lottie English. In her life with her brother she'd been a lady denied recognition as she sang upon the stage, and as the married Duchess of Newark, he'd done nothing more to give her the acclaim she deserved.

Give me the world and I'll stay . . .

He now understood exactly what she wanted—his name *and* his love. She wanted it all, and with great pleasure, he would give it to her.

Chapter 23

Near the end of the second act, Colin rose from his seat and exited his box unnoticed. Just as he had all those months ago when he met the marvelous Lottie English, he made his way through the curtain and down the hallway that led to the backstage area. This time, however, he didn't need to announce himself, so he simply nodded to the young man guarding the wooden door before walking into the darkness and on toward Sadie's dressing room.

His nerves were afire, his heart pounding in anticipation as he listened to the chorus from behind the curtain, knowing time was valuable and the second interval would soon begin. But unlike the last time he ventured into the backstage area during a performance, tonight no one paid him the least bit of attention. Everyone associated with the production had grown accustomed to his presence as Lottie English's lazy nobleman lover. A benefit made useful, for now.

After walking by the closed door of Lottie's dressing room, he glanced around him to make certain nobody watched him, then turned the knob on Sadie's door and opened it.

A small lamp burned by a vanity at the far end, though he saw no one inside. Swiftly, he closed the door behind him and took in the room as it was.

Much smaller than Lottie's, Sadie's dressing room contained only the small vanity with a mirror, and one small chair placed beside it for cosmetic application. Not only was it modest in size, it had no window, no room for a wardrobe, and not one flower to offer a scent or a hint of praise.

It only took Colin a second to surmise that Sadie's jealousy had to be greater than he or Charlotte expected. She clearly possessed the ambition of his wife, but not the talent, not the fame of an adoring public, and always being in Lottie's shadow made the Frenchwoman's desperation all that more understandable to him.

Suddenly cheers and applause broke out from the audience, and Colin quickly moved back to the door, standing behind it in a desire to surprise the entrants who would, hopefully, be arriving at any minute.

It didn't even take that long. Within seconds, the knob turned and Sadie walked in—followed by Charles Hughes, Earl of Brixham.

Colin had never been more shocked in his life. In the tiny room, next to the Frenchwoman, stood his brother-in-law, clearly dressed for the opera as he wore an excellent evening suit in navy, with high collar and cravat. For a moment he seemed confused. Then the earl turned and spotted him, his eyes growing wide with alarm as his mouth dropped open and the color drained from his face.

"Well, Brixham, I'm surprised to see you here," he said pleasantly, keeping his own anger in check as he closed the door and positioned himself in front of it to block an unceremonious exit. "And with a woman of the stage, no less. I thought being in the company of such ladies was beneath you."

Charles Hughes's instantaneous rage permeated the air like a tangible thing as he began to put the pieces together. His nostrils flared as his skin went from white to an unsightly shade of red. Sadie remained at the man's side, though her eyes had narrowed with suspicion.

Colin just smiled at them both and relaxed against the door, his arms crossed over his chest.

"Your grace," Sadie began, her accent laced with heavy sarcasm, "I had no idea you could be so very deceitful."

"I adore fine music," he returned with a shrug, though he never dropped his hard gaze from Brixham.

"Where is it?" Sadie charged. "What kind of deal do you want, bringing us here when you can sell it yourself?"

"Stop talking," Brixham finally uttered, his tone low and raw. "This isn't about music."

The Frenchwoman momentarily glanced at the earl, pulling a face of distaste. Then she turned her back on him, effectively ignoring his demand.

"Why did you bring us here, Colin?" she asked, moving slowly toward him. "Where is the music?"

"I want answers from him," he said, keeping his voice light in spite of his resentment and tightly controlled fury. "Why are you here, Brixham?"

"How do you know each other?" she asked with a growing suspicion.

A sudden knock at the door interrupted them. Colin reached behind him to turn the knob, never taking his eyes off his brother-in-law. "How convenient for us all," he said jovially. "The police have arrived."

Both Sadie and the earl took a step back in a brush of panic as Sir Thomas entered, pulling down on his cuffs.

"Your grace," he said with a nod and his usual stately flair. Then he turned and acknowledged Brixham. "My lord, you seem disturbed."

Indeed, the man looked increasingly uncomfortable, his face red, his lips almost white as they stretched across his teeth.

"He's not disturbed, Sir Thomas," Colin replied for him, closing the door again. "I just don't think he's enjoying the opera very much, especially when someone might notice just how closely he resembles the leading lady."

Sadie recovered herself quickly. "I think I need to be on the stage—"

"Not so fast, miss," Sir Thomas cut in, smiling. "I'm here at the request of his grace, the Duke of Newark, and I think he wants this party to continue." He glanced at Colin. "Am I right?"

"Oh, absolutely," he agreed. "And since you're only in the chorus, I don't suppose anyone will notice your absence if you don't return for the final act."

Sadie blinked, made speechless as she looked him up and down.

He ignored her, staying focused on his brother-in-law as he discarded the pretense of humor, his expression turning to one of contempt. "I'll ask you a final time. Why are you here, Brixham?"

The sudden commotion of Lottie's arrival, the sound of her voice outside the dressing room, kept the man from an immediate answer, though sweat had beaded on his forehead and he pulled at his collar as if it choked him.

"Sir Thomas is not from the police," he said, his voice pinched, "and this little inquest is a sham. I am here only for the welfare of my sister because I heard someone is trying to steal her priceless manuscript."

Sadie gasped. "That's a lie. Lottie's not his sister—"

"Shut up, you ignorant girl," Brixham spat, his eyes narrowed to slits.

"What is going on?" she asked, anger replacing her confusion.

Colin shrugged. "Let's ask Lottie, shall we?"

According to plan, he opened the door a second time and his wife entered, eyes sparkling, her cheeks dewy and pink from her exertion on the stage—until she beheld her brother standing next to Sadie.

She stopped short at Colin's side, casting a quick glance to everyone in the room, her face going pale as she suddenly realized just who was behind the treachery. She started shaking, and he reached down for her hand and held it tightly.

"You were saying, Brixham?" he repeated. "Please explain to your sister why you did this."

"I did nothing," the man said in a whispered fury.

Sadie took two steps back and dropped into the chair at her vanity, gaping at them. "My lord, she is not a lady," she murmured, seemingly in an effort to convince herself more than anyone else in the room.

Colin drew in a deep breath and acknowledged her for the first time. "Not only is she a lady, Miss Piaget, she is my *wife*, the Duchess of Newark. And I believe it's time you showed her a little more respect than you have thus far."

Sadie's eyes grew round as saucers, and she appeared, for the first time, as if she might faint.

Brixham suddenly straightened, pulling down on his coat tails, and began walking toward the door in an attempt to leave the room. Sir Thomas quickly positioned himself in front of the man, his own expression now hard with distaste.

"I'd like you to explain yourself as well, my lord," he said coldly. "Did you, in fact, seek to harm your sister in an effort to secure a rare piece of music?"

Brixham took a step back, appalled as he looked the older man up and down. "Of course not."

"He wouldn't hurt me," Charlotte said at last, her voice dampened by shock. "But you would steal the Handel masterwork, wouldn't you, Charles? Did you think to sell it to pay off your debts?"

Brixham wiped the sweat off his expansive forehead with the back of his hand. "This is not the place to discuss this—"

"Oh, I think it's the perfect place to discuss this," Charlotte chided, color returning to her face as she grew more incensed by the second.

"We're all here and dressed for the occasion,"

Colin added. "You have about five minutes to do so before your sister takes the stage again."

His wife released his hand and planted her fists on her hips as she moved closer to her brother to confront him. "How did you know I owned it, Charles?"

"He saw it," Sadie replied for him, her composure returning. "At least that's what he told me."

"Shut up!" Brixham bellowed.

"I will not," she countered, standing again and facing him. "You told me you saw it once, but you failed to tell me the details. Is this why? Because Lottie English is your *sister*?"

The Earl of Brixham looked as if he might explode.

Colin crossed his arms over his chest as he slowly began to walk toward his brother-in-law. "How did you find out about the music? Charlotte had it hidden and said she told nobody."

Still, the earl refused to answer until at last Sir Thomas cleared his throat. "Perhaps you'd be more comfortable discussing this with a detective, my lord—"

"Absolutely not," he cut in, the fear of disgrace loosening his tongue. "I want nothing to do with the police."

"Good," Sir Thomas replied, clasping his hands behind him. "Now, you were just about to say?"

Brixham swallowed so hard his Adam's apple appeared to get stuck. Then finally, seething, he looked directly at Charlotte and replied, "I knew you had it. Your tutor came to see me soon after I forbade you to continue with your ridiculous lessons. I explained to him that you needed to marry, to quit your singing nonsense, and settle down as a lady of your *station*. The stage is not the place for the sister of an *earl!*"

Sadie winced; Sir Thomas dropped his shaking head. Even Colin was taken aback by the man's vehemence. But Charlotte seemed unmoved by her brother's confession, remaining self-possessed as she began to draw her own conclusions.

"Sir Randolph told you he was going to give it to me, didn't he, Charles?" she asked matter-of-factly. "He told you he knew of my dreams, that he was going to give me the music to secure my future." She shook her head in disdain. "But why look for it now? I've owned it for years."

Brixham glared at her. "Because you haven't sold it and left for the Continent, have you, Charlotte? And here you are again tonight, in London, risking our family name by appearing in this . . . costume." He threw Colin a look of disgust. "Even your husband hasn't been able to curb this indecency."

In controlled fury, Charlotte replied, "There is nothing indecent about opera. And my husband is a fair-minded gentleman who knows I *belong* on the stage."

"You *belong* at home having babies!"

Suddenly livid, Colin walked to his brother-in-law, grabbed him by his tidy cravat, and shoved him up against the wall. "What she does now is no longer up to you," he muttered through clenched teeth.

"Colin, stop it," Charlotte said from behind him.

Brixham looked startled and unable to speak.

Reigning in his anger, he loosened his grip on his

brother-in-law, but his gaze never left the man's face. "Why now?"

"I wanted Lottie English *gone*," he replied at once, seething through his words. "With the sale of such a rare manuscript, I could rid myself of the threat of her being discovered, then live in luxury the rest of my life, my debts wiped clean." He raised his chin a fraction and looked directly at Charlotte. "If you weren't going to sell it to save us, I would."

Colin released the man abruptly and took a step back as clarity washed over him. "You're responsible for her invitation to Italy, aren't you?"

"What?" Charlotte said through a fast breath.

Brixham's eyes narrowed. "Unhand me, sir."

Colin released him and stood back, but with one glance at Sadie and the smug, crooked smile on her face, he knew he was right in his assessment.

"And you knew about it, didn't you?" he directed to the Frenchwoman.

"I don't believe this," Charlotte cried out from behind him.

"It's true, isn't it, Brixham?" he murmured, fisting his hands at his sides. "What did you do, contact the theater managers directly? Offer to pay for her because you'd so soon have the funds? Having her leave for the Continent would be a relief to you, wouldn't it?"

"Charles, tell me that's not true," Charlotte whispered, moving closer to her brother.

"Of course it's true," Colin replied for him. "And he told Sadie, which is why she knew of the opportunities before you did." He looked at the Frenchwoman again. "What did he promise you? Money? And the ridiculous notion that you'd be left here to take her place?"

Utter silence reigned supreme for a long, tense moment. Yet even when faced with the evidence of his own deceit, the Earl of Brixham couldn't acknowledge it.

Finally, Sir Thomas inhaled a deep breath and blew it out loudly. "Unfortunately, although the two of you deserve to be fed to the ridicule of the lions of society, I see no crime here—"

"Yes, there is," Colin cut in, looking at Sadie. "Someone tried to hurt my wife physically."

"I had nothing whatsoever to do with that," Brixham blurted defensively. "I never asked anyone to hurt my sister; the thought appalls me."

"Because she's managed to help you out of debt by marrying me?" he returned snidely.

The earl said nothing, though his lips pinched distastefully, as if he had to force himself to keep his tongue in check.

The Frenchwoman fumed, looking from one to the other, realizing with only the briefest shadow of horror to cross her features, that she now had everyone's attention.

Crossing her arms over her breasts and lifting her chin, she fairly barked, "I challenge you to prove *I* had anything to do with it."

Colin supposed he probably couldn't, and they all knew it. Still, he couldn't help but goad the woman into incriminating herself.

"Prove it? Maybe not. But I think I'll have Lottie make a list of all the sundry 'mishaps' that have befallen her lately, then ask the police to check into them, comparing each instance to whatever you might have been doing during those particular times." His gaze narrowed to slits as one corner of his mouth twitched. "When questioned by the authorities, people tend to reveal all, Miss Piaget. You would do well to look into your affairs. I suspect you're about to find yourself in very deep water."

"Or arrested," Sir Thomas chimed in good-naturedly.

Eyes wide, Sadie took a step back, licking her lips. Then a sudden knock at the door startled everyone, and before a response could be made, one of the cast members peeked in, her painted brows rising high when she took in the strange view.

"Uh, Lottie, two minutes," the girl mumbled hesitantly. "And you need to change costumes."

Colin glanced back at his wife. She looked pale and anxious, and utterly beside herself with anger and dejection. He could read her face like a book.

The muffled sound of music began anew, saving Colin from taking three steps forward and killing his brother-in-law for causing her so much hurt for so many years. Instead, he reached for Charlotte's hand and turned her around to face him.

"We'll finish this later," he said with a tentative smile. "Right now, you're needed on the stage."

He could see the hesitation in her eyes, the shock and confusion and frustration in her features. He cupped her cheek with his palm and murmured, "Go and sing and make me proud, my beautiful duchess. You are the star."

She nodded and tried to smile in return. Then glancing back to her brother, she hissed, "We're not through with this conversation, Charles."

Brixham scoffed and looked away as his sister walked from the dressing room. Sadie stood and brushed her palms down her costume. "I'm needed as well."

"I don't think so," Sir Thomas chimed in. "In fact, I think it's high time we began investigating your involvement in this scheme."

Sadie glared at him. "I need to sing."

Colin replied, "As I said before, you're in the chorus. You won't be missed."

"How dare you!"

"I suppose I could follow you," Sir Thomas interjected, "make certain you don't corrupt the performance with any antics."

The Frenchwoman gasped. "Antics?"

"An excellent idea," Colin said. "If you must be on stage, Sir Thomas can watch you from behind the curtain, and then the two of you can continue your little chat when the performance ends."

"This is ridiculous," she spat.

"Not as ridiculous as your thinking you could ever compare yourself to the grace, beauty and talent of Lottie English," he murmured, his words overflowing with contempt.

She gasped at his gall.

Colin ignored her, glancing a final time to his brother-in-law. "I'm sure you'll not want to miss the third act, Brixham," he said wryly. "It's time for the world to discover who Lottie really is."

His eyes opened wide as the sweat began to roll down his reddened cheeks. "You wouldn't," he warned in a choked whisper.

He shook his head and chuckled. "Oh, I would. With pleasure."

Then he turned his back on them, nodded once to Sir Thomas, and quit the dressing room.

Chapter 24

Even after all the turmoil she'd just endured, with a new anger and sorrow bubbling up in her heart, Charlotte would always be a professional singer, the star of English opera, beloved by her country. Although her identity would remain a mystery for now, she would never give anything less than her best with each performance, regardless of place or part.

And so she didn't.

The third act went as perfectly as she could have ever dreamed; even Porano, oblivious to what had just transpired with her behind the stage, sang flawlessly. The night was indeed magical, made even more so because her husband had stood beside her, in every possible way, defending not only her honor, but her choices as a woman, to her scoundrel of a brother and the ignorant girl she'd actually considered a friend.

She had no idea what her future would bring

now that she'd learned the truth behind her offers to perform in Italy. But as she sang her last this night, at the end of the opening night for Balfe's *The Bohemian Girl* revival, it hardly mattered to her anymore.

As the cheers erupted, Charlotte curtsied deeply to the adoring public with tears in her eyes as they one by one began to stand to salute her performance. She'd never felt more revered in her life as minute after minute passed with unending applause, some shouting "Bravo!" and ladies in finery handing her flowers from the edge of the stage.

Charlotte acknowledged the orchestra, then Porano and Walter as they took their places beside her, bowing to the crowd, Adamo making a grand example of Italian joviality as he grabbed her and kissed her once on each cheek.

And then as sudden as it was odd, a hush fell upon the audience, as the cheering and clapping turned to murmurs, the roar of adulation swiftly changing to a low drone of whispered conversation.

Charlotte turned, noticing at once what had caused the commotion.

From the side of the stage, her husband appeared, stately and dashing as always as he began to walk toward her.

"What is your lover doing on the *stage*?" Porano whispered through his forced smile.

Charlotte didn't answer him. Excitement and a surge of tenderness welled up inside of her to the point of nearly overflowing when she caught sight of the enormous bouquet of red roses he held nestled in one arm.

In all the years he had admired her from afar, he had never given her flowers. That this night was his first to do so made the gesture so much more meaningful, and it instantly brought back the memory of the evening they met in her dressing room all those months ago. That night she had been nervous and overwhelmed by the handsome man who gingerly propositioned her. Tonight, with his gaze locked with hers, looking more handsome than she'd ever seen him, he emanated a devotion for her so powerful it took her breath away.

For seconds, she couldn't speak. Then, her throat closed tight with emotion, she whispered, "Colin . . ."

"My darling Lottie," he replied, his eyes filled with adoration and a trace of amusement. "You are, and will always be, the prima donna of the London opera."

As if escaping a trance, Charlotte became aware of the crowd once more, staring at her, some of them undoubtedly appalled that the married Duke of Newark so callously took the stage to salute his lover.

Recovering herself, she curtsied, then took the roses he offered as she replied, "Thank you, your grace. I'm—so glad you could attend this opening night."

Nobody moved. Several long, uncomfortable seconds passed as the audience, consisting of nobles, the elite of society and dignitaries, grew quiet, some of them gaping, some whispering.

Suddenly she heard a loud gasp, then a squeal from the balcony.

Colin winked at her, then stepped to his side. In a rather loud voice, he said, "Mr. Michael William Balfe, may I present to you my wife, Charlotte, the Duchess of Newark."

For a long moment of absolute incredulity, the entire Italian Opera House in Covent Garden stood silent and transfixed. Charlotte stilled as a wave of panic coupled with astonishment washed over her.

From behind her husband, in walked the portly form of Great Britain's most celebrated composer of the nineteenth century, his oiled hair smoothed down atop his head, his beard outlining his jowls, now widened with a smile.

Her knees suddenly went weak beneath her as the man strode slowly to her side, then reached for her hand.

"You have done my music proud, madam. I'm honored to meet you," he said with complete sincerity before dropping a light kiss on her knuckles.

Charlotte thought she might faint, though she did manage a curtsy. "Mr. Balfe," she murmured, her throat unnaturally dry.

She could hear Porano behind her mumbling in Italian, and she made her best effort in introducing him, coming to her senses as she realized everybody in the cast and orchestra, even the audience, remained at a complete loss for words.

Balfe evidently understood the reaction, for he waved once to the crowd, then leaned in to say,

"Your husband invited me several weeks ago to sit in his box this opening night. I think he thought to surprise you."

She gazed back to Colin, who stood to the side a little, his hands behind him, watching her with a wicked grin on his mouth.

"Then I shall thank him later," she replied, her nervousness finally fading.

Balfe chuckled. "Truly, madam, you have a magnificent instrument. Perhaps you'll do me the honor of singing for me in a new production one day." He scratched his side whiskers. "I am, in fact, returning to St. Petersburg in the coming months, and probably Vienna as well. Perhaps you and your husband can join me so that you can sing on the Continent for a season."

She fought back tears of utter joy. "It would be my greatest pleasure, sir. But . . . um . . . I would need to discuss it with him, of course."

"And on your behalf, so will I," Balfe returned, his eyes sparkling in good humor. "But I don't think it will require much persuasion."

Charlotte laughed as the atmosphere grew more relaxed around them. The audience had begun to disperse, some in the crowd hesitantly stepping onto the stage, presumably to meet the great composer, others leaving through the back as they exited into the foyer. The cast and orchestra started to encircle them now, all wanting their chance for introduction as well.

"Open the card, Charlotte," Colin interrupted in murmur as he moved closer to her side.

She blinked, uncertain at his change in subject. "The card?"

"With the bouquet," he clarified, nodding to the flowers in her hand.

She dropped her gaze to the beautiful roses he'd given her only moments ago, at least two dozen of them, wrapped in a white satin ribbon. It took her only seconds to find it, tucked into the ribbon at the base of the flowers.

She shot him a quick glance, then offered another smile to Balfe, who watched with his arms closed over his chest.

The whispers around her died down once more, and she suddenly felt a grave sense of anticipation course through her.

Colin took a step even closer, and she could feel his gaze on her face. Then she opened the card and began to read.

Your soul is my only treasure, my greatest joy.
   The world is now at your fingertips.
   Love me, Charlotte, as I love you and will
love you always.

                    Your husband, Colin

For seconds, she couldn't move, couldn't look away from the handwritten note. Then she started trembling, and very, very slowly, she raised her lashes to look into his eyes.

She saw only a trace of uncertainty in his candid gaze, and then he whispered, "Love me?"

His face became a blur as tears filled her eyes. In a voice barely heard, she breathed, "I do. Always."

Then oblivious to everything but him, she dropped the roses and walked into his arms.

Epilogue

Penzance
September, 1864

Colin stirred from what he supposed was a nap, glancing up to the late afternoon sun, then squinting as he cleared the fog from his head and searched for his wife.

It took him only a moment to find her, down by the sea, holding Olivia and Sam's second child, Matthew, a baby of only eight weeks, in one arm while she spoke to Gracie, Matthew's three-year-old sister, who appeared to be building a sand castle. Or attempting to. He watched them for a moment, taking note of the children, as Will and Vivian's son, Henry, suddenly jerked his hand free from his mother's and ran up from the shoreline to kick the clumps of sand, then jump up and down on the creation to his own great amusement.

Gracie began screaming, which in turn made the

baby cry, and Charlotte looked at him and waved, a huge grin on her mouth which no doubt came from the fact that they, as yet, remained spared from the torture of shrieking children.

Colin turned on his side, resting his head in his palm as he took in the scene. Will and Sam, who stood a short distance away, talking to each other by the sea, only briefly glanced over their shoulders at the commotion, then returned to their obviously more important conversation. Vivian scrambled up from the shore to scold her son, who then began crying and throwing a fit of his own for all to enjoy.

It amused him, really, when he considered how their lives had changed through the years. He had been the one to avoid marriage the longest, deathly afraid of losing his independence, and now he found it difficult to remember what it felt like when he didn't have Charlotte by his side, to comfort him, get angry at him, make love to him. In many ways, he and his friends had grown closer since he'd married, probably because their wives had all become great friends themselves. They only saw each other once or twice a year now, but they always made a point to holiday in Penzance together before the end of summer. And he truly looked forward to these times. Even screaming babies didn't bother him anymore. They were simply part of life, a joy of growing older, and one he'd begun to wish he could experience for himself.

They hadn't really talked about children, as Charlotte had been touring the Continent to great and growing acclaim these last few years. True, they had been careful in their lovemaking, but somewhere inside he'd begun to feel a spark of concern that she might not be able to conceive. He hadn't mentioned his thoughts to her, and she'd seemed enormously content just knowing he stayed by her side when she traveled, and so up until now it hadn't really mattered.

He'd accompanied her abroad, naturally, and had thoroughly enjoyed the experience himself, meeting and dining and conversing with various dignitaries, members of the aristocracy, and just those individuals who adored the opera and admired the gift that was his wife. If he'd been proud of her before, nothing compared to watching her take the stage in the grandest opera houses in Italy, Austria, Russia. She was magnificent, and every day his love for her deepened.

As if knowing he suddenly needed her beside him, Charlotte handed Matthew to Olivia and began to walk toward him, brushing her unruly, gorgeous hair off her face as the breeze pulled it from the ribbon at her nape. He grinned, feeling a surge of lust as he watched the wind pick up for a few seconds to sweep her skirts to her side, outlining her curves from breasts to ankles for his view.

"I think I slept," he drawled as she approached.

"Hmm. Would you be shocked to know you snored so loudly, my darling, that you frightened the birds from the shore?"

He chuckled. "I did not."

She sat beside him, pulling her legs up and under her skirt, then wrapping her arms around her knees. "You did."

He remained quiet for a moment, gazing out to sea. "It's lovely here, as always."

She sighed. "I know. I think I could live here."

Reaching for her hand, he began stroking her fingers. "Charlotte, I've been thinking . . ."

She turned her head, gazing down at him. "I thought you were sleeping," she replied lightheartedly. "Well, until Henry destroyed Gracie's marvelous architectural achievement," she amended. "I don't think anyone for a mile could nap through that."

He chuckled. "That's exactly what I was thinking about."

"What? Screaming children?"

He shrugged. "Why not?"

She laughed, throwing her head back, her strawberry-blond curls brushing his arm. "You mean have one of our own, Colin, my love?"

Grabbing her around the waist, he yanked her down onto the blanket beside him, pinning her there as he began to nuzzle her neck. "Let's have five or six."

She screeched. "Stop that, it's indecent."

"I don't care," he murmured against her skin.

She tucked her palm under his chin and pushed him back a little, holding him a few inches away. After a moment of skimming his face with her gaze, she whispered, "Do you know how much I love you?"

He absolutely adored it when she asked him that. "How much?"

She ran her thumb along his jaw. "Enough to give you the world."

"My Lottie," he teased, rubbing his nose on the tip of hers. "You've already done that."

"Then how about a baby," she whispered, "next March?"

He pulled back a little and looked at her strangely.

She gave him a crooked grin. "Why talk about it when I'm already carrying?"

On March 25, 1865, their daughter, Sophia Victoria, entered the world, strong and healthy and wailing louder than any child he'd ever heard in his life. Every night Colin would stare at her while she slept, his love profound, his joy beyond description, wondering, with her piercing voice, how he would be able to afford her tour when she begged him to sing upon the stage in twenty years.

Avon Romantic Treasures

Unforgettable, enthralling love stories, sparkling with passion and adventure from Romance's bestselling authors

Avon Romances

the best in

exceptional authors and unforgettable novels!

AVON

978-0-06-083120-2
$13.95

978-0-06-057168-9
$13.95

978-0-06-082536-2
$13.95

978-0-06-078555-0
$13.95 ($17.50 Can.)

978-0-06-112861-5
$13.95 ($17.50 Can.)

978-0-06-085995-4
$13.95 ($17.50 Can.)

Visit www.AuthorTracker.com for exclusive
information on your favorite HarperCollins authors.

Available wherever books are sold, or call 1-800-331-3761 to order.

ATP 0507